The Two Pearls

An international science mystery
of climate change
Pandemic Mysteries #3

J. Oestreicher
&
D.R. Oestreicher

Omega Cat Press — California

Omega Cat Press, independent publishing since 1990

"But the pearls were accidents, and the finding of one was luck, a little pat on the back by God or the gods both."
– John Steinbeck

"A legend grows around a grain of truth, like a pearl."
– William S. Beagle

Dedicated to our grandchildren,
And their planet.

Also by J. Oestreicher and D.R. Oestreicher

Pandemic Mysteries #1: Darwin's Paradox
#2: Plague of Equals
Suramarti Saga #1: Kitane, Bull Jumper

By Joy Oestreicher

Legends of Azureign #1: Dragon and Oracle
#2: Raka and Secrets

Table of Contents

0. PREFACE

The authors know that climate change is a serious threat to life on earth, specifically complex life, such as humans. We did our best to imagine the impacts of climate change and potential responses.

The story highlights the importance of scientists and non-scientists working together.

The conclusion is fiction and not intended to lessen the urgency of real-world actions to address climate change today.

PART I — 2045

1. PROLOGUE—SNÆFELLSJÖKULL ICELAND

He climbed to the top of Snæfellsjökull in bare feet but otherwise wearing his park ranger uniform. The blue pants, red shirt, and white slouch hat matched the Iceland flag. He hadn't eaten in two days, nor had his younger brother and sister. He prayed to Freya that the cruise ship would be on schedule and the tourists and crew would be generous.

He opened his pack and took out his binoculars, the most valuable thing he owned. He scanned the horizon across Faxaflói Bay toward Reykjavik to the south. There it was: a modest-sized ship. He estimated less than 500 passengers. He thanked Freya for his good fortune. A small ship meant rich tourists. He checked his pack: two half-liter water bottles, his empty bowl, and a dozen empty silicone sacks to carry food back home.

Sitting on a warm rock, he reviewed his tour guide speech, starting with the famous *Blue Marble* photo of earth from space. "You are here."

"I do not work for the government. I even have to buy my uniform."

"This volcano, ironically named Snow Fall, last experienced snow before I was born."

"The hike to the top is steep in places, but the panoramic view of western Iceland is one of the best you will see."

He again checked his binoculars, and the ship had advanced farther than he expected. He jumped up and ran down the volcano. Even though today was his day, with such a small ship, if he arrived late, the other guides might have claimed all the available groups, leaving his family hungry until his next slot. Another six days from now.

He arrived at the temporary dock—the sea-level had risen again—just in time. A crew member from the ship handed him the last flag—the propitious number nine, the number of surviving deities of Ragnarök.

He started with eighteen tourists, but only a dozen, plus one more, completed the full hike. He accepted their tips, but he was more interested in food than money. The *Hot* had upset agriculture in Iceland, and food was scarce. He had heard about farmers around the world migrating to more favorable climates in places like North America or Asia. Iceland, an island, did not offer such an easy escape.

As he collected the generous tips, he left his empty bowl on the ground. The visitors knew it requested food donations. By the time they returned to the ship, the bowl overflowed with energy bars, packets of milk and juice, and, much appreciated, fresh fruits. He quickly packed everything into his silicone sacks.

One last step meant the difference between fasting and feasting. He ran to the smaller crew gangplank. There the kitchen crew had stacked small cartons of discarded food—meats, vegetables, desserts. If he had been earlier, he'd have opened each one to select the most nutritious alternatives. Again, he was late. He took the last three packages and thanked Freya for her bounty.

That night his family ate well.

2. ABBIE, MIKE—CHEROKEE OK USA

"You'd think farmers would have plenty of food to eat, wouldn't you?"

Sasha lifted her large head and gave her tail two lazy shakes. She opened her mouth in a big smile at the mention of food.

Abbie found a rag to mop up a puddle of drool. "You're a good girl, but it's not dinner time."

Abbie had plenty of Newfoundland chow for the 130-pound dog. Feeding the rest of her family presented the challenge.

They grew wheat, thousands of acres of wheat, but they couldn't eat that until a large corporation ground it into flour. *What would she prepare for dinner?* She stretched their shrinking budget with a kitchen garden. She went down to the root cellar and surveyed the shelves of mason jars with tomatoes, carrots, green beans, and blackberries. One wall was stacked with bushels of apples, sacks of onions, and dried corn. Dried herbs hung from the rafters. She picked up a quart each of carrots and berries. Berries could make a pie. Everyone liked pie, but what else?

Abbie prided herself on managing the farm. Buying food for her family had become more difficult each year and she had records to prove it. They showed income falling and prices rising.

While the blackberry pie baked, she planned the meal. They hadn't had rice in a couple of days. She checked the cupboard and found a mostly full fifty-pound sack of white rice, and a similar one of brown, though it wasn't as full.

Carla, her eldest, almost in college, would have liked a steak, but the budget called for ground chuck. She'd get hamburger gravy. Mike, just starting high school, had recently been off meat. She'd prepare rice with cheese and some chopped jalapeños for him. That just left Redbird. Fortunately, he'd eat anything, complaining regardless. She'd stir up some fried rice to share with him.

Once she had dinner under control, her brain switched over to the farm. The *Hot* meant Oklahoma no longer provided the ideal climate for winter wheat. Unfortunately, the McGilverys were committed to this crop, with generations of experience and heavy investments in equipment. Discussions of farm finance led to angry silences and hurt feelings. Abbie found it easier to shoulder the responsibility than to deal with the resentments. She had enough self-awareness to acknowledge she liked it that way. This arrangement suited her.

"Mike. Carla. Redd. Dinner is ready!"

Sasha was the first to arrive. Abbie picked up a few treats. "Here you go. Good girl."

Sasha wagged her tail.

The Two Pearls

Mike's Social Studies teacher dimmed the classroom and displayed his presentation: *Welcome HotGens.* "That's what they call you. Does anyone know how you got this label?"

Mike closed his eyes and listed synonyms for hot. *Boiling. Scorching...* The classroom faded away. *On fire. Tropical...* Funny, he thought, Oklahoma is now tropical. *Scalding. Febrile...*

Someone kicked his desk. "Wake up!"

Loud laughter greeted his return to reality. He startled. His comp slid across his desk, but he grabbed it before it crashed. He hugged it to his chest and made a small smile.

Without meeting anyone's eyes, he surveyed the forty-one Cherokee High ninth graders and a single girl who hiked over every afternoon from the eighth-grade building. They had taken their final exams and were now counting the few days until they were free.

The teacher repeated his question. This time a lanky boy wearing a red and gold baseball jersey and fancy boots shouted, "Cause our girls are hot!" He took his wide-brimmed hat off and waved it in the air. "Yee-haw."

The class laughed at this welcomed diversion and the cowboy turned around to blow an air kiss to the girl sitting behind him.

She punched his arm. "Forget it. I'm not anybody's girl!"

You tell him, Mike thought. That was Elzia, the lone eighth grader, a tall girl with a violet stripe in her brown hair and thick glasses. She was a head taller than him. He admired her. She didn't wear tight tee-shirts or a lot of makeup, but she was smart and friends with everyone.

Well, not everyone, he reminded himself as he pushed his red hair from his face. She was a Longhorn. One of the rich cattle ranchers who had moved into Oklahoma from Texas.

This was where the *Hot* became personal. Farmers like his family had grown wheat in Oklahoma for centuries, but now it was too hot and dry, on fire and arid, poached and parched. Many of his friends' families had gone bankrupt and moved away. Normally his mother didn't talk about money. So, when she hinted about selling out and moving, he knew their situation must be serious.

The cattle ranchers acted like they owned everything and were better than the farmers. They called Mike and his friends Okies and Dusters, referring back to the farmers who left in the 1930s for California. The Longhorns made fun of the Dusters as if the *Hot* was their fault and they were stupid to have farmed in the first place.

The teacher changed his slide: *Hot Impacts.*

Mike knew where this was going. He interlaced his hands behind his head and leaned back in his chair to watch the show. Forty-one students took notes or played games. The slides reiterated the news Mike had been following since kindergarten: *Extreme weather. Hotter, drier trends. Crop failures. Starvation. Natural disasters. Floods in India. Droughts in Oklahoma.*

The Longhorn boy held his hat over his face as if that would prevent anyone from seeing him. Behind his hat, he taunted the teacher with, "So what Okie. Who cares? That's the way it is!"

Mike deplored that no one expected anything to change. Cherokee High recycled. Solar panels covered the roof. The theater building displayed a weathered banner: *Oklahoma-certified carbon-negative school.* This sign embarrassed him. He couldn't bear to look at it when he came to school each morning. *Too little, too late.*

Something big was needed. Something bigger than electric cars and *carbon-negative* everything. He had an idea. A courageous idea. And it was growing in his bedroom, in recycled two-liter bottles.

●

When dinner ended, Abbie knew what her husband was going to say.

As expected, he questioned her planning. "Why do you make such large meals? What are we going to do with all these leftovers?" Redbird picked up his coffee cup and walked over to the piano. "You know that people are starving? Not here, not yet, but to the south and across the oceans, and even some in northern Canada."

No one planned more carefully than she did. Abbie embraced him and whispered, "Yes dear, I know about all those empty bowls." He gently wrapped her in his muscular arms while she rested her head against his chest and listened to his heart. *Ba bum, ba bum,* strong and steady, just like him.

She wondered if his father had cursed him by naming him after Redbird Smith, the 19th-century Cherokee who famously said, "My greatest ambition has always been to *think right and do right.*" Redd was obsessed with all the empty bowls around the world.

She returned to the dining room and sipped the last of her coffee while absentmindedly tracing the grain of the cedar table, a legacy of Redd's ancestors. She collected the leftovers in ceramic containers. Nothing went to waste in Abigail McGilvery's kitchen. With two teenagers, there could never be too much food in the fridge. She stepped outside the kitchen door to deliver the uneaten fried rice to the chickens, and plate scrapings to the pig.

At times she appreciated Redd's compulsion to *think right and do right.* Like when she'd mentioned that wind turbine noise was waking her up in the middle of the night. Without any further discussion, he hired a backhoe to dig a long trench from the house to the other side of the dairy barn. After a few months of chaos, the massive wind turbines had been exiled to a distant field, never to be heard from again.

The Two Pearls

The house reflected centuries of his family's philosophy to *think right and do right*. The plumbing was from the 20th century and the old part of the house from the 19th when the Cherokees arrived over the Trail of Tears. The original structure, a pioneer cabin, contributed the living room and sitting room in the front, and two bedrooms behind. The rest of the house sprawled in different directions depending on the whims of the previous occupants. It had always been easier to build out instead of up or down. No upstairs. No basement, beyond the indispensable root cellar.

With the food taken care of, she collapsed in a kitchen chair to listen to Redd playing a sad progression of minor chords. Sasha placed her huge slobbering head in her lap. She unbraided her red hair—her Scottish inheritance—until her curls covered her shoulders in an orange fog.

She looked into the old part of the house. She could just see the top of Mike's head peeking over the sofa. He hadn't benefitted from his father's tall genes. She'd have been happy if he were playing some video game, but he was reading science journals. Carla, who had gotten all the tall genes, was probably in her room doing homework. School was almost over, and she'd been accepted to college months ago, but she took after her mother, serious and hard-working. Abbie had great hopes for her.

With everyone settled, Abbie put on a shawl and walked out to her office in the dairy barn, the newest building. She reminded herself that Redd was not the only one with ancestors. Hers had survived the rugged terrain of Scotland through persistence and unflagging effort until they were forced off their land by English sheep farmers in the 19th century. While Redd worked with his hands, she made the budget and paid the bills. She didn't mind the bookkeeping since she enjoyed planning and knowing. However, the farm's finances kept her awake at night. In recent years, wheat farming in Oklahoma had become a money-losing proposition.

She tapped her comp, downloaded accounting files, and tortured the numbers. Climate predictions. Projected crop yields. Market prices. Interest rates. Mortgage payments. No matter how hard she tried, she couldn't make the numbers balance.

She scratched Sasha's silky ears. "What do you think girl?" Sasha looked at her with soft brown eyes and an expression of love.

Her husband worried more about hungry people on the other side of the world than the bank that was waiting to foreclose. Carla was leaving for college in Chicago. And Mike planned to save the planet with bottles of green pond gunk. *Dark green pond gunk.*

As much as they would all grouse about her decision, she knew what they had to do.

"Yes, Sasha. We're going north."

Sasha wagged her tail in support and agreement.

3. SULUK—QAMANITTUAQ NUNAVUT CANADA

Suluk froze when the entirety of Snow House rattled and shook around her. Earthquake? Noticeable quakes were uncommon in this part of Nunavut, but that's what it felt like. Everyone else in the restaurant had stopped talking and looked at each other, customers and workers alike— Suluk was not imagining things.

She could hear the dogs barking, and faintly, the roar of several slushskis starting up.

"Did the mine collapse?" Giqa wondered. His eyes met hers as he looked up from his breakfast plate.

Maybe, Suluk thought. But since his accident, Giqa thought everything bad happened at the mine. And how could an open pit mine just collapse, anyway?

The old man whose name Suluk could never remember seemed to think the same thing. "That was a 'splosion, not a rockfall," he mumbled around the unlit cigarette clenched in his teeth. "Ain't no rock cuts scheduled at the mine."

Besides, Suluk thought, every year the operational sections of the gold mine moved further and further away from Qamanittuaq town. The old section of the mine, that had been worked when her father was a child, was more than sixty kilometers away. When that had been mined out in 2021, the active section of the mine moved even farther northwest.

But she also knew the Kivalliq Inuit Association had approved uranium mining at Blackmeadow. That was closer, but then, operations were not supposed to begin for another six months.

She shook her head. It did not seem likely anything done at either mine could affect Snow House, whatever the old miners thought.

Meanwhile, Giqa scowled at the nameless old man, but said nothing further. The old man pretended to smoke his unlit cigarette, while Suluk bussed dirty dishes, then dried her hands.

She went through the kitchen to the mudroom and back entry and pushed the screen door open. She couldn't see anything past the low slope that bordered what they called the "parking lot." As she stood there, her half-son Tarkik pushed past her.

"Methane, I think. I'll go see," he said over his shoulder. She closed the screen and went back into the kitchen. She stirred the hearty bean soup she was preparing for lunch a couple times until she heard Tarkik's slushski start up and move off. She turned down the heat beneath the soup.

Back in the dining area, conversation had started up again. She cleared the tables of those who had left and then went back to her tiny office area to take another look at the menu. Her sister Meriwa was working today and could take care of any new customers. Suluk wanted to add something new to her menu. She wanted to make it more professional-looking too. It had stung when Tarkik laughed at the typed sheet.

"Even the dorms had fancier menus," he'd said, fresh back from his visit to the Aurora college. He imagined himself a big deal, since they'd offered him two scholarships. Apparently the menus there were printed with colorful photos of the food offerings. Snow House couldn't offer color photos, but she could manage a nicer printed menu. She could get one of the kids to make some drawn art to decorate it, maybe. Foreigners to the Snow House might like polar bears and fish art, and maybe some ulu, and tattoo designs.

"Wasn't at the mine," Tarkik said, kicking ice off his boots before stepping on the plastic mats in the mudroom. Suluk watched him set his boots aside and put on his fur-lined slippers from the bin behind the door. "Methane pocket up by Nalingmiut's place. Nobody hurt." He was scowling.

"Okay," she said. "Nobody hurt, that's good."

Tarkik grunted and served himself a cup of coffee, without paying, of course. He sat at the counter instead of dirtying up a clean table, at least.

She thought about methane and explosions as she watched Meriwa mixing up a batch of bannock. Once the soft dough was formed, she would drop it in the big iron skillet in hot fat and fry it up crispy outside, soft and warm inside. This batch was mostly plain, although she saw Meriwa chopping onion with her ulu, and then *uaguk* sprinkled a finger-pinch of chopped onion into her bannock dough when she added the salt and baking powder. The savory scent and flavor was Meriwa's secret. Caribou butter was Suluk's. Bannock was a staple food, though the wheat flour was becoming more and more expensive as the *Hot* basically burnt away farmlands.

Costly flour and methane pockets weren't the only problem the *Hot* caused the Inuit people. Now that the tundra didn't stay frozen, they'd had poisoning from anthrax bacteria in meltwater, arsenic leached from uranium mine tailings was getting into drinking water somehow, and heavy metals had been found contaminating their fish—even the ones caught way out in Hudson Bay water.

Originally, the mining operations throughout Canada, and especially Nunavut Province, were careful of the environment. It was in the mining companies' own best interest to care for the land and the people working it, not just to follow government rules. But no one had planned for the permafrost melting, and now contaminants were leaking out of what was supposed to have been permanent containment sites.

The entire Inuit community—all of Nunavut, as well as the rest of the Arctic peoples from Russia to Greenland to Alaska, were exploring ways to slow the effects of climate change. They knew, now, as she did, as her family always had, that if all the tundra melted, *all* the peoples of the world were going to be in trouble, not just those in Qamanittuaq. Permafrost wasn't permafrost anymore. The *Hot* was killing it, and everything that depended on it.

◡

The second methane explosion later that day was not harmless. The windows along the east wall of Snow House both cracked, and the larger one actually broke, scattering pieces of glass onto the empty tables. Fortunately, the startled customers tended to sit away from the cool windows. But that wasn't the worst of it.

Suluk saw beyond the cracked and broken windows, her mother waddling quickly towards Snow House as if on a mission. Breathless by the time she came in the front door, Osha stopped and gasped as Suluk reluctantly walked over to her.

"Opik," Mother managed. "The methane bubble at the caribou field…"

Suluk forced words past the lump in her throat. "Osha, Meriwa, you stay," she said, untying her apron as she moved toward the mudroom. She tossed the linen apron onto the washing machine, kicked off her slippers, and pulled on her boots.

"Be careful," Osha said from the doorway, wiping her hands on the red and white check apron that rode her hips. They'd worked hard on those aprons, made from the same fabric as their tablecloths. Suluk stared at the apron, then looked up at her mother. Opik had protested the cost, saying Snow House didn't need to be fancy. Opik, who had gone to check on the caribou.

Meriwa also said, "Be careful." She walked up to Suluk, resting her arm on their mother's shoulder. "There's another methane bubble rising by the road at—"

"Your house. I know."

When she got to the "Parking Lot," she realized there were no more of their own Ticasuk family slushskis in the lot. Tarkik hadn't come back from whatever errand he'd left to run, and everyone else had walked to work that morning. She eyed Giqa's machine, but that wouldn't be right. The man could hardly walk; she couldn't borrow his vehicle. She moved on past the lot to the dog pens.

They kept the dog teams so Snow House could run tourist rides. The dogs were upset, she could see; Sivoy, her much-younger brother, was out with them. He worked most days as a hunter and guide and dog-wrangler.

"Set me up a sled, Sivoy. I need to go out and check on Opik."

He looked up from the harness he had just slid onto pack one's Aput. The lead dog was wagging his tail, eager to go. Aput was always ready to go, one of the reasons he was the lead.

Sivoy nodded. "Figured," he said. Once the team was rigged up, Sivoy handed her the ice hook. "Haven't been out in a few days, likely to be ragged," he said. Warning her the dogs might misbehave.

She snorted, but took the hook and fitted it into the holder tube by her feet. Enough to worry about getting the pontoon-fitted sled through slush and half-melted permafrost without having to deal with overly frisky dogs. The ice hook would stop them, she could hope. She clasped the reins in her gloved hand, impatient to be off.

She was too worried about Opik to think about dogs and sleds, that was all. She set one foot on the left runner and shouted, "Hup!" As the dogs headed off, she gave a firm push with her other foot, wishing she'd tied her boot tighter. The sled slid away from Sivoy and the dog runs full of barking dogs.

She took the back track, paralleling the road, where the slushskis going back and forth that day had packed up the ice a little. She'd let the dogs carry her for now, okay to be riding until they left the track. Once they hit the rougher path that led to the caribou ranch, she'd have to run alongside. It would take longer, but just because she was getting old, slowing down, didn't mean she needed to put the burden onto the dogs. They were doing their best for her, pulling hard.

There hadn't been enough snow this year, like every year lately. Not enough cold days, either. Instead of firm permafrost—firm enough to drive a jeep on—all the ground was slushy. Suluk gritted her teeth as the dogs splashed through another low puddle and the sled slowed. She pushed, and the pontoons slid across the watery gap onto colder, drier dirt.

She noticed a fair amount of smoke in the air as she left the town behind. Was the tundra on fire? Besides methane pockets, tundra fires had become almost commonplace as the permafrost melted, the peat dried out and became vulnerable to fires. Just as Siberia's taiga burned year after year, former areas of moss and algae-covered permafrost had caught fire all across the arctic, releasing what scientists estimated as "tons" of carbon back into the air. Nature's fine system of carbon sequestering had become part of a degenerating cycle as human-caused climate change affected every biome on the planet.

Suluk wiped her eyes with the back of her hand. She sneezed and coughed and used her sleeve to wipe her nose. The smoke was patchy, coming at her like a braided stream.

The sun sparkled on meager snowbanks and melting ice as the sled moved through the silence. Toward what? She did not think about it. The news would come soon enough. She was very much afraid it would not be good.

4. XIANG BO—DONGLAN COUNTY CHINA

Xiang Bo wished she had been able to get her usual rental car. This one had a strong pull to the left. She had to fight it all the way from Hechi to Aidong on the main highway and then on the curvy roads through the mountains of Donglan County. But while she was wishing, she might as well wish again to have her two research centers closer together. She felt like she was traveling as much as she was getting any research done. Geography was not her friend. *No*, she decided after a little thought. It was *distance* that was not her friend. Geography was why she had two sites to begin with.

Eventually, she neared the Hongshui River bridge. She signaled for her left turn, but had to wait as two long truck trains roared past in opposite directions. When the road was empty again, she turned onto the pot-holed half-gravel road. The asphalt disintegrated a little more every time she came. Eventually it would be re-classified, downgraded to gravel or dirt, and she would not be permitted to drive her rental car on it at all. She frowned as she wound along the riverbank toward the village. She had no plan for what to do then. She and her husband, Dr. Cheng Li, had discussed buying a vehicle and leaving it parked in Hechi. Perhaps she should follow through on that.

She negotiated the narrow strip where the road had washed out the previous monsoon season, and arrived, at last, at the Changle Post Office. She pulled to a quick stop as the children swarmed her car, eager to greet their teacher, happy to be at school today.

"Dr. Bai! Dr. Bai!"

Little Zi Min was jumping up and down so fast, Xiang Bo's head felt like it could snap off trying to follow her. She finally just laughed, and shepherded the children into the small room at the back of the post office sorting gallery, where they held their school on the days Xiang Bo could come there.

She taught the older children a lesson in the proper structure of a scientific study. As usual, she found the concept of control groups to be a hard sell. Magical Thinking was pervasive among the Zhuang, and combatting it was one of her goals. Scientific exploration was one of the best ways she had found to do that: that procedures could have replicable results was fascinating to these children.

The younger ones, including Zi Min, she gave several pages of arithmetic drills. Before she gave them the algebra lessons she had developed, they must demonstrate they knew their times tables and could quickly and accurately manage the basic arithmetic skills, including writing their numbers clearly. Zi Min was eager to get to algebra. She was only seven years old, but she could keep up with the teenagers. That was what initially attracted Xiang Bo to the tiny girl.

Other teachers came here to teach history, languages—each child here learned Han Chinese as well as Zhuang and English—and government and physical education. The Zhuang children were regularly assessed for gymnastic skills, having produced several world champions.

Xiang Bo taught science and math, as often as she could. The government had good intentions, but they still had poor textbooks and under-trained teachers for the Zhuang children of remote Donglan County.

After class, she crossed the road to the orphanage. She greeted the housekeeper with a nod and walked toward the commissary. She felt a tiny hand slip into hers. With a smile she grasped it. Zi Min. They weren't supposed to show favoritism to the mostly female, mostly abandoned girls. Unwanted female children, leavened with a few genuinely orphaned ones and even fewer males.

While the one-child laws had been relaxed, and indeed had never been enacted against China's minority groups like the Zhuang, still many couples had found having only one child a good thing. It meant they could get ahead—financially, politically, socially.

And of course, Xiang Bo thought, *there was always a preference for boys.* Until suddenly those boys had no young women to marry. They were poaching wives from other countries, now, still not acknowledging their mistakes.

"Are we going to *Ya-ya's* house now?"

She smiled down at Zi Min. They sat down together at one of the less-ruined tables. It had cheap picnic chairs instead of a bench, but the tabletop still had all its gray Formica covering, cracked and stained though it was.

"Not this time," she told the little girl. Zi Min's bright eyes dimmed and she looked back at her plate of rice. "I will ask my mother, Jiao, if that will be okay, next time. It is her house, after all."

Zi Min bit her lip and nodded.

Xiang Bo snuck Zi Min one of the extra shrimp the cook always gave to her. When the child on her other side looked longingly at Xiang Bo's plate, she slipped her last shrimp to that one.

⌣

As much as she enjoyed coming here and teaching the class and visiting Zi Min, Xiang Bo felt like a wrung-out towel by day's end. She still had to drive across the river and south through the rugged mountains to Nalai, where her mother now lived. She was not going to have either the time or the energy to visit her friend Mo Chou in Donglan.

When her father had been alive, Xiang Bo and her parents lived in Donglan town itself. Her father had fields behind their house where he grew monk fruit, bamboo, and pigs that were sold each year at the Donglan auctions. Then their products were shipped all over the world. Her father had spent many days with a world map, and eventually a globe they were able to buy at the trade fair one year. The globe had a tiny nick and a scratch over Antarctica, but the rest of it was good. Papa had shown her cities in Switzerland and France and Norway where their bamboo went for furniture and flooring. She had seen the location, and later, photographs, of cities where the monk fruit and pork ended up, mostly in China and parts of southeast Asia: Viet Nam, Cambodia, and even Tibet, once.

Those geography lessons had helped fire her imagination, and both her parents' determination that she received a good education. Ultimately, she believed, those early beginnings had led to her scholarship to Oxford and graduate school at Scripps.

That was why she was willing to spend hours and energy teaching the orphanage children. Perhaps she could set a spark alight among those girls— and even if not, she would have the satisfaction of knowing they'd been exposed to more than they would have been without her efforts.

Abruptly the car dropped into a pothole that she was going too slowly to drive out of. She was stuck; her wheels spun but the car didn't move. She got out to see exactly what had happened. The passenger rear wheel was in a hole filled with watery sand. There was nothing for the tire to push against. She opened her suitcase and got out the new hand trowel she had gotten for her mother to use in her garden. She used it to scoop some sandy dirt from the roadside into the soggy pothole, packing it around the tire as firmly as she could. She wasn't sure that would work, but it was the only thing she could think of.

Then she remembered Cheng Li teaching her how to rock the car to get it out of a slippery clay patch he'd driven into once, near Huixian. She put the trowel away and got back in the driver's seat. She copied what her husband had done, gently rocking the car forward and letting it roll back. After the fourth rocking motion, she pressed firmly on the gas pedal and the car lurched out of the hole. With a sigh of relief she wiped her gritty hand on her pants and continued driving, more alert for troublesome holes.

The mountain environment was different from the flat wetlands at the Cheng family compound. Part of the Huixian Wetlands, the ever-experimental integrated fish farms were her first research project.

She'd had to completely change directions with her algae for these mountains. In the wetlands, she enjoyed the steep upthrust karst hills that framed flat rice fields and ponds. Here, she was focused on a direct food source that could be easily grown in the many rocky streams. An algae that people would eat.

She nursed the rental car along the last meters of pavement on the road to her mother's village at Nalai. The tiny "village" comprised five distantly-spaced houses or compounds. They were deemed too small to need a road. She parked and took her suitcase and computer bag out of the trunk. The last two hundred meters she had to walk.

Perhaps she should obtain a four-wheel-drive vehicle that would get her all the way in. Her own 4WD: it sounded like freedom. She walked quickly, hoping to get under her mother's roof before the afternoon rains began. There were no trees here to shelter her.

There were still rice terraces on the rocky hillsides, but rice would no longer grow in them. Too hot now in summer, when the monsoon came and everything literally steamed in the sun, and too cold in the winter, when icy snow fell. Even the few remaining fir trees were failing.

At the Huixian Wetlands site, the weather remained tropical, but a little warmer each year, so she and her husband continued to try different forms of algae to incorporate. Her job there was to find an algae that fed the fish while cooling the water, and provided a food source in its own right, as well as allowing vegetables to be grown in the enriched water.

His job as a biologist was to gene-splice fish and vegetables, to help them survive with the fish and the *Hot*.

She did not walk fast enough to avoid the rain. It came down in torrents, warm torrents as though she stood in a fancy hotel shower. But not one in California, where she had done her graduate work. Those showers had metered water; freshwater was rare and expensive there, despite the desalination plants built along the Pacific coast.

The chickens were clustered together beneath the henhouse for protection against the rain. The silly things could go inside and be completely dry, but Xiang Bo had long ago decided they'd rather be wet and be able to snatch up worms or other creatures also escaping the rain. Their feet got wet in the mud, so what?

She stepped beneath the lean-to behind her mother's house and stripped as much water from her hair and arms and cases as she could. She kicked off her shoes and went inside. As usual these days Jiao sat drowsing on her one good chair, a faint smile on her face.

"Mother, I am here," Xiang Bo said.

Jiao's eyes popped open and she smiled. "Daughter," she said, and ridiculously bowed her upper body, honoring Xiang Bo as she would a respected acquaintance. Xiang Bo frowned, noticing her mother did not attempt to stand up right away. *She must be getting weaker.*

They made dinner together, chopping vegetables and fruits grown in the garden beside the house. They stir-fried the sturdy celery and onions, and Xiang Bo chopped tofu made from her most-successful algae, to add some protein. They enjoyed monk-fruit for dessert, using some of the half-spoiled fruit that Jiao would not be able to sell.

"Mama," Xiang Bo said softly, in her 'asking a favor' voice, "next time I may bring a little girl here. One of the orphans. Would that be all right?"

Jiao looked at her from beneath drooping eyelids. "I would enjoy meeting her. You have talked about her many times," she said.

Xiang Bo smiled. *Nothing wrong with mother's memory.* Gradually her smile faded as she thought of the work ahead of her.

Early in the morning, she needed to repair the sedum planted on her mother's roof. She'd noticed a couple bare spots in the sod as she'd walked up. The living roof worked just as well as she'd hoped, insulating the small house, and absorbing rain and controlling runoff far better than the sloped tin they'd had previously. She'd planted a variety of sedum that could be eaten, adding to salad greens her mother gathered from her garden. Jiao had even begun to trade some, getting honey or fish in exchange for her greens and eggs.

After fixing the roof, Xiang Bo would drag herself through the bamboo crop down to her research site to see how her algae were doing.

5. KARINA, KACZKA—EAST PACIFIC RISE

The ship's PA system sounded three short alarms follow by an announcement, "Attention. Attention. Betty has landed."

"Finally!" Karina cheered in the cabin she shared with her father on the research vessel RV Riftia. She loved adventuring with her father. As the only child on board, not even a teenager, the adults ignored her, giving her many opportunities to explore. Most compartments and decks were restricted, but that rarely impeded her activities.

The PA sounded again, "All crew muster to watch duty. All crew muster to watch duty."

This was her chance. With the deep-submergence vehicle DSV Betty underwater, most areas of the RV Riftia would be abandoned. She headed for deck zero-two, the final location on her itinerary, the center of operations, and the most secure.

She put her ear to the door and listened. The small ship pitched forward and like an experienced sailor, she automatically put her hands out to avoid banging her head against the gray metal bulkhead. The coast was clear. On her toes, she ran up the ladder and through the hatch to the main deck.

Her heart rate accelerated as she excitedly scouted up and down the central passageway. She checked out the electronics lab, the biology lab, and the shops, where friendly scientists had already given her tours. She passed these up in favor of the salty and rotting low-tide odors wafting from Betty's hanger, off-limits to scientists and twelve-year-olds alike.

She entered the metal frame that reminded her of monkey bars. The titanium track sparkled in the sunlight. A clear lubricant coating its surface gave off a surprisingly medicinal odor. At every meter around the bulkhead, a hook-and-chain connected to an electronic winch awaited Betty's return. She opened her comp and took pictures of the track, chains, and compartment, even climbing the superstructure to capture aerial views. She considered posting copies until she remembered that she wasn't supposed to be there.

She could have spent the whole day exploring the main deck, but the elusive deck zero-two called to her. She scaled the ladder to zero-one deck, containing the galley, mess, and library. These were known territories as her father, a visiting food scientist, spent much of his time in the galley.

A chain and a *Restricted Area* warning blocked the ladder to zero-two deck and the aft control station, but she didn't let that deter her. She waited for a diversion. With Betty on the East Pacific Rise, two and a half kilometers under the RV Riftia, the crew was on alert.

After a few minutes, an alarm sounded. She counted. Three shorts. One long. She didn't recognize this sequence, but footsteps heading aft echoed overhead. *Now!* She scrambled up the ladder but stopped halfway when she spied a lone sailor running toward her. She promptly swung over the railing and hid under the ladder.

The sailor skidded to a stop. "Hey you! What are you doing there? It's not safe and you are in the way."

She quickly sized up the man addressing her. *Young.*

He did a double take. "You're a—" He paused like he couldn't find the word. "Girl."

She'd recently discovered that such guys responded to smiles. She climbed back up the ladder, stood facing him, and flashed him a big smile. "I was so bored in my cabin. I didn't think I'd be in the way." She moved closer and opened her eyes wide.

He stepped back. "You can't be up here."

She nodded assent and stepped back down the ladder. He resumed his mission, sprinting toward the aft control station.

When he was out of sight, she ascended the ladder slower this time. Having been warned, she wouldn't be able to play innocent if caught again. She didn't want to get her dad in trouble. Her heart pounded and hands sweated.

She entered a now unoccupied area of her destination, deck zero-two. She still worried because high above on zero-four deck, the bridge overlooked her position. *Now or never.* She took a deep breath and ran. She stopped at a winch, bigger than a car. It hid her from the aft control station, but the bridge could still see her if anyone happened to look. Fortunately, her luck prevailed. She stared at her goal, the aft control station roof. She scrambled for it but tripped on a cable.

Her mind raced as her body sprawled to the deck. She remembered her comp in the cargo pocket of her pants. With her knee and elbow, she protected her valuable electronics at the cost of a terrible bruise on her side. She gasped and pursed her lips. She mustn't yell.

In pain, she crawled between two winches to assess the damage. She woke up her comp and rubbed her hip. Nothing had broken. She waited. After what seemed forever, another alarmed sounded and she sprinted up the ladder to the top of the aft control station. Now safely hidden from the bridge under the radar dome, she relaxed for a pleasant afternoon of observation. The ocean stretched to the horizon inviting her to imagine a limitless future.

What is that? Looks like a splash! She made a tight circle with her finger and brought it to her eyes improvising a telescope. *A small grey whale breached. And another. A pod with calves. And a pod of dolphins!* High upon deck zero-two, she had a clear view. The whales rolled around playing with each other, seeming to ignore the pesky dolphins. But the dolphins loved the whales, swimming around, between, and under them, like so many playful kittens. They were too far for pictures, but she was happy to just watch the majestic mammals.

Pontoon rafts rang against the ship like clappers of a giant gong signaling the main event. Betty emerged from the deep. The A-frame crane whined, track clamps clanked, and the hangar door squealed wide open, releasing its *Eau de Davey Jones* fragrance.

Karina turned her attention to the recovery operation. She watched the crews move into position. The medical staff opened their red equipment chests. The deck crew checked the track. Below her, in the control station, the officers issued orders with a staccato tempo.

A recovery specialist scrambled aboard Betty and plugged in a phone to talk to the dive team still sealed in the personnel sphere. Plugging in a phone seemed so 20th century, but she hypothesized the sphere must be like a giant Faraday cage impervious to wireless technology.

This thought was interrupted; this wouldn't be an ordinary recovery.

First, the dolphins arrived, and then the whales, circling Betty like she was a long-lost friend. The recovery operation halted. The pontoon crews scrambled aboard Betty while the dolphins head-butted the rafts. Karina and everyone else watched the action. Now they were close enough and Karina took video. No one would believe this without the video record.

After fifteen minutes, the dolphins and whales grew bored with their unresponsive friend and the operation resumed. Betty was attached to the A-frame lift cables. While the winch screamed, Betty slowly rose. At the proper height, the A-frame rotated, moving Betty over the deck, lined up with the track. Karina held her breath until the swinging DSV was clamped in place. When she heard the last clamp snap, she smiled. *Good job.* People swarmed Betty like precision marchers or maybe a ballet troupe.

Amidst all the frantic activity, scientists recovered milk crates from the collection platform. They poked their gloved hands inside and examined the plants and shells. *I'm going to be a scientist.*

She'd need college money to do this. Good thing her mother had left a trust fund. *Thank you, Klara.* At twelve, the trust seemed unreal. All she knew was that it was for her education, not to live the life of a rich heiress.

She searched among the crowd for her father. He emerged from the galley with his two assistants. They stood out, being the only people in chefs' hats.

Two white milk crates remained for her father, Dr. Kaczka Kowalski. Karina's chest swelled with pride as the sailors made way for him. She doubted they cared about food science. More likely they appreciated his flair adding flavor and zest to their everyday fare. He led his entourage back to the galley. The sous-chefs followed bearing the milk crates in their outstretched arms like a pair of religious acolytes.

While Betty rolled into her hangar, Karina returned to her cabin. She spent the remainder of the time until dinner narrating the video and writing in her journal.

Kaczka had imagined this moment of discovery many times before boarding the RV Riftia in San Diego. After Institutional Review Boards and proposals, he had secured the necessary approvals and funding. His non-profit, Future Foods, received the bulk of its support from the U.N. Food and Agriculture Organization. Future Foods also depended on smaller groups, such as Empty Bowls organized by a farmer from Oklahoma.

His assistants looked to him, each holding a white crate full of Betty's deep-sea bounty—dripping seaweed, wriggling crustaceans, and sections of tube worms looking like amputated arms and legs. "Do you still want these on the center table? There's rather a lot of them."

Kaczka surveyed the ship's galley where he'd been preparing meals. Suddenly the two aisles between the walk-in cooler and the pantry felt confined, nothing like the spacious test kitchens in the U.N. Technology Innovation Labs scattered around the globe. The long wooden counter dividing the galley was dangerously close to the cooktops and ovens on one side and the sinks and prep tables on the other. "Yes. Plate them out."

The tube worm segments were collected to be taken to the scullery, while the remaining seaweed, crustaceans, and fish were sorted. Kaczka's mouth watered at the fresh seafood scent. He delighted at the colorful cornucopia bestowed by Betty. This had been an expensive gamble, but it had paid off. The deep-sea benthic flora and fauna looked similar to their shallow-water relatives. He looked forward to testing these ingredients in his favorite recipes, starting with a special farewell dinner for the crew. They could be important sources since the shallows were being depleted. These alone could justify the expedition. The tube worms could be the silver coin in the Christmas pudding.

He followed the crate of severed limbs to the scullery with anticipation. He'd found ways to serve Antarctic krill, forest kelp, and phytoplankton. He'd find recipes for these alien worms too. Someone had to track down new food sources. Proudly, he thought: Today, that someone is me.

His comp interrupted him. Annoyed, he reached for the flashing device.

The caller ID signaled *Roshni*, the chief scientist on his most ambitious project. She came ahead of tube worms, as did Karina. He couldn't forget his daughter. She had no one else.

"*Namasté*, Roshni. Are you calling to announce the birth of a mammoth calf?" he asked expectantly.

Future Foods' plan to bring back the woolly mammoth superseded the benthic exploration in cost and potential. Future Foods had raised many grants, each time promising "cattle" for the Arctic, along with other environmental benefits. Unfortunately, after many years, he still had nothing.

She ignored his question. "You forgot the money transfer again. Can't you set up something so the payment is automatic?"

He had placed the research in India because the well-educated population offered a steady supply of inexpensive doctors and biologists, even though the mammoths, when they arrived, would prefer a cooler climate. Dr. Roshni Teertha had the perfect *curriculum vitae*, educated in England with a doctorate and a medical degree—Biochemistry and Reproductive Endocrinology. Before joining the mammoth program, she ran a large laboratory at IIT New Delhi dedicated to cloning extinct species. Cloning mammoths would be the pinnacle of her research.

"I've been busy exploring the ocean depths. I'll send the money right now." An automatic transfer had been on his to-do list for years, always preempted by something else.

"Kaczka, as we've discussed many times, Jurassic Park was a Hollywood fantasy. Cloning extinct species is cutting-edge research."

He nodded. He'd read her papers, confirming her expertise and respect in the field. If she couldn't clone mammoths, no one could. He reassured her. "I'm in this for the long run."

"I'm glad to have your support. You understand we could redirect our efforts to dodo birds. My research has shown that it is easier to clone birds than mammals."

"Dodo birds? Are you serious?"

"Absolutely! Like the mammoths, they can be both a food source and a cultural icon or tourist attraction."

He had established the Mammoth Research Station with expectations that Dr. Roshni Teertha could clone woolly mammoths in a few years. Without a single mammoth birth, he considered her proposal: *Dodo birds? Surely, she's joking. He imagined everyone laughing at him.* He wondered why she was willing to give up after dedicating a decade to the work. *Was cloning mammoths that difficult?* "Let's not quit. Your rupees have been deposited. Let's get back to work. You birth some mammoth calves and I'll find a way to make tube worms edible."

His assistants prepped the tube worms in a scene that reminded him of an abattoir—blood everywhere. First, metal shears cut open the hard tubes. The worms were basically blood, bacteria, and sulfuric acid—a corrosive, smelly mess. The sous chefs puréed and packed the worms into centrifuge tubes. It took skill to extract the blood, the only edible part of this alien. He would start with the many recipes that used blood like Scandinavian blood pancakes and blood sausage from everywhere. Masai and Mongols drank blood straight from the source. He eagerly anticipated experimenting with all these recipes and inventing new ones.

Still, he wondered: Have I overextended myself? Tube worms. Mammoths.

What about Roshni? Was she disturbed by the Hindu protesters camped outside the Mammoth Research Station? As worshippers of Ganesh, the elephant-headed god, they wanted to shut down the use of elephants as surrogate mothers. He discarded this concern. *She may be Hindu, but she's a scientist first.*

And what about my daughter? Karina loved the excitement and novelty, but he often worried about her safety and lack of peers. When Klara was alive, life had been simpler. He hadn't needed to think about what to do to keep his daughter well and happy and safe while he tried to feed the world. Now as she approached her teen years, he felt unprepared. His itinerant lifestyle was wrong for a maturing teen.

At the farewell dinner, everyone praised his *Paella*, the classic Spanish shellfish dish. He surely could find something similar for tube worms. When he returned to his cabin, he opened his comp, and a notification grabbed his attention: Call for Speakers. South Africa had a conference on invertebrate foods—*konferensie vir ongewerwelde voedsel.* I'm an invertebrate expert he thought—squid, clams, crabs, shrimp. Fascinating, but he needed to figure out how to cook tube worms first.

With Karina snoring gently in the adjacent bunk, he turned off his comp and fell asleep enumerating an endless list of invertebrates.

Blood can substitute for eggs! Kaczka awoke. His eyes popped open, fully alert. He struggled to hold onto this subconscious vision before it faded away. He repeated to himself, "Blood equals eggs," over and over until he could write down his gift from Morpheus. He found his comp and recorded his revelation a second time.

In an instant, he'd solved the tube worm challenge. As an egg substitute, smaller quantities would be needed for each serving; the tube worms would stretch farther. Ideas flooded his mind. Blood cakes. Blood frittata. Savory blood custard, *chawanmushi* in Japan, and *la povera cucina* in Italy. He sent an email to his chefs, currently borrowing lab space at the U.N. Technology Innovation Lab in Finland, with a detailed plan. *Tube worms were solved. What next?*

He looked at the time. Three in the morning. Full of energy, he contemplated his next venture. What about South Africa? With a few taps, he determined it was early afternoon. He found the Call for Speakers.

"Lesedi Marais. Can I help you?" She spoke very quickly.

He couldn't believe his luck. She was the conference chair. He could hear her talking to several people in the background. He started cautiously. "I am Dr. Kaczka Kowalski. I am a food…"

She interrupted him. "*The* Dr. Kowalski? Antarctic krill popcorn? Forest kelp tortillas? *That* Dr. Kowalski?"

Taken by surprise, he found himself uncharacteristically lost for words. "Y…yes."

"I thought you were exploring black smokers, hydrothermal vents, tube worms."

"I just finished that project. I was wondering if you still needed speakers. I have quite a bit of experience with invertebrates."

"Oh yes!" She paused, adding, "You understand our meeting is on land animals like earthworms and crickets."

"No problem. Your attendees would still benefit from my experience with invertebrates of the seas. From the food prep point of view, there are a lot of similarities."

He heard her whisper, "Just a minute," to the people with her. "Mdudu Nyama looks forward to hosting you in Stellenbosch. I will send you the logistical details."

Kaczka had been waiting for a natural segue, but the conversation was too rushed to provide an opening. He couldn't let it end like this. "Perfect. By the way, I always travel with my daughter Karina. Her mother died. She's twelve."

As she replied, he knew there was a problem. Her voice dropped in pitch, volume, and tempo. "Our area has experienced a small outbreak of equine encephalitis spread by mosquitoes."

He'd never heard of this. "Is it bad?"

"The greatest risk is to children under fifteen and old people over fifty. The fatality rate is one out of five, so yes, it's pretty bad."

He didn't tell her that even though his daughter was twelve, he was fifty-seven. He'd already set his sights on the conference. "You said it is a small outbreak?"

"Yes, a dozen cases and two deaths. We've been able to keep it out of the news. Life goes on as usual, but most parents have sent their children to Cape Town."

"I understand." He could be careful, wash his hands, slather himself with DEET, etcetera. However, there was no way he'd take his wild child, thinking of her uncontrollable adventures aboard the RV Riftia. He thought more about Karina. "Are you sure you'll be able to keep this quiet?"

"Yes. Is that important?"

"Karina would be upset if she knew I visited during an outbreak. I'd don't intend to tell her. The trust of a daughter in her father is in your hands."

"No worries. We'll keep it quiet. Besides, Stellenbosch is not Cape Town or Johannesburg, few people care about our idyllic town in the countryside…unless it impacts the wineries."

He'd made his decision. "Okay, I'll expect your email and see you soon."

After the farewell dinner prepared by her father, Karina returned to their cabin. She packed her suitcases and put out a clean top and jeans for embarkation the next morning.

In the lovably clumsy way, she'd come to expect from her father, he started a discussion with no introduction or preliminaries. "I've hired a new teacher for the school at the Mammoth Research Station."

Good, she thought, but why mention this now? She hated the old teacher. He just gave them lessons to memorize and couldn't answer any questions beyond the scope of the textbooks. She constantly lamented, "He is not very bright. We could learn just as much without any teacher at all."

Her father smiled like he was about to disclose some amusing secret. "You and the other prodigies will not outsmart this one. She's Dr. Priya Agrawal with a Ph.D. in History, and an M.D., board-certified in Pediatrics." He paused as if just remembering something. "You're growing up... becoming... a woman."

She could see her father struggling. He could be a lot of things, but always stumbled when he needed to stand-in for Mom. She hugged her awkward father. "She can explain the birds and bees. Right?"

He returned her affection with a chaste pat on her shoulders. "Yes. You're correct." Then he stepped back and made another of his conversational leaps. "I received an invitation to speak at a conference on terrestrial invertebrates in South Africa."

"Terrestrial invertebrates? Like snails, spiders, and slugs?"

"Exactly! Especially worms and crickets."

"You don't know anything about *earth* worms. You've been prospecting the oceans."

"That's exactly why they want me. I am an expert on the invertebrates of the sea. They expect a lot of crossover."

She didn't want to argue. "Sounds like fun. I assume I'm going with you."

"They only invited me. Besides, you've already missed too much school. I'll catch up to you in a couple of weeks." Before she could reply, he continued. "I've arranged for your transfer from the San Diego docks to LAX, where you'll fly to Cochin. I'm sure you'll like the new teacher."

She went to bed more concerned about missing the trip to South Africa than the new teacher.

6. MIKE, ABBIE, CARLA—CHEROKEE OK USA

Mike had looked forward to his first day of Calculus. The teacher wrote her name on the board: *Miss Perry*. He doubted anyone needed the reminder since the short woman with grey hair and steel-blue eyes had chaired the math department since the beginning of time. Both his sister and mother had warned him about her strict rules. Even his father, who had taken woodshop instead of calculus, knew her reputation.

Her soft voice started the class with, "Everyone stand up. When I call your name, take the next available seat." She stood by the front row and tapped the desk nearest to the door. "Starting here." Mike studied the student work from previous years decorating the walls. He noticed a poster titled *Turbulence and Navier-Stokes* with beautiful illustrations. It was three years old and the author was Carla McGilvery. He frowned. Sometimes he hated having an older, smarter, taller sister.

"I'm starting with the ninth graders. Elzia."

Mike hadn't noticed her, but there she was walking to the front of the class. She had let her hair grow over the summer and now it was a pale blue. Her thick glasses hadn't changed.

Miss Perry didn't wait for her to take her seat. "Only a single ninth grader this year. We have five tenth graders. She paused before she read the next name. Mike cringed, praying she wouldn't mention his sister. "Mike you're next. I'm expecting great things from you."

There was a murmur of laughter, especially among the Longhorns with their big hats. Mike heard a whisper, "Way to go, short Duster. Keep your eyes on that tall Longhorn. Her grades are going to stampede over you." After some appreciative guffaws, someone added, "Leave you in the dust."

Miss Perry put a stop to the frivolity. "Silence! Remember where you are. This is not a required class, and your attendance is conditional on your behavior." Hushed quiet followed.

"Mike, your sister was the only student to get a perfect score on the final since—" She interrupted herself. "She's in college in Chicago, isn't she?"

Mike walked towards his seat and responded with a polite, "Yes ma'am." Mike expected to do well in this class but wanted to do it on his own, not because the teacher remembered his sister. He sat down thinking it couldn't get any worse.

"Now that I think about it. The only other person to get a perfect score was your mother."

The room broke out in guffaws with people whispering, "Your mother," and "Yo mama." Mike thought he saw Miss Perry smile and that she let them go too long before she smacked her ruler on her desk. This was a disappointing start to what he hoped to be one of his good classes.

25

At lunch, Mike went to hang out by the theater. It was the best place with the most space and the fewest teachers. His mother told stories of cheerleaders practicing on the padded benches and learning the latest dance moves in front of the revolving doors.

He approached a crowd in cowboy hats. Longhorns. More cattle ranchers had bought out wheat farmers over the summer. The Dusters had lost their prime real estate. He retreated to the gym thinking: It's not just climate change. Everything is changing.

When he reach the gym, he muttered under his breath, "And nothing's getting better."

After school, Mike stood with a group of Dusters who had known each other since kindergarten when there were few Longhorns. Everyone waited in front of the office for an air-conditioned ride home.

He had exciting news from the summer. "I went to the state science fair in Oklahoma City. My algae won first prize in the *productivity and power* competition. When mixed with all the other algae, they dominated. Dominated! After a week, they took over the bioreactors."

"Did you win a cash prize?"

"No, but my algae genome gets sequenced and registered in the national database. I named it "Mike's Mighty 00147." It's my 147th strain. Can you believe it started from our pond?"

Polite silence greeted his pronouncement. Still better than those Longhorns in math class, he thought. Undaunted, he continued, "I knew I was going to win because 00147 is a different color, darker. Did you realize that the chlorophyll color is the light that is *not* converted to energy? A darker chlorophyll absorbs more light energy. Black would be the best. I think I've discovered a new type of chlorophyll. This would be the first new one since *chlorophyll b*, over twenty years ago. I'm going to name it *chlorophyll m*."

Someone interrupted. "There's my mom. See everyone tomorrow." Three students ran from the air-conditioned school to an air-conditioned pickup truck. Groups of twos and threes left as more cars arrived.

"It uses ninety-six plastic bottles, all cascaded together—" Mike was explaining his latest bioreactor design when the last of the Dusters departed.

He wasn't alone for long. Elzia and her herd of Longhorns—boys and girls wearing their uniform of ponytails, camo shirts, leather jeans, and brightly-colored boots—walked by. She came so near that he felt her breath on his forehead. He could smell her lemon scent.

She taunted him. "Shouldn't you be finding a cure for *global warming* or whatever excuse you Okies use to beg for more money from the government?"

He smiled at her. "I am. My algae hybrid won a prize at the state science fair."

She smirked. "Algae? Really? Will algae stop the *Hot*?"

He stood tall and tilted his head back to look up into her green eyes. "Absolutely. I'm in a national contest to breed a strain of algae to capture carbon and sink it to the bottom of the ocean. My algae could win."

A boy standing next to Elzia interrupted. "We better not be late for football practice."

Elzia didn't seem to hear him. Still looking at Mike, she said, "Good luck with your contest." When the others headed to the gym, she ran to catch up with them.

He waved and shouted, "Thanks." At that moment it felt like she was the only one interested in his science. Stupid school, he thought.

His eyes followed her blue hair until she reached the end of the corridor and disappeared. He didn't think she'd stay until football practice ended, so he sat on the floor and read research papers on his comp. The first report he found was from China, about diatoms. The next one concluded that global temperatures had risen 2.7 degrees centigrade, well beyond the 1.5 scientists had recommended at the beginning of the century.

After an hour, the air conditioning switched off. Elzia hadn't returned. He walked home alone thinking about ways to improve his bioreactor and which strains to cross to improve survivability. Unfortunately, his dominant algae decayed and released their carbon shortly after they died. If algae were to end global warming, they needed to take their accumulated biomass to the bottom of the ocean and preserve it.

Stupid algae, he thought.

⌣

Abbie heard the thunder of cattle. A cloud of dust engulfed the yard and filtered through the open windows. She ran around the house closing them cursing the encroaching haze as it mixed with Sasha's fluff. At times like this she imagined the massive Newfoundland shed her undercoat year-round. She leaned out from Mike's room and shouted. "Redd! Cattle! Dust! Come help me close up the house." Sasha ran to the front door to greet Redbird, and Abbie could hear windows closing.

She yelled, "Thank you!" With the house secured, she noticed a new stack of bowls on the piano. She offered him an opening to talk about his pet project. "More donations?"

He proudly counted them. "...ten, twelve, fourteen, fifteen! This has been our best fundraiser yet. People are lining up to donate a hundred dollars in exchange for a hand-carved bowl with our *Empty Bowls* logo branded on the bottom. All that money goes to discover new food sources, to relieve food insecurity around the globe."

She was glad he'd found this network of woodworkers. He didn't like to socialize, but he fit in well with these people. As he headed back to his workshop—his sanctuary—she delayed him. "Redbird, our time in Oklahoma has come to an end."

He stopped mid-exit, holding the screen door open. "I thought we had decided to stay put."

She'd mentioned moving several times, but he'd ignored her. She had his attention now. After years of research, she'd considered every alternative. "Just the other day, you told me how dry the fields were. This is our final year for wheat. Ag extension investigated cotton, more drought-tolerant than wheat, but they rejected it. The cattle have won!"

He let the front door close, slowly turned back into the room, and dropped into his chair. Sasha promptly curled up at his feet. A thick book about the Trail of Tears sat nearby. "My family was driven out of Georgia. I don't want to leave my home again."

She didn't want to have this discussion, especially if he was going to start two centuries back. She ran her fingers through her curly red hair. "Yes, and mine were cleared from the Scottish Highlands at the same time."

He was silent.

One more time she explained. "If we don't sell, the bank's going to foreclose. This is about mortgages and droughts. It has nothing to do with distant people—other continents and centuries—empty bowls in Asia, 19th-century Cherokees in Georgia."

She pointed to the empty bowls. "If you want to feed people, we should keep growing wheat. We're good at it."

He ignored this. "I like it here. We could raise cattle like the others."

"Unfortunately, we have a heavy investment in wheat farming equipment. If we try to sell it here, we'll lose a fortune. In the north, the Dakotas, or even Canada, seed drills and harvesters are still valuable. There's still a living for wheat farmers up there."

He reached down to scratch Sasha's ears. "Some things are more important than money."

That was the last straw. "This is *exactly* about money! Without money, we lose the farm. Our only choices are to get thrown out or to sell. We don't have enough money to stay."

He didn't reply. She heard his feet stomp across the wood floor and the front door opened.

She followed, raising her voice. "You can't ignore this anymore!"

"I can't talk as well as you, but can you think of my ancestors? Some are still buried here in unmarked graves under the kitchen garden. If we sell, cattle will sleep on their graves. Not good!" He took a deep breath like he was going to say something else, but he didn't.

Then she saw someone in the doorway. *Mike! Had he seen the entire thing?* Mike closed his eyes and covered his ears. She recognized his look, disappointment, fear, sadness. Sasha's tail wagged once, then stopped.

Before she could say anything, Mike patted the Newfie, "Let's go, girl." The boy and dog went out together.

Redd stepped forward and gently hugged her. She stood with her arms at her side. He pressed his lips to her forehead and whispered, "Sorry. Of course, we'll do what you think is best."

She hoped that would be the last discussion. She returned to the kitchen to chop fresh vegetables, a luxury of the season. She raised and lowered her favorite knife with care, fearful she might cut off a finger.

Carla waited until Mike took Sasha out and ran to join him, "Mike! Wait up!"

Carla stood next to him gazing across the newly planted fields, bleak in the grey autumn light. "Tell me brother, what happened while I was away saying goodbye to my friends?"

Mike answered in that bored tone teenagers use when they don't want to talk. "I was gone most of the afternoon myself. Mom cooked. I think dad carved some more empty bowls."

Carla pressed. "Yes, but what else? I saw them at dinner. They were too nice, too polite. Something is wrong."

Mike threw a ball for Sasha.

Carla continued. "I saw you too. You were on your best behavior. You wiped your mouth with your napkin after every mouthful, a sure sign of trouble."

Sasha returned and Mike grabbed the ball.

"Mike, I'm your sister. You can tell me." She put her arm around his shoulder. "You know I'm leaving for Chicago tomorrow."

When his shoulders slouched, she realized reminding him of her imminent departure was not the best approach.

Fortunately, he didn't retreat into silence. He snapped back at her, "I'm not blind. I can see the rental car charging in the driveway." He threw the ball over the barn and while Sasha ran around to find it, he closed his eyes. "Forget about it. Nothing happened while you were gone."

His response encouraged her. She held his head against her chest and rested her chin on his curly red hair. "Come on Shorty. Tell your sister about it."

He took a deep breath. He recounted how he'd come home from school and saw mom shouting. "She was angrier than I've ever seen."

Carla reached for her brother, but Sasha had returned, and Mike knelt down for the ball. "You're leaving. I have to take care of myself."

She smiled at him. "You're right and you can do it."

After a few tense minutes, he asked, "Do you think they'll get divorced?"

Carla laughed. "Oh no!"

She saw a frightened look on his face. "When we were little, they argued a lot. There was a lot of shouting."

Mike shivered.

She continued, "I'm not sure what changed. I was too little to understand, but the fighting stopped." After considering what he'd told her, she added, "Until today."

Mike gave her a crooked grin. "In my family life class, they told us that the first disagreement was the hardest. I was frightened that this was that. If they've had other fights, I guess they'll be okay."

"I think you're right." She encouraged him, and added, "You know, brother. You worry too much."

"Yes, I know, but if they haven't fought in a long time, maybe this is like the first one. I don't want them to get divorced."

Now Carla worried, not about her parents, but about her brother. She took his hand and they walked back to the house with Sasha and her wagging tail showing the way. "Sasha's a good girl. She'll take care of you."

●

A month later, Abbie served dinner making two trips to carry the pot roast, mashed potatoes, cauliflower, homemade biscuits, and gravy to the table. *Why am I still using serving dishes when there are only three of us?* She reflected that since Carla left, dinners had become quiet affairs. *But then again, maybe it had nothing to do with Carla. Is he still mad about moving?* Abbie had committed to not broach the subject again.

She studied the two quiet men at her dinner table. Mike behaved like a scared child. He took small bites, chewed forever, and wiped his mouth after each one. If he didn't look so sad, she would have laughed.

Redd moped and sulked. His knife and fork made angry clicking sounds as he cut up his pot roast and mashed potatoes. His pulse throbbed along his tense neck. More click-clack. She resisted telling him he didn't need a knife to cut her pot roast and certainly not the mashed potatoes!

It had been too long for this to drag on. As usual, the responsibility to clear the air fell to her. She collected her courage and did her best to sound neutral, "Is something wrong?"

She noticed gray streaks in Redd's straight black hair as he looked down at his plate and kept cutting. She didn't ask again. If he didn't want to talk, that was his choice.

When dinner was over, Redd sat silently while Mike, still on exemplary behavior, cleared the dishes. She served homemade pie, pumpkin this time, and poured Redd a cup of coffee. He cut his pie, click-clack-click, just like the pot roast. A cloud of flaky pie crust surrounded his plate.

Without looking up, he began, "I had the seed drill all scheduled, and Howie forgot to order his seeds. We are all on no-till planting. There's not much preparation."

Yay! He's not brooding about the move, it's just the planting. Abbie relaxed. The tension ebbed from her shoulders. She could feel herself sitting taller. Her relief didn't last long as she flashed back to her second pregnancy.

"I am exhausted, every day, all the time. Can you help with little Carla?"

Redd exploded. "Do you think you're the only one with problems? It's planting season and I have to coordinate with a dozen farmers to use the communal seed drill. Each one is more disorganized than the next!"

Toddler Carla woke up crying. Abbie shouted as she rushed to the bathroom to throw up. "Now you woke her up. Can you go check on her?"

"No, I can't check on her. I have to check on Howie. He was scheduled to deliver the seed drill here early this morning, and now it's noon! How am I supposed to get my fields seeded by the end of the day? I'm going to be out there until midnight."

Abbie returned from the bathroom, calmed Carla, and let her rest her head on Abbie's little bump. She stroked her curly red hair and sang to her, "Hush little baby, don't say a word."

Eventually, she bought Redd his own equipment to shield him from such difficulties. He didn't have to coordinate with the other farmers.

Redd took a forkful of pie. She liked how the tart-sweet flavor with her secret blend of spices put a smile on his face, but after he swallowed it with a slug of coffee, his scowl returned. "Darn Howie had one thing to do, and he messed it up."

She murmured, "It's our equipment. You don't have to deal with the neighbors, especially not Howie."

They owned the seed drills for just this reason. She managed the money, therefore they never discussed this. She invested in equipment to relieve his anxiety during planting and harvesting. Somehow his creed of *think right and do right* meant he had to help everyone even if it drove him crazy.

She shook her head. *All that money spent, and he's still upset.* After all these years, he was still something of a mystery, but her mystery. She hugged him and didn't say anything more.

7. Xiang Bo—Huixian China

The man in the car rental office yelled at her for getting mud on the fenders. "Where have you been driving this? You are supposed to stay on the paved roads. Only paved!" he said in a loud, hard voice. He tried to loom over her, but since he wasn't any taller than she, Xiang Bo decided he'd had entirely the opposite effect. She almost laughed aloud at him, but instead looked at the floor, hiding her mouth that kept curling into a smile.

Somewhat mollified by her apparent shame, he flicked the papers on the countertop and declared, "I will not charge you extra for the cleaning this time, but this cannot happen again."

Xiang Bo knew she should keep her mouth shut, but it just seemed unfair. The words came out, though she did at least manage to keep them gentle. "How is one to keep mud from splashing from the paved road when it is always raining here?" she asked. "Am I supposed to not drive it in the rain?"

"This is thick mud, not from major highways, where the surface is only wet, not muddy. You drove on much smaller roads."

"Ah."

She noticed he charged her a cleaning charge after all, probably because she dared question him. She went ahead and paid him, vowing to not return to the small storefront where the clerks were always angry. She did not need to come here. She *would* not come here.

She boarded the bus to the airport, clutching her computer bag and a small suitcase in her lap to take up as little room as possible on the crowded bus. People were jammed in so tight the standees did not even tilt when the vehicle stopped abruptly. She could see a couple of young adults—adventurous students, probably—clinging to the closed doors outside the bus. Their toes must be barely on the entry steps. She worried for them, but they hopped off after only a couple blocks.

She rested her chin on her computer bag, thinking of how to enter the most recent data into a legible table. Grant committees liked easy-to-read tables. And charts. She was good at presenting her information clearly.

Her latest grant had come in for the full amount she had asked for. She would have been pleased to have even half that. It was unexpected, but welcome. She had not told Dr. Chen this. She still did not know exactly why; it was a bragging point to show him, to prove to him her doctorate, her work, and *she*, were all just as good as his were.

But she hadn't told him. She had almost one hundred thousand Canadian dollars. It would buy her a small lab, separate from his. She was still not entirely certain he had not sabotaged one of her most promising genotype trials. *Some*one had. He and his lab assistant claimed animals had gotten in, but animals did not open bottles and drop a milliliter of ammonia into each of her Petri dishes. She tried to believe he had not known of the attack, but it was very difficult when he remained so contemptuous of her trials.

She sighed, and waited her turn to get off the bus. The little airport at Hechi was small and clean. She found her gate and sat down.

The grant money could also buy a four-wheel-drive vehicle, with enough left over she could increase the number and thus the diversity of her algae-diatom samples. She could even hire a technician, so she needn't make these back and forth trips so often. She dared not ask Dr. Chen or his assistant to help.

She now had one working genotype suitable for the lowland ponds. She had added it to the water of one of her test pools, next to others with failed genotypes. Or, perhaps not *failed*, precisely. Just less efficient than she'd hoped. She was trying to persuade it to do too many tasks: cool the water, provide not only shade and food for the fish, but also a screen that might help keep the cranes from feasting—all while being inherently tasty or at least amenable to cooking with spices and herbs.

The fish, and indeed the algae itself, were intended as food for *people*, not their beloved but overpopulating birds. The ecology was self-sustaining—if nothing interfered from outside. The sturdy *Hot*-proof rice grew in mud rich with algae and fish defecation. The algae also used the fish droppings and the oxygenated water to grow. The fish ate the algae and microorganisms that grew with the rice. They sustained each other. But would they provide more food for humans than plain rice? Plain fish? Algae alone? Were vegetables a better choice than rice?

Ponds existed already all over China, in the terraced rice fields and bottomlands. Most of the country had sufficient water, but because of increasing temperatures in all "temperate zones" of Earth, even Guangxi Province could barely feed itself.

She along with most of the world was convinced the problems would only get worse as temperatures continued to rise. Saltwater rice fields covered the lagoons and former swamplands of areas bordering the Yellow Sea, like around Qindao. Even so, half of China was going to bed hungry.

Of course she would go straight to the fields when she got home that afternoon to see how the new genotype trial was doing. Was it the answer? Well, no reason to speculate; she would see soon enough.

She took advantage of the airport's free Wi-Fi to look up used four-wheel-drive vehicles. Nothing in Hechi fit her needs, but there was a possible vehicle in an auction lot just outside Guilin. She would go take a look. She'd have to drive the thing to Hechi, if she bought it, but that was easily done. She used to get rental cars in Guilin and drive the entire route, but since it took an extra day, she had switched to the short air hop to take her halfway.

Li was right in one respect, her second research site was remote, and annoyingly distant from the one in Huixian. But she had the benefit of being in Donglan to see her friend Mo Chou, her mother, and Zi Min and the other children. She wasn't willing to give any of that up for the sake of a few less travel days each month.

◠

Dr. Chen Li stood in the doorway, arms folded, a scowl on his face. He stepped in front of her, blocking her attempt to sidle past him. "You didn't answer me," he said. "Where did that hideous *jeep* thing come from?"

"It's not a Jeep. It's a FAW four-wheel drive. It's a used police car with special safety features for driving on country back roads and cross-country. The rental place in Hechi will no longer let me take their cars where I need to go."

"Is it rented, the jeep?" Li said, his face expressionless.

"No." Xiang Bo stopped trying to get past him and instead raised her gaze to meet his dark eyes. Dark angry eyes. "It's mine." She said.

"You dared take our money to buy this monstrosity?"

"It's from *my* grant monies."

"You never had enough to buy that."

"I did."

From behind Li, his mother's voice came, strong and amused, "Xiang Bo, it is such a practical solution for your studies. Will you drive all the way to Donglan next time?"

"Yes, Di'e," Xiang Bo said. "I will leave it in Hechi and fly home. That way it will be there where I need to drive on the gravel and dirt roads."

"That is a better solution than paying for the rental cars, I would think," Di'e said, with a small smile.

"In any event, they won't let me rent a car there now. Both rental companies require staying on paved roads, and that just isn't practical."

"If you would move your second site closer to Guilin—"

"Li, we have discussed this many times. The whole point of the Nalai site is to experiment with other micro-ecologies. I cannot do that here."

Dr. Cheng Li, in all his vaunted superiority, threw up his hands.

Xiang Bo darted past him, into the kitchen. Di'e stood in there rubbing her wrinkled hands together, as she did whenever Li and Xiang Bo argued. Xiang Bo gave her a small bow, as to an honored elder, and moved back into her tiny office. It was a closet, really. A pantry they'd removed the doors from. Her chair in front of the board "desk" was perpetually in the way of anyone passing from either bedroom to the long-ago retrofitted bathroom with its composting toilet.

The Cheng compound was ancient, but Di'e and others' care had kept it livable, practical, and clean for nearly two centuries. It was probably held up more by layers of paint than the brick of its walls, these days. Despite its age, the graceful lines of the buildings, painted pure white against the sun and heat, were still a lovely refuge. Xiang Bo opened her computer and began entering growth numbers and observations.

Di'e's soft voice asked if she wanted tea. She must have said yes, because Di'e's favorite gray-glazed small pot appeared on her table, along with a pair of tiny cups. Xiang Bo glanced up to see Di'e dragging a stool from the kitchen so she could sit beside her. Xiang Bo jumped up and helped get the stool placed, then they sat down together. Di'e poured, and they sipped the first sip together. Then Xiang Bo returned to her work. Di'e watched.

Li was still complaining about the "jeep" at dinner. "Surely something more efficient and less expensive could be found," he said.

"But this is what I wanted," Xiang Bo said. "To be safe, and have always available without having to fight the rental agency each trip." She took a bite, chewed it without really noticing what she ate. Di'e's food deserved better attention than it got, she thought, while also trying to think about arguments for Li. "And," she said as he began opening his mouth for another salvo, "it's going to be less expensive in the long run, since they keep charging me extra for mud, or rock dings, or cracked windows or some nonsense."

"Why is there so much damage? Are you driving crazy?"

"No. The damage that they're finding is minimal, they just choose to view it as things that wouldn't happen if I stayed on the main highway."

Li shook his head, frowning. Again, as he opened his mouth to speak, she pre-empted him.

"It is mine. I bought it with grant money that was expressly provided for the purpose of continuing my research," she said. "It will help me continue my research."

That should have concluded the discussion. That it didn't was just one more example of Li's insistence that he was supposed to be "boss" and all decisions were his. Even the ones involving *her* research.

Xiang Bo felt uncharacteristic rage rising as Li pattered on with repeated iterations of his same previous arguments. She had answered his objections. She had spent her own grant money as she saw fit to continue her own research! She stood up and left the table. Dr. Cheng Li, in all his Han authority, rose and demanded she sit back down. She left the room.

◠

"I told you to use the Chlorospermac," Li said looking over her shoulder at the pond. He pointed his finger. "These are clearly not green algae. What are they?"

"Diatoms," she said, tying her straw hat under her chin. "Green algae does not block enough sunlight. It doesn't cool the water."

"It could if you had blended the genotypes properly to begin with."

Xiang Bo felt the rage rising again. She could not stop herself from letting it explode. It was as if her will to control herself had been eaten away to nothing, chipped off bit by bit by the little hammers of Li's contempt.

"I *did* blend them!" She grabbed his arm by the elbow and dragged him across the embankment to the next row of pools. "This is the result." Surely even in his blind arrogance, Li could see the murky water of the pool, including a couple of silvery-green streaks that were the bellies of dead fish. While they watched, a small gas bubble erupted from the water, as though the entire pond had burped its discontent. "It *works* in one way," she said in sarcastic tones. "The herons and cranes stay away! They won't touch anything in this pond."

She let go of his elbow and went back to re-measure the temperature of the diatom-filled pond, leaving him to stare at the disaster.

This water was definitely staying cooler. She wrote the temperature down in her log book. She felt the deep green rice leaves. They looked and felt healthy. Last, she dug the fish net out of the gear she'd brought out from the field-shed and scooped up a net full of fish—and algae-diatom. The fish were a good 15 centimeters in length, and half of them were so energetic they managed to flop themselves out of the net and back into the water. She prodded the remaining two fish; the gills were healthy, their scales were shiny and clean, no slimy residue coated them, like in the Chlorospermae-treated pond. She set the net back below water level allowing the fish to swim out.

She felt the net, to see what the texture of the diatom-algae blend felt like. Rather than typical slippery algae, she rather expected a gritty texture, like broken pottery. Instead it was smoother than that. More like very fine sand, or polishing clay. She scooped a few water samples into tubes, to look at in their tiny lab.

Next she examined the edges of the pond to see what kinds of residue the water might be leaving on the embankments. "Levees" her classmates at Scripps had insisted on calling them. Of course these were not at all the great sloped walls—levees—that had held back the Mississippi that she had seen when she visited New Orleans. These were more like the little dams children liked to build in streamlets. Without care to pack them tight again each spring, the embankments holding the pond water in would gradually erode back to nothing. They were made of mud, after all, sometimes with a little sand or gravel bed beneath to support them. She took samples of the dirt and algae-diatoms there as well.

She stood up and smiled at the happy little pond. She saw no evidence of invasiveness which meant her genotype design had held true. The algae-diatoms would grow to fill their space, naturally. But then they would stop, not bloom into disastrous world-eating sludges, like the Chlorospermae had a tendency to do. This was a good result, as far as it went.

She might try Azolla again next, but it did not have the same ability to drastically reduce the water temperature. It was working at the Nalai site. And Jiao's pigs and chickens loved it. It was probably even better at converting atmospheric nitrogen into a natural fertilizer than the diatom-algae were going to be.

—

Di'e had asked to go with her when she went to check on their bracken "farm." They were laughing over Di'e's tart observations about the compound's neighbors as they bounced across the creek-bed ford in her 4WD. Xiang Bo wondered again at her ability to get along with Li's mother better than she did with him. Perhaps she should have married Di'e. But that wasn't done openly in China, of course.

She and Li had planted the bracken together, in a happier time. The small farm lay on the site of one of the Great Leap Forward's most infamous failures. Backyard furnaces were small steel blast furnaces that were supposed to be used by untrained ordinary people to smelt steel and other ores, a part of making each commune self-sufficient in Mao's crazy plan. Instead, the best results were low-quality pig iron, and some of the worst were toxic waste dumps, resulting both from the ores, and the fuels used to smelt them.

While at Scripps Institute of Oceanography, Xiang Bo had learned of bracken fern projects, where bracken were planted to purify heavy metal mining sites. After the plants matured, they were harvested and burned. The ash contained the heavy metals, in some cases in pure enough form that they could be re-used.

Even if their fern farm never *produced* any ores, they were at the very least plants that would grow to cover the ugly slag heaps.

She and Di'e harvested the most mature plants from the field. Xiang Bo would burn them and test the ash at their small lab set up outside the living quarters, back in the corner of the fenced compound of Di'e's home. Xiang Bo still did not consider it hers, though of course she recognized that was partly because her own mother did not live there. Maybe if she stayed there more often, it would begin to feel like a place of refuge. Di'e certainly welcomed her.

She had hoped Li would as well, but he seemed more interested in picking apart her research. At first there had been some mutual respect between them, but now it was more like a competition. Was that her fault?

8. KARINA, PRIYA, KACZKA—KERALA INDIA

The pilot's announcement woke her up. "Look out your windows for one of the seven wonders of the 21st century. Indian engineers have built over 300 kilometers of levees to protect the barrier islands separating Vembanad Lake from the rising sea. The Kerala Backwaters Project cost over two million crores."

She was still mad at her father for sending her away while he visited South Africa. She felt like she'd been kidnapped. However, the massive construction piqued her interest. She activated her small window. The concrete and steel walls glowed in the sunrise, holding back the Arabian Sea to the west and containing Vembanad Lake to the east. It reminded her of Los Angeles International Airport where she had just flown over the Pacific Coast Barriers on her way to Cochin.

After she cleared customs, Karina scanned the arrival hall until she spied the khaki uniform of the research station security staff. She waved and he came forward. "*Namasté*. Did you have a good flight?"

No flight that lasted over twenty-four hours could be considered good, but she put on her best manners, "Yes, thank you."

She napped during the short drive to Muvattupula, the closest city, where they stopped to pick up a woman, also in a khaki security force uniform. Karina stared at the woman's rifle, "Is the research station under attack?"

The woman answered. "The demonstrators have gotten more militant. We've had intruders, painted slogans, broken windows, and once the elephants were let loose. Vadish just wants to be prepared."

Vadish was the head of security and paranoid. "Do you really need guns?"

The man locked the doors and rolled up the windows. "You're Kaczka's daughter. We don't want any surprises."

She found this supposed threat hard to believe. She recalled families camping outside the gate: men playing drums, children chasing each other, and women in colorful saris waving signs, mostly painted in the beautiful spirals of Malayalam script. On her previous visits, the guards joined in the party-like atmosphere ignoring the formality that they were "opposed" to the "protestors.".

Soon enough, they arrived. The Muslim Arch marked the entrance. She admired the mosaic artwork, tiles glazed in bright colors and arranged in geometric patterns, typical of Islamic art. In contrast, she frowned at the miles of fencing topped with surveillance cameras and motion detectors— more of Vadish's paranoia. As she expected, a colorful group seemed to be having a party. Over the objections of her escorts, she opened her window to greet the families. She handed out candies she'd saved from her flight and the children gave her small bags of rice while repeating in English, "For Ganesh." It would have been nicer if armed guards were not posted atop the arch.

A short distance beyond the gate, beyond the reach of the protestors, stood a five-meter-tall elephant, with four arms and three eyes—a shrine to Ganesh, the god of science, wisdom, and many other things. He was the reason for the crowds. Even though Ganesh opposed research using elephants, he was her favorite. She asked the driver to stop so she could place the children's rice into the elephant god's offering bowl.

Once they passed the commotion, the car picked up speed as they drove through coconuts, bamboo, pineapples, bananas, pastures for the elephants, and a field of solar panels. Adjacent to the solar panels was the power plant, today buzzing and smelling of ozone. She grimaced at this relic of 20th-century technology. Unfortunately, solar panels didn't provide enough power during monsoon season, which had been particularly wet this year—an ominous reminder of the changing climate. She thought windmills could help, but no one listened to a twelve-year-old.

Through the haze, she reacquainted herself with the main buildings. On the west side of the main road, she recognized the western-style laboratory of glass and concrete, painted a dull grey. In sharp contrast to the lab, on the opposite side of the road, the administration building resembled a pagoda with tiers of steeply pitched tile roofs and painted a bright red. It contained offices, meeting rooms, the communal dining room, and the library. The west-west, east-east layout was her father's little joke.

Continuing north, a smaller copy of the lab contained a combination of infirmary and veterinary hospital. Across the road were the barns for the elephants and equipment. Finally, they entered the village with its maze of narrow roads. On her first visit, there were only three bungalows, for her father, Roshni, and Vadish. The others lived in tents or commuted over an hour each way to Muvattupula, the closest city. Now there were almost a hundred bungalows along with a small shopping center and a pool. Only her father's bungalow was still the original grey. The others were a cheerful array of tropical hues, every pastel color of the rainbow.

When the car stopped in front of her father's bungalow, she carried her luggage to the veranda and waved goodbye to her armed escort. Kaz would expect an email reporting her arrival. "Safely delivered to *Fort* Mammoth. LOL. Vadish has turned the place into an armed camp. Enjoy your worm conference. Don't eat too many crickets. Off to school tomorrow."

A warm meal from the dining room and her comfortable bed called to her fatigued body. However, as a seasoned flyer, her brain resisted the urge to crash. Putting off sleep as long as possible, she ate dinner at the local time.

Priya's heart cried for the awkward twelve-year-old blond girl with her comp pressed against her chest who could only be Kaczka's daughter. "Welcome Karina. This is your desk." Kaczka had requested that she be taught with the teenagers, surely thinking that his precocious offspring would benefit from the more advanced material. Priya recalled when her grandparents had subjected her to the same well-meaning torture. She still shuddered reliving the taunting she received each time she was awarded a top score.

She had placed Karina between Sarita, the daughter of Vadish, and Niraj, son of Roshni, imagining that these children of senior people would know Kaczka's daughter and treat her well. Her mistake was immediately obvious.

Niraj extended his legs in the aisle blocking Karina's way. "What are you doing sitting with the big kids?"

Sarita hissed, "Oh look. The baby is back."

Karina stepped over Niraj's legs and sat at her desk not responding to Sarita at all. Her blue eyes stared into Priya's brown ones as if to say, "Just ignore them. Just ignore me."

Priya accepted the implied criticism and advice. She taught her one-room school with students from lower primary to higher secondary as if Karina were invisible. As she anticipated, Karina received the top scores, but the results were never announced. Priya took hope when the other students eventually ignored Karina.

◗

Karina arrived early to an empty classroom and took her seat between Sarita's and Niraj's desks. She checked her comp to be sure she had all her homework. Unsurprisingly, all her assignments were there. Also, unsurprisingly, she received an email from her father, copied to Priya, Vadish, and Roshni, delaying his return from Africa again. She open the *Lord of the Flies* eBook, anxious to see what next misfortune would befall her favorite character, Piggy.

Niraj smiled at her, "Good morning! Could you help me with my maths homework?"

Since he hadn't spoken to her since that first day, she was suspicious, but she could see no harm. She knew he needed the help.

While she explained the quadratic formula, Sarita arrived. Karina tensed up as she approached.

"Thanks for tutoring Niraj."

Karina listened for sarcasm in her voice but didn't hear it.

"We're having a barbeque in the pineapple field tonight. Would you like to join us?"

Even though she suspected some nasty prank, she welcomed the alternative to eating alone. "Sure."

Karina enjoyed the barbeque. It was followed by other social events with the older kids and additional delays by her father. When Sarita and Niraj invited her on an overnight excursion, she accepted and looked forward to more good times with the teenagers.

◡

After teaching her last class on Friday, Priya returned to her bungalow. She exchanged a silk jacquard sari for loose cotton pants and a blouse. A simple jute bag she'd purchased in the Muvattupula market for a few hundred rupees held her comp. A plain umbrella from the same market completed her outfit. She admired herself in the mirror. Ordinary. Forgettable. Almost invisible. Perfect. She didn't want to attract any attention waiting for the bus amid the protestors outside the Muslim Gate.

As a final step, she checked her list. She had forgotten the ripe pineapple she'd picked for *Achachan*. It was her grandfather's favorite. She put it in her bag and headed out the door.

As she walked to the gate, she noticed someone standing at the Ganesh Shrine. She thought it might be one of the many security people. Unexpectedly, it was Roshni!

"Good evening Priya. What brings you all the way out here?"

I should ask the same question, she thought. What's Roshni doing by the gate? She has her own Ganesh shrine in her lab. Though Roshni wasn't her boss, she still felt obligated to offer a polite answer to the query. "I am here every Friday afternoon, waiting for the bus to spend the weekend with my grandparents."

When Roshni took two long steps in her direction, Priya backed away. Roshni looked down at her, staring directly into her eyes, and asked, "Are you sure you're not here to stir up the protestors? Is that why you're disguised? I almost didn't recognize you."

Now Priya had enough. She'd been polite, but Roshni had gone too far. "I visit *Achamma* and *Achachan* every weekend. Now get out of my way." When Roshni didn't move, she added, "I could ask the same of you. Are you here to encourage the protests?"

"I'm just offering some rice to Ganesh."

She looked directly into the chief scientist's eyes, below her wild eyebrows. It surprised her when Roshni didn't return her gaze. *Is she hiding something?*

"Vadish and I researched your background. You're overqualified. Board-certified pediatrician? Did Kaz hire you to replace me?"

Such crazy talk. Priya just wanted to not miss her bus. Her grandparents would worry. "Obviously not!"

Roshni crossed her arms, moved closer, and blocked the way.

Priya considered smacking her with the jute bag or poking her with the umbrella. Instead, she said something which she regretted later. "I have been reading the literature on cloning extinct species, much of it authored by you." Her hands shook, almost dropping her weapons. "Dr. Kowalski might not notice, but I can see you're not using your latest techniques." She realized she'd raised her voice, something she never did. She continued with a controlled delivery. "Your experiments fail because you don't even follow the best practices from your own papers. He didn't hire me to replace you, but maybe he should have!"

Now humiliated and in tears, she side-stepped past Roshni and ran to catch the bus that was approaching the Muslim Gate, all the while wondering how Roshni had succeeded, since she was such a sloppy worker.

When seated on the bus, she was soothed with the thought, I always do my best, just as *Achamma* raised me.

◗

Karina woke up to Niraj and Sarita banging on her door. She pulled on her clothes, grabbed a poncho, and opened the latch. Sarita yelled, "Let's go, *baby* sister." Niraj barged in and grabbed her backpack. "Big adventure today."

She stuck her tongue out at Sarita. "Don't call me that! Just because your dad's head of security and you're fifteen, you have no reason to treat me like a child. I can be as grown-up as anyone."

Niraj, whose mother was Roshni, stepped in front of Sarita. "Calm down girls. Let's not start off fighting."

They took off on ATVs, splashing through puddles. Karina reflected on the difference a few weeks made. At first, the teenagers would have nothing to do with her, and now they were going on an overnighter together. She enjoyed the freedom of being on her own. Kaz wasn't expected to return until tomorrow afternoon. She didn't even send him an email!

"We'll be back before my father arrives, right?"

Sarita replied, "Don't worry."

Niraj added, "We'll be back by breakfast. Your father's not expected until afternoon, or maybe the next day."

Karina joined in the joke. "Or even next week. No one sets their clock by my father's schedule. Anyway, where are we going?"

"We're going to take kayaks down the river."

"What river?"

"The Kaliyar. It's just a short way. I'm sure you've seen it driving to the research station."

Karina had a vague recollection, but she was usually jet-lagged when she arrived, so she couldn't be sure.

They drove uphill. When they reached the eastern perimeter, Niraj turned off his ATV. "We'll be on foot from here."

They left the station through an unattended gate and headed into the forest. The trees looked familiar, like the northeast United States, but the undergrowth displayed the bright pinks and reds of ginger. As dense trees blocked the sun, Karina recalled researching the Western Ghats, home to panthers, leopards, tigers, and wild dogs—all dangerous—all exciting. "I hope we get to see some big cats."

"Me too," agreed Sarita.

She shouldered her backpack. Niraj and Sarita each wore their own packs and carried a hamper between them looking like a sweet couple going on a picnic. After a short uphill stretch, the trail branched. Karina turned downhill, sure that had to be the way to the river.

Finally, they reached two kayaks beached on the bank of a fast-moving river.

Sarita exclaimed, "Look at that! I've never seen the Kaliyar so high."

Niraj added, "Named after the Goddess Kali. That's where it gets its power."

"Power?" Sarita made a face. "Power comes from Allah! Kali is a myth!"

Karina ignored the religious tension between the teenagers. Him being Hindu, her being Muslim didn't explain why the river was beautiful. Instead, she marveled at the whitewater splashing against the boulders along the banks. This reminded her of spring in the Alps. She took a seat on the sandy shore while Sarita opened the hamper and removed a *dabba* of stacked aluminum pans. Karina had skipped breakfast, so she watched intently as Sarita spread the food before them. Rice, naan, and tandoori chicken, her favorites. Niraj handed out bottles of cold beer.

She hadn't had beer before but didn't want to give Sarita a reason to call her *baby* again. She sipped the cold bottle slowly and ate a big lunch. She found the beer refreshing.

After lunch, they embarked, Niraj in one kayak with the packs, Sarita and Karina in the other. Sarita maneuvered them through the swift currents. Karina felt nervous as the river rushed them farther from home. Thick vegetation enclosed them in a green tunnel. Soon enough the river flattened and widened, and Karina relaxed.

By evening, Karina wondered where they were going. Two other rivers joined the Kaliyar. Gradually homes and boats lined their route. The buildings became larger and they entered a city.

"Welcome to Muvattupula," Niraj called out.

Karina gasped when her kayak tipped. Sarita laughed and made a sharp turn. "We'll spend the night here."

Karina couldn't read the swirling Malayalam script, but other boats were tied up and the teenagers that swarmed all around gave her a safe feeling. A few spoke English, but the rest spoke something else, maybe Malayalam.

Karina felt grown up with all these teenagers. After a communal dinner, someone brought out a comp to play music. The music channel changed many times until the group settled on one that Karina thought might be a fusion of Indian movie soundtracks and American pop.

She asked Niraj, "I didn't think we had cellular coverage. Where are they getting all that music from?"

He pulled out his comp and showed its signal. "No signal up in the foothills where the research station is, but now we are in the big city."

"If I had known, I would have brought my comp. I've gotten out of the habit of carrying it." She added, "Obviously, it's no big deal. We're heading back to the foothills tomorrow."

She had another beer and started feeling sleepy. She turned to Sarita. "I'm getting pretty tired."

"Me too. Let's get our packs out of the lockers and go to the girls' dormitory. It's early. We'll get our pick of the beds. You'll want your pack first thing in the morning. You can keep it safe by using it for a pillow."

They selected a bunk bed in a far corner. Sarita took the top bunk and climbed up with her pack in hand. As soon as Karina's head hit her pack, she fell asleep.

In the morning, there was a breakfast of muesli, rice, sliced pineapple, and yogurt. A side table had tea, coffee, and warm milk. As she tried the coffee, she thought, another grownup meal. It was bitter. When no one was watching, she left it and got some tea. Later she noticed that the kids added a lot of sugar and warm milk to their coffee. She promised herself to try it that way next time.

Sarita stood up. "Time to go."

Niraj added, "We should get out our ponchos. Monsoon. Let's do our best to stay dry."

Karina thought Niraj's comments unnecessary. Though this was only her second day, she felt confident and prepared, much relaxed compared to yesterday. Here she was on her own on a real adventure, traveling without her dad. Sleeping in a hostel. Drinking coffee and beer. She threw her sandals into her kayak. Waving her paddle like a flag, she called to the others, "Let's get this show on the road."

The kayaks headed downstream. She waited a few minutes for them to turn around. When they didn't, she cried out, "What's going on? I thought we were going to be back by breakfast, but especially before my dad arrived. We're headed the wrong way."

Sarita looked back at her with a serious face, "*Baby* sister! Just shut up and paddle!" She was yelling so loud people back on the dock turned to look. Sarita lowered her voice. "This will be fun."

Karina picked up her paddle, but when Sarita turned around she put it back down. The river had become wide. The lotus blossoms that lined both sides seemed far away. She saw ducks navigating between the lotus pads, cormorants drying their wings, and a single heron watching the water for fish. Lots of birds, but no sign of people. It would have been beautiful, if the kayaks hadn't been going in the wrong direction.

The monsoon rains started as soon as they pulled away from the hostel, even heavier than yesterday. Karina held her poncho tight against the storm. Cold rivulets ran down her back. She shivered, and her teeth chattered. *What's happening?* Tears mixed with the rain on her cheeks. She didn't feel very grownup anymore.

Why had Sarita yelled at her? Even her father never yelled at her. She wiped her face with her wet hand, pursed her lips, and took a deep breath. She stopped crying long enough to ask, "Where are we going?"

Sarita paddled with strong steady strokes. "You really don't understand, do you?"

The tone offended her worse than being called *baby*. She didn't deserve this. What had she ever done to Sarita?

On the distant shores, the wind shook the rain from the tall tree ferns, playing a frantic drum roll on the philodendrons. The wake from the kayaks speeding down the river dominated the wide midstream channel, moving rapidly away from home.

She didn't want Sarita to yell at her again. "Sure. I don't understand. Tell me."

Sarita paddled a long stroke. "For years we've been trying to stop the elephant torture. Do you know what your father does? He rapes elephants to feed people.

She looked at Sarita. "Elephant torture? My father rapes elephants?"

When Sarita didn't respond, Karina reflected that the teen's little speech had sounded memorized. *What's going on here?* She began again with a more deferential approach. "What does this have to do with me?"

"When people refuse to pay attention," Sarita began, but she was interrupted by a flash and an explosion of thunder. "Just like that. You are our thunder. You are the instrument of Shiva, the Destroyer."

"Sarita, you're Muslim. Why are you even invoking Shiva?"

"Doesn't matter."

Karina had no reply. It seemed clear now that they were not her friends. She should have known. They had only taken her to get at her father.

But wait. This still didn't make sense. Their concern was elephants. Why? "What do you mean by 'torturing the elephants?'"

Sarita kept paddling. "How old are you?"

"Twelve." She felt young when she said it.

"Well, you may not be old enough."

She'd seen more of the world then these Kerala kids had. "Try me!"

"They're forcing elephants to be impregnated and to carry genetic-engineered embryos. Can you even imagine being forced to carry an alien baby?" She took a few strong strokes. "We're not talking some special-effect science fiction video. This is real!"

Karina thought about it. She'd read college-level biology texts. She knew about in-vitro fertilization and artificial insemination. Now she felt like the adult. "Are you serious? This happens all the time, all over the world. To make more food, so people can eat."

Sarita slammed her paddle down and crossed her arms, "You've been brainwashed. If they did this to humans, it would be a rights violation. Imagine forcing women to be impregnated with monkey babies. Would you like a monkey growing inside you?"

Karina wanted to laugh, but instead, she got scared. She had to get out of here. These kids were crazy. But how? *I don't know where I am or how to speak the local language.*

She searched for a route of escape, but only saw crocodiles with their open jaws awaiting on the shore.

The river widened and became glassy. The plants and settlements faded in the distance until all Karina could see was water, smooth, still water.

"Where are we?" she asked, but there was no response. Had they reached the Arabian Sea? Not likely. No waves.

When the sun sank low, she could make out something on the horizon between the sky and the water. At first, it was just a dark line, but then she saw trees, thin trunks, and a crown of palms. Vembanad Lake! The inland waterway she had seen from the airplane—so not yet to the ocean, but still far from where they started a day ago.

"We're here." Sarita roughly pulled her onto a dock.

She looked around. The levees confirmed she was on the Kerala backwaters, as she'd seen from the plane. Sarita handed her a fresh water bottle and a bowl of rice. Not knowing what the future would bring, she ate, ignoring the remains of gutted fish surrounding her on the bamboo pier.

Soon Niraj returned with a machete. "We need to prove we have you. Put your hand on the deck."

She put both hands behind her back and screamed, "No!"

Sarita pushed him away. "I thought we were just going to take a picture!"

Niraj yelled, "Grab her wrist. Pictures are no good. We need something with DNA, like a finger...or a toe." He turned to Karina. "Finger or toe? Your choice."

Her fingers hid into a fist and her toes curled. This was like a bad movie. She couldn't believe this was happening.

Niraj's comp buzzed. He turned to her. "Shut up! Be quiet!"

The call was short. "No. Not yet." "Yes, right now." He returned angrily. His green eyes flashed like some evil monster. Karina cringed when he slapped Sarita. "The courier is almost here. Let's do this!"

Sarita pulled Karina's foot and pushed it down, holding it so tight it hurt.

Karina watched as the machete swung toward her foot. Before it reached its target, she screamed and kicked, knocking Sarita over. The machete missed her foot and stuck into the dock.

After shouting in Malayalam, a voice said. "Courier, courier!"

Karina saw her opportunity. She leaped up, pried the machete from the bamboo, and threw it in the water. The courier ducked and fell from his canoe. The machete missed him and was lost in a tangle of reeds.

She screamed, "This is a bad movie and you kids are just stupid." She tried to dive into the water, but Niraj caught her legs and her head bounced against the dock. She was dazed but could still hear the frustration in Niraj's voice as he screamed at Sarita, "What do you expect me to do with scissors?"

Karina smiled for the first time since breakfast. "You can have my ponytail. Plenty of DNA there!"

Sarita agreed, "I'll cut her hair and wrap it up."

Karina took some small satisfaction knowing that the mitochondrial DNA in her hair wasn't what they were looking for and she had saved her phalanges. Thankfully, these Kerala kids weren't that smart.

Kaz arrived right on schedule. Karina usually met him in the dining room, but it was empty. As he walked up the stairs to the library, he yelled, "Karina. Karina! Anybody? Anyone here?"

Just then Vadish arrived, out of breath. "Your daughter, and my daughter, and Roshni's son have all been kidnapped. I have my forces assembled. We're going to rush the mob at the Muslim Gate."

Kaz couldn't believe his ears. "You're going to attack all those women and children? And then what?"

Vadish smiled like he'd been waiting for this. "No worries. I have a contingency plan for just this situation."

'Really?"

His chest puffed out and he stood at attention. "Absolutely. We'll move the elephants outside and house our hostages in the barn. I have a supply of blankets and shackles."

"Stop. There will be no attack, No hostages. No women and children in shackles. Just slow down! Are you sure they were kidnapped?"

"Obviously, they're gone. There's no other possibility. Everyone knows the first twenty-four hours is critical."

He thought, this must be why Karina kept going on about Vadish's paranoia. "They're teenagers. Don't jump to conclusions. We'll investigate and if those protesters did this, we'll notify the authorities."

Vadish spoke into his communicator. "Abort. Abort, but hold your positions."

Kaczka was glad his plane hadn't been delayed, but it did mean he had more time to worry. Where was his daughter?

9. SULUK—QAMANITTUAQ NUNAVUT CANADA

Suluk was passed by several small packs of caribou running the opposite direction. That was bad. It meant the fence was down. The sturdy concrete block and steel post fence Opik and Sivoy had built. However panicked the herd had been, caribou alone would have had a tough time knocking that fence down. They'd tried and failed, before. It was a good fence. Had been.

She guided the dogs away from some rocks that stuck up past the thin layer of snow. Rocks could puncture the pontoons they'd had to add to the dog sled runners. They'd been kind of a precursor to the slushski solution, a way to convert the ski-like runners of sleds and snowmobiles to something that would slide along on top of the mixed slush and ice that the permafrost was turning into. The pontoons were tough, like army boats, but they weren't tougher than rock.

The land was white and brown and black. The smoke added gray to the chiaroscuro effects.

The smoke thickened as she and the team approached the pasture. She could see some frosty brown dirt and moss scattered over the top of the slush. It had been thrown out of an enormous hole in the pasture floor.

She flung out the ice hook into the firmest ice she could see, and called the dogs to halt. Aput skidded on his butt as the sled slowed and the rest of the dogs came to a stop. She stepped off, moved the ice hook to a firmer spot and dug in her feet, one hand tight on the sled's handle, the other firm on the ice hook brake. The sled came to a stop before it overtook the dogs.

The fence *was* down. Most of the south end of the fence was...gone. There was no sign of Opik. She could see blood on the snow, and a severed caribou leg rested at the edge of the hole. Heart pounding, Suluk ran toward the southern end of the pasture. Maybe Opik had been and gone.

Maybe he hadn't been here when it blew up.

She heard a commotion behind her as more sleds and slushskis approached. She left the noise behind as she began to walk. She walked, slowly, all the way around the pasture. There was no sign of Opik, nor his slushski. The explosion indeed had ignited a tundra fire, which was burning north, as the onshore breeze pushed the mostly smoldering flames away from the river. She stared at the smoke as her boots crushed the fragile burnt plants with each step. Then the crunchy sound diminished as she arrived at unburnt sections. After a long while, she returned to her starting point. She had not found Opik, nor any sign he had ever been there.

"Suluk!" someone called. Her sister's voice. She scowled. Hadn't she asked Meriwa to stay at Snow House? Osha could not manage things all on her own. Numb, she turned and saw Meriwa as she shut down her own slushski.

It penetrated Suluk's mind that others were here, too. But none of them were Opik.

"He's not here," she said as Meriwa stumped over and gathered her in a hug. "Opik's not here."

"I know, *uaguk*. I know." Meriwa continued to hold her while some men walked around the pasture, studying the ground. When had the men come? Suluk did not remember.

Over Meriwa's shoulder, she looked at the empty corral. Where had the caribou gone?

"We lost the caribou," she said. "The experiment is ruined."

"Yes," Meriwa said. "There are more caribou. We will try again, Suluk. It is too important to give up on."

Suluk saw Sivoy and Tarkik looking at the ground inside the fence, talking and pointing at the ground.

All the men had been eager to have caribou meat available all year round. Snow House could have fresh steak instead of frozen remnants they'd managed to save in their tiny freezer each year. The meat was just one small benefit of the caribou pens.

The men—all the people, really—had been less sure about the other part of the experiment: that the caribou hoofs would churn up the permafrost so it would refreeze better each year. Everyone said caribou hoofs wouldn't be enough to stop the *Hot*. Everyone also said you couldn't domesticate caribou, but that part of the experiment had been working fine. They'd been calm as reindeer, most of the time. Opik had been pleased.

The soil under the caribou field had, in fact, churned up and refrozen faster than the rest of the permafrost. They needed more fences, more pastures. But they also needed more feed, and Suluk couldn't figure where that was going to come from. Other than that, the re-freezing experiment had been going pretty well.

The caribou were safer and in a place where they could be fed regularly, instead of out in the wild, trying to dig a bit of edible moss out of smoldering peat, or wildflowers and lichen. The people had thought the caribou pens were part of the tundra's future.

They hadn't counted on exploding methane pockets as the tundra decomposed. Opik would be sad to see it, after all his hard work.

"Where is Opik?" she asked. Meriwa did not answer. Instead she led Suluk to her slushski.

"Come, Suluk," Meriwa said. "They're all looking for him. I'll take you home."

"The dogs!" Suluk waved her hand at her team, her sled.

"Sivoy will bring them, they'll be fine."

"Sivoy's here?" Suluk shook her head. When had he come?

Even days later, Suluk still clung to hope.

Maybe he tried to ride one of the caribou again. She could imagine it, Opik atop the wild animal as it kicked and spun and tried to buck him off. Then the methane sink had exploded and the animal had run mad with the rest, carrying Opik off into the wilderness with the herd.

Opik would come walking back any day now.

Except he did not.

Suluk sat at the Snow House counter, staring at her bowl of soup. She'd been waiting for it to cool down, watching the steam rise above the heavy white U.S. Navy-surplus bowl that had somehow made its way to them. Fat congealed at the edge of the bowl. She picked up her spoon and broke the fat into tiny floating 'bergs. Meriwa came and sat down on the stool next to her.

"You should eat that, *uaguk*. It is cool now."

"Yes," Suluk said.

"Listen, my sister," Meriwa said putting a hand on Suluk's shoulder. "Those men have called again, the ones about the mammoths."

"Fools." She set her spoon back on the counter.

"Yes, but they are rich fools. We should maybe listen to them this time. We may have to give up on the caribou experiment, but maybe the mammoths could work the same way. They are offering us a lot of money to just try this thing. I think we should."

"Leave her alone, Meri," Lusa said.

"Leaving her alone isn't working," Osha said as she waddled in from the mudroom, tying on a red and white apron. "Meriwa is right."

Mama always had liked Meriwa best, Suluk thought. There was no bitterness in the realization, simply observation of a fact. Meriwa's opinions mattered to their mother more than anyone else's, though Suluk was never ignored either. Osha's parenting standards were very high, something to be aimed for, Suluk thought. She did not think her own ways matched up, but she tried.

She picked up her spoon again and set it lightly on top of the thick *minestrone*-style soup. She pushed it just deep enough into the liquid for it to fill with broth, but no vegetables, no beans or noodles. She sipped the broth. It was good. Maybe this was the new thing she could add to the menu. It was expensive, though; all the ingredients were costly.

Or maybe—maybe Meriwa was right. Maybe they should try to raise the mammoths. Mammoth soup ought to be good. Mammoths should be more effective at churning up the tundra than caribou—they were much bigger.

But she ought to leave that decision to Opik, since he would be the one herding them, feeding them, making sure they were not ill. How could you tell if a mammoth was sick? Maybe Opik knew. Maybe the mammoth men could tell him, if he did not.

"I think we've found a way to drain off the pressure from the methane bubbles," Meriwa said.

Suluk stared at the soup. A green bean stuck out above the surface of the broth. She took her spoon and pressed the bean back down, thinking, *the natural world should take care of itself.* They shouldn't have to raise caribou or mammoths. They shouldn't have to poke holes in methane bubbles to keep them from exploding. The *Hot* wasn't right. It was a failure of all mankind.

The *Hot* had taken Opik, and now she must fight it without him.

She bit her lip and looked up at her sister. "How can I do this alone?"

"Oh, *uaguk*. You are not alone." She waved her arm around, indicating all the family in Snow House. "We are here. And soon Maatalii and Amaruq will be back home, too."

That did not seem like enough people to fight the *Hot*. Suluk shook her head and put down her spoon. She used her apron to wipe her eyes. "It is too big for us, Meriwa. The *Hot* is too big."

After Halloween, Abbie interviewed realtors. She started at the larger towns: Enid and Stillwater. Those agents weren't interested in wheat farms. She didn't let this discourage her. Venturing farther out to Oklahoma City, the big offices in OKC told her, "Your best option is to stay put and raise cattle." A long drive to Tulsa and fast food on the highway just reiterated the depressing story.

She wanted the best for her family, and these meetings drove her to reconsider Redbird and his ancestors buried under the kitchen garden. *Maybe the great spirit wants us to stay.* She spent the night in the dairy barn drinking coffee, analyzing numbers, and trying to find a way to make it add up. "What do you think Sasha? Could we open a Bed and Breakfast, tell Carla and Mike to get jobs, and only eat every other day?"

The ever-supportive Sasha pushed her massive head into Abbie's lap and wagged her tail. She scratched her ears. "Don't worry girl. You can eat every day. I'll figure out something."

The next day, walking downtown, she noticed Pamela Properties, a small office tucked between the pawnshop and Abbie's favorite bakery. Abbie examined the *For Sale* flyers displayed in the front window. She noticed too many acreage properties for her comfort until she realized that some of the listings were from as far away as Iowa or Montana. She walked in. The office was spartan with more flyers on the faded orange walls, a desk, and some chairs.

Pamela immediately got up from behind her desk and walked over to the two nicest chairs—orange upholstery with wooden arms. Abbie took the offered chair and after some polite preliminaries got down to business, "It's gotten too hot and dry to grow wheat in Oklahoma. I want to move north."

"I understand. I have six other wheat farms already listed. Each year more cattle move in and more wheat moves out." Pam unrolled a map. "Where to?"

Abbie contained her excitement; she hadn't gotten this far with any of the other agents. Maybe the great spirit was on her side. "I was hoping to move to North Dakota. Wheat farming should be good there for another decade."

"How large a spread are you looking for?"

Pam seemed to be a miracle worker. In Abbie's exhilaration, she asked for the best she could imagine. "Given our equipment and overhead, I think we need at least two thousand acres."

"Plus, I assume, a farmhouse, outbuildings, and a kitchen garden?"

Abbie smiled, "Of course, no one can get by anymore without growing some of their own food."

Pam tapped on her comp. "You have 3,200 acres now? Right?"

"Yes, Redd's family, original Cherokee settlers, have added pieces for over two centuries. We also have a small dairy operation, new barn, and the kitchen and bathroom have been updated."

"I'm afraid North Dakota is still doing well. The *Hot* hasn't impacted the farms that far north. Prices are still high." After some more tapping, Pam frowned, "Most likely your property will be purchased by a corporate cattle operation. Fortunately for you, two large operations abut your land. They'll both be interested. Of course, they don't pay top dollar, and care little about your buildings."

Abbie stayed upbeat and sent a little prayer to the great spirit to remember that Sasha wanted to eat every day. "I understand. What's the bottom line?"

Pam tapped some more. "Wait! Here's an opportunity. Let me connect with the listing agent."

Abbie waited while the realtor chatted online.

The tapping increased and Pam's frown turned into a smile. "Here's the deal. I see a nice 2,200-acre operation in South Dakota."

This morning Abbie would have taken any offer, but now she felt optimistic. "I was hoping to be farther north."

"You should consider this one. The owners are retiring, and their grandkids live in Enid. They would be willing to swap for your setup."

Maybe South Dakota could be okay. "How big is their house?"

More tapping. "Same as yours. Four bedrooms, three and a half baths. Also, recently updated. No dairy, but they have an acre of greenhouses." More tapping. "Wow! They have solar, two wind turbines, and a working well."

"Impressive. What are they growing now?"

Pam chatted with the other agent again before answering. "Flowers under the plastic. Soybeans and corn in the fields. Of course, with the *Hot*, it should be good for wheat."

"Furnished?"

Another short chat. "Yes, if you'd like."

Abbie thought for a while. This deal was too good to let go. She stood up and offered her hand, "Let's do it."

After the two women closed the deal, Abbie sighed in relief. She felt like doing a little dance.

◡

At dawn, Redbird took out his special wood-turning chisels, the ones he'd milled and honed himself. They were L-shaped, single-purpose tools. The blackjack oak he used for the handles once grew in the front yard. His great-great-grandmother had seen the tree and declared that the house should be built in its shade. When it died, he saved the wood.

He rolled the handles between his palms, enjoying the shape and patina. Before he started work, he took out a whetstone and sharpened the delicate edges. He attached another piece of the heirloom oak to the chuck, put on his earplugs and safety goggles, and entered a solitary trance.

When he turned on the lathe the barn cats Mischief and Trouble hissed and retreated to a high perch on top of a stack of hay bales. For the first step, he'd turn the cube into a sphere. Many steps later, he'd have a Chinese puzzle ball, a novelty invented in the 14th century, a ball within a ball within a ball. The puzzle? How was that made?

This project took time and patience. After hours of slow progress, a very fancy cat toy emerged. One slip, too much pressure, or even a defect in the wood, produced kindling. He looked forward to winter when the wheat rested under the snow and he had welcome days of isolation and silence to watch a puzzle ball develop from his gentle prodding.

The desired orb still hid within the oak block when he looked up and saw Abbie. He had no idea how long she'd been standing in front of him, but he turned off the lathe and took out his earplugs.

"It's past 10:00, and you haven't had breakfast." She set a tray down on a hay bale and waved her hands at the dust in the air. "Where's the face mask I got you?"

He ignored this familiar query. The mask made it too hard to breathe. Trouble jumped down to investigate, but Mischief just looked suspiciously at the suddenly quiet lathe. Redd recognized the wooden tray; he'd made it for her on the first Mother's Day after Carla was born.

He hadn't eaten. He couldn't argue with breakfast. He said, "Thank you," but didn't move. He looked around. Both cats now circled the tray. She smiled at them and shooed them away with a friendly, "Silly cats, that bacon is not for you." Glancing from the cats to the tray to Abbie, he noticed the big red SOLD signs on his lathe and planer/joiner, the ones he tried to ignore. He sighed and took off his safety glasses.

She looked at his lathe. "That's going to be another Chinese puzzle ball, isn't it?"

He nodded, waiting for what would surely come next.

"I'm sorry about selling your lathe, but we are downsizing and it's hard to move such heavy equipment. We're swapping farms furnished to avoid the expense of a moving company."

It was money. With Abbie it was always about the cost. *Think right and do right*, he reminded himself. In this situation, he needed to support his wife. The move already gave her enough stress. He sipped his coffee. "Thanks for the lovely breakfast." The red signs again caught his attention. "If we can move the combines at twenty tons each, another couple of thousand pounds for my lathe and planer/joiner is nothing."

When she took a deep breath, he knew he wouldn't like what was coming next. "We've contracted with a farm equipment shipper to disassemble the combines and seeder for shipment on their custom trailers. Everything else is going in your truck or my van."

When it came to money, he couldn't change her mind. "Okay." He sat down to his breakfast. After she left, he gave the cats their share of the bacon.

◡

Mike opened the door and Sasha jumped up to greet him. He scratched her floppy ears. "Mom! Mom! I'm home."

"Oh, there you are. I've been meaning to talk to you. It's time to get rid of all these bottles of pond gunk."

"They're going to win the Algae Challenge. I've contacted the South Dakota Science League. I'll compete there after we move."

His mother made her stubborn face. He gathered his strength and was stubborn right back. "This is my research."

"It smells."

He mumbled, "Dad let you sell his lathe, but I'm keeping my algae."

Mom gave him her frustrated face and looked at him like he was a disappointment. "We've been over this before. Do you know how many laws you'd be breaking transporting pond scum across state lines? All those plastic bottles, tubes, compressed gases, pumps, have to go."

"They're my future. My algae are Earth's future. They'll encircle the world removing carbon from the atmosphere and ending the *Hot*."

"Algae are dangerous. Algae blooms poison fisheries. State and federal authorities are on the lookout for invasive species. You'll be arrested as a bio-terrorist."

He walked up to her, face-to-face and shouted, "You never support me. You're like everyone else here, only interested in farms, crops, and tractors, or football and cattle. Other things are important!" He turned around and went out with Sasha. "Let's go girl. She's just having a bad day."

Outside he hid behind the barn feeling bad for yelling at Mom. When Sasha brought her ball, they played fetch. Each time Sasha returned, she looked at him with her large sad eyes. "You're right Sasha. We have the best Mom and I can grow new algae in South Dakota."

◡

Carla returned home for Christmas. She dropped her duffle in the sitting room, petted an excited Sasha, and looked around. The Christmas tree looked bare, as did the fireplace. "Mom! Where are all the Christmas decorations?"

Mom came out of the kitchen and wiped her hands on a blue-and-white checked apron. She looked tired and somehow even shorter than Carla remembered. "I've been sending you emails. You do remember that we're moving? Right?"

56

Carla snapped back, "And you remember that I'm in college? Taking classes? Getting an education? Right?"

The university offered more classes than there were people in Cherokee. And Chicago had museums, libraries, theaters, architecture, everything.

"I know Carla dear. We're glad you could find time to visit for the holidays."

"I love Chicago. Lake Michigan is just enormous. I can't imagine that an ocean is any bigger. And I've been sledding and skiing. Mom! I went skiing."

"That's great. Can I make you some coffee? I'm sure the trip was long and cold."

Carla continued telling her mom about life in the big city. "In the morning, I go jogging along the shore of Lake Michigan. Even with the *Hot*, winter is still *winter* in Chicago!" She sat at the dining table. "Sure, I'd love some coffee." She scratched Sasha's ears, and the Newfie's tail wagged like crazy.

"Pie? I have apple and pumpkin."

"Sure, I'd love some apple."

Along with the pie came Mike. He took a big slice of pumpkin.

After a couple of bites, she again looked around. "Where are the Christmas dishes?" Every place she looked; things were missing. No pictures on the piano. No piano!

Mike forced a laugh. "You missed all the excitement. Every Saturday is flea market day. Usually Enid or Stillwater, but for Christmas, we went to OKC and Tulsa. That's where the holiday stuff went."

Carla secretly searched from room to room, opening closets and cupboards. Empty and empty. The linen cabinet had bare shelves. She even snuck into her mother's closet. Unused hangers. Vacant shoe racks.

Mike noticed what she was doing and whispered conspiratorially, "Before you leave for Chicago, you should take whatever you want. Your room is next."

The next day Carla went through the house recording everything on her comp's camera, and then outside. Swiss chard in the kitchen garden. The cows and chickens. The big green combine.

Her father met her in the barn and hugged her. She thought she saw a tear in his eye. "That's okay Carla. We're taking the combine…and Sasha."

She hugged him harder. "What about Trouble and Mischief?"

"Your mom says they'll be happier staying here. We'll inherit new cats in South Dakota."

"Mom—" She didn't say any more.

After a long silence, he stepped back, wiped his face, and smiled. "We'll be closer to Chicago."

She returned his smile—feeling especially close to her dad at that moment. "That's good anyway."

Christmas eve, Carla stared at the paper plates on the dining room table—paper plates with printed red and green designs of ribbons, bells, and holly. Her favorite Santa Claus salt and pepper shakers were missing. The holly-trimmed serving platter was gone.

She knew her mother bought those paper plates to make up for the dearth of traditional decorations, but all those paper plates reminded her of dead trees, carbon emissions, and ecological decline. Carla broke down. "This isn't Christmas! People move all the time without throwing everything away. I could have taken the Christmas dishes to Chicago. You're all acting crazy."

The men just looked down at their hands in their laps.

When no one responded, she got frustrated. "If this is what's happening, I'm never coming home again. Never!" Carla then laughed. "Isn't that a joke. There is no home to return to!"

Her mother set the roast turkey on the table with a thump. With everyone seated, she stayed standing, "That's enough. You three remind me of little children worried about your toys. Redbird wants his lathe. Mike wants his algae. Carla wants Christmas decorations."

Carla looked around the table. Everyone still had their heads bowed, as in prayer.

"You're all comfortable, with a roof over your head and regular meals. All that comes from a farm that is losing money every year while you all enjoy yourselves. Our choices were to move or be moved. The bank is not going to loan us any more money."

The three looked at each other as if to ask, did you know this?

Her mother continued, not yelling, not even seeming mad, just disappointed. "Don't give me your sad faces. You're not little children learning there's no such thing as Santa Claus. Grow up."

Carla shut up and ate her dinner off the paper Christmas plates while exchanging embarrassed looks with her father and brother. She promised herself to be less of a brat and imagined the others doing the same.

After that Christmas dinner, Redbird did his best to *think right and do right*. The next day, over pie and coffee, he told Abbie, "I said goodbye to my great-great-grandparents, cousins, aunts, and uncles buried under the garden and buildings, but I have one final responsibility."

Abbie took an impatient breath. He hurried to explain. "I inherited original copies of the Cherokee Phoenix from 1832. I sent queries to the newspaper, which is still publishing, and to various museums in Oklahoma and Georgia. I even contacted museums in Washington, D.C. and several national parks."

He put down his fork and picked up his coffee. "You know why no one wants them? The Internet. Everything is online; no one wants old newspapers. I have space in my pickup. I'm keeping them to honor my ancestors."

She smiled at him. "That's a good plan."

He smiled back.

A group of Longhorns circled Mike. "Tell us Duster, are you leaving?"

"Yes, my family isn't waiting around until it's too late, like the Okies during the dust bowl. We're packing up. And we're not going west either. California's no better…droughts, fires, earthquakes."

A guy in blue and green boots pushed him, "You're right. Oklahoma is cattle country now. Might as well annex it to Texas."

The Longhorns laughed and a few yelled, "Yee-haw."

He replied with a "Moo," as they moved on.

Elzia stayed back. When it was just the two of them, she moved closer and spoke softly. "I'm sorry to see you go. We could have been good friends."

He looked up at her. *Is she making a joke?* He saw no trace of a smile, and it was only the two of them. *Was she serious?* He considered asking her.

Instead, he said, "I want to see snow drifts again. I don't want to wait for the next drought or earthquake. Besides, I'm not going to be a farmer. I'm going to find a solution to the *Hot.*"

She looked like she might believe him, and she squeezed his hand before she walked away.

11. XIANG BO, DI'E—HUIXIAN CHINA

"This!" Li shook the handful of papers, "this is not a result! This is an observation! We cannot write a paper based on this, Xiang Bo. You know that!" His face was alarmingly red. "You claim results, but there is nothing here even of interest to the self-serving bureaucrats that pay you!" He tossed the papers contemptuously to the floor.

"I will send it to the grantors without your name on it then, if that is what you want."

"I want— aggh! I want real science, with real results. I want data, pages of it! I want not to be the laughingstock of Chinese biology!"

Too late, Xiang Bo thought. *They already laugh at you behind your back.* Laugh, because you send pages and pages of data about nothing very important at all. She tried again to convince him.

"This is important work. These results will *feed people,* Dr. Cheng Li!" She could feel tears of frustration welling in her eyes. Furious, she wiped the tears away with the back of her hand and picked up the pages of their draft article from the floor. She only realized she had been speaking to an empty room when she stood back up and saw he was gone. She sighed, half growling, and put the pages back in order. She would print another copy, without his name.

When she sat back down at her desk, she discovered that Di'e had brought her tea and some spring rolls, still warm from the kitchen.

***

Pretty much a copy of their earlier argument, Xiang Bo's request to bring Zi Min home resulted in a shouting match. She had brought up the idea before, that the girl needed a home, and they needed children. For some reason Li resisted, just as he had resisted creating their own child, pointing out how much it would slow or delay their work.

"A Zhuang child in our household, with her own language, her own beliefs, how much time will that take from our work? We will have to start as if she was an infant to teach her manners and language and proper thinking."

Or else she will be an embarrassment to the Cheng household, he did not say, but Xiang Bo heard.

"I am Zhuang. I speak five languages and read and write in four of them," she said. "There is no reason to think Zi Min will not do likewise."

"Meanwhile we have to hire a nanny and a tutor," Li groused. "Or give up our research grants to teach her ourselves."

"Di'e wants a grandchild. She is happy to have a companion and someone to—"

"She has my brother to care for! She does not need a little girl on top of that."

"Cheng Ming-Hua is doing fine. He only needs guidance when he travels to performance venues, and his fellow musicians have been doing that. Why do you persist in seeing him as helpless? He's blind, not incompetent."

"Don't try to tell me how to care for my brother!" Li actually picked up a vase that sat on the fireplace hearth and threw it across the room. It smashed to pieces, splashing the water and the stems and blossoms of purple iris everywhere. It also smashed the old boxy television screen, she noted with secret delight.

Xiang Bo actually smiled at his childish temper tantrum and its result. Now she could go buy the new flat screen television she and Di'e had been wanting. Even Ming-Hua was interested, because he could listen to what they watched and imagine the picture show.

Li misinterpreted her smile, as she might have guessed.

"Don't you *dare* mock me," he said, and stomped out of the room. "You are far too immature to raise a child," he snapped on his way out the door. "My answer is no."

⌣

"You are going to lose her, you know," Di'e said. "Is that what you are trying for? Do you want her to leave?"

Li shook his head. "I don't know any more, Mother."

"You told me when we began looking for a wife, that you wanted children. More than one. I even found a Zhuang who could have as many babies as she wanted. A smart one, an educated one. Why is she now so terrible in your view?"

He shook his head again. Di'e scowled. It was clear to her that he was the bigger half of the problem. Xiang Bo was a trifle more independent than she had expected, yes, but then, the woman had gone to university in England and the United States, where she had been exposed to many more ideas than just scientific ones. Had Di'e overlooked too many flaws when she had arranged this marriage? Now she shook her head, as if mirroring Li. She did not think Xiang Bo's stubborn femininity was the problem. More that Li's intolerance was the culprit. He'd expected a *Han* wife, with Han traditions and humility.

Di'e shuffled across the compound courtyard to the ancestors' shrine. She prayed for patience and understanding. She asked for their help with Li. The ancestors had sent aid before, when she had entreated them for help with Ming-Hua. He had, literally, stumbled upon her grandfather's ancient pipa, and sat down and tried to tune it. By the time he was completely blind, he could play like a professional, and they had thus discovered what he was meant to do with his life.

Perhaps Li could find something, likewise. She could see he was suffering, but yelling at Xiang Bo was not going to help. She rose from the ground and exited the ancestor's niche. Li was standing in the courtyard, looking like a small, lost child.

"My research grant has been canceled," he said in a very low voice.

Oh, Di'e thought. *That is the problem.*

"I have no income but hers." He sat down abruptly on the wicker drum stool by the fountain. The last of the rosy peony blossoms rioted behind him, framing him in dazzling pink. The contrast between their bright color and his sad, pale face was shocking.

Di'e rested her hand on his shoulder. Lost his grant. Well. That explained a lot. He was shamed, and that was the one thing he could never tolerate. His pride was mighty, and when things were bad, his shame tilted all the way opposite his pride. What had happened to unbalance him so? He had been grim for quite some time. Had he seen the loss of his grant coming?

"They think I am not getting anywhere. They are putting more money into salt-water rice, and *Hot*-hardy corn." He shook his head. "What am I going to do, Maman?"

"We will think of something."

"I had to let Wei, our lab assistant, go; I still owe him back wages." He shook his head, looking forlorn.

Di'e had never seen him like this. Disappointed, yes. Shamed, too, but he had survived. This was different; it was *despair.* It caught at her heart.

"I sold the car; I offered it to Wei for his wages, but he already has a better car. I didn't get much for it, it is too old.

"Ming-Hua volunteers more than he gets paid; therefore, he is no help. Our gardens produce enough for us, but none to sell. I suppose I could clear and begin farming more of our land." He groaned and rubbed his temples, staring at the stone paving of the courtyard. "What if I have to sell the compound, to pay for us to live? The Yangshuo Council already has its eye on us. They want to make a tourist hotel. It's a nightmare."

Di'e bit her lip. Would he be willing to hear her suggestions? Or did he just want to suffer?

"Perhaps..."

"What, Maman? Do you have an idea?"

"They may still need you at the Yangshuo campus of the Guanxi Normal University. There's even a tram that stops just down the road, that could take you directly there. We can use the bicycles to get to town once a week or so to get whatever else we need." He lifted his head and looked at her, his mouth turned down. She went on, "You used to enjoy teaching, do you think you could again?"

"I suspect they've filled the position long ago, *Maman.*"

"But isn't it worth looking to see? Especially in your field of expertise?"

He nodded, pulling out his cell phone. "You could be right. They were pretty desperate. I think I still have the contact information. Even if I could only do a couple classes now, I might be able to pick up more later on. It at least would be something—something to do, some way to earn."

She smiled at him. This was more like her younger son. Maybe if he wasn't faced with failing experiments every day, his attitude would improve.

If he went to teach, he would be less grouchy. He could woo Xiang Bo back.

Di'e certainly wouldn't agree to him selling the compound. It had been in her family for centuries. She had brought it to her husband Dr. Chen Wang as her dowry. She would not let Li let it go; things were not as bad as that. She patted his shoulder, and walked back into the house.

Di'e smiled wistfully at the photograph of the two boys as children. She had been permitted to have a second child, since the first had been born with the vision defect that meant he would be blind before he reached adulthood. The two boys had gotten into cartloads of mischief when they were little, managing to sneak out of the compound more than once and find their way into the rice fields, where they played at being ninja warriors.

She smiled at the memory, and snorted when she remembered the time Li had broken his arm, trying to "fly" through the bamboo forest, when they'd traveled to Longji. Ming-Hua's vision was failing even then, so he had been a bit more cautious than his younger brother. She'd probably let them watch too many movies about fighters flying through the bamboo, but had thought it would build their imaginations.

It would be nice to have a little girl to raise, she thought. Well, *help* raise, because she knew Xiang Bo would have strong ideas about that, as she did about pretty much everything. But Di'e was certain she, as grandma, would still be allowed to brush Zi Min's hair and twist up sticky-bun hairdos. With bows and sparkly pins and sticks, like she herself had always wanted. They were not so poor that they couldn't afford a few sparkly pins.

She walked further back into the house, and stopped outside Li and Xiang Bo's bedroom when she saw what her daughter-in-law was doing. Packing a suitcase. And a box. Several boxes, in fact.

"Please, Xiang Bo, little daughter," she said lowly. "Please give him more chances to think, to change his mind."

"I am hoping he will do that, when he sees that I am gone," Xiang Bo answered in reasonable tones. She flicked her queue back over her shoulder in irritation as it kept catching in the midst of the clothes she was folding. "Do you mind if I borrow the children's books, Li and Ming-Hua's books you kept? I would like something for Zi Min to read besides her schoolbook."

If she borrowed the books, she would bring them back, Di'e thought. "Of course," she said. "Bring Zi Min back with them," she suggested, with hope. "You know I would welcome her, don't you?" she asked.

Xiang Bo stopped packing and straightened up, meeting her eyes. "I do know that, *Maman,*" she said.

Di'e was comforted by the endearment. She and Xiang Bo had always gotten along better together than Xiang Bo and Li had. It was a puzzle. "Ming-Hua would welcome her also," she said. "He is always looking for more audience for his music." She smiled, wishing she had more words, more power to coax. But even so, she could be warmed by the thought that Xiang Bo intended to come back. She hoped it would be while she was still alive to enjoy a granddaughter.

12. Kaczka, Karina—Kerala India

Kaczka ran in the direction of Vadish's whistle, anticipating good news. "Did you find them?"

"No, but three ATVs are missing. They left a clear path." Vadish kept moving while he explained the obvious. "Look at the wide tracks through the grass over here, and on the other side, a groove dug into the gravel. Those things wreak havoc on the environment, so they're easy to follow. They headed toward the Western Ghats, wild territory."

Kaczka jogged after Vadish until they reached three vehicles parked inside the eastern perimeter fence. Kaczka leaned over an ATV and struggled to catch his breath. Meanwhile, Vadish sprinted through the gate and disappeared up a narrow path into the dense undergrowth.

"Hurry! They took Tiger Trail."

Kaczka imagined tigers and leopards, and dangerous snakes. What was Karina thinking, a twelve-year-old girl roaming through the jungle? Vadish surprised him when he got down on his hands and knees. "This is an important fork in the trail. We don't want to get it wrong. Left is up the mountains. Right is down to the river."

Kaczka waited, still trying to catch his breath, as Vadish ran uphill and got back on the ground. Vadish pointed to the trail. "Can you see that? A small pack of wild dogs chasing a squirrel."

Kaczka didn't see anything. "Are you saying they went the other way?"

"For sure. I don't see any shoe prints, but with the rain, their tracks could have been washed away."

This pronouncement did not inspire confidence, but Kaczka followed Vadish, downhill.

"Look at that! Three different shoe prints and broken branches. We're on the right path." Soon Kaczka could hear a river. The path became narrower and the plants lusher. Vines and roots crisscrossed the way. He tripped and scraped his hands and tore his pants. He brushed a mixture of blood and dirt off his hands and kept going.

He bargained with the gods. Please let her be okay. I'll take her on every trip, never let her out of my sight. I'll get married so she can have a mother. This last promise shocked him. He hadn't even had a girlfriend since Klara died.

He heard Vadish's whistle over the sound of the cascading water. He kept going, wary not to trip again. He appealed to the thirty-three million Hindu gods. Let her be alive. Please let her be alive. He swore to bring some rice for Ganesh.

When he arrived at the river, he didn't see anything. He could feel a tightness in his chest and an urge to explode at Vadish. Where are they? What happened? He wanted to shout over the roaring of the water, but he just clenched his fists and waited for Vadish's next round of pronouncements.

"All the signs are clear. The discarded *dabba*. The long deep tracks on the bank. The moss-covered boulders rolled over." Vadish pointed. "They had lunch here. That *dabba* is from our kitchen. They pulled kayaks into the river. They could be anywhere by now."

He collapsed and cried into his hands. "So, she might be okay?"

Vadish admitted, "Yes, this could be a teenage escapade as you suggested."

Karina heard the door that separated the stable from the house slide open. "Sarita, get out here." She recognized Niraj's tone, enjoying his position of power—head warden assisted by three adult guards.

Sarita rose from her pallet and shuffled out of the cell the two girls shared. Sarita's situation baffled Karina. *Why is she also locked up? Is she here to spy on me, or is she a fellow victim?*

When Niraj locked her in by herself, Karina moved her laundry basket and returned to the slow work of tunneling under the wall. Her years as an only child had taught her independence and discipline. She smelled the stable's former occupants—pigs and goats, but she refused to let the kidnapping overwhelm her.

In addition to Sarita, Pucca the cat and an assortment of geckos occupied the repurposed stable. The geckos controlled the bugs and spiders. Pucca assumed responsibility for mice and the occasional snake.

Karina scratched the unyielding earth, slowly expanding the tunnel. Once she had a hard-fought handful of dirt, she sprinkled it into the hole that served as a latrine. Pucca immediately squatted down to cover up the evidence. Karina scratched Pucca's ear, "Good kitty."

The door unlocked. She rushed to replace her laundry in front of the nascent tunnel and dove into her sleeping space. She feared that lock. She had worried about being trapped by a fire until she realized that before the roof collapsed, the walls would burn through.

Roshni, their true jailer, entered. "*Urmi, uraruka,*" she yelled. Karina continued to feign sleep until she remembered, *That's me. I'm Urmi.* Roshni had named her Urmi and prohibited her from speaking English. Urmi had learned enough Malayalam to get by.

"Urmi! Get out of bed." Roshni dropped a basket of dirty clothes. "Laundry day!"

Urmi had been expecting shopping day, her only chance to leave the compound. On shopping day Niraj and one of the guards escorted the two girls to a small shop to buy rice, spices, and some small necessities, such as tampons. The latter so embarrassed Niraj that he didn't enter the store with them. Urmi always took this opportunity to pilfer a few coins. She hid them under her sleeping pallet and called them her *escape money*.

When Urmi didn't immediately start the laundry, Roshni barked, "No breakfast until the clothes are washed and hung to dry."

Breakfast! Urmi held her stomach. Her hunger never went away. She thought, my diet of rice, and whatever I can scrounge, matches most of the planet. I am no longer consuming more than my share. This thought didn't soothe the emptiness in her gut.

Sarita stood quietly next to Niraj. Both smiling, until Roshni noticed. She ignored her son, but yelled at Sarita, "You too. Laundry!"

Sarita looked to Niraj, but he stopped smiling and backed away. She crossed her arms, "Roshni, why do I have to do laundry. I thought I was your friend."

Roshni raised her eyebrows. "Really? I doubt that. Your father has been working against the elephants. He's just as evil as that—" She used a Malayalam epithet that Urmi couldn't translate, but she could tell from the tone that it wasn't nice. "—Priya, the witch that wants me to force my elephants to birth abominations. As long as I'm in charge, that won't happen!"

Urmi silently repeated Roshni's words. "That won't happen." She blinked twice. Roshni had been sabotaging the mammoth research! She pursed her lips and squinted her eyes at the nasty woman thinking, when I get out of here, you're going to be fired!

Roshni was mean and Urmi doubted the woman would ever give Sarita special consideration. Regardless, Sarita pleaded with Roshni, flirted with Niraj, and made friendly overtures to Urmi. She wanted to be everyone's friend. Where did her true allegiance lie?

On her way out, Roshni spoke to Niraj. "Make sure they do a good job."

Urmi watched the front door slam followed by the putt-putt of Roshni's motor scooter. *She's going back to the research station to undermine the mammoth cloning.* Urmi kicked the laundry basket in anger, causing Pucca to jump.

Urmi snapped at Sarita. "Let's go Cinderella. Laundry day."

For the rest of the morning, Sarita sat on a stool in front of the steel laundry tub and cleaned clothes with a washboard. Urmi's job was to pump water and heat it over an open fire. She also mixed ashes and cooking grease to make the harsh soap they used for everything. When the water was warm, she dumped it into the washtub and hung clean clothes on the rope strung between two trees: a lemon and an orange. As she ran around the yard from pump to fire to tub to line, she looked at Sarita sitting on her stool. "Look at you, sitting there like a queen on her throne."

Sarita held up her raw, red hands. "These aren't queen's hands."

It was another monsoon morning, wet and gloomy. Kaczka joined the other parents, Vadish and Roshni, along with Priya, for breakfast. The chai was cold, and the *appam* burned. Vadish spoke first. "I convinced the Kerala Forest Department to initiate a search. They checked on all their large cats with radio collars. Good news there, no sign of our children."

Kaz wondered why Vadish had gotten Kerala Forest Department involved when the evidence pointed west, not east.

He noticed Priya's eyes and nose were red. Caring, but weak, he thought. She spoke in a soft voice. "I've organized the students into groups. They are searching the cultivated lands for clues. They searched the coconut palm groves yesterday, the bananas—"

Roshni cut her off. "I've recovered DNA samples from the kids' rooms. I also want swabs from the parents. I'll personally drive everything to the Intelligence Bureau in Cochin. It'll take a couple of days."

Vadish scowled. "Don't you have all that equipment here?"

"Obviously, but the IB have their own procedures."

Kaz went to exchange his cold chai for hopefully hot coffee thinking that the search wasn't going anywhere.

After a couple of days of steady rain, not much had changed. He sat in another meeting, struggling to imagine something else to try.

Vadish reported. "Muvattupula have sent police to every place frequented by young people…arcades, parks, video theaters, hostels, fast food, markets."

Roshni continued. "The IB now have DNA profiles for everyone." She raised her wild eyebrows. "I have some good news." He looked at her expectantly. "You are all parents to your children."

He frowned. This seemed like inappropriate humor. "Well, Priya. Have your kids found anything?"

"No. Nothing among the bananas or the bamboo. We'll search the pineapples today."

Kaczka was desperate. How could three teenagers just disappear? He took some rice from the kitchen and walked toward the Muslim Arch. All around were cultivated fields reminding him that India was an ancient civilization. People had been farming this land for millennia.

He had intended to offer rice to the elephant god, but there was already something on the offering plate, a package. It felt like it was empty and had no shipping label. On one side, written in black marker was his name, just his first name: KACZKA.

He tore it open and found three packets of hair, two dark and one blond, and a demand for the research station to be closed and the elephants released.

He crushed the ransom note and reached in his pocket for the rice to place in the platter. He continued putting his fingers in and retrieving one or two kernels at a time. It seemed important to give Ganesh every grain. As in a trance, he checked the corners and the seams and even his other pockets.

When he was sure he had offered every grain, he sat on the ground in front of Ganesh and wondered what he was supposed to say. A gentle rain slowly filled Ganesh's platter.

He'd lost Klara. He had to find Karina.

The next morning, his head of security welcomed him to the meeting. Vadish put his hands together, "*Namasté*, Kaczka."

He'd come to hate these bureaucratic, time-wasting exercises as much as the depressing rain. So many reports, so much activity, but no word of the children. He poured himself a cup of sweet filter coffee popular in Kerala and sipped slowly, waiting for an idea to bubble up.

While the pointless discussion droned on, he poured some honey on a warm naan and studied maps of the triangle between Muvattupula, Alleppey, and Cochin. There were pictures of the missing children and multiple versions of flyers in English, Hindi, and Malayalam tacked to the wall. Vadish summarized as he'd done every morning, "Our three children have been missing over two weeks, without a trace." He solemnly repeated their names, "Karina Kowalski, Sarita Qureshi, Niraj Teertha," as if this incantation would return them.

Roshni harrumphed, "Not completely without a trace. I returned to the IB and they declared those hair samples belonged to our children."

When the meeting ended, Kaczka sipped his coffee and considered malevolent explanations. If Vadish is so thorough and organized, why hasn't he found even a single lead?

He also wondered about Priya. Why would someone with her education take a job at a small school? Is she involved?

And Roshni? Her life was cloning extinct animals. This had to be her dream job. Besides, she'd also been so helpful, volunteering to drive back and forth to the Intelligence Bureau.

Later that afternoon, when tea arrived, the unexpected scent of fried chicken emanated from the kitchen—not tandoori chicken, but American fried chicken, garlic, and pepper, with hints of thyme, paprika, and ginger. He was wiping the grease from his hands when Roshni exploded into the room, followed by a bruised and dirty young man.

Even covered with dirt and scratches, needing a haircut, Kaczka immediately recognized him. Niraj! One of the three missing children. He ran to the child and hugged him. "We're so glad to see you." He stepped back and examined the boy, just to make sure Niraj had really returned. Thank you, Ganesh!

Then his eyes darted past the mother and child, searching for Karina. He didn't see his daughter. He grabbed Niraj by the shoulders and shook him. "Where are the girls? Why aren't they with you?"

Niraj just stood mute.

Kaczka pushed him. Niraj fell to the floor. Kaczka howled. "Why aren't they here with you?" A chill ran through his arms. Almost in tears, in a pleading voice, he asked, "Are the girls alive?"

Roshni assisted her son to his feet and protectively put her arms around him. "He just showed up. I brought him here immediately." She turned to Niraj and gently asked, "Can you tell us what happened?"

Niraj looked at the table. "Can I have something to eat first? I haven't eaten in days."

To move things along, Kaczka spread his arms wide. "Of course. Help yourself."

Between bites and swallows of half-chewed mouthfuls, the boy's story unfolded. "So, we were kayaking down the Kaliyar River, still above Muvattupula, when they attacked us. Men with automatic rifles and helicopters. They drugged us."

Kaczka waited impatiently as the boy opened a bottle of beer. He knew high caste Hindus discouraged drinking. He glanced at Roshni. She pursed her lips but didn't say anything. Vadish and Priya looked at each other. Whatever had happened, the boy had changed since the kidnapping.

"Well, when we woke up, we were high on the Western Ghats, surrounded by a fence to keep wild animals out. Obviously, it also kept us in. A small creek ran through our open-air prison and they tossed food scraps at us each morning like we were chickens."

Kaczka stared in silence, examining the boy, trying to decide whether to believe him. His mother hugged her son, but Kaczka still needed news of Karina. He interrupted this tender scene. "So, this is all interesting, but what about the girls?"

Vadish added, "Are they here with you?"

Niraj grabbed a handful of chips which he ate ravenously. "Well, I'm getting to that."

This time Vadish shook the boy. "Get to it!"

"At night we could hear tigers roaring, so when I'd dug a hole under the bars blocking the creek entrance, they were afraid to leave with me. I escaped and ran downhill. I've been alone in the forest for six or eight days. I lost count."

Vadish spoke through clenched teeth, "Are you saying my daughter was so afraid of the tigers, she preferred to stay in a yard living like a chicken?" Niraj didn't answer and Vadish added, "She's trained on military-style missions in those mountains since she was little." His voice dripped with scorn and doubt. "This sounds like the plot from some cheap video game."

Roshni held her son tighter. "Do you want him to lead you back into the Western Ghats?"

No one replied. Kaczka suddenly felt cold and empty. He didn't know what to do or where to turn for advice. Ganesh? He needed to confer with

Vadish who seemed to share his suspicions. "Roshni, your son needs medical attention."

Priya, who'd been silent, assumed her rarely used pediatrician persona, "Please accompany me to the infirmary." She left, speaking to mother and son in comforting tones. Before she closed the door, she looked back and raised her palms upward and rolled her eyes, indicating she shared their confusion and disbelief.

"So Vadish, we have our first lead. What do you think?"

Vadish leaned across the table and whispered. "I've had some other leads that I kept to myself, just for a situation like this."

Kaczka felt like Alice in Wonderland. Nothing made any sense. He dropped into a wooden chair and spoke to the floor. "You didn't even tell me? Did you think I kidnapped my Karina? Why didn't you tell me?" He slowly raised his head and pointed an accusing finger at Vadish. "You deceitful, untrustworthy—"

He stopped, too confused to continue.

Vadish crossed his arms and took the abuse stoically. "Kaz, you must understand that none of our communications here are secure, and now you should be glad I took precautions."

His pulse beat hard; he could feel it in his chest. He looked into Vadish's eyes. "It's just us now. Tell me what you know!"

Vadish whispered so softly Kaz could hardly hear over the blood thumping in his ears. "I have reliable information that the kids spent the first night sleeping at a hostel in Muvattupula and left headed downriver in the morning."

Kaczka tried to understand. "Are you suggesting no automatic rifles or helicopters?"

Vadish added. "And no mountain hideaway."

He perked up. "Good work. So, we can ignore Niraj's fantasy and know for sure they headed west." He put his arm around Vadish's shoulder and gave him a half hug. "I'm sorry I got upset with you. You're one of the good guys. Why do you think he made up the story about helicopters?"

"Well, India is still conservative, especially out here away from the big cities. Spending the night with two unchaperoned girls is not allowed...taboo."

"But helicopters and automatic weapons? Surely he could have invented an aunt or something less dramatic?"

"Certainly, but he's a teenage boy. They imagine soldiers everywhere."

"I see." Kaczka headed back to his bungalow, still wondering what to believe. Had Vadish withheld the report from the hostel to protect his daughter's reputation? How was Roshni involved? He could understand how loyalties would be divided between professional responsibilities and parental ties, but it certainly made finding the truth more difficult.

The next morning, Vadish declared, "Roshni is gone. She and Niraj left in the night. That is highly suspicious, don't you think?" He leaned back and crossed his arms.

Priya suggested, "Do you think she organized the kidnapping? Has she used her trips to Cochin as a cover to meet with the other terrorists?"

Vadish nodded. "That's exactly what I think. She's been against us all along."

Kaczka thought, well that confirms our guess that Niraj's story was fabricated. How much the protests at the research station were Roshni's doing was an open question. But she was gone. His chief scientist was gone. The Mammoth Research Station was as good as closed. Roshni had won.

Was he just giving up, or had his dilemma solved itself? Could it be as simple as that: Close down the research station? At least Karina would be released. He'd abandon the mammoth research. Release the elephants. He had his answer.

With that decided, he expected to feel better, but he didn't. Something was wrong.

With Roshni on the lam, only Vadish and Priya sat with Kaczka around the breakfast table. He asked, "Do you think we can trust the people who took Karina and Sarita? Do you think releasing the elephants is the answer?"

Priya said, "Well, as a Hindu, I can assure you that if the kidnappers are devout, they won't harm the girls."

Vadish added, "I'm Muslim, but I agree with her assessment."

This didn't satisfy Kaczka. The answers sounded too easy, too simplistic. He was frantic about his twelve-year-old daughter. "And if they are not devout?"

Vadish frowned. "Then, anything is possible."

Priya stood up. "Young girls on their own, are always in danger. For every good and decent person, there is a desperate one and a few who are just plain evil. Let's not fool ourselves. We cannot sit here and do nothing. We need to find them."

He shivered. That was the strongest speech he'd heard from the diminutive teacher. He looked at her in a new way. Her plain face and short hair didn't indicate any transformation. She was no taller than he'd recalled, but he noticed how straight she stood and how her sari appeared to wrap her in great power.

She continued. "I know Karina and Sarita. They are capable and intelligent young women. I do not imagine them waiting to be rescued by knights in shining armor. I also think the mammoth research is important. It is here. Protect it. Don't sacrifice it to some fantasy that releasing the elephants will magically return the girls. That is not the way the world works."

Kaczka returned his attention to Vadish, who was also studying Priya intently. His green eyes were open wide. Nothing had happened, but somehow everything had changed. Vadish looked to Priya as if she was in charge, as if he needed her permission. "Tomorrow, I should trace their voyage down river and Kaz should go to the U.S. Embassy in New Delhi."

Priya nodded and it was decided.

The morning meeting convened beside a trailer in the parking lot where one driver towed a riverboat for Vadish, and another stood by to take Kaczka to the Cochin airport. He had invited Priya to see them off. She held a hot chai in one hand and an umbrella in the other. "Vadish and I might both be on fool's errands, but I'll be glad to fly away from this incessant gloom and rain."

Priya turned toward the pagoda and Vadish headed for the tow truck.

"Wait!" Kaczka called. "Before we separate, I have one thing to do. Priya, without those three senior students, I don't think we need you at the school anymore."

Priya stood tall and her face showed no emotion. "I understand. I was happy here and am sad for Satita and Karina. If there is another way I can help, I'd be happy to assist." She added. "This is a good time for me to move home. My grandparents are getting older and need me."

He felt clumsy. He'd done this thing poorly. "No. No! I don't want you to leave. With Roshni gone, you are the best qualified to continue the research. I'd like you to be the chief scientist."

Vadish looked surprised and squinted his eyes as if to say, Are you crazy?

She smiled. "You won't regret this. I have some ideas. I can do this."

While Kaz had been uncertain about Priya's promotion, now he thought: There's more to this quiet schoolteacher than I realized. Maybe she'll surprise me, maybe surprise us all.

His optimism was short-lived. Vadish's surprise had turned into a frown. Somehow Priya's promotion had offended his sense of his place in the hierarchy. Kaczka couldn't have a demoralized head of security. He needed him to defend the station and find Karina.

As if it had been his intention all along, he announced, "And Vadish, I'm also promoting you to General Manager Operations. Your additional responsibilities will include finance, facilities, logistics—" He took a breath and searched for something else to include. He thought of the farm and the power plant. "— agriculture and utilities. Congratulations!"

Now they both smiled and Kaczka could head for the U.S. Embassy confident he was leaving everything in good order.

13. MAATALII—QAMANITTUAQ NUNAVUT CANADA

Maatalii slid her suitcase under the bed and watched as her *uaguk*, Amaruq, hung up the last one of her school uniforms in their tiny shared closet. The Twins, everyone called them, although they were simply cousins who looked alike. They weren't even the same age, having been born two months apart. But they had grown up in the same house together, and were *uaguk*, sister-souls, best friends.

This was the third year they had gone away to school together. This year they'd been joined by Maatalii's own little brother, Yuka. They hadn't seen him much at school, since he was in Junior High School and they were first-year High Schoolers. Well, second year, now. Or they would be after the summer break.

Lusa, the oldest of the family children, had graduated and would be finding an apprenticeship, since he was not interested in college but instead wanted to work with his hands. He had come home two weeks before they had since he was finished. He helped out at the family restaurant a lot; Maatalii wondered if Mother would miss his help if he got a job elsewhere.

She fluffed her pillow and tossed it onto her bed.

Being away from home for nine months wasn't as much fun as Maatalii had originally thought, though their classes were inspirational. And useful. When the world economy collapsed, dozens of the smaller schools were closed throughout Nunavut. They'd been given a choice between going away to the Consolidated School in Iqaluit, or a school of their choice in one of the adjacent Provinces. After a great deal of research, the family had decided on a highly rated school in southern Manitoba. It wasn't really any further away than Iqaluit would have been; they had to fly no matter what, taking the tiny plane to Yellowknife, or Churchill, then transferring onward.

"I'm looking forward to being home awhile," Amaruq said, echoing her thoughts. They both sat down on their beds, looking at each other across the narrow aisle between. "Why did Mama give up the family house? I know our home is Snow House now, but my heart can't accept it."

"I think without Papa it was too much. She had to give up something, and it wasn't going to be this, which is the whole family's livelihood," Maatalii said, waving her arm to mean the whole of Snow House Inn and Restaurant. But that probably wasn't what Amaruq meant. "I think it just hurt too much to walk home to an empty house every day."

Ama nodded. "I guess."

"She brought our things, and put them here for us—she was making sure we feel welcome here," Maatalii pointed out.

"Yes," Amaruq said. "But still…"

"It was a surprise to me too, Ama."

Her "twin" nodded again, then brightened. "At least we get to share our very own room, now."

"No more annoying Yuka and his annoying dogs running through all the time."

"Smelly, drooly, clumsy dogs breaking things with their waggy tails!"

"Eww!" they said, at the same time, and laughed.

"Come on, I want to tell Mama about our greenhouse project," Maatalii said, jumping to her feet.

"Do you think she will let us do it?"

"If it's for school, I think she would let us do anything!"

Maatalii took off her gloves to help hold the board down while Sivoy hammered the staple in. Yuka held on to the other end of the bendy board to keep it from flopping in the breeze. Then they moved it into position in a hoop shape over the floor. Once all the hoops were up and braced, they'd staple on the heavy plastic. Supposedly the flexible cover would withstand the winds of a blizzard, but Maatalii still wasn't certain the scientists who had designed it understood arctic weather. The whole thing might collapse in the first storm. Or blow away.

Anyhow, that was why they were making a small one to begin with. If the greenhouse survived, next summer they'd make a full-sized one. Or maybe two. Then Snow House could offer farm-to-table fresh veggies. And Maatalii and Amaruq would get *beaucoup* extra credit in their Practical Biology class.

She looked over to where Amaruq and now Yuka were mixing a pile of home-made compost into some store-bought potting soil. It seemed ridiculous to have to buy *dirt,* but tundra didn't work. It was mostly peat or rock. Yuka dumped the last small bag of sand into the mix while Amaruq used her shovel to turn the planting dirt over and over. She also dug up a shovel full of compost and added it to the pile, mixing it in. Their plants would have rich soil to grow in.

There was a reason not much grew in their lands, and it wasn't just the cold winters. Moss and algae had to work hard to make a go of it, and that was before the peat fires had become a threat to the whole tundra. That was why the caribou moved all over the tundra; there never was enough food to stay in one place. Not until the people penned them, attempting to solve several problems at once.

The Twins' extra credit last year had involved turning Snow House's kitchen scraps and caribou dung into compost, and it had turned out well, even though Mama had forgotten to keep turning it. Maatalii suspected Uncle Sivoy had done it, so the girls' work setting it up would not go to waste.

Sivoy had also been the one who had gone out and rounded the wild caribou back up after rebuilding the pasture fence. Mama was still not back to normal at that time.

Sivoy, who now cleared his throat, waiting for her to set the end of the next bendy board against the frame so he could staple it.

"Sorry, I was lost in thought," Maatalii said. "Mrs. Gunderson said we should cut slits into the plastic to let the house "breathe" to prevent mold from growing. Do you think the slits would also help the wind go through? So it doesn't blow down?"

"We'll see," Sivoy grunted. Not much of a talker was Uncle Sivoy. But he was a good solid worker. You never had to ask Sivoy twice to come help, unlike Tarkik, who never did anything, even if his sister Amaruq begged him. Except maybe flirt, if you could call that *doing* something. He and her brother Lusa were both big flirts. But whether they were flirts or hard workers, they were all going to enjoy the fresh fruit and vegetables she and Amaruq would grow.

Well, *someone* would grow them, she hoped. She and Amaruq would actually be back at school. Maatalii still had not convinced her mother to do the job; Suluk had enough to do. She didn't think they could ask Grandma Osha, although she might enjoy working in the relative warmth of the greenhouse. She was just too old.

Maybe their grouchy Aunt Meriwa could be coaxed into it. Hers was the only household in Qamanittuaq that had house plants, after all. Fresh parsley couldn't be much harder to grow than spider plants, right? And Aunt Meriwa-mother's-sister enjoyed a challenge, which was why she had helped raise Tarkik and Ama.

Many times the girls had been grateful Suluk had taken in the orphaned girl while Meriwa had taken the boy. Of course they took in the orphaned children of their older sister and her husband, who had died suddenly of a mysterious disease. That is what family did amongst *The People*. But splitting up the siblings could have happened the other way 'round. Tarkik could have grown up with his cousin and Maatalii's older brother Lusa. *Wow. Then they really would have had a pair of hopeless flirts!*

Maati realized she was being unkind to compare the two, though. Her brother Lusa might flirt, but he also worked. He was out feeding caribou, right now, or he'd be helping her and Sivoy, she knew.

They attached the last board to the sturdy frame and decided to take a break before tackling the plastic. They'd need more people for that anyhow, and someone taller than Yuka, if one could be found. Maybe Uncle Ujurak was around or Lusa would come back. The plastic had to be unrolled, then stretched over the bendy hoops, and stapled down everywhere.

Then, she needed to look at the instructions again to see how to frame the ends and build in the door or doors. Maybe this little greenhouse only needed one door, but probably when they made the big ones, they would want two, one at each end.

The greenhouses would end up looking like plastic Quonset huts like they used at the weather station and at some of the ranger stations in the arctic. They were poorly insulated, but cheap. The hope was that the slight snow they got nowadays would stick outside on the plastic and help insulate the greenhouses, kind of like the Inuit's old igloos had. The problem was with the *Hot* still expanding, they were unlikely to get enough snow for that to work. The greenhouses might need to have hay or moss spread on them, at least at the base, to help hold warmth in. Eventually a solar panel or two could run little heaters, but Suluk had not been willing to spend the money for them. Yet.

Maatalii was determined to make a go of the project. It would be her contribution to the family's income, expanding Snow House's menu and hopefully generating a strong reputation to attract more customers. Tourists were becoming interested in the area. Some people had never seen snow, or wild ice, or the northern lights.

"Do you think Spencer will come and do a food review for us?" she asked Amaruq that night as they got ready for bed.

"I don't believe he's going to risk his internship at the magazine for the sake of Snow House," Ama said. "And we don't really want him to come until we have plenty of fresh foods to add to the...*cuisine,* right?"

"I'll suggest it next year, then." She squeezed toothpaste onto her brush.

Amaruq sat on her bed, braiding her hair. "Is Mama going to do the mammoth project?"

Maatalii stopped brushing her teeth to spit in the sink. "She keeps looking at their brochures, and how much the project will pay. Plus if we could get the mammoths to increase, they'd probably buy them for zoos and stuff too, not just for meat and tundra trampling."

"I think the meat is going to be the most worthwhile thing. They're saying more cattle is impossible, it's not worth it to lose 25% of their herds each year to the *Hot.* And cattle have always been bad for the environment."

"I think the part Mama likes best is mammoths might help keep the permafrost frozen."

"If it works."

"Yeah. If it works."

"Did you talk to Aunt Meriwa about running the greenhouses?"

"You know, *she* came to *me* about it!" Maatalii said, still marveling.

Amaruk's eyes widened. "She *volunteered?*"

"Pretty much. She said if she got to choose some of what we're planting, she will bully Tarkik or Lusa into helping, since Lusa's done with school. Or maybe one of the Uncles will help."

"Lusa's really not going to college?"

"Not if Tarkik goes. Anyhow, Lusa may have found an apprenticeship at the machine shop. Even with scholarships paying their way, we can't afford to hire help if they both leave for school."

"Not that Tarkik ever does anything to help."

"Actually, Mama said he's been taking care of supplies, ordering things, and picking them up, making sure the kitchen and Inn rooms are stocked up."

Amaruq mimed fainting. "*J'en doute*," she said tartly. She loved her Conversational French classes, did Amaruq.

"Methinks thou lovest thine own brother *not* too much," Maatalii said, laughing.

"Oh no! That reminds me," Amaruq said, "I've still got a thousand pages of Shakespeare to read before we head back."

"Ugh, that's a lot!" Maatalii pointed her finger. "You can do it!"

"Uhm. Maybe. You're much more dedicated than I am."

"You always look better than I do."

"Blaine Andresson doesn't think so," Amaruq countered.

"Ha!"

Maatalii had long thought she and her cousin-almost-sister were equally attractive. Her papa always had something nice to say to her about how pretty she was—just one of the little things she missed about him. But at school, it was Amaruq who got the most attention. Slightly plump, long glossy black hair, shining eyes, dimples framing an outrageous smile: that was Amaruq.

Maatalii, if she was indeed beautiful and not just the daughter of a kind man, had slightly less to work with. She studied the mirror. With her hair pulled back into a single long braid, the oval shape of her face became prominent. Supposedly, symmetry was what made faces beautiful, and she could always see how crooked her eyes were, the left one much higher than the right, though at least their tilt was at the same angle. Her nose was okay, but her mouth was too small, and her teeth, while white and strong, were also crooked.

I think we are not twins anymore, she thought. Amaruq had surpassed her in looks. She sighed. Well, looks weren't everything. Maybe I'm supposed to be the smart one.

As if reading her mind, Amaruq said, "Did your grades come in today's mail? Mine did. I hope yours are better. Mama is not going to be happy; even Meriwa may say something."

"Actually, I think she is less worried about grades than she is if you are getting pimples, or dying your hair blue."

"You may be right. Stop changing the subject. Grades?"

"All A's except for that stupid typing class. B-minus."

"*Cherie*, how did you manage that?"

"Trying to go too fast, I suspect. But at least I can type with all my fingers, now."

Ama nodded. "It makes doing reports much easier. And even texting, though I still have to do that with two fingers."

"The keyboards are *still* too small." Maatalii, staring at herself in the mirror, tried wrapping her braid into a fat bun. She took a picture with her phone and looked at it. Kind of like a round Aztec temple, or a beehive.

"I'm going to see if Mama needs help in the kitchen," Amaruq said.

Maatalii nodded. "I'll be along soon."

But she wasn't. Searching for her hair ties, she came across the box of keepsake photos her mother had put under her bed with her bins of clothes and hair things.

She picked up the family photo Uncle Sivoy had taken during the previous winter/holiday break. She and Ama stood with their arms across each other's shoulders, big smiles on their faces. Mama and Papa held hands, gentle smiles on their faces. In front of them, Yuka knelt with a hand on each of his dogs' shoulders, a proud grin showing his perfect white teeth. Behind their parents, Tarkik and Lusa stood awkwardly in front of the fireplace, serious expressions on their faces, as though they were deciding the future of the world.

But what caught and held her eyes were her parents. She stared at her father's face, which was quite symmetrical. She could see her crooked eyes came from her mother, not him. He was both handsome and wise. And kind.

Had been.

She felt tears slip down her cheeks, and then just burst into a wailing cry, missing him terribly.

14. XIANG BO—DONGLAN CHINA

Xiang Bo actually enjoyed the drive from Guilin to Hechi in the four-wheel drive. She planned to spend half a day finding an inexpensive place to leave the vehicle so it was always available when she flew into Hechi. Taking a note from the big international airports, Hechi's airport administration charged hefty fees for all parking anywhere near the airport. She looked for a place near one of the regular airport tram services, checking out driveways, and especially new houses with two- and three-car garages. Eventually she found one that was not being used by its owners and made an agreement to pay a small amount to park there. From the garage, it was three blocks to the airport tram. That would work.

This time, though, she still needed to drive on to Donglan, to the school and Zi Min, and then to her mother's. She would need to make a place for herself and Zi Min—either part of her mother's house, or separate somewhere on her farmland. Xiang Bo could sleep in Jiao's kitchen, but with Zi Min too, Jiao's house was simply too small. She needed to have a long visit with Mo Chou also, but her friend was busy hostessing Council meetings all week.

After teaching her class at Changle, she crossed the road to the orphanage with Zi Min at her side. Her heart pounded surprisingly loud in her chest, enough so that she was certain someone would notice. Someone would know she was about to defy her husband and adopt a little girl who needed a home. Once she thought of it in those terms, her rapid heartbeat slowed and gentled, and she was able to smile at the head mother. How could this be wrong?

"We need to go to your office, Liang," Xiang Bo said, feeling awkward as always, to refer to the woman by just her personal name. Liang was an orphan as well, never adopted, never given a surname.

Eyes alight, Liang led the way. She had been in charge of the orphanage for many years. Xiang Bo had always hoped to introduce the woman to her mother, so Jiao would have a friend not too far away, but that had never happened. Her mother refused to leave her little house and plot of land, and Liang needed to be always at the orphanage; she lived in a tiny room at the back of the small compound.

"How may I help you, Dr. Bai?" Liang said, after showing them to chairs beside a table she used as a desk.

"I am adopting Zi Min. I would like to have the papers I need to make it official."

Liang's smile was kind, and she looked at Zi Min, then back at Xiang Bo. "Of course," she said. "I am glad."

It took surprisingly little time to accomplish what felt like a major, life-changing event. Not quite like giving birth, but equally complex. When Xiang

Bo walked with Zi Min back down the hall, she was an official mother and guardian of the little girl whose long black queue bounced as she skipped beside her new parent. As they passed other children, Zi Min was looked upon with envious eyes, and Xiang Bo received a few pleading stares. Alas, she could not manage more than Zi Min. Giving all these orphans a home could never be as simple as sharing a shrimp.

Liang had worried, "Will you continue to teach here?"

"Yes, certainly," Xiang Bo said. "And perhaps Zi Min will come with me to visit her old friends?"

Wide-eyed, Zi Min had nodded yes, and everyone smiled.

It was done, Xiang Bo thought. She had made her own family.

⌣

Xiang Bo helped Zi Min compress the last of the bamboo chips into a fire brick, squeezing the press tight. She cleaned crumbs out of the brick press, and poured a bucket of water over it, rinsing the binding glue off so the simple lever did not stick itself together.

Then they took a rest before carrying their batch of bricks to the house. She sat on a rock, while Zi Min squatted among the last crumbs of bamboo on the ground, poking at a beetle with her finger.

"Sometimes those are stinky, Zi Min," Xiang Bo cautioned. She remembered once as a child having to wash her hands a dozen times to get the nasty odor off. That beetle had been a different shape and color, as far as she could recall, but she was no insect expert. Li was better at that, even though it was not his specialty either. She felt a pang, thinking of him. She had not even telephoned when she had been in Donglan, where cell coverage was good. But then, he had apparently not tried to call her either.

Her visit with Mo Chou had been revivifying for the most part. Mo Chou had, of course, strongly suggested an official divorce, in case Cheng Li got nasty about money or other legal issues, but Xiang Bo was reluctant.

"I still think we can work it out," she told her friend over tea. "He's been worried about finances and his own grants, and that has taken a toll on his patience."

"You always make excuses for him," Mo Chou said, a frown distorting her pretty face. "Men can be pigs."

"You say when you use them so adroitly," she snapped, suddenly tired of Mo Chou's constant dismissal of all males.

"That is how I know how piggy they can be."

Xiang Bo shook her head. "It's different for me. I never regretted my marriage, just the timing."

"What you are describing is bullying and disrespect," Mo Chou said. "And those I know about." She leaned forward, speaking more softly. "My Donglan Councilman is easy to manipulate, but he can be just as much a bully as your Li." She rapped her long shocking pink fingernails on the table. "I know."

"Li doesn't like you any more than you like him, so it has always been a struggle for me to talk to either of you about the other." Xiang Bo shrugged and went on, "Yet I still talk to both of you. I can see the value of what both of you say, however much you disagree with each other."

Mo Chou received this with a grunt. She poured more tea into each of their cups. "When do I get to see Zi Min?" she asked.

Xiang Bo sighed. "Soon, I hope. I could not come into town and leave mother all alone, so daughter is staying home with her today."

Mo Chou nodded. "Bai Jiao is not doing so well?"

"No, she gets weaker by the day."

They discussed Jiao's failing health, and Xiang Bo's proposed vat algae project and the doings of Donglan Council, and ended by coming back around to Cheng Li.

"I just hope you don't regret leaving him without divorcing him," Mo Chou said.

"I still have feelings for him," Xiang Bo said. "He can be kind when he's not so worried."

They hugged, and then Xiang Bo drove home, thinking of the Chengs.

She *had* received a letter from Di'e hoping she was well and that she might come back to visit. Di'e herself was not getting younger, she said. Of course, neither was Jiao, whom Xiang Bo was here with. Could Di'e survive until after Xiang Bo's own mother had passed on? She certainly wasn't abandoning her mother now.

Di'e had her own two sons, while Jiao had no one but Xiang Bo. And now Zi Min. Xiang Bo smiled, thinking about her mother's reaction to having a sudden granddaughter. It seemed to have given her new life, at least for a few weeks.

She came back to the present when the first raindrops hit her face. She glared up at the clouds. "Time to get these inside," she said, looking at the bricks under the darkening sky.

"Will rain make the bricks come apart?" Zi Min wondered.

"Yes. They have to dry before they become hard and sturdy."

"We will hurry, then," Zi Min decided, sounding very adult.

Xiang Bo smiled at her and bent to pick up bricks. They filled the small handcart, and each ended up carrying a sack full as well, as they clambered up the hill, shoving the handcart through the remaining stands of bamboo. The rest had been harvested by a professional crew the week before, bringing into the Bai household enough cash to last the winter, even without Xiang Bo's research grant monies. She needed to write her paper, and a progress report, to satisfy the grant requirements, before she could hope to see any more money from them. The bamboo earnings were a big help, cash in hand.

Once the bricks were stacked in the kitchen, Xiang Bo went back outside and looked over the remaining work needed on their bedroom beneath the main portion of Jiao's house.

Built up on stilts in the traditional way, Jiao's house consisted of two rooms on the main floor: her mother's bedroom, and the kitchen-sitting area. The back of Jiao's house rose almost ten meters above the ground while the "front" where the entrance was, was very nearly at the ground level of the steep hilltop.

She'd laid a floor below, floating it off the sturdy stilts about halfway up the empty space and partly dug into the sloping hillside. There was a room with a nearly three-meter high ceiling—which was the floor above, of course. The new floor measured almost four meters by six. There was plenty of room for a bed for each of them, as well as some closets or cabinets for their clothes. She had almost completed the walls, sealing out the wind and rains of autumn with a layer of insulation between the inside bamboo-strip walls and the outside walls of wood laths to be covered with stucco-like plaster before the winter snows fell.

She already had extended the covered pathway from the house to the outhouse, making a turn and adding a few stairs down to their room's entranceway under the main house. It would not be warm getting from the upstairs house to their room, but it wouldn't be any colder than using the outhouse.

Xiang Bo had plans to add a composting toilet indoors for Jiao, but they hadn't figured out where it should go; her mother's bedroom was too small, and the kitchen wasn't appropriate. Xiang Bo's plan now was to increase and close in the lean-to by the entrance door and make a small toilet room there. Eventually the little room could be sealed up and made more a warm part of the house, but in the interim it would mean Jiao did not need to walk outside through the snow.

Climate change meant weather extremes. While the rest of the world seemed to be heating up, there were a few places where winters were colder, and Nalai was one of them. Xiang Bo had been horrified to discover two meters of snow piled up around her mother's house the previous winter. If she could not get this extra bedroom sealed up before snowfall, she and Zi Min might have to sleep in the main house after all, simply to stay warm.

She could hear Zi Min and Jiao talking about something, overhead, but not quite clearly enough to understand what they said. After a few moments, the sound of Zi Min's feet pattering on the boards of the kitchen floor dwindled as the little girl came outside to help Xiang Bo. They put on matching masks, then seized by sudden foolishness, Xiang Bo began making silly faces, wiggling her eyebrows and scrunching up her nose beneath the mask. Her new daughter laughed and tried to copy her. She looked so silly when she crossed her eyes that Xiang Bo laughed out loud. She could see laugh lines at the corners of Zi Min's eyes as well. Still smiling, she waved a hand at the work they had left to do, and they refocused.

Zi Min shook up the yeast-based spray foam insulation bottle while Xiang Bo got the guide board into position. They had the bottom meter done all the way around the room, and were now working on the next section. By the end of the week, they should have it all sprayed on and dry. Then Xiang Bo could put up the finishing boards inside—beautiful siding made from their own bamboo.

She scowled as Zi Min reached past her to spray the next section while she held the board. Even through the mask, she could smell the chemicals of the foam insulation. Was she exposing Zi Min to something harmful?

Zi Min swirled her straw in the *milkshake* Mo Chou had bought her. Xiang Bo watched her friend and her daughter interact, wishing she could show Li how wonderful having a child was. It was like revisiting her own childhood in some ways, recapturing the wonder of discovery. That sense of wonder was something she thought they had both lost, her and Li, somewhere along the way.

It was, she thought further, perhaps an explanation for why Li's research had stalled out, although hers seemed to be going well enough. She had driven into town to mail her project progress report and buy a few supplies. Zi Min loved Mo Chou, so of course Xiang Bo had arranged to see her friend and give her daughter the rare treat of Mo Chou's sassy tongue. Mo Chou's outspokenness was what Zi Min liked best about the woman. It was also probably what had kept her friend from marrying, but everyone in Donglan seemed to love her company, despite it. Mo Chou knew everybody. Sometimes Xiang Bo envied her friend's easy affability.

But Mo Chou was also an irrepressible gossip and would tell everyone everything. She was fun, but Xiang Bo had learned long ago to be cautious what she said to the woman. Their mutual friends claimed telling Mo Chou something meant that in a scant week, the story would come back to them from someone living in Suzhou. That seemed like hyperbole, but one thing was certain: it had never hurt Xiang Bo to guard her tongue, even though Mo Chou had been her best friend since they were in diapers.

Now Zi Min used her straw to noisily suck up the last bits of her dairy treat that Mo Chou had insisted she must try. Xiang Bo hoped her daughter wouldn't become ill from it. Many non-Americans were lactose intolerant. She wondered if her college friends were still able to get milk and other dairy products. She'd read the United States was not enduring the *Hot* well, that many of their traditional food sources were becoming unreliable.

Not that they weren't experiencing problems of their own here. Guangxi province was no longer able to grow enough rice to feed its own peoples, much less export it. She needed to focus more attention on her algae research.

"Have you heard how they are doing with the water projects in Qinghai Province?" she asked Mo Chou.

"Oh, it's stupid. They have taken so much water, the output from Three Gorges Dam has actually gone down. They had to stop until monsoon season."

"That seems impossible," Xiang Bo said.

Mo Chou shook her head. "Worse, they sent all that water up there, and they never did anything with it. It all soaks into the ground, as much a desert as ever. The people are starving. Millions of *kuai*, for nothing!"

"Mm," Xiang Bo said. "I thought they had prepared rice fields."

"Hui and Tu peoples don't eat rice," Mo Chou said in a tart sarcastic tone. "Let them eat wheat," she said, misquoting.

Xiang Bo laughed.

"So, have you divorced him yet?"

Xiang Bo made a face and shook her head.

Mo Chou said a rude word, then apologized to Zi Min immediately.

"He hasn't even met Zi Min yet," Xiang Bo said. "Besides, Zi Min should meet her other grandmother. I feel sorry for Cheng Di'e."

"She seemed nice enough," Mo Chou allowed.

"I cannot leave Jiao just now," Xiang Bo finished, and Mo Chou nodded her agreement.

"I understand. Is there anything I can help with, my friend?"

Xiang Bo shook her head. "No. Our room is almost finished, and cozy for winter."

Mo Chou stood, reached for her car keys, and Xiang Bo remembered one last, important thing.

"Were you able to find recipes for my algae?"

"Oh," Mo Chou said, sitting back down. "You are right, it makes a decent substitute for tofu, and my Indian friend used it in place of tempeh. No one is fond of the taste, but everyone agrees eating it is better than starving for protein. Are they really having so much trouble with soybean production?"

"It's affected by climate change the same as everything else. The *Hot* is pushing soybean production far north—or south in the Southern Hemisphere, of course. Everyone is running out of room in their arable zones. I'm growing this locally, so we can go out to the lakes and stream pools and scoop it up."

Mo Chou nodded. "I know," she said. "It just takes many spices to make it good, and spices are *expensive!*"

Xiang Bo sighed.

"Figure out some cheap ginger and pepper, then we'll be happy," Mo Chou said.

"Thank you. I'll try to get up here again soon. Mother is a little better than last week, so I am hoping her improvement will continue."

They hugged, and then Xiang Bo watched as perfumed and coiffed Mo Chou also hugged little Zi Min in her denim dress and messy braids.

"She wears a lot of makeup," Zi Min said in the car as they headed home.

Xiang Bo chuckled. "Yes. She always has."

"Can I wear makeup?"

"Not yet. You are too young by many years."

Zi Min sighed. "I would like some makeup. But not perfume," she said. "That is too much perfume. I can still smell it on *me*."

"Yes, I can smell it, too. I prefer fresh air bamboo scent."

Zi Min nodded. "Me too."

15. Urmi, Kaczka, Karina—Kerala India

Urmi listened to Sarita snoring. Ever since Roshni sent Niraj on an errand, Sarita had been staying up late trying to make friends with the guards.

With Urmi's cellmate asleep, she shoved her laundry basket aside and reached her hands into the cool dirt. Little by little she extended her tunnel. Sarita snorted and rolled over. Frightened that Sarita had awakened, Urmi covered the excavation and feigned being asleep herself. Eventually, gentle snoring returned and the tunneling resumed.

She cursed the ground, full of rocks, seashells, and ginger roots. Then a whiff of refreshing night air blew through the spicy foliage into her stuffy cell announcing that the tunnel had broken through to outside. Widening the tunnel would take more work. Once she escaped, she'd go north to Cochin. She didn't worry about getting lost, as her humble prison rested within sight of the Vembanad Lake. She'd just follow the levees.

Come morning, the sound of river taxis taking children to school murmured through the open tunnel. She hoped that no one would notice. Sarita's morning routine occupied her, so no worries there. But Pucca rubbed the laundry basket, purring loudly and pawing at the ground around it. Urmi threw a piece of knotted cloth to distract the observant cat.

Her meager progress gave her hope. She didn't have any reason to trust Sarita, but no one had shown up to rescue them. No knights in shining armor. She got impatient, so she took a risk. "Sarita, I've been working on a tunnel." She imagined what it would take to interest her roommate. "If we work together, we could be out of here in a week, perhaps before Niraj returns."

Sarita gave her a smug look when a big crash came from the house. Urmi thought it sounded like thunder but more metallic. Sarita smiled, "No chance. That's him."

Urmi heard the stable door unlatch and Niraj swung it wide open. "I'm back. Look what I have!" He dragged a white metal barrel past the girls' room. Urmi recognized it: a washing machine, with cranks and a wringer, like she'd seen in a history book.

He continued out the back door and dumped the machine next to the old washtub. He smiled and waved to Sarita.

She waved back and then turned to Urmi, announcing in a loud voice, "Too bad, I found out about your tunnel and told him. He kissed me and promised to help with the laundry. No more soaking my hands in soapy water."

That night, Niraj locked Urmi alone in the stable. When she went to work on the tunnel, she discovered it had been filled with concrete. Urmi had hoped the other girl would be her friend. Now that possibility had vanished, and her isolation filled her with sadness. She held Pucca while the monsoon drummed on the roof. "I love you, kitty. I promise to take care of you."

Her plastic sack of escape money and dried fruits still hid under her sleeping pallet. In the dark, she counted her coins. 2,531 rupees. Not much, but better than nothing. She didn't know how she'd escape but felt sure she would.

○

Kaczka looked out from the twenty-third floor to admire India's *Arc de Triomphe*, simply called India Gate. His meeting with the U.S. Ambassador had exceeded his expectations. On his final day in New Delhi, he celebrated with room service. Dressed in white from turban to slippers, the waiter delivered a British breakfast—bacon, sausages, eggs, black pudding, baked beans, tomatoes, mushrooms, and cold toast, each on a separate dish. *There's no shortage of food here.* He spread some marmalade on his toast and connected with Vadish.

"I have good news. Though she can't admit having agents in India, the ambassador assures me that they will search for Karina. Also, her intelligence briefings will now list Roshni as a terrorist."

Kaczka expected congratulations, but Vadish seemed distracted by something else. "Yes. Yes! That's all nice, but don't you ever watch the local news?"

Why doesn't he just state his concern? Why ask about the news? Attempting to disguise his frustration, Kaz echoed back, "No. No! Obviously not. Why should I?"

Before Vadish answered, the connection went dead. Kaczka knew the problem wasn't from his hotel. He worried. What's going on in Kerala? Why is Vadish acting so strangely? I better check the news when I arrive at the airport.

○

Grateful for the second day of clear skies after the darkest monsoon clouds passed over to the east, Urmi did her laundry day chores. No one spoke to her. Sarita and Niraj laughed and worked together using the new washing machine, turning the agitator and cranking the wringer, their hands overlapping. Every few minutes, he ran into the house to check on his comp until he returned with three bowls. "Early dinner!"

Urmi thought this was odd. The sun was bright and high. "Dinner already? We haven't finished the laundry. Should I hang the rest of the clean stuff first?"

Niraj shoved a bowl at her. "No! I said early dinner. Just leave everything where it is. And you're eating in your room."

Now she was scared. What's going on? She wished her new tunnel was complete as she sat on her blanket. Pucca sat next to her. She tore off some bread which the cat happily ate.

Niraj slammed the door and closed the bolt. Urmi put her bowl down. She wasn't hungry yet, so she went to work.

Unfortunately, a boulder blocked her progress on the new tunnel. She widened the hole to get around it. The wider she dug the hole, the bigger she discovered the rock to be. After an hour, she hadn't found the edge. It was time to eat.

She wiped her hands on her shirt. Dinner time. She sat with her cat and shared her rice with bean curry and a couple of *roti*.

She heard the front door slam. Then a roar in the distance moved closer. Water seeped up from the ground.

She upturned her pallet and dug up the plastic bag with her escape money and food. She attached it to her belt.

She thought that she should be scared, but also thought that she didn't have time for scared. Instead, she went to pick up Pucca, but by the time she reached the cat, she had scampered up the wall and was hiding in the thatch. Geckos also sought refuge in the thatch.

Pucca hissed and stared down at her as if to say, "What's happening?" Or, "Fix this!"

"I don't know kitty. I'll try to figure it out."

But she didn't have time. The water rose inside the room. It rose fast; it was already at her knees when she jumped to her feet. The water was cold and swirled ominously.

In just a few minutes, the room flooded to the ceiling, and she was up with Pucca holding on to the thatch.

"Help. Help!" She yelled in English and Malayalam. The stable had seemed so flimsy, but now it proved itself to be solid. No amount of pushing and kicking offered any chance of freeing her. The walls were firm. She struggled to stay afloat and find a firm handhold. Then she realized the water had stopped rising. "Thanks for that. Now I won't drown until I exhaust myself or starve." She had said that out loud, and hearing it just upset her more.

Even if I can't save myself, I can save Pucca. Her fingers bled as she dug a small nest into the thatch for her furry companion. "Here, rest. It's dry. We'll think of something."

All night she held onto the roof. She stroked Pucca with her cheek. "Wait here. I'll be right back." The cat purred. "Thank you for believing in me." *That cat has more faith in me than I do.*

She took a deep breath and dove down to the door. She put one hand on the door handle and the other on the wall. The door didn't budge. No amount of effort made any difference. When she ran out of breath she kicked hard for the surface.

The water constantly moved, sometimes calm and other times choppy. Once she dozed off and woke up coughing. In desperation, she broke the thatch one stick at a time, dropping the tiny pieces into the water. "Hang in there, Pucca. I can't escape, but I can get you out." The cat bumped her head against Urmi's hand as she worked through the thatch.

As the hole grew, she raised her mouth and yelled. The cat yowled in unison. By afternoon Pucca escaped to the roof, but Urmi was so tired, she feared she'd soon fall asleep and drown.

She felt something grab her leg. Crocodile? Watersnake? She kicked free, but her leg was grabbed again. She pulled herself against the roof and kicked, but the grip was too strong. She took a big breath as her head dropped below the water.

An arm grabbed her and pulled her through the door. How did the door get open? She had no energy. She was limp as someone pushed her onto the roof. The dry roof. Out of the water. She was either rescued or dead or hallucinating.

Pucca licked her hand.

She collapsed, coughing and trying to catch her breath.

When she opened one eye, she saw a kayak. She wondered, have I died? Then she opened the other eye and concentrated, recalling that people near death became delirious, "Sarita?"

She closed her eyes. She opened them again. Sarita was still there.

"Rest, Urmi. Niraj wanted to leave you. I never liked him, so I pushed him overboard. He's probably in the Arabian Sea by now. I came back for you. Sorry, it took so long, but the flood currents are strong and there was only me to paddle."

Urmi hugged Sarita. "Thank you. Thank you. Thank you."

The kayak pulled on its mooring. The roof rocked back and forth with the current. "Sarita! The house is breaking up. We need to cut loose." Urmi didn't wait for her answer. She reached to untie the kayak.

"Stop! Stop! Don't do that. I've been paddling against the current night and day to reach you. I have to rest." Sarita stowed her paddle on the deck with bungee cords and put her head down on her folded arms.

Urmi thought, I need a rest too, but we're tied to the roof, and it won't be part of the house much longer.

Suddenly there was a loud crack. She watched the roof on a nearby shack speed away in the current. She shook Sarita in panic. "You can't rest yet. Did you see that roof? It's gone."

Sarita raised her head. "What? What are you talking about?"

Urmi looked again. Everything was gone. She hadn't realized how fast the water was moving. She tried to imagine where the water was going. "So, can we just let the water carry us to safety?"

Sarita rested her head again. "Urmi, you just don't know anything."

"Maybe. But I know we can't stay here, tied to a building that's going to wash away." She tucked Pucca into the cockpit, grabbed her paddle, and spoke English, aloud, for the first time in weeks. "Sarita, you've been out in this. Where is all this water going?"

Sarita started in Malayalam but switched to English. "The ocean. From here everything flows to the ocean."

"What happened to the hills? There are hills between us and the ocean."

"Not *are* hills, *were* hills. The flood has broken through."

Karina thought faster in English. She immediately knew what to do. She untied the rope. The kayak quickly left the house behind. "Paddle. Paddle before the roof breaks free and swamps us."

Sarita didn't move. "Are you crazy? We can't paddle against this current. It is washing us to the sea, just like Niraj. No one will find us in the ocean. Now that you untied us, we're lost!"

Karina didn't have time to argue. She shouted over the rushing water. "To the right. To the right! We don't need to go against the current, just enough across it to hit a surviving hill. Steer to the right."

Sarita picked up her paddle.

Karina watched valuable supplies float past them. A bowl of rice sailed by with, unbelievably, the rice paddle still in place like a small mast. A bunch of bananas with two monkeys enjoying a snack like first-class cruise passengers. A mother duck and seven ducklings floated by on a raft of thatch. She even saw a comp in a thick waterproof case, the screen still playing some video. She didn't try to do anything but look. They were headed for a hilly shore, but even a moment of inattention would pull them into the maelstrom storming out to the Arabian Sea. *Adrenaline do not fail me.*

Pucca crawled down to her feet.

Sarita cried. "My arms! My arms are so tired!"

Sweat blinded Karina, but she kept pulling across the flow, each stroke moving the kayak just a tiny bit out of the main current.

This lasted forever, and then she jerked forward. They had hit land. She scrambled out and pulled the kayak ashore with Sarita's help. Pucca waited patiently to disembark on dry land. They left the kayak well away from the water. Perhaps it would help someone else.

Then came a big wave and the kayak was gone.

It was getting dark. They walked up the hill and collapsed well above the waves.

Karina blinked her eyes at the rising sun reflecting off the expanse of water. She felt the plastic bag. She was amazed to find it still hanging off her waist.

She jingled the coins. Useless, where could she spend money in a flood? She untied the sack and retrieved some dried papaya and banana and gave half to Sarita. Not far from her Pucca purred loudly with a breakfast of gecko.

They hiked up a little farther to a wide road signed NH66 and found a small town, Kommady, and their first view of the ocean stretching to the horizon. The vista persuaded her to forget the flood and, instead, imagine a limitless future. They ran into the first market they saw and grabbed water bottles, sweet cakes, and crisps. Water, sugar, salt, the basics of life.

The town was deserted. Karina left her cache of 2,531 rupees in the cash box, which wasn't locked, and still contained a stack of five-hundred-rupee banknotes.

They walked into the office and started making 1-1-2 phone calls.

Buzz! Buzz!

"Vadish! Why did you disconnect?"

Kaz took a deep breath. "Have you found Karina? Have they captured the kidnappers? Did the protestors give up?"

Vadish spoke slowly. "Can you calm down?"

Kaczka could feel his blood pressure rising and his heart beating in his neck. He cried out, "Vadish, you're scaring me. What's going on?"

"Please relax. I'll explain everything."

"Come on. Quit stalling!"

"A dam failed, actually several dams, and we've been hit by a flash flood!"

"Seriously, I've seen floods. They are not the end of the world. Water damage can be repaired."

"*Flash* flood. A wall of water rushed out of the mountains leveling everything in its path—crops, buildings, animals. The Idukki Dam failed, the Periyar overflowed into the Thodupuzhayar and the Kothyar."

He had no idea what Vadish was talking about. "Bottom line. What happened? Is the research station okay? Was everything lost? Were the elephants drowned?"

"Research station? It's now an island. Muvattupula and everything west of it washed to the ocean."

"Where are you?"

"Fortunately, I got out. I'm at the airport."

Kaczka reviewed in his mind. U.S. agents? On the job. Research station? An island, but fine. Vadish? At the airport. Karina? "Vadish. Any leads for Karina?"

He heard a sigh. "My best information is that our daughters are in the direct path of the flood."

He didn't know what to do, except to get back to Kerala. "Wait at the Cochin airport. I'll meet you there and we'll find them."

He changed planes in Bangalore, where every monitor displayed the Kerala disaster. Each story eroded his hope for Karina's safety. Everyone waiting for his flight wore a uniform. Military. Medical. Emergency services. He called Vadish. "Give me some news. Some good news."

"Sorry, Kaz, my friend. The flood has broken through the Vembanad Lake levees. Everyone was evacuated to higher ground and north to Cochin."

He already knew this. "Yes. Yes! But any word of the girls?"

"Well, I sent their pictures to all the emergency teams. Nothing yet."

"I'll be in Cochin in three hours."

"I'm already there and I have an all-wheel-drive amphibian with the batteries fully charged and a satellite phone."

"On my way. Find them before I land. Okay?"

Vadish's laugh was harsh.

Kaczka sat in the amphibian Vadish had rented, three meters above the road. He could see in all directions but had no idea where to go. Vadish received a connection from one of his contacts. He put it on speaker.

"Evacuation Center KB04 reported two Indian girls claiming to be your daughters. However, Sarita and Karina have been in the news. We think these are pranksters."

Vadish replied to the comp. "Thanks. Let us know if you hear anything solid."

Kaczka mused, "Every picture of Karina shows her long blond hair and fair complexion. Why would two Indian girls even pretend? It doesn't make any sense."

Vadish tapped on his comp. "KB04 is in the Kerala backwaters. My last intelligence placed our daughters in that area."

Kaczka couldn't just wait in the airport parking lot. "That's it. Let's go there, whether it's them or not. Even if it's not, that's where we need to be, isn't it?"

"Don't get too optimistic. It's chaos down there."

"All the more reason to get going."

They drove for hours, through Cochin and south on NH66.

All the traffic moved in the opposite direction. Their rapid progress encouraged Kaczka. "See, Vadish. The roads aren't that bad."

"Yes, NH66 follows the high land, at least ten meters above sea level, well above the floodwaters."

Just then Kaczka was pulled back by his seatbelt when Vadish jammed on the brakes. Barriers and police cars blocked the road. They pulled the huge amphibian onto the verge and went to take a look.

Just past the barricades, the road had been cut by a cascade of water rushing to the ocean. Kaczka had never seen anything like this. The road had been replaced by a forty-foot deep canyon. "What do we do now?"

They went to an emergency worker. "Is there any way to go south from here?"

She looked at them. Kaczka imagined her thinking, what are these two old guys doing here?

She politely asked, "Not sure. Do you have a helicopter?"

Vadish frowned and pointed to the amphibian, "That's all we have."

She smiled, evidently impressed that they had come somewhat prepared. "So, if you go downhill to the beach, the surge might have widened enough for you to cross in that thing."

As they walked away, she added, "If you get stuck, don't call us. We're really busy."

Vadish drove straight down toward the beach. Halfway down, their comps lost all signals.

Driving along the beach, Kaczka noticed how calm the ocean was in contrast with the Vembanad Lakes. When the floodwaters reached the ocean, they formed a broad delta.

Kaczka was encouraged as they turned south along the Arabian Sea. As the lady had predicted, the water streaming across the beach was only a meter or two deep. "Good work, Vadish. Nothing else would have made it through here."

Vadish shifted into a lower gear. "Here we go."

Kaczka saw the water streaming down the hills and into the ocean. Now he was worried. "Can we do this without getting washed away?"

He relaxed when Vadish laughed. "We have five tons of Indian engineering. We'll be fine." Whitewater roared over the boot and bonnet.

Kaczka thought, I think he's having fun.

Vadish was still laughing. "I changed my mind. Maybe we should have gotten a couple of elephants. We've got plenty of those, don't we?" He laughed louder and hit the accelerator. "I just love the torque on these electric motors."

The splashes rose above the roof. Kaczka got into the spirit. "Look at you. Moses. Parting the seas."

Soon enough they had forded the delta. Their comps had no signal, but they had turned uphill to return to NH66.

The sat phone rang. Kaczka jumped. He forgot that sat phones worked everywhere, even on the top of Mount Everest. He put the call on speaker.

"Hello? Vadish?"

Kaczka answered. "Yes."

"We've had so much trouble connecting to you."

"Do you have any news?"

"Well, maybe. We're going to give this number to those two girls. They'll call you."

Kaczka shook his head. "I thought you said they were just troublemakers."

"Uh. Umm. Well." Kaczka thought the guy on the other end seemed nervous.

"You see. They were at an evacuation center, in pretty good health with a pet cat even."

Kaczka encouraged him to get to the point. "Yes. I understand."

"We had so many people needing serious medical attention. We were doing field surgery for broken bones, inhalation of water. We even delivered a baby."

Vadish smiled at Kaczka, as if to say let him go, he'll get to the point eventually.

"And they had that cat. We had so many rescued animals. Not just cats and dogs, but cattle, sheep, and horses. There were even pet snakes and geckos. We were just so busy."

"So?"

"You see, one of those girls…her hair was dyed. She had blond roots. Blond roots! And she was Anglo, darkly tanned, but definitely Anglo. American Accent."

Kaczka said. "Thanks. We'll await their call."

He disconnected the sat phone.

Vadish pushed down on the accelerator and screamed over the roaring engine, "It's them. They made it!"

Kaczka tightened his safety belt and grabbed anything he could reach, as they bounced over the uneven terrain.

They cried and laughed. "They got themselves out!"

The sat phone rang.

"Dad? Is that you?" Sarita said.

"I'm here, too!" Karina's voice rang out.

"Yes!" Vadish shouted.

"We're coming!" Kaczka yelled.

Both men grinned, in awe of their daughters.

Kaz feared he might be thrown out of his seat, as he yelled, "Faster, faster!"

16. CARLA—WASHINGTON SPRINGS SD USA

"Lake Shore Drive." Carla instructed the rental car to take the scenic route. Lake Michigan reminded her of home—of Oklahoma—with uninterrupted vistas to distant horizons. Even the marinas were deserted, the boats all in winter storage. She could imagine dormant sprouts of winter wheat sleeping beneath the acres and acres of cold white. The city to her left presented a stark contrast—taller, darker, and warmer.

In Wisconsin, she took a video of a flock of cranes flying south. By the time she reached Minnesota, a crystalline white powder completely covered the roadside and fields beyond. A yellow warning light suggested she take control of the car in the snowy conditions, but she ignored it. She'd never driven in snow.

An eagle cruised the warm updrafts over the highway, right side, left side, back and forth, but never in a good position for a picture. She thought the predator's patrol was futile until suddenly it dropped out of the sky into a mound of snow. Shortly it was airborne again carrying a rabbit. Circle of life, she thought, but she also looked away and turned up the music to block the squealing rabbit.

Entering into South Dakota the wind picked up and snowdrifts were as tall as the car, now more snow than she remembered from her childhood. Crossing over the Missouri River she spotted a group of whitetail deer unperturbed by the traffic passing their watering hole. This time she got a picture.

The car's navigation system announced, "Dignity statue on the left," and Carla admired an enormous Native American woman. While negotiating a tight curve exiting the highway the nav system added, "Almost there."

"Mom, Dad, I'm home!" Carla dropped her suitcase inside the front door. During her ride from Chicago, she had promised herself not to repeat last Christmas. The move was over. This wasn't her house anymore, but she still couldn't help comparing. Everything was different. This house had stairs. A thumpity-thump grabbed her attention as Sasha cascaded down the stairs with her tail wagging against the balusters.

Immediately behind the Newfie, clomped her brother.

"Merry Christmas *big* sister."

She laughed for she was still a head taller. She reflected that sometimes genes had a funny sense of humor, giving Mom's shortness to him, and Dad's height to her.

"Shall I show you *up* to your room?"

"Not so fast. First, we have to plug in the rental. I get a credit if I recharge it."

Mike laughed. "You are in for so many surprises. Did you see those ugly—I mean retro—no, really ugly—garden gnomes? Those are the recharge stations. Just tilt back their silly hats."

She headed back outside. "You might as well follow. There's more to bring in."

She tilted a gnome's cap and plugged in the car.

A computer voice acknowledged. "Thank you. I was hungry. I can disconnect myself when I'm ready to go. Your receipt will show you recharged."

Her room—well not really *her* room—must have belonged to a boy. The walls were painted green and brown camo, scratched and dented everywhere. An undamaged circle surrounded by a cloud of pinholes was the one exception, the shadow of a dartboard.

She looked out the window. One story up extended the horizon, so different from being in the car. She looked down wondering: What happens if there is a fire? Or a tornado?

The next morning, Christmas Eve, brought more surprises. Outside her window, pristine white snow stretched to the horizon, reminding her of Lake Michigan. Close to the house, a black spot and a striped spot, the new Trouble and Mischief, scattered a cloud of snowflakes. The two balls of fur enjoyed the White Christmas as much as she did.

"Breakfast, sleepyhead." Mom called from downstairs.

She followed her mother's voice to the dining room. The furniture they left in Oklahoma was cedar, pioneer style, some handmade by her great-great-grandparents. This house came with more modern furniture with lots of steel and plastic. Ugly, she thought, but she didn't say anything. She reiterated her vow to not repeat last Christmas. She almost broke her pledge when she realized that all the curtains were plastic. She knew they were in style, but all she could think was hideous shower curtains. When she took off her shoes, she realized the carpet was also plastic.

Mike ran up with a girl at his side. "This is Elzia. She's visiting from Oklahoma."

The girl's eyes fixed on Carla through thick glasses. Carla rarely met girls as tall as her. Between them, Mike looked like a garden gnome. Elzia's hair was green with a red streak. Christmas, Carla imagined.

Carla offered her hand, "Nice to meet you. Is your family also moving north?"

"No. My family raises cattle." She said softly.

Mom jumped in. "Oklahoma's a good place for that."

Elzia turned to Mike. "Did you show your sister your new algae set up in the greenhouse?

Mike gave Elzia a quick hug. "Not yet. She just got here."

The table was set with wooden serving platters etched with Christmas designs. She picked up a stuffed egg and looked to her father. "Did you make these?"

He laughed. "The eggs? No."

"No. You knew what I meant. The platters."

She noticed a smile and a spark of pride. "Sure did. Sioux Falls Woodworking Guild. I go every Sunday. They have the best equipment. They even have CAD machines and laser engravers. Those platters were decorated using the engravers."

He picked up another platter with celery and carrot sticks. "Look at this. What do you see?"

"Veggies?" she replied echoing his dad joke.

"Touché. The platter." He looked at Mike and Elzia. They laughed.

She knew he was proud of something, but she couldn't imagine what. "Am I looking at the holly leaves? They are delicate and detailed."

His smile got bigger. "No-o-o. I gave you a hint already."

"The wood. Is that some special rare wood?"

"It is a very nice piece of walnut, but no-o-o again."

Carla laughed, happy to see her dad excited. "I give up!"

He spun the platter around. "It's kidney-shaped! I used the robotic router. I could never make something like this on my old lathe."

She ran her finger around the irregular shape and for lack of something else just said, "Wow."

Her mother grabbed her elbow and led her to the kitchen warm and smelling of cinnamon buns and sausage. "Let's get some flowers."

Flowers? She thought, then she remembered seeing the greenhouses. She reached for her coat from a hook in the mudroom.

Her mother gave her a conspiratorial look. "It's close. We'll just run. After all, it's really warm once we're inside."

In their slippers, they sprinted across the short distance. As fast as they were, the cats were faster. By the time they were comfortable among the flowers, the cats were already rubbing against their legs. Her mom reached for a bag of kitty treats and dropped them on the floor for the purring felines.

"They have their own door, so they always have a warm place to stay. There's a litter box in each unit and we keep them very clean—not that these outdoor cats use them often, but we can't have them using the planters."

She followed her mom with a pair of clippers and a basket. For Christmas they collected red and green roses. She had never seen green roses, but they looked lovely next to the red ones.

"Did you see that snow? That means a good winter wheat harvest. And this flower business brings in cash all year round. I sleep much better, knowing the bills can be paid. This is a wheat farmer's paradise."

She hugged her mom. "I love you. I know you are always thinking about us, even if I sometimes forget."

Christmas morning, she felt like a child again, the first one downstairs. Peeking at the tree through the balusters reminded her of holiday movies. She sat on the stairs with Sasha until stirring throughout the house sent the dog to the front door, ready to go out.

"Is it really morning already?" she asked herself.

She ran back to her room to get her presents. She had taken advantage of Chicago's exotic Christmas bazaars to find interesting gifts. A granite cutting board and rolling pin from Mongolia for mom. A collection of exotic woods from Southeast Asia for dad. Catnip kickers for the new cats. A tag with her new address for Sasha displaying the University of Chicago phoenix. A student subscription to a gene sequencing service for Mike.

Mike read the subscription terms and conditions twice. "Will they sequence my algae? Most services only sequence people and pets."

Carla explained. "They'll sequence anything! The more exotic, the better. The professors use the submitted samples for class assignments."

She felt proud of her selections. She had also found some unique wrapping paper from Japan, but otherwise, her packages blended in with the others, with two exceptions. Dad had made fire escape ladders, which he had not bothered wrapping. She smiled that she and her dad agreed about the dangers of sleeping on the second floor. There were also two uncharacteristically large packages for her and her brother from mom. The tags said *Santa*, but everyone knew what that meant.

When Santa's presents were opened, Carla was shocked. She received a new computer with a detachable full-size keyboard and an oversized monitor. She had been getting by with her comp from high school. While she was figuring out how to respond to this extravagance, she saw the other gifts. Mom had purchased an Amazon River cruise for her and dad with first-class airfare from Sioux City. Mike received one of the new home-scientist gene sequencers.

She made a wild guess. "It's wonderful to have a white Christmas."

Her mom took the bait. "Yes, we've outrun the *Hot*. That depth of snow in December means a good, no...a great, winter wheat harvest in June."

The others didn't say anything, but she could see those half-smiles that suggested everyone was thinking: the seven years of famine are over; many years of plenty ahead.

She thought back over her visit. Dad had not been talking about empty bowls and food insecurity around the world. Mike still hadn't shown her his algae setup. He was more interested in Elzia.

What a difference a good harvest makes.

PART II — 2048

17. Xiang Bo—Donglan China

The micro-algae Xiang Bo designed as a food source for the mountains of Guangxi was a definite success. She reread the concluding paragraph of her *Food Sciences & Generation* journal article with satisfaction. She had already sent basically the same article as a report to her research sponsors and now hoped to get the news out to other researchers and food production specialists—as well as add another research paper to her resumé—which might ultimately help her successfully receive *another* grant, for a new study.

The completion of her mountain algae research was both good news and bad news. The world could certainly use more alternative food sources, and her algae was easy to grow in many mountainous, well-watered regions. Of course, that meant she would no longer receive grant monies to support her research here. The project was finished.

The only income she had left was the small grant extension she had received for further study in the flatlands and rice fields of Huixian: her diatom-algae which presumably could be used for all types of integrated fish farms worldwide. She needed to go back to Guilin and check on the project that she had abandoned when she left Huixian to return home.

She'd left for good reasons: to adopt Zi Min and care for her own mother Jiao. She knew it was long past time to introduce Zi Min to Li and Di'e. But how could she leave Jaio alone for so long?

"Look, *Ya-ya*!" Zi Min's excited voice made Xiang Bo turn around with an interested smile. What new treasure was her daughter showing Jiao now? From her usual chair in front of the fireplace, Jiao looked up with a febrile smile. Zi Min was displaying a small garter snake she'd evidently found in her grandma's garden. Jiao hadn't been outside to even look at the garden in months, another sign of her decline. It was really Zi Min's garden, now.

Zi Min turned toward Xiang Bo and showed her the snake, too.

"That is a good thing, little one," she said. "It means vermin are being naturally removed from your little vegetable patch."

"Should I put it back?"

"That would be a good idea. Let it do its work. But Zi Min, you must be careful with snakes. There are some which bite and inject venom."

Zi Min nodded, hopping from foot to foot while the garter snake dangled. "We saw pictures at school, but this is not a *bad* snake. I knew that from its colors!"

"Good for you. Please put it back safely now."

Zi Min ran out the door and from the diminishing sound of her footsteps, headed to the garden to presumably put the snake back.

Between Jiao's ill health, and Xiang Bo's business with her papers and research results, the little girl had become the sole proprietor of the garden, pulling weeds and undesired volunteers, making sure the "good" vegetables were watered and fertilized, and even picking, cleaning and offering "finished" vegetables for meals in the little house of women. Xiang Bo smiled to herself, thinking of how carefully Zi Min described her knowledge of vegetables that were "finished" but not over-ripe.

The orphanage garden had been someone's wonderful idea, teaching the children how to produce at least a part of their own food, and giving them a good outdoor project. Zi Min had taken to the communal plantings with enthusiasm, and now turned that energy to her family's very own garden with pride.

When Xiang Bo turned back to her paper, her computer screen had dimmed, going to energy-saving mode. She needed to get more solar panels emplaced and connected. She had ordered them and they had arrived, and there they sat for almost two weeks now, waiting for her attention.

With a sigh, she saved her work and shut down the computer. That was her next project, then.

The third time Cheng Li called, Xiang Bo answered, leaning back in her seat in the tiny Donglan tea shop. They were able to talk for almost five minutes before interference from the thunderstorm caused Xiang Bo's cell to drop the call. She regretted they had talked that long, because Li had convinced her to return to Guilin, "at least for a few days," as he'd asked. To give him credit, he seemed as much concerned about her diatom-algae as anything else. And she did need to go check on that project—or give up the funding.

She sighed, fiddling with her teacup. Mo Chou arrived, Zi Min in tow.

"Look!" Zi Min chortled, spreading her fingers to show her new deep red fingernails. It was entirely too dark a color for a ten-year-old, but Zi Min was so delighted, Xiang Bo decided to say nothing.

"We match!" Zi Min said, grabbing one of Mo Chou's hands and holding it out next to hers. Their nails indeed matched in color, if not in shape. Mo Chou's nails were much, much longer.

Xiang Bo smiled and said, "Very nice." What good would it do for her to chide Mo Chou for the inappropriate gift? And to her friend, it *wasn't* inappropriate, Xiang Bo acknowledged. Mo Chou had worn nail polish for as many years as Xiang Bo had known her. That, and weirdly colored hair were Mo Chou's trademarks. She supposed she should be glad Zi Min hadn't gotten moldy-green hair. She ordered more tea and a light lunch. The tiny restaurant was the nicest one in Donglan, but that wasn't saying much. Even the worst of Guilin's many restaurants—developed primarily for the town's many international tourists—served better food than this. Nicer food was definitely one of the things she missed.

She paid for lunch, then asked Mo Chou her favor.

"Mother has been doing about the same for several weeks now, so you shouldn't have too much trouble," Xiang Bo clarified. "We should be gone only a few days…a week at most."

Mo Chou nodded, a slight frown on her face. "He talked you into visiting," she said.

Xiang Bo shook her head. "No. I must gather samples and observations at my research site, Mo Chou. That money doesn't come to my mailbox for nothing."

Mo Chou bit her lip, but said nothing further. She was kind enough to go stay with Jiao while they were gone, but she still viewed Dr. Cheng Li and his mother as a trap.

"Besides, Zi Min is eager to meet her other grandmother."

Mo Chou's grunt was barely distinguishable from a burp.

◡

She was glad, for the first time, that she had kept the rented garage in Hechi. She used the opener and pulled the four-wheel-drive FAW inside. Zi Min got her own little rolling suitcase from the back seat and was ready to go by the time Xiang Bo had her own suitcase out and locked up the car and garage.

"Is the airplane noisy? Mo Chou said it would be noisy."

Xiang Bo led the way to the tram stop. "It will be pretty noisy, yes. That is why I said you should bring your headphones; you will not be able to hear your MP3 music without them."

Zi Min put her hand on the headphones hung around her neck. "Will I be able to download more music, at the Guilin house?"

"Do you have enough money for more?"

Zi Min licked her lips. "I have some allowance left, but I can still get some songs for free. Some of the old ones are free on the site Mo Chou found."

Inquiring whether that site was legal or not was probably futile, Xiang Bo knew. Mo Chou would just find another "download mp3's for free" site if she blocked this one. "The Cheng compound has good WiFi," she said. "But Cheng Di'e will want to talk to you most of the time, and you should not be rude with your headphones on."

"I know. I'll do it at night, when they're asleep."

"That's good."

"Is Dr. Cheng mean?"

"What? No. Whatever gave you that idea?" But Xiang Bo knew *who* had given her that idea. Mo Chou wasn't such a good influence, particularly regarding Li.

The tram ride was new and fun, and Zi Min craned her neck looking at the city, the shops, the people.

The airplane ride was also new, of course, but it was not fun. Eyes wide, body trembling ever so slightly, Zi Min leaned against Xiang Bo from the time they left the ground until they landed. She never once looked out the window, which Xiang Bo had always enjoyed doing. It was just a sign, like so many others, that Zi Min was not truly her own.

Then she became annoyed at herself. Children were not *possessions*. And how could she possibly know what effect bearing one's own child had on how their parents perceived such children? Maybe all parents looked askance at their offspring's individuality, adopted or self-borne. Maybe Jiao had felt that way about Xiang Bo as she grew up and became her own person.

Who wanted to raise an exact copy of themselves, anyway? Xiang Bo shuddered, imagining a diminishing line of Xiang Bos fading into infinity.

No. She would take delight in Zi Min's idiosyncrasies. That was what made her so intriguing, wasn't it? The delight of discovery, the celebration of differences and similarities—they were all part of raising a child. Some things about Zi Min would always be a mystery, the whys and who of her, and that was *good*.

Zi Min bowed to Li just as Xiang Bo had suggested. He seemed amused, and bowed back, smiling with his eyes as much as his mouth. He nodded at Xiang Bo and reached as if to hug her, but bit his lip and stepped back, instead. He drove them home in a tense silence.

Zi Min was delighted with the Cheng compound. "It's just like an old movie!" she said.

Di'e seemed charmed, bending down for a kiss on her cheek from Zi Min, when Xiang Bo introduced them.

"It is a very old place," Di'e said. "In fact, they were going to use it in a movie once."

"I never knew that," Li said, disbelief in his tone.

Di'e nodded. "They ended up using something just west of Guilin, where there were fishponds right up next to the compound, because it seemed more 'colorful,' the film people said."

Zi Min laughed. "Like in *Mulan*," she said. But that was such an ancient, American movie, Xiang Bo wasn't sure any of the Chengs knew what she was talking about. Zi Min had watched it over and over when Mo Chou had given her the beat-up old copy. Xiang Bo had just gotten a television and a player, bringing the "magic" of Walt Disney into their little mountain home.

"Well, *Mulan* was animated," Xiang Bo felt compelled to explain. "I'm not certain it was based on a real place.

This didn't dampen Zi Min's enthusiasm in the least, as she gasped and bowed to the ancestor shrine.

"Let me show you your bedroom," Di'e said, taking Zi Min's hand and leading her off.

Leaving Xiang Bo and Li alone in the courtyard.

He smiled at her. "Well," he said. "It's good to see you. And to meet Zi Min."

Suddenly faced with him, his presence, she lost all her words and stood there in silence. *Was it good to see him?* She cleared her throat and managed, "You said the diatom-algae had spread?"

His smile faded, and he nodded. "It's in all our ponds, as of yesterday. And I'm afraid it's going to spread into others, and from there into the river."

She stood thinking, scowling at this news. "It should not have. The governor should have diminished reproduction once it filled the one pond."

"Well, something has broken," he said. "And I'm very much afraid that even if we can fix it, it is too late."

"You think it has escaped, already?"

He nodded.

"I'll need to spend some time in your lab."

"It's *our* lab, Xiang Bo. Always."

She met his eyes, saw the hurt there. Also the determination, and perhaps, love? She clenched her jaw and stared at the paving stones. Could they salvage this marriage? Or should she give up on it?

See how he is with Zi Min, she temporized. Then decide.

She looked up and gave him a gentle smile. He smiled in return. She saw no judgment in his eyes. That was a good beginning, to détente...and whatever would happen afterward.

18. Maatalii—Qamanittuaq Nunavut Canada

Maatalii stood on the low ridge beside the Qamanittuaq airstrip, her suitcases on the crumbling asphalt beside her. *Back home. For good this time. Maybe.* She had to make a decision about that: stay home, or go off to college. But she didn't have to decide just yet. She took a deep breath and let it out slowly.

One of the last three people on the tiny plane from her connection in Churchill, she felt like she had come to the end of the world. Winnipeg was a megalopolis compared to Qamanittuaq. The most astonishing difference was the complete lack of color: no neon, no posters or billboards. All the houses painted white, or not painted at all, just concrete and tin or grey tile. Making it worse was a layer of gray smoke from the latest tundra fire. Even little Churchill had had more color.

Churchill, where she had left Amaruq behind.

How could she still call her cousin and best friend, *uaguk,* if she wouldn't even come home?

She stared another moment at the black and white and gray village she called home, then picked up her suitcases and walked toward Snow House.

She stomped her feet on the mat outside the mudroom, fumbled her suitcases and dropped one as she opened the screen door, then the inside door. She noticed the paint was flaking off the door and the threshold. Somebody should have painted that, to protect the wood. She saw other signs of disrepair as she set down her luggage and rooted through the slipper box, finally finding her own pair at nearly the bottom.

By the time she had her boots off and her slippers on, her mother had come in from the restaurant kitchen. Suluk wrapped her in a warm mama's hug and kissed the top of her head.

"It is so good to see you!"

"Mama, I missed you so much."

Her mother saw the suitcases crammed on top of the boots and other snow gear. "Oh. I forgot to tell you I had to move you to room Five."

"I noticed Seven and Eight were boarded up." Maatalii hung up her coat and turned to her mother, forehead crinkled. "Why? What happened?"

Suluk threw her arms out in a helpless sort of shrug. "They're sinking. The foundation has tilted and cracked."

Two of the Inn's eight rooms were ruined? And it didn't help that the family was using at least one more of them. Soon they would have nothing left to offer guests.

"What are we going to do?" Maatalii asked.

"Sivoy has some plan or another. For now, we just need to work on caribou meat. And not sinking. Snow House must survive, for all our sakes."

Maatalii thought about survival as she held the ceramic straw Sivoy handed her, ready to insert it into a bulging methane bubble. Sivoy set up the biofuel collection canister and made sure the hoses were straight and connected tightly around the filters to the tank. They would deflate the bubble and at the same time, collect the gas for fuel uses.

"You said Lusa invented these?" she waggled the glass-like straw, which now had a rubbery tube connected to the un-pointy end.

"He did," Sivoy said, double-checking the fittings. "We have it down to a science, now, but the first few months we were probably just lucky we didn't have any disasters. Lusa realized the metal straws we were using could strike a rock in the permafrost and cause a spark."

"Then the bubble would explode," Maatalii said, "just what we're trying to stop."

"Yes. So he figured out how to make a ceramic straw, and he convinced the machine shop it would be a good idea to get a ceramic-making 3-D printer to make the straws…and other things."

Sivoy looked at how she was holding said straw in her fingertips and shook his head. "You're going to want to hold it under your arm to warm it up," he said. "Then it'll just slide right through the slush and any ice that might be in there."

"Okay," she said, doing so.

"Your mother then convinced Giqa and some of the other old men to run patrols and look for growing methane bubbles. It was a job the whole town needed done, and that their pay would be free meals."

"Which they were getting anyway, half the time," she said.

He nodded. "I think it has helped Giqa, at least, to feel more like he is doing something useful. They go out every morning through and around the town and along the roads to the mine and the caribou pasture and the airstrip."

"It uses a lot of fuel, though. As much as we gather?"

"Nope. I've got them taking our dog teams out. The dogs get to run, the old men feel useful, and no fuel use at all. Just meat is the cost, and that we would have to feed them anyway."

Them being the dogs, she presumed, not the old men. Maatalii nodded. "How's our caribou production going?"

"Pretty well. We've got some major buyers interested. The price we get keeps going up, because the availability of other meats, especially pork, is really low. Beef is expensive, but it's still more available than pork or lamb. Chicken and rabbits are much easier to produce in the *Hot* than the bigger animals, so our caribou are special."

Maatalii had seen their captive herd earlier in the week. It looked to her like the herd was two or three times as big as it had been before she went away to school, but of course that was unlikely; caribou couldn't reproduce that fast. They'd had to build more corrals. "Have you been gathering more wild animals?"

"Yes. We found a couple orphan families." He indicated she should insert the straw. She did so, jiggling it a bit as she pushed, until she met no resistance. He started the pump and she was delighted and a little awed, to see the bubble going flat as the canister's gauge showed an increase in methane. Methane they could use to run slushskis and heaters, stoves and machines. It wasn't much, but it was something.

"That's got it," Sivoy said, once the bubble was flat. They dismantled everything, replacing it on the small sled behind Snow House's two-man slushski. "Just the one today; the bubbles are slowing down. One week we had six we had to empty; lately just one or two."

"Less methane? Colder temperatures?"

"No, it's warmer than ever. But we think less methane is building up. It takes a certain composition of rotting permafrost mosses and fungi and dirt to produce a bubble."

"It's a great recapture system. Lusa should be proud," Maatalii said, thinking how good it was to turn a public health issue into a benefit. Thinking also how much better it would have been if they could have discovered it before Papa died.

Grandma Osha joined Maatalii in the greenhouse the next day, as they needed to weed and fertilize and harvest. While she had been gone at school, Aunt Meriwa had done a good job of upkeep on the two big greenhouses Maatalii and Amaruq had put in, after their small trial one had been such a success. They'd needed to add gro-lights to counter Nunavut's winter sunless-ness, and some heaters run by sun and wind. The vegetables and herbs *grew,* and Meriwa had been proud of them.

But now Auntie had a big wall-hanging order she needed to finish weaving, and Maatalii could do this work with the plants. She'd been surprised to see her grandma shuffling out to join her. The reason became apparent after they'd worked a few minutes. Osha had questions.

"So," Grandma said in her shaky old voice, "what have we done that has made Amaruq flee her home?"

Maatalii grimaced. "I wish I knew." She used her muddy fingers to tuck a wisp of tickly hair back into her braid. "But, I *think* she was more running *to* Niki than she was running from us."

"Niki is this boy she says she is in love with?"

"Niki Pitka."

"So he is Inuit, at least."

"He's from Alaska, so he mostly speaks some kind of Yupik, not Inuktitut. And English, of course."

"She didn't even want to come home to tell us?"

"He wanted her to look for a job in Churchill right away, before all the other graduates flooded the job market."

Osha scowled at this. "Job is more important than family?"

Maatalii had been over and over this in her own mind, after several weeks of confrontational arguments with Amaruq, with no answers. Her own *uaguk* had abandoned her, and she didn't understand it any better than Osha apparently did.

"I guess Niki is now her family, her first importance."

"She abandons all this," Grandma said, "You, your greenhouse project, and Snow House and Ticasuk family?"

Her heart feeling especially frozen today, Maatalii responded the only way she could manage. "Yes. All this," she said. "Like it was nothing."

Osha grunted. They worked in silence for a while, clearing the soil around desirable plants, filling their bucket with weeds.

"Are you going to run off, also?" Osha asked, tone hard, words clipped.

"Me?" Maati blinked, then realized her grandmother was thinking how close she and Amaruq had been. "I have no reason to leave." She shook her head. "I don't understand Ama, but it is her choice to make. *This* is my home." She waved an arm, meaning the greenhouses, Snow House, Qamanittuaq.

Osha grunted again. Eventually she came out with her real concern. "I was planning to begin teaching you both the Keeper histories. The stories, the laws and methods of *The Peoples'* life." She cleared her throat. "Your mother is too busy; Meriwa is not suitable, so it falls to you."

Maatalii felt her soul quiver: how could she be worthy? Osha was saying she, *she* was to become Keeper of the Ways.

She felt young, then. Too young. Yet, how could she refuse? Her grandma would not be around forever.

"I am here," she said, and Osha grunted.

Osha went back inside to the Snow House kitchen, clutching the mesh bags of herbs and vegetables they'd harvested. Maatalii watched her, feeling sad. Her grandma was getting very old. Before too long, they were going to lose her, too. Hence the old woman's worries about teaching the Ways, before she passed on and they lost all her knowing.

Maati stayed in the greenhouse, pulling weeds, setting a few new trays of seeds, and mostly comforting herself with the mindless work. As a last step for the day, she tossed the weeds into the composter, and then went to the decomp bins and pumped out two one-gallon buckets of bio-slurry to spread on the plants in the second greenhouse. She'd noticed the cabbages looked pale and some of the carrot tops were scrawny. The nutrient-rich sludge would perk them up. It was even more intense and effective than their compost had been.

Snow House was building a reputation for flavorful, honest food, built from their greenhouse produce and their caribou herds.

On her way out, she saw and pulled another weed, and trimmed the tops off the two basil plants, tucking the leaves into a mesh bag she put in her pocket. She walked back to Snow House.

After swapping her boots for her slippers, she washed up and then took the basil into the kitchen prep room, where she washed and chopped it. She'd make some basil and tomato bannock later.

She found the bags of profuse *haricot verts* Osha had brought in, washed and blanched one batch and froze it, and prepped the rest for the dinner rush. The French name for green beans made her think of Amaruq, and her love for French words, but she squelched the instant battle that sprang up in her mind. Ama was in Churchill. She was here. There was nothing she could think that would change that.

She put on a clean apron. She'd help in the serving area, not waste time wondering about her cousin. She picked up an order as Suluk finished plating it, and brought it to the customer's table.

Were she and Amaruq still even *uaguk*? She did not know. But she shut the thought down as she walked around the dining area, concentrating on just what she was doing: Picking up a soiled glass and sandwich plate. Wiping down the table. Setting a dirty mug on the dishwasher's pre-wash conveyor. Chopping basil leaves and tomatoes into a fine paste and adding them to her bannock dough.

◠

The sun flowed so warm over the new pasture that Maatalii took her jacket off. She finished tying off the wire they'd just strung, replacing a section of the fence that had snapped when a caribou bull had charged it, demonstrating his prowess for the ladies.

Sivoy moved to stand next to Maatalii, watching the animals churn up the pasture. That ground consistently refroze at night, just as they had hoped. But it was such a small area, it seemed insignificant compared to the vast reaches of tundra that were *not* freezing. Like beneath Snow House. They needed more than caribou.

"I sure hope the mammoths can do bigger areas," Sivoy said, echoing her own thoughts.

"Meanwhile, we need to expand this pasture."

"I'm thinking we should just make another one," Sivoy said, "closer to Snow House." He sniffed. "I'm not sure we can put the mammoths and caribou together, so we'll need a separate pasture for them...eventually. Lusa's trying to figure out how to make strong, easily-movable fences."

Maatalii didn't know if the two animals could mix together, either. Just one more little fact she needed to learn. Somehow. Maatalii glanced at her uncle. "You have a place picked out for the mammoths?"

"Yep," Sivoy said. "I'll get Tarkik and a couple of his friends to help build the new fence, before he goes. Though I think before long we're going to need the portable fences, so we can move their pasture area every few weeks. They'll probably eat a lot, so they'll need fresh tundra growth, and the churned-up pasture needs time to refreeze."

"Do we have enough money for that? How can we afford to build fences and buy mammoths when we have to rebuild Snow House?"

Sivoy sighed. "I don't know. But the next fence isn't for mammoths—those animals won't be ready for months, yet. It's for the expanded caribou herd. We've been doing so good with the meat sales, Ujurak bought the packing plant, where we process the meat and freeze it. We ship it from there."

Uncle Ujurak: Sivoy and her mother's oldest brother. He was kind of a recluse, so this was a surprise. "Oh, good for him. I hope it is paying for itself."

"It is. Maatalii…" he looked across the herd, at the calves and elders milling around the adult animals.

"What?" He was going to ask her to stay, wasn't he?

"I need help. Your mother needs help. *Her* mother, Osha, needs help. Tarkik is leaving for his turn at college. Meriwa's other boys all have good jobs, steady work so they can't contribute much here. We were expecting that you *and* Amaruq would be here together after you graduated. That you would both be here to help. I know the things you have learned have been helpful to all of us, but maybe now we need your hands, not your ideas?" He looked sad as he said it. As if he knew he was treading on her dreams, of college and maybe more.

"Osha has begun teaching me the Ways. What else does she need help with?" she asked, curious. The old woman had said nothing about other projects.

"The Sisterhood wants to produce a music album, to preserve and popularize the throat singing, as well as maybe earn some money. Jissika says a group from Greenland made several thousands of American dollars with just an EP, as well as some Euros and other money. They are, most of them in the Sisterhood, getting too old to work. And Snow House…"

"Needs more money itself, not to give money away for projects like that. I know."

"Lusa supports himself, and now I guess Amaruq does, too. But the rest of us rely on Snow House for room and board. We all need to work to support it. Your mother-my-sister, is working hard to expand the business, but we cannot attract tourists when we have tilted fun-house guest rooms."

Maatalii thought of the cheesy tourist attractions that claimed to have "different gravity" because they were built crooked: causing illusions like visitors walking on walls, and fooling the eye with perspective.

Their tilted Inn rooms weren't crooked as that, but they were bad enough. And now the plumbing leak from a broken pipe in room Six was encouraging mildew to grow. They'd have to destroy all three of those rooms soon, before they ruined the adjacent ones. Three rooms gone, leaving just five guest rooms, one of which Maatalii slept in.

"We're shrinking, instead of expanding," she said.

"The mammoths should help, if they ever get here," Sivoy said. "We've buyers already interested in mammoth steaks, since beef is so costly. Maybe we can sell mammoth hair, fur, and skins, too. And Osha has been looking into the ivory trade, if we can find some way to tag mammoth ivory so it can be distinguished from illegal elephant and narwhal and other endangered-creature tusks."

She thought about Osha doing research. "Can Grandma use the internet now?"

Sivoy grinned, making his slightly plump face look crinkled and very ethnic, like some of Meriwa's felt art faces. "Yes. Tarkik actually taught her." He cleared his throat. "She's embracing the new along with the old, and is encouraging her children to as well. So, besides needing to record their music, the Sisterhood has been tattooing each other, in the old way. Osha is the last to do so. I think she would be thrilled if you would join her for that."

Skin stitching, that was the old way. She had thought about doing her arms. The lacy look of the traditional bracelet-like designs was so pretty. Plus she had created some stylized flowers in art class that she could incorporate into her own *kakiniit* or arm-bracelet design. She might even do bands on her upper thighs like Suluk had done many years ago.

Mama had been a bit embarrassed by the old tradition at one time; now she was coming to be proud of them. Which, come to think of it, might explain why Grandma Osha was interested, too. When Osha was young, it just wasn't done. Too *tribal*, too not-a-white-people's thing. Now, when native peoples were feeding the world, everything tribal was deemed wonderful. Grandma was seizing the chance while it was trendy.

But that was probably not fair; at the very least, it was too simplistic. She had never known the kind of prejudice Osha had suffered. Tattoos probably would have signaled her out for all kinds of oppression. In fact, Maatalii realized, tattoos may have even been illegal in Osha's day, like speaking Inuktitut had been for a time.

She and Sivoy finished loading up their gear and turned the slushski back toward Snow House.

Maatalii continued to think about Sivoy's words, how he hoped for her help. Of course, Osha had already asked.

Aunt Meriwa had asked for Maatalii's help also, in stitching wall-hangings and dolls.

The Two Pearls

Over a century ago, a woman of the Qamanittuaq community named Jessie Oonark had become famous for her native crafts, especially her wall hangings and other fabric arts. Meriwa was determined not to let that tradition die out from Qamanittuaq. Not only did it help keep *The People's* traditions alive, but Meriwa actually earned quite a bit of money from selling them in galleries and at the Canadian government craft cooperatives. She had also begun selling them online; that was where this big order had come from. Some museum wanted huge wall hangings to decorate their Inuit section of artifacts.

"Well," she said as they unloaded the slushski. "I can help the women, of course. But Sivoy, I know nothing about demolition, or plowing, or foundations."

"If I can get someone to help with the dogs and tourists, I can take care of the rebuilding. Yuka is learning about everything he can, to help me, but he has to go back to school soon. I'm trying to coax Tarkik into taking over. You could encourage him. Help get him trained up and married off, so he doesn't waste all his time and energy flirting and dating. Settle down when he finishes college. He likes the dogs and being a guide, so that's a good start. He likes them almost as much as he does girls."

○

Thinking back to that conversation, Maatalii realized that was probably more words than she had ever heard from Sivoy. Was that what meeting his new girlfriend—now fiancée—had done for him?

He was maybe a little old for a first-time marriage, but that didn't seem to bother the fiancée. Maatalii had interacted with Hitty several times now, and had found her to be a good woman. A widow, she had three nearly-grown children that she would bring into Sivoy's home. Perhaps some of them would stay in Qamanittuaq, to help—that was worth following up on. If they could be made to feel a part of the Ticasuk family and Snow House, maybe they would be happy to stay, and to help.

She was proud of what Sivoy and her mother and the others had accomplished. It especially delighted her to see the positive they'd made out of the negative methane bubbles. Solving more than one problem at a time in such a creative way signified just how well her community worked together to deal with the *Hot*.

Her heart seemed to drag as she re-considered leaving the village to go off to college. Did she really want to leave this energetic community to learn more? Weren't the bulk of the people of Qamanittuaq doing perfectly well without college educations?

"Maatalii?" her mother's voice reached dimly into her thoughts.

Did she really need more education to make a useful contribution?

"Maati!!?" Mama's voice sounded angry. Maatalii realized she'd been staring at the dishwasher, lost in thought, for who knew how long.

"Yes, mama?"

"Can you come help?"

"Yes, of course." There was a clear limit to how much help standing around thinking could be, that was certain! "On my way!"

Mama was better now, after the shock of losing Papa. But like herself, there were long moments when Suluk was simply lost in thought, missing him, missing those happier days.

Maati went out to the dining room, folding up a damp towel to clean tables.

Sivoy was having a cup of coffee and a plate of bannock when she walked by. He looked up and waved at her. "I was thinking," he said. "What if we quick build a couple of rooms onto the back of the restaurant. Then—"

"We could move me and Mama into those rooms and have two more open to rent."

Sivoy nodded. "I think I can get a discount for materials; they owe me favors at the lumber yard. That, and we can pay for it with some nice caribou steaks instead of cash. The new rooms wouldn't be fancy, but we wouldn't need them for long."

"That's a wonderful plan, Sivoy."

"Then I can demolish the broken rooms and plan something really nice to remake the Inn, bigger and better."

Maatalii nodded.

"Last spring, we had two families here, looking for polar bears," Aunt Meriwa said from her booth by the door. "And some photographers were here to get pictures of melting permafrost for some fancy magazine." She was working on the wall hanging, pieces of colorful felt, woven segments, and embroidery threads laid out in a rainbow in front of her on the table. "We can probably fill twelve rooms at least some of the time. Miners on their way up, filmmakers on their way back. Fish counters and weather scientists."

Sivoy frowned. "I need to find a way to stabilize the ground before we pour new foundations. I think the restaurant and supply room are okay for now, but the way things are going, we're going to have to plow or something before we set new foundation posts and rebuild everything from the bottom up. I already know we need to make our stilts taller to keep the warm rooms higher up off the permafrost."

Maatalii thought about that, about how expensive that was going to be. If it was even possible. "Can taller stilts even help?" she asked. "If it…if the permafrost keeps melting?"

"Many of the bigger buildings in town are having the same problem. Lusa's shop expanded, and when they built the addition, they plowed deep and compacted the earth before pouring new foundation posts. It hasn't been up for long, but it definitely is higher off the ground, and more level than the old building." Sivoy took a big bite of bannock and chewed, meeting her gaze. He swallowed. "We're going to have to do that too."

"Maybe we could paint new Snow House a pretty color," she said.

"What, red?" Meriwa grumbled.

"No, like a pretty ice blue, or turquoise."

"I'm sure we can manage a can of paint, Maati," Sivoy murmured.

"Water level keeps rising, we gonna have to move some houses," Giqa said, leaning over the back of his booth and staring at Meriwa's work. "Town's going to flood if it gets much worse."

"I was away when the second part of the Antarctic ice sheet collapsed," Maatalii reminded them. "How much rise did we get?"

"River went up two, almost three meters from it," Giqa said, before anyone else could.

Between rising water and the encroaching tree line and fires burning the tundra, the permafrost that they knew and depended upon was shrinking to a narrow strip. So far, they were scrambling to cope, but if the land that they knew disappeared, then what would they do?

Mike held tight to his paddle as his kayak bounced down the rapids. *Through a gap in the spray, he caught a glimpse of Elzia. She reached out her hand to him, but he shot past. The current catapulted him over the precipice.* He screamed and woke up happy to be safe in bed, but sad that Elzia remained out of reach.

Sweating, his heart beating fast, he rolled over and picked up his comp: *1:00.* He tapped Elzia's picture. *No connection.* He tapped frantically. *Washington Springs SD to Cherokee OK.* Oklahoma wasn't that far from South Dakota. He looked for the cheapest way, then the fastest way. Bus. Car. Air. Nothing worked. Oklahoma was too far from South Dakota.

Then his screen flashed. She had returned his call. "Elzia. Elzia!"

A sleepy voice replied over a voice-only connection. "What's up. Why are you calling so late?"

He looked at the blank screen hoping he hadn't awakened her. He almost asked if she'd been studying, but he remembered it was Friday night. Maybe she'd been out on a date.

He listened to her and tried to imagine her sitting beside him. Her voice wasn't enough. "Can we share the sky?" He placed his comp at the window and adjusted it until the new moon was in the center of the screen. She didn't reply, but soon he saw a matching image from her comp.

The computer connection didn't bring him comfort. "The moon is so dark and lonely."

Her disembodied voice filled his room. "Think of those space pictures, a pearly white moon with the earth in the background, *Blue Marble* rising. I have that poster with South Dakota highlighted. We're not that distant and the far side of the moon is glowing right now."

"Nice science, but I wish I could reach through my comp and hold you."

"We will be together soon. Just not tonight."

He couldn't help sounding desperate. "What about tomorrow? Tomorrow is prom. Can you drive up?"

She sounded frustrated. "Prom? Again? Why are you up thinking about prom? Forget prom."

He knew she thought prom was silly, but he still pleaded. "We've been together over two years. You can do it."

"You know I can't. I have exams."

In two years, he'd never changed her mind on anything, but this was Senior Prom. "You can study while the car drives. It's almost all eRoads. I checked"

She replied in her frustrated, you-should-be-smarter-than-this voice. "You know I'm applying to college in September and these exams are

116

important." She paused and took a deep breath. "You should understand. Aren't you sorry you didn't study more last year?"

"I'm not worried about college."

Now her voice mixed anger and sarcasm. "I know. You never even applied."

"Don't worry. When my algae wins, schools will be lining up to recruit me."

"You said that last year in San Francisco and the previous year in Boston."

He was sure her family didn't want her going out with a Duster. "It's your parents, isn't it?"

"Good night Mike. I love you." The screen flashed into an explosion of hearts and then went black.

He went back to his comp trying to find a way to visit her. *If I had a car, I'd leave right now.* Before the sun rose, he fell asleep without a plan.

Carla planned to begin her summer internship when her classes ended, but here she was in South Dakota. "Mom, where's my birth certificate?"

"It got misplaced when we moved. Have you looked at the unopened boxes in the basement?"

Carla stomped down the stairs. She scowled at an assortment of boxes stacked floor to ceiling, some labeled, and some not. She opened all the likely ones, those with her name and others simply marked *papers.* Empty-handed, she grabbed the handrails and pulled herself up the stairs that seemed steeper than on the way down.

She sat at the strange kitchen table. "They're not there."

"Are you sure you need a passport?"

Carla didn't want to have this discussion again. "Yes."

"Are you really going to South Africa for six months to work in a factory that raises worms for people to eat?"

She took a deep breath. "This is a great opportunity. Mdudu Nyama is one of the most advanced protein processing companies in the world. I was lucky to get this internship."

Her mother hadn't wanted her to go to an out-of-state college. "I thought you were going to study climates, maybe work for a weather channel, like the one in Sioux Falls."

"Everyone studies climate science. I'm going to be a Chemical Engineer."

"Who's ever heard of chemical engineers?"

Her father walked into the kitchen followed by Sasha. Redd opened a cupboard to get some treats for the dog and a handful of cookies for himself. He sat down in the seat closest to Carla.

He winked at her and whispered, "I've got this."

He finished the two cookies in his mouth and stacked the others on the table. "Chemical Engineers are the future. If we're going to feed everyone on this hotter, drier planet, we need to process biomass into food. More people have to eat worms, bugs, and algae."

Her mom turned back to the stove to stir a big pot of beans. Like everyone else, the family ate more vegetables than meat, but still none of the more modern foods, like manufactured meats. "We're farmers," she said. "Our grains feed people, but also are for feedlots, for *real* meat."

Her dad sat back. "Chemical Engineers are also required for desalination plants."

Her mother turned to Redd. "You should spend more time at that Woodworking Guild, or reading, or playing with Sasha."

At the sound of her name, the great Newfoundland ran to the door.

"Look at her. Look at you. No one is starving in this house. We've had nothing but bumper harvests since we moved north. Both of you could use some exercise."

He followed Sasha. "Let's go girl." They both went out leaving Carla with her mother.

After some noisy pot-stirring, Abbie handed a large wooden spoon to Carla. "Here, stir this. I'll go look for your certificate."

A few minutes later, she returned with a tattered envelope. "I had it with my marriage license."

Carla grabbed the birth certificate, all the while thinking, I could have saved a trip home and why didn't you mail this to me a month ago when I asked for it? Before she said anything, she recalled last Christmas in Oklahoma. *Don't give me your sad faces. You're not little children learning there's no such thing as Santa Claus. Grow up.*

She restrained her exasperation, and replied with, "Thank you, mom, for finding my birth certificate. This is just an internship. I'll be back I promise."

She hugged her mom. "By any chance, do you have any pie?"

Her mom gave her a little laugh and a big smile. "Peach rhubarb."

20. Karina, Kaczka, Roshni, Priya—Kerala India

When Karina stepped off the Muvattupula bus, she was immediately recognized and surrounded by the ever-present demonstrators. They clamored at her in Malayalam. "Free the elephants! Close down the research! No more cloning!"

Before her kidnapping, she'd supported the crowd as non-violent protestors, and blamed any belligerence on Vadish's paranoid behavior. What could be expected from these peaceful families provoked by armed guards and barbed wire? Now three years later, she agreed with Vadish and considered the mob to be troublemakers under the direction of Roshni.

Roshni had sabotaged the mammoth cloning and organized Karina's abduction. Now she was a wanted terrorist who didn't dare show herself. Even after years in hiding, she still led the mob that appeared every day. Regardless, under Priya's direction, the Mammoth Research Station lived up to its name with new mammoths being born each week.

Karina yelled back at them in Malayalam, "You can tell Roshni, we're never leaving!" She walked straight at the mob. Just daring them to give the guards a reason to shoot. Once through the Muslim Arch, she continued to the Ganesh Shrine, out of reach from his worshippers. She looked back at them with disdain. "This is what I think of your elephant god!" She picked up some dirty stones from the ground and threw them into the offering plate. They made a harsh metallic clang instead of the gentle whooshes from the rice ordinarily offered. The mob rushed forward but were held back by Vadish's guards. Karina ignored their anger and walked away.

Later that day Karina sat with a sullen Sarita on the paddock fence watching the baby mammoths enjoying an afternoon romp. The clones filled her with pride in the science and delight in the exuberance of the calves. She invited Sarita to join the fun. "Do you have a favorite?"

Sarita scoffed. "A favorite mammoth? They're just hairy elephants."

Karina knew better than to confront her friend with Cheer up or Don't be such a grouch. She continued as if nothing was wrong. "Well, my favorite is Indrakshi because her hair matches mine, blonde."

Sarita didn't let go of her melancholy that easily. She grumped, "Well, she's not going to look blonde much longer. She's heading for that mud hole."

Karina didn't give up either. "Oh my! Did you see that? She fell in! She's just like a human child."

Melancholy Sarita slid off the fence and walked away.

Karina yelled after her. "Watch this! I taught her a new trick. She hopped into the paddock and yelled, "Indrakshi! Hug!"

The juvenile mammoth rolled out of the mud hole, waddled over, and wrapped her little trunk around Karina's waist. Karina held the big round head and wiggled the floppy ears. "You are a scientific wonder, a happy scientific wonder." Indrakshi concurred, shaking her rump and wagging her tail.

Sarita kept walking. "Big nothing. Look at you! You're all dirty."

Karina pried herself from the affectionate mammoth and vaulted over the fence, "Wait. Sarita, wait!" She ran to join her friend, but Vadish, taking long strides in their direction, reached Sarita first.

"Why are you out here wasting time with those animals? Why aren't you in school studying for your college entrance exams?" He grabbed her arm and pulled her toward the admin building.

Sarita protested, "Daddy! Let go of me. It's Saturday. No school today!"

Karina felt uncomfortable witnessing this. She did her best to placate Vadish. "Mr. Quereshi, we were just going to the library to study."

Karina reflected that she preferred an absent parent like Kaczka over an angry one like Vadish.

When they were out of earshot, Sarita squeezed her friend's hand. "Thanks, and you're right. Indrakshi is pretty cute."

Karina asked, "Do you want to spend the night at my bungalow? Kaczka is still gone and who knows when he'll return."

Sarita seemed hesitant. "Maybe."

That evening Karina arrived late for the regular meeting. She'd come to dread them because of the tension between Vadish and Priya. She took a seat next to Sarita, as far as possible from the feuding adults.

Priya reached across the table to pour tea for the girls. They each grabbed a chocolate biscuit. Priya turned to Vadish. "I sent a report to Kaz: No change. More mammoths. More demonstrations."

Karina tensed. She'd seen this interaction play out before. Vadish clenched his jaw and frowned. "Did you tell him the demonstrations were under control? *Why* do you even report on my activities?"

Karina cringed when Priya gave a familiar response. "Kaz has asked me for regular reports."

Vadish stood up and leaned over Priya. "Are you trying to take over my job, or are you just stupid? You know very well; he was only asking *you* for reports on the cloning. Anything that happens outside *your* lab is *my* purview. I'm the General Manager."

Karina dropped her biscuit and looked to her friend. Sarita was concentrating on the steam rising from her tea, embarrassed by her father's outburst. Sarita gently elbowed Karina and whispered, "For sure, I'll spend the night at your place."

Vadish grabbed Priya's hand, spilling her tea. "Just keep cloning those babies. That's *your* job. And stay out of *my* business."

Priya pulled her hand back, *accidentally* splashing tea on Vadish. "You need to control your temper!"

Karina thought: I'm glad Priya is standing up for herself, giving as good as she gets, but she's not helping things. She should mind her own business.

Karina looked around the table. Vadish, Priya, Sarita, all sat silent, drinking their tea, and staring at the plate of biscuits. Any new direction would have to wait for her father, but she feared he wouldn't show up before one of these two did something regrettable.

Kaczka started with a slide show of baby mammoths. The audience laughed as two-hundred-pound calves bumped into each other, tripped on invisible obstacles, and made soft cooing sounds. "Look at those colors: bay, chestnut, palomino. Wouldn't you like them living here?"

He had returned to the Svalbard archipelago in Norway with high hopes. Surely a mammoth breeding program would fit with their seed vault. A few years ago, Future Foods had worked with them to develop recipes for extinct plants, so whenever changing conditions required withdrawing seeds, they would have recipes on hand. That had been a mutually beneficial collaboration. He expected they'd be open to another one.

When he started in Provideniya, the closest Russian town to Alaska, he had high hopes that many Arctic communities would soon be competing to receive a herd of mammoths. Kaczka didn't let himself get discouraged even though none had been interested. The mammoths couldn't stay in India; he had no choice but to carry on. Each morning he told himself, "Today's the day. They're going to love them!"

He extolled the virtues of woolly mammoths. Resistance to extreme cold. Trampling the snow conserves the permafrost. Valuable fibers. Lean meat. Ivory tusks. Cultural icons. Tourism. Everyone listened attentively. He was heartened when they took notes and whispered encouraging comments to each other. His heart raced and he thought, this is it, they're going to bite.

With their enthusiasm high, he made his offer. "We have enough calves and surrogate moms for you to have your own herd." The room went silent. He recognized the signs. People leaned back in their chairs. They turned away from him and faced their neighbors. Avoidance. They had forgotten about the cute babies. Starting in the back, they headed for the door.

He forced his smile and held the podium to keep from visibly shaking. He was a veteran of many sales campaigns and grant presentations, so he'd get up tomorrow and do it again. Still, it hurt each time he was rejected.

Back in his hotel, he reviewed emails from India. Vadish reported all is well, except for Priya being out of control. Priya reported another mammoth birth and Vadish not being able to curtail the demonstrations. These two fighting like little kids didn't make his job any easier.

The U.S. Embassy sent a classified memo disclosing widespread resistance to the mammoths throughout India. With each report, the pressure increased to find them new homes, pressure he didn't need. He'd put so much into the cloning and now that the project was successful, he couldn't let it die.

Instead of sleeping, he reviewed his slides, looking for a better way to entice people to adopt the mammoths. He booked arrangements to continue the roadshow beyond Iceland, only to realize he'd already done this. How am I supposed to concentrate on marketing when everything is crazy in Kerala?

He didn't like to complain to Karina, but he had nowhere else to turn. "Svalbard Seed Vault wasn't interested. My Siberia to Iceland tour hasn't turned up anything."

"Cheer up dad. You still have the Inuit in Nunavut and that ranch in Maine. Right?"

"Yes, but they're both so small. I had to get a grant to subsidize the Inuit. I was hoping for a richer sponsor." He was grateful for Karina's support. Even though she was only fifteen, she seemed to understand his difficulties. She reminded him of Klara.

Just when he was feeling better, she added, "We may not have enough time. The protests are growing. Roshni's been in hiding, but I'm sure she's behind it all. With popular opinion on her side, she's been urging them to greater violence."

He hit the desk with his palm. "I can't fathom why they haven't caught her yet."

At a small restaurant in Nuuk, Kaz enjoyed the *suaasat* sampler, a tourist specialty showcasing the many variations of Greenland's national dish. He had started with a cup of reindeer *suaasat* and then loon. For the *pièce de résistance*, he selected musk ox. That final cup of soup justified him extending his Arctic tour beyond Iceland and would certainly be an inspiration for new Future Foods recipes.

Around the table, Greenland Inuit told him stories of hunting from dog sleds and kayaks. He enjoyed their easy friendship and open manner. They reminded him of the people in Qamanittuaq. After dinner, he retired confident that he'd found a third home for the beleaguered mammoths.

"Oh dear, Karina."

"What's wrong Kaz? I thought you'd found a receptive audience."

She spoke calmly, reminding him even more of Klara. Since the flood, he'd been treating her as a friend instead of a child. He took a deep breath and blew it out making a whistling sound. "Yes. Yes! They immediately understood how trampling the snow would preserve the permafrost."

"That's great! Why do you sound so discouraged?"

"One problem. They already have a similar program with the local musk oxen, so no interest in mammoths. Do you think we can keep the Mammoth Research Station open a while longer?"

"Oh, Dad! Don't you see?" He thought he could hear her stamping her feet, and then she shrieked, "They can't stay here!"

She sounded so emotional and immature. He almost said, don't be a silly girl, they have no place else to go.

She spoke first. "Do you think he just doesn't like women? A Misogynist?"

Now he realized she wasn't concerned about the mammoths. It was something else. "He? Vadish?"

She didn't answer his question but went off in another direction. "Do you think Priya hates Muslims?"

He knew that if he let her continue, she'd explain herself, so he just waited.

"It is past innuendos and insults. They are at each other's throat at every meeting. I'm scared."

So that's it! He hadn't realized it had gotten so bad. Indirectly, she'd answered his question. The elephants couldn't stay in Kerala. The problem wasn't Roshni and the protestors, but the growing strife between Vadish and Priya. He had to do something even though he was five thousand miles away. If the mammoths had to leave immediately, Qamanittuaq and Maine would have to do. He'd just hope for the best.

This left him with a different problem, transporting them to North America.

He had an idea. "I hear you. I have to check with my contacts at the U.N. I'll call you back when I have something concrete."

Then he remembered who he was talking to and added, "I love you."

"Me too, dad."

Roshni sat cross-legged leaning against her bundle of belongings wrapped in a spare sari. Once again, her visit to the Cochin Port hiring hall had offered a modest breakfast of *appam* and beans, but no employment. She ate slowly contemplating the empty time ahead.

Not all empty time. She recognized trouble when two well-dressed women approached her. "*Namasté, ranis.* To what do I owe the honor of your visit? Do you need my advice?" She waved her arm to the floor. "Have a seat. I'll call the *chai wallah* to bring us some tea."

The women stayed standing. "The Ganesh Committee voted to remove you from the board."

Roshni stood. "After all I've done? After all these years? After all I've sacrificed?"

"There isn't a tree in the world that the wind hasn't shaken. You no longer lead. You just loiter around the docks and pray to Varuna for your son's return."

The other woman added, "Your ideas are too old and tired. You're too timid. We've all made sacrifices."

"You silly hens! Now that India supports us, do you want more violence, more kidnappings? That is not the way!" She threw the last of her *appam* to the floor. "You ungrateful— Varuna will return Niraj, and I will be here for him."

"We're kept from our goal not by obstacles, but by a clear path to a lesser goal. Niraj is your lesser goal." One of the women handed her some 500-rupee notes which she let drop to the ground.

The other woman said, "May you find your right path," and they both left.

When they were gone, Roshni stuffed the money in her bundle, uncertain what her future might bring.

◡

Priya cringed when Kaczka exclaimed, "You deserve a trophy for saving the mammoth project."

Back in school, she'd received too many unwanted awards. It made her wonder about the other students. Did they forget to do the reading or not bother to study? She didn't need to be in the spotlight. She brushed him off with, "I just followed the protocols. Cloning's not the mystery it was when they cloned Dolly over fifty years ago."

He persisted, "Priya, you're too modest."

She knew this but didn't dwell upon it, so she changed the topic. "Are you still in the Arctic?"

He responded about China. "Did I tell you about the algae from China? It's called *Nofu*, like tofu. Get it? It is very nutritious and they're ramping up production. The problem is people don't like the taste. Like tofu, right? Future Foods will solve the palatability problem."

She never got used to him jumping from topic to topic without warning. She tried to get him back on track. "Thanks for that information. Is that why you contacted me?"

"Oh. No! I need you to save the mammoths again."

She thought: Oh. No! What is your crazy idea this time? She mentally braced herself.

"The mammoths can't stay in India. We have to get them out of there. The Parliament will soon pass legislation making them illegal—an abomination against nature."

"So Roshni has indeed won?" she mused aloud.

The mention of Roshni set him off. "No! Never! And we will find her and bring her to justice." He stopped, took a deep breath, and sighed, "Just forget Roshni. I'll take care of her."

Again, she guided him back on track. "I see. No problem. Where would you like them sent?"

Kaczka lower his voice and spoke slowly, as to a young child. "Not that easy. No Indian port will accept them. The sentiment from Punjab to Tamil Nadu is against us."

Frustrated that he wasn't getting to the point, she sharply asked, "Surely you have a plan. How are we going to rescue the mammoths?"

"Through my U.N. contacts, I have a ship to pick them up in Sri Lanka, a refugee ship."

"Sri Lanka? Do you know how far that is?"

"Not really, but I've been told that it is the closest port not in India."

At least, this will get me away from Vadish. "I'll do my best." *I always do my best.* "Thank you."

With that, she had a new assignment. *Achachan* had taught her to do her work without wondering why it was her work. He always said, "You can't do your best if you waste energy questioning your fate."

Priya discovered that no trucking company would transport the mammoths, even without mentioning the pregnant elephants. Kaz had been correct about national sentiment. She'd have to herd them over the mountains like an old-time drover.

She asked her comp how to walk to Sri Lanka. It announced, "Cannot find a route." It presented her with paths all blocked at the Palk Strait. So close, yet so far.

She went to bed to the sound of Vadish's soldiers outside her bungalow. *I'll be glad to be free of him.* She fell asleep confident she'd figure out how to part the seas and reach Sri Lanka.

In the morning, she remembered a friend in Tamil Nadu. "Hello, Huma? This is Priya. Do you remember me? We did our pediatric residency together."

Huma replied in a high-pitched voice. "Oh yes! I remember you. It's been five...no, eight years. You're the one we all went to when we got stuck. Are you married? Children?"

She could visualize Huma, round cheeks, smiling, and always wearing a headscarf. Priya continued the small talk long enough to be polite. Huma, sure enough, was married with three children and working as a pediatrician.

"No husband. No children." Priya was glad she didn't have to say she was a teacher. "I'm a research scientist. I have fifty baby mammoths born using elephant surrogates."

"Wow. Like *Jurassic Park?*"

Priya proudly replied, "Exactly."

Huma was quiet for a while. "So, what about Ganesh? You're Hindu. Don't the Hindus object to using elephants?"

"That's why I'm calling. We can't stay here. I'm moving them, smuggling them to North America—fifty mammoths and fifty elephants. I have a ship in Sri Lanka. I am going to herd them across Tamil Nadu, but how do I get over the Palk Strait?"

"Really? Why so many elephants? Why elephants at all?"

"I wish I didn't have to have the elephants. Like you said, anything with elephants can bring the wrath of Ganesh."

"Yes, you're asking for trouble."

"Well, some are surrogates, pregnant with mammoth babies. The others are nursing mothers for mammoths too young to be weaned."

"I see. I may be able to help you. Let me connect us to my brother."

After a silence, the video screen split, and a rugged-looking guy appeared.

"Basu, this is my friend from school. Priya, this my brother. He studied Archeology but became a fisherman like my dad."

Priya explained the situation to Basu.

He asked, "How many animals?"

"We're starting with fifty mammoths, but they're young and some may not survive. Also, we have twenty-five pregnant surrogates, so I expect a few more mammoths will be born before we see you."

"Baby mammoths! Sure! I'd love to see them and would be glad to help. I know just how to do it. Get your animals to Thondi and I'll take care of the rest."

"Thank you. Thank you! Over the Western Ghats, across Tamil Nadu will take some time. Will you still remember us when we finally arrive in Thondi?"

"Don't worry. How could I forget Huma's school friend and fifty mammoths?" He murmured, "Fifty mammoths," several more times before breaking the connection.

Priya shook her fists in the air. That was the best news. She sang a silly song she'd learned from American children. "She'll be coming around the mountain when she comes."

She began preparations by constructing lists. She could hear *Achamma* reminding her, "Make a list and cross off each line until you're done." She started with categories: food, shelter, security. Each category exploded. Food expanded to people and animals, and people became storage, cooking, serving. She was feeling confident until she considered contingencies like weather and accidents. Before she got discouraged, she flashed back to long nights in med school—so much to remember, so much to organize. I did it before, and I can do it again.

She looked around the dining room until she spotted Karina and Sarita. She expected they'd be happy to join the mammoth migration. "I'm taking the mammoths out of India."

The fury of their responses surprised her.

Karina hissed, "So Roshni has won? I can see her reclining on silk pillows watching our struggles on her comp, orchestrating the mammoth resistance from her hidden lair."

Sarita added, "After all she's done, I wish I could have thrown her overboard instead of Niraj. Maybe I'd have fewer nightmares."

She poured the upset girls some tea. "Your time in captivity must have been just awful."

They were ready to talk because with that simple prompt, they recounted their ordeal.

Priya listened silently, just refilling the teacups. Sarita's contribution ended with, "The worst thing was having to choose between Niraj and Karina when Roshni made him leave Karina to drown in the flood. I'm glad I chose Karina, but I still blame Roshni for making me choose."

The two girls hugged.

Priya waited a few minutes and then leaned forward to whisper. "I'm going to show her. I'll steal the mammoths. They'll be moved to safety before she realizes it, but I need help."

Karina replied, "Okay. When you put it that way, you can count me in. Anything to help those majestic mammals."

Sarita expressed some concern, asking, "Is my father coming."

Priya didn't want to offend her, so she just answered with a simple, "No."

"Good. Count me in too. I'm tired of him trying to turn me into a soldier. I'm so ready to leave his perpetual boot camp."

Priya was glad for another ally against militaristic Vadish. "However, without your father, I don't know how we'll handle security."

Sarita laughed. "I wasn't joking about boot camp. I'm proficient with many weapons and own several. I'll take care of security."

Priya basked in the satisfaction of her thorough preparation. Before the sun rose, the animals and supplies were herded to the eastern pastures. Everyone had a job. Karina led the way, following the same path her kidnappers had taken her three years ago. Priya carried a case of 5,000-rupee banknotes "for emergencies." Sarita wore a sidearm and had a rifle over her shoulder. The three women were prepared for any eventuality.

All went well until they reached the eastern perimeter fence.

"Halt!"

Priya was surprised to find security patrolling these remote reaches of the station. Two men blocked the gate. The gate to nowhere. There were no settlements or roads for miles in all directions.

The three women looked at each other. Priya hadn't even considered a contingency for this absurd situation. Something had to be improvised, not her strong suit. Still, Dr. Kowalski had left her in charge. This was her responsibility, but she didn't know what to say.

One of the two guards stood at attention and addressed her formally. "Chief Scientist Agrawal, where are you taking this valuable livestock?"

Priya looked to her left and said, "Sarita." She did her best to compress: *These people work for your father. Say something to them,* into that single word and an urgent stare. Sarita either didn't get the message or had no idea what to say.

The awkwardness abruptly ended when Karina stepped forward. "Kaz wants the animals moved. Roshni's terrorists have acquired helicopters. We have to take the animals to the forest for safety. We'll be back after you repel the attack."

"But— But Vadish didn't leave us any orders."

Priya admired Karina's poise and confidence as the young girl pushed forward without a plan. Karina took out her comp and thrust it toward the guard like a weapon. "Do I have to wake up my father? He's in China and will be unhappy to hear we were delayed."

The other guard responded. "That's fine. Be sure to return after the attack."

Karina laughed. "Obviously, where else would we go?"

Priya grabbed the girls' hands and urged them through the gate thinking: I can't believe that worked. Once the guards were out of sight, she turned to Karina, "Helicopters?"

"I got the idea from Niraj. My dad has told me that story like a hundred times."

Sarita said, "Cool bluff. There's no signal for your comp out here."

And Priya added, "And it's later in China, so Kaz wouldn't be asleep."

Karina laughed, "I don't even know if he is in China."

Priya returned to her plan, expecting that to be the end of surprises.

21. Maatalii, Suluk—Qamanittuaq Nunavut Canada

The snow all melted away long before it should have again that spring.
Maatalii scuffed her boot over the slushy mud in the parking lot, thinking
they shouldn't even call it permafrost any longer. Just tundra. At least it would
be tundra until the tree line crept all the way north to them. *Then it will be
forest,* she thought, *or taiga, like Siberia.* An environment her people knew next
to nothing about.

It already felt like they had adapted too much to the changing climate.
They were changing their ways.

It took a good eight inches of ice atop water to ride a snowmobile over a
frozen river or lake, and at least five inches over earth. When they consistently
got slush instead of ice, they'd converted the snowmobiles to the pontoon-
skid slushskis, and used boats over the water: there was not enough ice to use
the old ways.

They'd built *greenhouses,* to provide local food that was far too expensive
to import these days. They used more fresh vegetables and herbs than Inuit
ever had.

Maatalii chewed on the end of her braid, deep in thought. It was a vicious
circle: The air was no longer cold enough to freeze the ground solid in winter,
and in summer there was scarcely any snow at all, so the feeble sunlight
thawed the permafrost even deeper down. There *was* no one-to-three feet of
permafrost. Maybe a few inches at the bottom of a mud and slush dirt
topping, that was all. They were doing everything they knew how to do to
reverse the effects of the *Hot,* but it was never enough.

She looked to the area Sivoy had fenced off on the side of the parking lot
opposite the dog runs. They'd found a starving, abandoned polar bear cub
on the tundra several weeks ago, and had made a home for it here. They tried
to feed it caribou meat, which it didn't really have the teeth for, yet. They'd
chopped and ground some up, and the cub only nibbled it. Maatalii herself
had discovered the little bear would suckle caribou milk from a human baby
bottle, and that seemed to be nourishing it at least a little. They'd built a tiny
hut and lined it with caribou skins and straw, but the cub sat outside it and
cried. Poor solitary little beast; they all hoped, but did not believe it would
survive much longer.

She gritted her teeth and made her way back to the row of greenhouses
behind Snow House. Her latest greenhouse experiment, a cavern-like hut,
covered in black plastic to keep light out and moisture in, had produced a
bountiful crop of mushrooms. Like the other greenhouses, they had put a
solar- and wind-powered temperature control system in; the mushrooms

liked a cooler and more consistent temperature than ordinary sun-loving vegetables.

She'd learned mushrooms also liked untreated caribou poop, mixed with a little dry grasses or straw. They grew practically overnight: she needed to harvest again. She would be able to sell some at the little "fresh veggie" booth she and Suluk had constructed just outside the Snow House restaurant.

Villagers were slowly getting used to the idea of different kinds of fresh vegetables, something that had been very rare in their cuisine before now. Maatalii still had to give verbal cooking instructions with many bunches or tubs of produce she sold. Most of the homes had never seen fresh spinach or fungi before. Even those brave enough to buy them had no idea what to do with them once they got them home. Maatalii or Osha explained sautéing, or making soups, or stir-frys. Sometimes she thought the women ended up throwing the food away out of sheer perplexity.

She kept meaning to print up a few pages of instructions—she could make them in both English and Inuktitut—for the most common vegetables they over-produced and had available to sell. Right now it was mushrooms and a few herbs. The herbs were easier: they could always be chopped and tossed into bannock. Maatalii bit her lip, thinking, as she stuffed a big canvas bag with her harvest. Would bannock be good with some mushrooms in it? Maybe sautéed in butter and then added to the dough? She'd have to try a batch and see.

◗

"I think we have a solution for the plowing work," Suluk told the **women clustered around her.**

"How's that?" Osha wondered, watching as Suluk dragged the tattooing thread through the ink, soaking it.

"Or, well, Sivoy and I found it together." She squeezed out excess ink from the thread with her already black-tipped fingers. "Erne-Auco is barging in some big earth-moving equipment for the next stage of their mines. It is coming up here from Churchill."

The Gathering Room in the building behind the small all-sects chapel was cool and well-lit. It had many tables and chairs to accommodate the *potluck* dinners the new minister held every month, and other gatherings, like Alcoholics Anonymous meetings, and their own Sisterhood group. It thus was perfect for the Sisterhood's tattoo and wall-hanging projects with plenty of space to spread out the various pieces across the navy-blue vinyl-covered tables.

"How soon will it be here?" Maatalii asked, looking up from her sewing. Suluk saw Meriwa scowl and jerk the wall-hanging back flat, bringing Maatalii's attention back to their project.

"I don't know the details," Suluk said. "But it's coming. So Sivoy asked the shipping man about if we could borrow it for a day. We were both amazed when the man said we could. He was actually *happy*, because he is worried about if it still works after coming so far, on the railway and then, I suppose, on trucks and then on the barge."

"So we can test it and get our own job done, too?" Maatalii asked, without looking away from her stitches this time. Meriwa hummed a little in content.

"Yes," Suluk nodded. "Though they have to bring their own driver in, since we can't do it."

"And that's going to work, to pack it down for the Snow House foundation?" Meriwa said, a sarcastic tone to her voice.

"I don't know, but Sivoy and the shipping man both think so."

Osha made a funny face, but then Suluk realized it wasn't because of her comment, but was instead because she had inserted the needle a little too sharply beneath the skin of Osha's wrist.

"Sorry," she said, and Osha hissed, then tightened her lips.

At the next table, Maatalii looked up and watched the skin-stitching procedure closely for a few moments. She would be next.

The Sisterhood's newest member, Hitty, meanwhile, pressed a chilled towel on the fresh stitches in Osha's wrist while Suluk dabbed at some dripping ink on the table.

"Ready?" Suluk then asked.

Hitty removed the towel, Osha nodded, and Suluk took another stitch, pulling the ink-soaked thread through, adding another tiny element to the design. She referred to the paper where Osha had drawn what she wanted. The thread would leave behind the ink, tattooing a permanent design. Suluk needed to be careful with each stitch she placed, being sure to match Osha's plan.

The men claimed their method of puncturing the skin with tiny dots was a more authentic method of tattoo, but Osha had only snorted her opinion of that. Skin stitching was the true way, all the women knew that. And Osha, Keeper of the Ways, knew best of all.

Meriwa and Hitty both nodded their approval of the latest stitches. Osha bent and looked closely at her arm.

"That's going to be very delicate," Meriwa said. "I'm glad I went with something stronger for my design."

"Yours suits you," Suluk told her sister. "Wouldn't suit our Mama."

Osha snorted. "Have you *seen* what Maatalii drew up?"

"It's old and new," Maatalii said. "I used an old design and made it more modern. It still looks like snow lilies," she said, a defensive tone to her voice. Suluk glanced at her daughter, worried. Maati hadn't been the same since Amaruq had abandoned the family. They hadn't even had a phone call from Churchill; it was as if Ama had vanished from the earth.

Working alone, Maatalii had spent weeks on her design, adding her own elements to the traditional ones.

"Snow lilies with zig-zags and mountain-tops!" Osha crowed. Suluk couldn't decide if her mother was shocked or pleased. Or maybe, both.

Maatalii shrugged. "Those are both old fashioned designs, grandma. Even you said so."

Osha snorted her opinion of that, as she did often. "Maybe not the way you made them, eh? *Stylized.*"

Hitty smiled as the comments and laughter went back and forth and then spoke her judgment on Maatalii's work: "It is a perfect design."

"Osha's is, too," Suluk put in.

Meriwa made a wry face. "Not mine?"

"Of course yours, Meri. Of course," Hitty said, and everyone laughed.

Hitty applied ice after Suluk finished four more stitches in the tattoo. Then Suluk took a break, thinking Osha needed one more than she did.

"Oh!" Hitty said, startling everyone with her sudden outburst. As a new member of the Sisterhood, Hitty was still earning her place in the town and among the women. Most of them considered her to be somewhat…erratic. Perhaps eccentric was a better word. A widow, with teenaged children, Hitty seemed to act like a young woman half her age.

Osha's judgments of the woman were the harshest. Being Keeper of the Ways, or wise woman, did not necessarily mean even-tempered, and certainly not kind.

Nevertheless, Hitty was making a place for herself.

"Oh," Hitty said again. "I have news!" When she had all their attention, she smiled. "Our music CD sold 25 copies last week!" she turned to Maatalii, "and I think it was your advertising idea that did it!"

"Which idea was that?" Suluk asked.

"I linked it to Aunt Meriwa's Etsy page," she said. "I also filled in a Wiki article about *kakiniit* and other skin-stitching information, and showed the CD cover as an example of the art, with a link to the CD. I also added our link to the throat-singing article. I put the Norway women's CD on there, too; the Greenland one was already linked as an example of throat singing."

"Did we make any money?" Osha asked, peering at her wrist again, then up at Hitty.

"Yes, since the boys let us use their recording setup for free." One of "the boys" being her own son, she did not say.

Suluk glanced around at the other women. "I decided we should give something back to them for that, though our earnings are still small. "I've already given them each a package of caribou steaks, and Maatalii made some herb and vegetable packets. That all seemed to make their families happy," she added with a sly look at Hitty.

Hitty smiled and nodded. "Yes. Thank you."

Maatalii looked up from her stitchery. "I could make some advertising links for *their* CDs too," she said. "The boys have some set up already, but I think there are categories they missed."

"Rapper rock and roll!" Meriwa said, rolling her eyes.

Maatalii and the others laughed.

Suluk smiled, remembering the boys' faces when the Sisterhood had spent fifty minutes blowing throat songs for the recording. They had seemed intrigued, asking Maatalii if she would come and sing background for some of their songs when they recorded next. So her daughter had played one of the boys' songs for her. It was very loud, of course. She'd tried to be open-minded, but to Suluk's ears it had sounded like Snow House Inn being torn down: scraping, raucous, discordant, and as irritating as fingernails on a chalkboard. To her, it seemed to carry the sound of their Inuit culture being wrecked, like the permafrost. How could Maatalii's throat-singing be heard behind all of that?

"It's more melodic than Norwegian Death Metal," Maatalii said, "which is making a comeback, by the way. But it's still not what we would ever call *pretty*."

Suluk just shook her head.

The Sisterhood all thought this was funny, too.

Maatalii watched in fascination as the *kakiniit* was begun on her left arm. They would let that arm heal up before doing the other one. Then she could decide if she would do more.

She felt sad, thinking she had always planned to do this with her *uaguk*. But Amaruq had turned her back on Qamanittuaq and everyone in it. Maatalii took a deep shuddery breath while the women of the Sisterhood looked at her design. They had many comments. But none of them were Amaruq's.

After the first band of simple lines, Meriwa took over the stitching, as Suluk had been working many hours already that day and her hands ached.

"Now, there is plenty of time, Maatalii," Hitty said from where she sat, stitching a seal form onto the water area of Meriwa's big hanging. "Tell us what happened with Amaruq."

Osha nodded. "I need to hear everything, too," she said. "It just seems unlike her."

"It *is* unlike her," Maatalii said, feeling tears spring to her eyes.

"Have you met this man she has run off with?"

"I met him. He is a boy, not a man." Maatalii felt the tears slip free from the corners of her eyes, sliding down her cheeks. "He's okay, I guess, though...I do not trust him."

That brought everything to a halt. Needles froze in the wall hangings, Meriwa set down the inky thread into the soaking pan, and Hitty dropped the chilling towel onto the table with a thump.

"I did not know this, Maati," her mother murmured.

Maatalii kept her left arm still even though they weren't working on it just now. She used her right sleeve to wipe her eyes and cheeks dry. "I cannot say why, which is why I did not say anything before now." She bit her lip, and looked up, around at all the women's faces surrounding her. She felt safe. *So the opposite of how she had felt every time she had been around Niki.*

"Even when he put the pretty ring on her finger, I felt like it was a trick. I thought at first I was just angry because he was stealing my *uaguk*, but I've come to believe it is more than that. I've caught him in at least one lie. And...his shadow...*shifts*. I cannot make it any more clear than that."

The women muttered, Osha especially, chanting what sounded like a prayer.

"Then I learned that he had convinced her to support him while he took classes from the Manitoba Institute of Technology there in Churchill, at the outreach campus. Which means Ama needs to work to support them, instead of going to college herself, never mind coming home."

Maatalii brought her gaze up from her arm. She met each woman's eyes, gauging if she had made her unease clear.

"Amaruq was flattered by Niki's attention, she didn't think about anything or anyone else." *It was as if Ama was entranced.*

She suspected deep in her heart that Niki was using her *uaguk,* and would drop her once he had taken from her all that he could...including Amaruq's innocence and trust.

But what could she do?

"Ama is blind in love. She's not listening to her *uaguk*, that's certain." She stared at her bracelet pattern, drawn in blue ink on a piece of Ama's sketching paper. "She did not care about this," she pointed to her design, "when I tried to get her opinion. And then suddenly she was gone to Churchill." She hiccupped, fighting back tears. "It's a thousand kilometers from here!"

◖▬◗

Maatalii glanced around the Snow House grounds, and to the tundra beyond. Now, in summer, the scrubby bushes and springy moss were green. A batch of saxifrage was still blooming, a purple blanket that covered the little valleys in the tundra. She sighed and went into her room, turned on her comp.

She read through the list of online classes she had put together again. They covered a range of large-animal agricultural sessions that should be applicable to the mammoths. Of course, none of them were *about* mammoths, because they'd gone extinct 3,600 years before she had even been born. But they should give her some general background, at least.

She dawdled in front of her laptop, exploring design ideas for *tunniit* facial tattoos, including especially the traditional three radiating lines on the chin. It was something she would have asked Amaruq about.

Amaruq who hadn't answered any of her texts or emails.

Amaruq who just seemed…gone…like Papa.

Suluk knocked on her door. Maatalii looked up at her mother, and it stabbed at her heart, that her mother felt she must knock before breaking in on her daughter.

"Mama," Maatalii said.

"I did not want to interrupt you when you were deep in thought," Mama said.

"I'm brooding, not thinking," she said. "I think." She laughed, a grim, tight little sound.

"I wondered if you could perhaps help out at Snow House tonight. One of our servers has called in sick, and I'm not feeling that well today, either."

"What's wrong?" Maatalii said, immediately worried.

"Just tired, I am thinking."

This was something she needed to think about too: twice now, her mother had asked for her help because she was tired.

"I wondered," Mama said, voice low, "Are you staying home, or leaving us, too?"

Maatalii rolled her chair around to face her mother. "I will not leave," she said. "I think that is the best idea for me, for us. I thought about it a lot. Considered: would I be more help if I got more education and then came home? Or would it be better if I got a degree and a good job, and sent home the money, because more cash is always helpful? Or should I stay now, just as I am and help as I can?"

"Those are good questions. Important questions," Suluk said, nodding her head. With a pang, Maatalii noticed how many silvery threads had crept into her mother's deep black hair. When had Mama gotten so old?

"I found some online classes I can take from right here," she said. "It's mostly the mammoths I'm worried about. No one knows anything about how to take care of them. I can't learn much about mammoths directly, but I can find out about raising buffalos, which are similar in size and preferences."

Suluk nodded, resting her hand on Maatalii's shoulder. Maati tipped her head to rest it atop Mama's wrinkled fingers, broken nails. Broken, but clean from hard work in the kitchen.

"You think maybe your cousin decided leaving home was *her* right idea?"

"I think Amaruq is thinking with her tiny baby heart, and is going to be quite sorry someday," Maatalii replied. She grimaced, and shrugged. "*Ajurnamat,*" she said. "It can't be helped."

Mama pulled Maatalii's head against her soft chest. Maati could smell the fresh herbs Mama must have been chopping. She thought about Amaruq, knowing Niki was never going to hold her cousin with such love as Suluk always had held them. It made her unutterably sad.

Abbie shuffled across the yard scowling at the puffs of dust. The *Hot* had caught up with her. She peeked through the barn door to spy Redd's legs jutting out from under a green tractor. She marveled that the massive tractor could automatically navigate up and down the rows, but still required her husband to crawl underneath for regular maintenance.

"It's hotter and drier than last summer," she shouted into the barn.

"You worry too much," came the reply.

She licked her finger and with one puff it dried. She turned back to her husband but remembered he didn't think about the farm much. As long as they had food on the table, the news of starvation in faraway places occupied his thoughts.

She didn't want to worry about the weather either, so she went into the greenhouses to prepare her raised flower beds for the fall season. Working her home-grown compost into the soil, she appreciated how good it smelled—earthy, fresh. It slid through her fingers like warm dough as she mixed it in with her bare hands.

She enjoyed her role as marketing manager for the flower business. The job mirrored wise women of the past, knowing the cycles, foretelling the future. She sorted through her collection of seed envelopes, selecting orange flowers for the fall season: marigolds, zinnias, chrysanthemums, and daisies. She *prophesized* they'd sell well for back-to-school, Halloween, and Thanksgiving.

The chickens interrupted her reverie pecking on the door. They could have squeezed through the cat door, but Trouble kept a watch and attacked any chick that came close. By the time they were grown, they naturally avoided the area around the cat flap.

When she opened the door, the timid chickens backed away, but when the door stayed ajar and no broom appeared, a few brave hens entered. They scratched the damp floor and celebrated every thrip, beetle, or worm devoured. Abbie chuckled at them. "You are from our future, living on bugs."

They just cheeped and peeped in response. Soon the entire flock swarmed over the dirt floor. The yard dried out in the summer heat, yet the greenhouse still offered a nice array of treats in exchange for their assistance with organic pest control.

It was too hot to cook, so Abbie put together a family favorite: Greek salad with avocados and hummus, and pita on the side. Thinking about the many choices she had for dinner, she had to agree with her husband, people in Asia and Africa were more impacted by the *Hot*.

When Mike and Redd finished their salad, she said to no one in particular, "I checked with the weather services. El Niño has returned. Winter wheat will be a struggle for the next few years."

She felt an affection for the two men as they wiped their empty plates with a piece of pita and looked towards the refrigerator.

She answered their implied question. "We have peach pie and fresh strawberries. You can have either or both."

Redd asked for strawberries, and Mike predictably said, "Both."

After dessert, Mike replied to Abbie's statement. "After I win the algae competition, I'm going to college. Carla's in Africa and I doubt she's returning. Can't you two retire?"

She smiled at her naïve son. "I'm only forty-five. I have more than fifty years to live. Too early, way too early to retire."

Mike took a forkful of pie topped with berries. "Are you going to raise cattle here?"

Redd acted as if someone poked him. "Cattle? Never. With the problems feeding people around the world, raising more cattle is not the answer."

She recalled that he'd considered cattle when he wanted to stay in Oklahoma, so now she rushed to support his changed position. "That's one thing your dad and I agree on. No cattle." She looked at Mike who seemed sad. "My apologies to your girlfriend's family, but no."

"Then what are you going to do? Move again?"

"Exactly. I've found an ideal location in Nunavut."

He looked surprised. "Wow. Isn't that really far north?"

"I wanted to move farther north the first time, but I let that real estate lady talk me into this. I won't make that mistake again." When he didn't respond, she added. "The land is outside a small village and the people are very friendly. I think we'll be happy there."

Mike spent the summer dividing his time between preparing for the algae competition and helping around the farm. Each night he connected with Elzia. He'd forgotten about missing Senior Prom and had no worries until he received an official-looking letter. He held it by the edges and turned it over a couple of times, then showed it to his mother. "What's this?"

His mom smiled. "It must be important. I had to sign for it."

He considered the possibilities. The algae competition wasn't for a couple of weeks, but maybe this was his first college recruitment letter. That would show Elzia. He had discovered a new chlorophyll. Maybe this was the confirmation of his name registration: Chlorophyll m. Even if he didn't win, some colleges might notice that. He had heard of some high school algae breeders being offered big corporate jobs *before* college. *That would* really *show Elzia.*

His mother interrupted his reverie. "Are you going to open it? It's from CSE. Who's CSE?"

He dropped the envelope. "How did you know that?"

She pointed to the top, left corner of the envelope now lying on the floor and laughed. "See that? It's called a return address."

He stared at the corner. *CSE. Washington, DC.* He thought for a moment and made the connection. "Corporate Science Events. It's from the science fair."

He picked it up, ripped it open, and read silently.

THIS YEAR'S COMPETITION HAS BEEN CANCELED. HOMELAND SECURITY HAS DECLARED A NATIONAL SECURITY THREAT FROM ALGAE BLOOMS. NEXT YEAR'S COMPETITION WILL BE ON PERSONAL POWER GENERATION. PLEASE CHECK OUR WEBSITE FOR REFUNDS AND DETAILS.

THANK YOU FOR YOUR SUPPORT OF CORPORATE SCIENCE EVENTS AND WE REGRET THE LATE NOTICE.

He couldn't believe they had abandoned the cutting-edge algae breeding for the mature technologies of wind turbines and solar panels.

He turned to his mother and did his best to remain calm. "It's about the algae competition." He went up to his room to call Elzia.

Elzia looked disappointed as she asked him, "So, you're really not going to college, are you?"

Mike balanced his comp on the windowsill and pointed the camera outside. He didn't want her to see his sad face.

She politely commented on the view. "Yes, I see the barn and the greenhouses, but we both know you're not going to be a farmer." Her voice picked up a slight tremor as the speakers echoed off the window glass.

"Elzia, you haven't sent in your applications yet. Wait until it's your turn. We'll see how you'll feel being judged and shoved into some narrow slot."

She responded with confidence, and he thought he could sense some scorn in her tone. "*I am* going to college. Physics. Climate. As soon as summer is over, I'll enter my applications. I've already started my essays."

He picked up the comp and panned a row of five small bottles. "These are my best strains, 202, 325, 451, 452, and 703. Best except for 147 that I had to abandon in Oklahoma. Even with the competition canceled, they still might get me into college. Someone will notice them."

"Mike, Mike! Don't you realize that the competition was canceled because no one cares? In twenty years, no one's ever won. It's impossible."

Mike put her back on the windowsill facing the yard and paced around the room. "Yes, I told you that. Algae that excel in *productivity and power*, decompose instantly upon death, sequestering no carbon. Algae that *sink and survive* grow so slowly that they are also useless. But...but, I'm close to a solution."

They had had this discussion before. She supported the conspiracy explanation. "Corporate science just set up the game to keep students from studying climate change."

He almost punched the row of bottles. "No! I've done it. My latest strains can grow and survive. One of these will stop the *Hot*."

"Waste of time. You should have studied physics. We could have gone to college together."

"I'm going to dump these algae in the Big Muddy. From there they'll take over the world and lower carbon levels."

"Remember your algae sequences are registered. You'll have Homeland Security after you."

Mike rubbed his temples. After so many years he was tired. Tired of sequencing algae. Tired of searching gene databases. Tired of splicing promising snippets. Even tired of the foul smell of growing and dying plants. "Elzia, some days I think I could be happy raising flowers. They grow inside, therefore I could forget the *Hot*."

"That's nice, but I'm afraid you may have a bigger problem. Look out your window."

Mike got to the window in time to see a South Dakota Department of Environment and Agriculture car stop in the driveway. A man and a woman walked to the front door. They looked very official, white shirts with collars and buttons, black pants with badges on their belts, and carrying comps. They walked with shoulders back, like marching soldiers.

"Elzia. Why do you think they're here? I don't think they've come to register me for college."

She whispered, "No time for a joke. This looks serious."

He heard the doorbell. His mother yelled, "Coming." He walked toward the stairs.

Elzia called him back.

He moved close to the comp. "What's up?"

"Look outside now."

Two more men exited the South Dakota car. These were State Troopers with their hands on their sidearms. They walked toward the greenhouses.

Mike and Elzia said in unison. "Not good."

Then a panel truck arrived with two more troopers and a German Shepard. They followed the first troopers.

"Let's not jump to conclusions. I'm going to the stairs to listen. I'll call you back when I know more."

The woman was speaking. "Mr. and Mrs. McGilvery, we're from the Department of Environment and Agriculture. Our information is that you moved here from Oklahoma."

Mike could see his father sitting in his chair with Sasha. His mother answered. "Yes, and we've been happy here. We just harvested a successful winter wheat crop."

The woman officer continued, "We noticed. With the *Hot*, we're encouraging more farmers to move from soybeans and corn to wheat."

"We're experienced wheat growers from Oklahoma. I'd be happy to assist you with the conversion."

The man interrupted and didn't sound friendly. "Thank you very much, but we're here about something else."

As soon as he started talking Sasha made a soft growl and galloped upstairs.

Mike hugged Sasha. "It's alright, girl." He petted her ears and she lay down next to him, just out of sight of anyone downstairs.

"We're dealing with a different problem right now. The area around Sioux Falls, a *very* large expanse, eastern South Dakota, southwestern Minnesota, northwestern Iowa, are all suffering from algae blooms. Livestock ponds, fishing lakes, small creeks, and most worrying, some tributaries of the Missouri."

"I know. We had a bloom in our pond. Someone from County Extension talked to us about fertilizer runoff, but I don't think that was our problem."

He continued. "You were right. We've traced this problem to a new virulent strain of algae. We sequenced it and checked the national database."

Mike didn't need to hear any more. He ran to his room and checked out the window. The troopers were carrying away his bioreactors wrapped with yellow biohazard tape. He packed bottles of his best algae strains carefully into his backpack. He again regretted letting his mom leave 00147 in Oklahoma. It had certainly found its final resting place by now—in some landfill or an incinerator. He looked around his room thinking, what else?

What else included a sleeping bag, a change of clothes, some underwear, all the granola bars he could find, a small, cast iron frying pan, matches, and some other camping gear.

He wondered whether he could wait until nighttime or if they would tromp upstairs looking for him today. He had just turned eighteen and didn't want to be arrested. He opened the window. The troopers had confiscated all his stuff from the greenhouses. They were walking to the house. He could hear words like *bioterrorism, interstate transport,* and *Homeland Security.*

When they rang the doorbell, he thought, Now or never.

He threw the fire ladder out the window, grabbed his pack, and flew down. He ran into the fallow wheat field and kept going until he came to an irrigation ditch. He jumped out of sight and lay down in the mud.

His first thought was to call Elzia, but then he realized they would be looking for him. He looked suspiciously at his comp. He remembered reading that some apps constantly reported his position. He turned off phone service, messaging, email, local weather, navigation, and multiplayer games. The list seemed to be endless until he found an advanced setup screen. "TURN OFF ALL TRANSMITTERS?" That was it! He said YES and confirmed three times after a couple of dire warnings.

He crouched down and took off his pack so he wouldn't be seen above the level of the ditch. He headed south. College or no college was a concern of the past. Today, he was a fugitive.

Dr. Bai Xiang Bo, the check's "To" line read: and $30,000 U.S. Xiang Bo stood staring at the amount in frozen wonder. Her mountain food algae had been a big hit with the Future Foods founder, who was always looking for new ways to feed the world. Like Xiang Bo and Mo Chou, he had found the ugly and tasteless algae paste could be transformed with numerous spices and different forms of preparation. It was sufficiently different from tofu in the nutrients it offered, and it was easy to grow.

Future Foods was able to turn the unpleasant green paste into a swirled creamy-brown curd which would appeal to anyone who used tofu. Soybeans were becoming harder and harder to grow, while the algae was tolerant of many different growing conditions.

Xiang Bo had months ago decided she was finished with the mountain algae, but now she was being asked to grow it in production quantities. And they wanted to know if she could find a way to make it grow stably in vats. What a project! She tapped a tooth with a fingernail, thinking through the process of designing and testing a vat-grown variety.

Future Foods had also suggested a few names for the product, since "mountain algae" was rather unwieldy and non-marketable. "Fu-fu" was idiotic, but some of the other ideas might work. She was pleased to be asked for her input on the name. She and Zi Min had been calling it "Nofu" for years now. She sent that name to the FF staff along with her preferences about the ones they'd suggested. Which was pretty much any of the others except Fu-Fu, which sounded like some kind of yappy dog to her ears.

She made a list of questions that needed addressing if it was to be grown in vats.

Would it taste the same without the pure mountain waters? The pond-grown type was spreading throughout Donglan Province, providing inhabitants with an easy-to harvest protein. It survived snowy winters and monsoon steam. It was, essentially, growing wild in the mountains now. Friends were sharing with friends and starting it in their own ponds and mostly empty rice paddies. It did not like saltwater, and preferred still water ponds and quiet eddies to swift-moving streams, but survived well the weather extremes and constant harvesting.

She had thought she was done with the stuff, and was planning to move back to Guilin to work with the diatom-algae there. Now she had a whole new project to try.

She looked at the check. Should she cash it? That would suggest to Future Foods that she agreed to his loosely written production request. Or was it that he wanted her to send him samples so he could grow his own? She needed to take an hour and closely read the letter he had sent along with the

$30,000 check. She could send a rough outline of her test parameters and see what they thought.

⬤

The first big winter storm was blowing in from the north. Zi Min kicked her shoes off under the new lean-to and stepped around the corner to the entry of the toilet room where they had installed the composting toilet. Xiang Bo had been happy that the thing didn't smell bad, but Zi Min had kept silent whenever the subject was brought up.

She could smell it. It wasn't horrible, but she was very glad the little room was *outside* the house. *Ya-ya*—Grandma Jiao—was happy it was much closer than the old outhouse had been. Everything in life had to be this sort of compromise, Zi Min decided. Part of growing up, being an adult, was deciding what compromises she could accept.

She knew she wasn't old enough to demand anything yet, but she had discovered the art of suggesting things. If she thought of each decision as a line with a slider on it, marking where compromises could be made, she—the family's young but only child—could have an effect on where the slider stopped. And thus the toilet room was outside the house under the lean-to, with its own little door, rather than being built into the main house as Xiang Bo had originally planned. Zi Min finished, closed the toilet room door behind her, and opened the door to the main house, stepping inside and into her warm indoor slippers.

She checked the stove, fitting one more pressed-bamboo brick into the pot-belly, and then setting the refilled teapot back on the cooktop. She stared at it a moment, wondering why it was called a teapot, when they never made tea in it. It merely boiled the water to be poured into the *real* teapot which held the tea leaves. She would have asked one of the older women that question, but she discovered *Ya-ya* Jiao was asleep, and Xiang Bo was working at her desk, which was covered in papers and her laptop.

Zi Min pulled the big bean-bag chair closer to the stove and picked up her electronic reader. Good, it had fully re-charged while she was out preparing her garden for winter snows. She had been able to download a few new books when they'd been in Donglan a few days ago. She explored the first few pages of each, and settled on which one to read first.

She was about 30 pages in, when *Ya-ya* Jiao gave a deep sigh, and then slumped down in her chair. Zi Min glanced up and saw that the old woman was tilting over the arm of the chair, looking very off-balance and limp.

She got up and dropped her reader when its cord came up short. She grasped *Ya-ya* by the shoulders and pushed her up straight. The old woman did not help her at all, like she usually did. It was like pushing on a heavy sack of rice. It was wrong.

"Mama," she called, feeling scared.

Xiang Bo looked over her shoulder and smiled, then frowned as she saw Jiao slumping down again. She jumped to her feet so abruptly her chair fell over. Two steps, and Xiang Bo was at *Ya-ya's* side, with a quick glance at her daughter.

Zi Min bit her lip as she watched Mama hold two fingers against *Ya-ya's* neck and then laid her head against the old woman's chest. Zi Min gasped when her mother let out a moan that made all the hairs on Zi Min's arms stand straight up.

"Is *Ya-ya* dead?" she asked.

Slow tears wet her mother's cheeks as she nodded. "Your grandma is gone."

"Oh," Zi Min said, rubbing her arms. She had touched her, touched the old woman and straightened her up. When she was already dead! It was too spooky, and sad. She burst into tears, knowing that now everything in her life would change. Again.

Ya-ya had died during the first snowfall. The snow and the cold made it harder for people to travel. Nevertheless, her mother, Xiang Bo held a traditional memorial at their little house; Nalai villagers and a few old friends from Donglan came by to honor Bai Jiao's life. Some brought food. Some stayed to eat it. They all shared stories of things they had done and seen with *Ya-ya*. Many Zi Min had never heard.

Bai Jiao, they said, had been a good neighbor. She and her husband had grown a lot of food, sent from Donglan to all over the world. She had saved a neighbor's dog, which had gotten itself stuck in deep water in the creek below the village. She had brought a bag of life-saving rice to a widow who had lost her husband, along with everything else.

Some Bai family—distant cousins, Zi Min thought, though she was confused by so many visitors—from north of Donglan came and stayed a whole day, telling how *Ya-ya* had been a good wife and mother. Too bad they had not had more children, but look how fine Xiang Bo was.

They went on for hours sharing Jiao and Xiang Bo stories, and Zi Min listened in wonder. It was like hearing fairy tales of long-ago days, back when they had used mules and goats to carry loads, instead of cars and trucks. Had *Ya-ya* been that old?

The visitors' only note of discontent was that Xiang Bo cremated *Ya-ya's* remains, instead of performing the traditional Zhuang rites, burying the body for a year or two, then digging it up, cleaning the bones, and storing them in an urn in the ancestor's shrine.

Zi Min had wondered about that. But this little house had no ancestor shrine; she knew not everyone believed or celebrated the same things, but she did not say anything to her mama. Instead, she took a small bottle and filled it with *Ya-ya*'s ashes from the big urn. She hid her little bottle, and later made her own shrine in her grandmother's garden—now hers.

She smiled and talked to *Ya-ya* when she worked in the vegetable patch It was her own tiny ancestor's shrine. She had never had one before, but she did it properly, burning aromatic leaves in a small bowl and leaving some of mama's algae on a leaf for Grandmother to eat.

◡

At last the mourners were gone, and Xiang Bo could take Jiao's ashes and scatter them into the big waters of the Hongshui River. Perhaps Mother would end up in the sea, which she had wanted to see, but never had.

Xiang Bo chewed her lip. She had tried to take Jiao to some of the places she had dreamed about, but there had been so many excuses flooding from Jiao's mouth, that she finally realized her mother did not really want to go travel. She had dreamt those places, and wanted the dream to remain her reality. As if seeing the actual places would be so much *less*, it would destroy her vision.

Xiang Bo had given up. She had brought travel magazines and brochures that Jiao enjoyed looking at—the tourist advertising was what matched Jiao's dream. She had told Xiang Bo she had always admired her bold daughter for picking up and going to school in Edinburgh and California. But she liked being where she was.

In some ways, it was a wonder Jiao had ever left the Donglan farm for Nalai. There had been some financial problems when Papa died, which was probably the only reason.

Xiang Bo walked around the entire house, feeling like she had done all that building over the last three years for nothing, since she and Zi Min now had the whole house to themselves. After a few weeks, she cleared her mother's things from the big upstairs bedroom and cleaned and painted the walls a fresh pale green. She gave the big old bed to the young couple that had recently moved into the biggest of the Nalai houses. That cleared up room for her and Zi Min to bring their separate, smaller beds upstairs, along with their cabinets and clothing.

She looked out the window to see Zi Min kicking snow with her new, tall boots on her way to the garden to see what might be ready to pick for dinner. Winter chard grew just fine under the snow, so Xiang Bo knew they would have at least that. A few leaves from the roof sedum, an egg or two, a couple cubes of mountain-algae-not-tofu—*Nofu*—and they would have dinner. Just the two of them, now.

◡

The next time she was in Donglan for supplies, she got a phone call from Li, apologizing for not coming to Jiao's memorial. They'd had an emergency at the university where he now taught classes: a fire had taken out

145

a good portion of the old classrooms, and he had barely managed to save his books and research papers from his office.

Besides, Xiang Bo thought, he hadn't ever really known or liked her mother. For all that he disparaged his own mother, Xiang Bo had always thought Li was simply more comfortable with Di'e's ways. The Bais were Zhuang; they and their traditions and their homes were too different for him. She also believed that was part of the problem between the two of them. Li had been happy to find a Chinese wife, but she wasn't Han Chinese, and that was almost like marrying a woman from Cambodia, or the Philippines, or Taiwan.

Di'e had counseled Xiang Bo to be patient. Cheng Li was tolerant; he would try to see someone else's point of view. But how long should she wait for that to happen?

At least in that call Li had verified that the diatom-algae were behaving. The evidence of the escape and spreading he thought he'd seen had been a false alarm. The fish and rice and vegetables maintained their almost-symbiotic micro-habitat in the DAS pond. Other ponds, without DAS, grew fewer plants and fish, but their water was clear. That was good. Her governing system was working.

She still had so much to do here.

She grunted, levering the hand truck underneath the big vat to move it into their downstairs room. She was converting their previous bedroom into a lab and experimental space to see if she could produce the micro-algae in vats, as the Future Foods's leader had asked. She had three big tanks, which wasn't enough, really, but at least would give her a way to compare three ranges of artificial sunlight and temperatures, then later, three water sources, to see what was going to work best.

Zi Min finally came in to help just as she had finished brute-forcing the last vat into its space.

"Bring me that blue toolbox, please," Xiang Bo said, trying to keep the annoyed tone from her voice.

Zi Min complied without a word, then stood by as Xiang Bo hooked up the water lines to the big tank. When she stepped back, the three vats did not seem all that big. She had gone to a chocolate factory in America once, with a bunch of other students at Scripps, where they had seen truly *big* vats, with automatic stirring mechanisms and the heady scent of chocolate and sugar suffusing the air. By comparison, these tanks were small.

"Well. They are ready for their first trial run," she said.

Zi Min laughed. "Why don't they just use their streams and ponds and rice fields, instead of these things?"

"Mmm," Xiang Bo said. "Can you think of some reasons they would do it this way?"

Zi Min shrugged and twisted her lips into her "puzzled" face.

"Do you think all of the Earth looks like Nalai or Donglan?"

"No, of course not," Zi Min said, affronted at either the idea or Xiang Bo's silly question, she couldn't tell which. "So," she said, "they don't have streams?"

"There is a fresh-water shortage in the United States, especially in the West, but they do still have streams, and probably a few ponds, also."

The still-small girl thought for a moment. "So then it's too hot outdoors."

"Their land has the *Hot* much worse than we do here. You have seen that no one here can grow rice any longer."

"Yes. The *Hot* makes it hard to grow food plants everywhere, I know that."

"This algae can grow in both very hot and very cold weather."

"Yes, I *know!*" Zi Min said, exasperated. "I don't understand why they don't try to grow mountain algae outside, then!"

"They hope to grow more food with less water, and less arable land, by growing it in tanks." She turned the handle on each of the three tanks, letting water flow in to fill them. She tried a different question, "Do you remember how the smallest pond dried up last summer?"

"All the water evaporated, or sank into the ground. Oh!" she cried, realizing what Xiang Bo meant at last. "In the tanks, it won't evaporate so much!" She smiled, pleased with herself. "But how does it get sunlight? Doesn't it need sun, like the vegetables do?"

"It will need some sunlight," Xiang Bo agreed. She pointed to the rack of gro-lights on stands she had constructed. "That is why these vats had to be translucent. We are going to see how much light is needed, and test other conditions."

"So we can make lots and lots of *Nofu!*" Zi Min said, bouncing on her toes.

"Just so," Xiang Bo said.

24. ROSHNI, KACZKA, KARINA, PRIYA—KERALA INDIA

Roshni thanked Varuna for the fine weather as she walked to the Sikh temple. With her belongings propped on her shoulders, she left Mattancherry Wharf in good spirits. Surely some of the younger, fitter women could complete the journey in half her time, but she was in no rush. There had been no work at the hiring hall, none for chambermaids, no laundresses, not any day labor at all. On days like this, she could only look forward to the free meal at the Sikh langar, and hopefully no panic attacks.

She meditated, concentrating on each step: lift, swing forward, heel, toe, shift weight, repeat. She observed the gentle swaying of her load as the balance shifted with each step. She remembered: "When meditation is mastered, the mind is unwavering like a flame in a windless place." When she noticed her surroundings, she was already on the Venduruthy Bridge, more than halfway.

In time with her meditation, Varuna, the god of the sea, splashed against the piers with a rhythmic refrain, "Niraj, Niraj, Niraj." The regular cadence echoed, building to a panic attack. Oh no! Her legs shook, almost tumbling her to the walkway. Her heart seemed to explode out of her chest. Her sweating hands grabbed the railing and she lost her small breakfast.

When her consciousness returned, she picked up her bundle and continued to the temple. No meditation this time.

At the temple, she wrapped the *pallu* end of her sari over her head and left her belongings and sandals outside. She followed the line into the langar hall and sat cross-legged on the floor. Even though the meal was available to all, no religious observance necessary, she always took the time waiting for her tray of roti, rice, dal, curry, and kheer, to worship.

"Ganesh, I have been a righteous warrior defending your honor. I beg you to beseech Varuna to return my Niraj."

She repeated this mantra until it was time to accept her tray of food with a small bow and tears running down her cheeks. Surely Niraj would be found and returned. Now that she was off the Ganesh Committee, this was all that remained.

Once Xiang Bo's cashed her check, Kaczka initiated a major project to supplement the earlier feasibility experiments. The Future Food team commandeered the test kitchens at the U.N. Technology Innovation Lab in Stellenbosch. *Nofu*, an unpleasant green paste packed in hundred-liter barrels, a cross between seaweed and hay, had replaced similar containers of manufactured meat from Mdudu Nyama.

Kaczka had flown to South Africa for the first tasting, confident the Future Food scientists could find the perfect recipes.

"Here we have *Nofu* caviar." A waiter, in formal dress and white gloves, placed crystal bowls on the table. "Accompanied by toast points lightly spread with fresh unsweetened butter. Kaczka and the chef-scientists dipped the toast into the salty concoction and took generous bites. He smiled. "Excellent. The fishy flavor works well."

They all chewed in silence, until a scientist reached for a shot glass of vodka and downed it with a quick swallow. He made a face pantomiming puking. "No. The after-taste is like a stable that needs to be mucked out."

The afternoon proceeded like this. Brief promises, but nothing to stock Xiang Bo's unpleasant green paste on supermarket shelves.

Tastings continued with dishes like Caesar salad, sushi, minestrone, chicken fried steak, barbeque short ribs, and three different desserts. The results were the same.

Kaczka knew that much of taste is olfactory, so he suggested. "Can we fix the odor?"

One scientist responded defensively. "We've tried everything, activated charcoal, baking soda, strong spices."

A woman in the back of the room stood up and the chatter stopped. He recognized Dr. Järvinen. an analytical chemist, over six feet tall with short hair and biceps like a butcher. "It's time for the big guns. I took the liberty to order a vacuum evaporator, the same one used to dehydrate food for space."

The next tasting featured offerings plated artistically, as usual. Dr. Järvinen, who was more scientist than a chef, added her contribution, green mush in a plastic bowl.

This time all the dishes won approval, even the mush.

Kaczka congratulated everyone, "You've done it! Marrying science and cuisine is what Future Foods does better than anyone else."

Dr. Järvinen somberly added, "We're only halfway there. Fractional distillation and mass spectrometry will identify the offending volatiles. Then we can optimize the process and save some of the good flavors and odors we've lost in this round."

Someone added, "It's all food engineering from here."

The self-congratulatory banter continued, but Kaczka left the room when his comp sounded a notification. "Morning, Vadish." He had to sit down when his General Manager Operations announced, "I've found Roshni!"

Over the past three years, he'd heard this every few months. So many false sightings. "Are you sure?"

"Positive this time. Intelligence Bureau have fingerprints and DNA, everything. Hiding in plain sight at the Cochin Port."

"Have they picked her up?"

"The IB have her health records. She suffers from PTSD and panic attacks. They are reluctant to arrest such an unfortunate woman. She's homeless and feeding herself with day labor and free meals from the Sikhs."

Kaczka had so many questions. *PTSD? Which Sikhs? How do they provide free meals?* His most pressing question was, "Does this mean she's not behind all our troubles?"

"Yes. Our terrorists are independent. Nothing to do with Roshni. She can barely feed herself."

Kaczka felt sorry for anyone who didn't have enough food. He had dedicated his life to feeding the hungry, and now Roshni was hungry.

"What do you want us to do about Roshni? Even if the IB doesn't want to capture her, we can force the issue by taking her into custody ourselves."

Kaczka was torn between revenge and empathy, not a recipe for action. "Don't do anything. She's hungry."

◗

With the mammoth calf Indrakshi at her side, Karina proudly led the world's best science experiment as they embarked on their migration. A gentle breeze stirred the grasslands, which the animals sampled while maintaining their orderly column. The dawn took on a green tinge filtered through the dense foliage of the foothills. Karina looked forward to the expedition, thinking of the Oregon Trail, a computer simulation she'd played in school. Such a glorious adventure.

The elephants balked at the dark track into the dense undergrowth of ferns and palms. They'd reached Tiger Trail. Karina became concerned when the animals bunched up into a mob around the trailhead. The mammoths pushed through the herd to find their mothers, except Indrakshi who stood beside Karina wrapping her delicate trunk around Karina's waist. Karina hugged the mammoth's head and whispered into her ear, "It's okay Indrakshi."

The elephants chirped and grunted. The narrow unfamiliar path had spooked them. Then Sarita ran up Tiger Trail, quickly disappearing. Karina wondered: Is she escaping from the impending stampede? Karina urged Indrakshi away from the crowd and shouted to Priya, "What's happening?" Certainly, Priya had a plan.

Sure enough, Priya led Vani, the matriarch, to the front. The chirps and grunts stilled as the animals watched. Vani reached her trunk out to smell the unfamiliar forest. Karina imagined her as a scientist collecting data. Vani trumpeted and turned around. As the others also reversed, Karina flashed back to the terror of the Idukki Dam Flood. The herd reached a frenzied peak sounding like the roaring water. Karina rushed Indrakshi to a sheltered glade at the edge of the forest.

Vani raised her head and extended her trunk. Here it comes, thought Karina. She's going to sound the charge. But just then, Sarita came running down the path dragging a huge branch scattering leaves, buds, and flowers in all directions. "*Kalikkuka! Kalikkuka!* Eat! Eat!" she shouted to Vani as she offered the matriarch the tender browse.

Vani paused and sniffed the unfamiliar offering. She tasted and responded with a deep rumble. The rumble spread throughout the herd as Vani followed Sarita in search of this new treat. The crisis had been averted.

The herd moved up the path, at first the elephants, and then the mammoths grabbed branches of new growth leaves, tentatively chewing at first, but after that, eating with gusto. A chorus of approving chirps echoed through the forest as the herd rambled up the trail.

Karina and Indrakshi followed the herd, once again on the Oregon Trail, and no one had died of dysentery.

⌣

Priya checked her comp. Even though there was no signal, the GPS still worked. Satellite images showed them approaching the end of the woodland. Right on schedule.

Just soon enough. Everyone had had enough of the perpetual dusk under the canopy. The animals had lost interest in the novel browse. The exclamations such as, "Did you see that green and red barbet singing in the tree?" and "Can you smell that sweet ginger?" had stopped. Everyone mirrored the silent boredom of the pack animals.

Priya was the first to notice the opening. She ran forward celebrating, "The Periyar River. We made it!" Leaving the forest for the river basin, they entered another world. The eucalyptus, sandalwood, and teak trees gave way to open fields and marshes. A tranquil gurgling river replaced the muted hum of the multi-story forest with its many birds, frogs, and insects. The open fields of green seemed to glow in the setting sun as the caravan departed the haze. Even the air smelled different, the sweet smell of flowers overpowering the musky odor of the forest.

She allowed herself a small moment of pride observing all of her charges expressing their approval of the campsite. The animals who had dragged themselves into the camp area after the long march now were playful; lifted ears and bouncy steps showed how happy they were. The elephants and pack animals formed small groups in the bright green grass, all heads down enjoying the change of menu from the strange jungle browse. The mammoths ran to the river to drink and splash where they were hidden by a dark green stand of reeds. They may have been out of sight, but their delicate trunks trumpeting their high-pitch squeaks made them easy to find. The people dropped their heavy packs and drank from their canteens, confident of a ready supply for refills.

Priya turned to Sarita, "Can you organize some feeding stations? The animals should get some corn and oats to reward them after today's uphill journey."

She assigned others to set up an impromptu corral and to position tents around the perimeter. With the ready water supply and the tender green pasture, she doubted there would be any tendency for the animals to roam. She made a note to keep an eye on the mammoths. Juveniles! One can never know what to expect. Kids are kids.

Once the animals were settled, she thought about dinner. They carried some food, mostly twenty-five-kilogram bags of rice and some spices, but she'd hoped to hunt and gather. She touched her backpack to check on her box of 5,000-rupee notes. For emergencies. A couple of guys had already started two big pots of rice.

She walked over to them rehearsing her we-must-conserve-our-resources speech. The food needed to last. She wanted to avoid eating roots and bugs. With a forced smile, she asked, "What's for dinner?"

"Rice and barbequed barramundi. The fish are plentiful, we might also have them for breakfast."

The thought of the buttery flavor and meaty texture replaced her anxiety about running out of provisions. "Sounds great. We're going to follow the Periyar for a few days. I hope people don't get tired of fish."

"No fear. I'd eat these three times a day."

Another cook added, "We can barbeque them, fry them, bake them, and even dry them."

After dinner, a four-wheel-drive vehicle with a canvas top pulled into camp. Priya recognized the emblem of the Kerala Forest Department from its elephants. Sarita and Karina followed her as she approached the man at the steering wheel. Seated next to him was a woman with a rifle across her lap.

When both rangers got out of the jeep, Priya stood between the girls and the rangers, hoping to keep control of the discussion. "I am Dr. Priya Agrawal. Can I help you?"

The man replied while the woman stood alert holding her rifle. "We received several alerts. We're usually sent after suspected poachers. Obviously, you're here for a different reason."

Priya smiled, "We're not poachers." She waved her arm to the elephants and mammoths while she decided how much to tell them. "We are bringing these elephants to Chennai for the festival, *Ganesh Chaturthi*. Can you advise us of the best path over the Western Ghats?"

The woman relaxed and pointed her weapon to the ground. "Just follow the river. The animals will have easy access to water and forage. You can cross over the top of the Kallarkutty Dam."

The man added, "That path will avoid all the construction. You remember the flood when the Idukki Dam failed?"

Sarita pointed to Karina. "We remember it well. We were—"

Karina interrupted, "—on holiday in the Kerala backwaters. It was quite exciting."

Priya didn't want to discuss the flood, the kidnapping, the protests, the mammoths, any of it. "I've got it. Just follow the Periyar to the Kallarkutty Dam, right?"

The man replied, "Exactly. When you get close to the dam, send someone ahead to clear your transit with the KSEB."

Priya nodded to indicate she understood his reference to the Kerala State Electricity Board. "Can we offer you some barbequed fish?"

They politely refused and were returning to their car when the woman stopped. "Those are strange-looking baby elephants."

After the Chennai story, she was more comfortable making stuff up. She quickly spun another story. "Those are a newly discovered elephant subspecies from Nepal. We've been breeding them." She elaborated further to bolster her tale, "You probably read about them when they were discovered five or ten years ago."

The rangers nodded and continued on their way. Priya relaxed, glad they were more interested in poachers than strange elephants.

This had been a good start and she looked forward to the remainder of the journey. Herding the animals to Sri Lanka was turning out to be more fun than shipping them by truck. She put her head down on her pack and fell asleep listening to the elephants rumbling.

Roshni sat among, but not with, the other women in the hiring hall eating her *appam* and beans. She rarely participated in their gossip, but today they were so loud, she couldn't miss overhearing their chatter.

"His skeleton washed up on the beach."

"I pray for his mother. Did she also drown?"

"Niraj—"

Roshni heard that "Niraj." She listened closely. *Are they talking about my son?*

"After all these years, the sea has returned her son."

"At least she has some closure."

Now she understood. *They are talking about my Niraj! He is not returning. I didn't want closure; I wanted him alive! Ganesh, have I offended you? Have I followed the wrong course of action?*

She reached into her bundle and withdrew a small Ganesh statue. She broke off each of the four arms and the trunk. She stood up and stomped him until he disappeared, embedded into the dirt floor.

Her decade of fighting the Mammoth Research Station and her three years of meditation had not brought peace. Varuna, the god of the ocean and the west, had not returned her son.

Another path. She needed another path. She picked up her bundle and her bowl and headed east away from Varuna. She repudiated her former goals: the downfall of Kaczka and his mammoths; the return of Niraj. Desire nothing, give up all desires and be happy. The wisdom of the gods would guide her on this new path.

As she traveled in the direction of the rising sun, she had no destination, no purpose, no desire. After so many years of striving, this felt strange, but also like her right path.

Kaczka's comp flashed and he clicked on *headlines*. "Body of Kerala kidnapper washed ashore. Terrorist mother still at large." He connected to Vadish. "Do you think the Intelligence Bureau will pick her up now?"

"They tried, but she was gone. No one knows where."

He gratefully thought: At least *my* Karina has been returned. Roshni's Niraj is gone forever, and she's all alone and hungry. He decided to do something in Roshni's memory.

"Vadish, the mammoths and Roshni are gone. It's time to make peace."

Vadish didn't argue.

"First, I want you to prepare a feast for the people at the Muslim Gate and invite them to visit the remaining elephants."

"If you want to make peace with them, you'll have to return. You may forgive them, but they won't forgive me. Maybe later, but not now."

Kaz thought of Vadish's troops, the miles of barbed wire, the trespasses in both directions. Vadish was right, and Kaczka guessed *he* was also not ready to forgive. "I understand. Make the preparations. When I return, I'll host an elephant festival."

"I can do that. Good timing. *Ganesh Chaturthi*, the elephant god's birthday, is soon."

Kaczka admired Vadish's positive attitude, even though he doubted that Vadish supported the plan in his heart. He's a good and loyal soldier.

25. Mike—SD USA; Carla—South Africa

Mike hid in the field. Sirens and flashing lights demanded his attention. He shivered curled up in a muddy ditch. Late into the night, each time more troopers arrived, he listened to the commotion until he could pick out voices.

One of his pursuers said, "I'll get pictures from social media."

The conversations among the assembled forces seemed so close that he feared capture before he could even leave the farm. He heard another voice from the crowd. "The pictures will help us widen the search. He's probably long gone by now."

That was good news. If they thought he was gone, he could sneak away. As long as he stayed alert, he could escape.

"We'll come back in the morning with the dogs."

He relaxed and wrapped himself in his sleeping bag to stay warm. By morning, he'd figure out a way to evade their dogs.

"Contact HomSec. They should be able to track his comp."

Now he felt confident. He'd taken care of electronic tracking. TURN OFF ALL TRANSMITTERS. He thought, *I'm smarter than these guys. Let me think about what to do next. Maybe, I'll just visit Elzia.*

The next thing he heard, shook his confidence. "Meanwhile, let's get those infrared drones in the air."

Oh no. He looked up as the sky lit up with a small fleet of drones carrying searchlights. Then he noticed other drones that were dark and barely visible. He assumed the dark ones had infrared cameras. He quickly figured out their search pattern and it was not encouraging. They performed an orderly ballet, following each other in an increasing circle. In a few minutes, they'd be directly overhead.

He did some quick calculations in his head. Daytime temps were in the high 90s. He'd be hard to spot against that background, but now the thermometer had dropped to the 60s and he'd show up like fireworks against the cooling soil and crops. The widening circle closed in on his position. He couldn't escape their net.

He formulated a plan. He pulled out his sleeping bag, threw it in the irrigation ditch, turned it over and over to get it completely soaked, and crawled inside just as the drones passed above. He lay motionless enclosed in his wet camouflage until the drones expanded their search pattern beyond his position. Faint conversations among his pursuers confirmed his cloaking had worked, but what next? Could he stay hidden until the afternoon heat when he'd be safe? Maybe, but the dogs would arrive long before that.

The drones became faint as he prepared to crawl away from the house. He desperately wanted to strip off the wet sleeping bag before his clothes also got soaked. He rolled it up and wrung out what water he could, but then the drones got louder. They were returning for a second pass.

Back into the sleeping bag. If they kept him pinned down, the dogs would find him at dawn—now only a few hours away. He was out of ideas. He curled up in a fetal ball to protect his core temperature and hoped for a miracle.

He felt light-headed and weak, thinking this is it. If I lose consciousness, I may never escape. Suddenly the crowd came to life. Their activity shocked him out of his stupor and forced him to full attention. *Thank you, adrenaline. What's happening?*

Three different troopers shouted. "We've got him."

Mike could pick out isolated voices from the excitement. "Direct the lights to drone Gamma, heading 330."

The drones and troopers headed away from his position. He didn't move.

"He's moving fast. He's now under drone Delta, heading 270."

"Get more drones in that sector."

The yelling and commotion increased.

"How can he move that fast?"

"He's back at heading 330. Two drones have acquired the target."

A familiar sound rumbled across the field.

He cheered silently, "Sasha! I love that dog!"

"It's the dog!"

"Who let the dog out?"

"Bring the drones back to base. We'll install new batteries. Our own dogs will be here soon."

With the drones temporarily grounded, Mike rolled up the wet bag and headed south, towards Oklahoma. He'd only gone a short distance when he heard a familiar panting. He whispered, "Sasha. I can't take you with me. Go home."

The moon reflected in Sasha's large eyes. She sat, catching her breath, but otherwise alert and not moving. Her eyes seemed to say, "I saved you from those bad men. I'm not leaving. You need me."

The troopers started shouting again. "Where did that dog go?"

Mike quickly realized there was no time to argue with a stubborn Newfie. He and Sasha headed south through a fallow field that offered little cover against drones and dogs. They ran for a mile, while Mike calculated how long it would take to walk 600 miles to Oklahoma. He didn't have a plan.

When he reached highway 34, his first idea was to cross and continue south, but he saw a pickup truck approaching from the east. He needed to put some distance between himself and those tracking dogs. Sasha barked at the oncoming truck. He patted her head, "Okay girl, let's see if we can get a ride."

He put down his backpack and waved his arms. Sasha jumped up and down in the middle of the road. The truck flashed its lights and when Sasha didn't retreat, it came to a stop.

A lady jumped out of the truck. "What are you two doing here in the middle of the night?"

Sasha went right up to her and gave her a big slobbery kiss.

"Down, Sasha. Down!"

The driver didn't seem upset. "She's big, isn't she?"

"I'm sorry. I don't know what got into her. She's just been crazy tonight."

Sasha sat at the lady's feet and looked at her with those big eyes as the lady rested her hand on Sasha's head and scratched her ears.

"You didn't answer my question."

Mike thought quickly. He had a backpack and camping gear and a dog. "We're heading for Fort Thompson to meet some friends camping on the other side of the dam."

She didn't look like she believed him, but she was still petting his dog and smiling. "In the middle of the night?"

Sasha rubbed her enormous head against the lady's leg. Mike gave her his best goofy smile, the one Elzia seemed to like so much. "Seemed like a good idea."

She smiled. "I don't believe you, but your dog is friendly, and you seem old enough to be on your own."

He might have answered too quickly. "Yes. I just graduated from Washington Springs High School. Go Emigrants!"

She laughed. "Throw your pack and that bear into the back. I'll take you as far as the dam. You can walk from there."

She didn't need to offer twice. Soon they were in the truck and rolling down the highway.

She spoke to the truck, "Big Bend Dam."

"North or south side?"

"North."

Mike admired the moon as the vehicle glided across the prairie.

◡

The pilot announced, "If you look out the window you can see the sunrise across the Namib Desert."

Carla craned her neck over the tall man in a black, red, and green dashiki sleeping beside her. Sure enough, a brilliant red expanse kissed the rising sun. Though she was exhausted and jet-lagged, the thought of concluding this thirty-six-hour ordeal lifted her spirits. In celebration, she accepted a cup of coffee, or maybe it was tea, and a stale corn muffin, or maybe it was a sweet roll. After so many naps and snacks, she didn't care. Her seatmate woke and also had some breakfast if that's what it was called. She gave him a sleepy smile and he returned with a high-pitched laugh, usually reserved for young children. "*Dumela* mama."

Another announcement. "Fasten your seatbelts. We have started our descent into the Winnie Madikizela Mandela International Airport. Out of the left windows, you'll soon see Robben Island."

She reached across the tall man and tapped the window. "Is that it?"

"*Yebo*. Robben Island. Mandela was there for eighteen years back in the twentieth century."

She recalled her World History. She remembered something about Gandhi and the Berlin Wall. "Mandela? I don't recall Mandela. Should I go there?"

"*Cha*. Don't bother. I've haven't been since primary school. It was important to my grandparents, but now it's just visited by schoolchildren."

The plane took a sharp turn and banked. He leaned back so she had an unobstructed view. "See that?"

She saw a high plateau. She guessed. "Table Mountain?"

He smiled. "*Yebo*. Go there instead. The views are spectacular, and you can walk around without fighting crowds. Since you've come during the rainy season the lines for the cableway should be short, though you better carry wet weather gear."

She didn't say anything.

He looked embarrassed. "I didn't mean to rain on your holiday."

She didn't like being mistaken for a privileged tourist. "Holiday? No. *Cha*. I'm here to work. I'm a Chemical Engineer. I'm going to work at Mdudu Nyama in Stellenbosch."

He reached out his hand. "You must be Carla McGilvery. I'm Ashur Chace, just returning from a Food Security and Sustainability conference in Glasgow." He showed her a bag with the conference logo.

That ended their conversation. She was thousands of miles from home, traveling alone, and suddenly this man knew her name. It was creepy, a little scary, and she was trapped beside him.

After she cleared the long non-citizen line at customs, the strange man who knew her name waited at the baggage carousel and offered to drive her to the hotel in Techno Park. All the warning signals went off. She hadn't ever mentioned Techno Park.

She tried to recall his name from when he introduced himself as they departed from Heathrow Airport. It was Ash something. She didn't remember ever hearing that name. All she recalled were cautionary stories about women traveling alone. She also recollected something about the separation of women and men. Even if he was from Mdudu Nyama, his suggestion seemed at least improper, if not dangerous.

Then she looked at his luggage cart. This was just getting worse. He had collected her baggage. How did he even know which bags were hers? When she saw a driver with a comp displaying her name in large letters, it seemed like a good time to separate from him.

"That's my car over there. I'll see you around." She waved to the driver and he waved back. She grabbed her bags and rolled them away from the tall man. She sighed in relief as her driver rushed over to take them.

But Ashur, if that was his real name, followed and talked to the driver in a language she didn't understand. Finally, the driver said in English, "I have to check with the company and Miss McGilvery."

The driver made a call while Carla wondered what she had gotten herself into. She'd only been in South Africa an hour and already she was uncomfortable. Should she have stayed in the Midwest as her mother preferred?

Then her comp buzzed. The woman's dark face was in shadow, and Carla struggled to recognize her features. Then the woman turned her head, and there on the screen was Lesedi Marais, her boss from Mdudu Nyama.

"*Sawubona.* Hello, Carla. I see you've finally arrived."

"Yes, I'm at the airport, through customs, and I have my luggage."

She paused, not knowing how to explain Ashur.

Lesedi broke the silence. "Did you meet Ashur Chace? He was on your flight."

She relaxed a little. "We were seated next to each other. He told me to avoid Robben Island."

"Oh yes, that's him. All engineering and no fun. Did he try to convince you to hike up Table Mountain?"

"No. He said I could take the cableway."

"Really? Point your camera at him. Let me check if you have the right guy."

She turned in a circle. Ashur appeared and disappeared on her screen.

"I guess he was just on best behavior. Can you let him share your car? I'll tell the driver to drop you off first, so you don't waste any time. I'm sure you're tired."

She considered her boss's request and the presence of the driver and that Ashur had been positively identified and her boss was a witness and agreed.

After a short walk, they were on the way to Stellenbosch.

After the airplane, the car felt luxurious, smooth, and quiet. The countryside contrasted with the endless fields of wheat she had grown up with. The rolling hills were broken up into patches of vegetables or pasture lands. She recognized cows, sheep, and horses, all in their own fenced areas. She didn't recognize the fields with long rows of plants supported by wires. She wondered aloud. "Are those grapes?"

The driver started to answer, but Ashur interrupted. "Yes. Some of the best wine in the world comes from Stellenbosch. Even with the *Hot*, the climate here is still perfect. You know the *Hot* has had less impact in the southern hemisphere. Less land. Less industrialization. More ocean."

She had grown up discussing the *Hot* daily. She wanted to change the subject. "What are those bright pink flowers?"

Ashur jumped in again. "Bougainvillea. They're vines, climbers, and if you're not careful they will take over with their two-centimeter-long thorns. Not from here. Originally from South America."

"Isn't this winter?"

Ashur laughed. "We're at the same latitude as Los Angeles, just south instead of north. So, don't expect snow or anything like that.

She took out her comp and took pictures. Vineyards. Bougainvillea. Mountains. Bright sun. Then she saw palm trees. Palm trees! She had never seen anything like this. Travel might have a reputation as an ecological destroyer, but she enjoyed seeing everything live and refused to feel guilty.

"I'm Lesedi Marais, welcome to Mdudu Nyama's mid-year internship program." Carla looked around at her fellow interns gathered in a garden of roses and tulips and more of the bougainvillea she'd seen for the first time yesterday. These lush gardens surprised her. She never imagined Techno Park would be a repurposed wine estate, looking more like an Italian villa than a Chicago industrial park.

"You can call me Lesi. You will be divided into two teams, but first, we have a tour and lunch." The crowd of about twenty stretched out as they walked along the stone paths. Carla found herself walking with another tall girl.

Listening to all the different languages, she felt self-conscious that she only knew English. She turned to the tall blond girl and spoke slowly. "Hello. My name is Carla."

The girl responded, "I'm Freja."

She didn't have any accent, so Carla ventured, "Are you American?"

Freja laughed. "No. Danish."

They stayed together during the tour and sat next to each other at the company cafeteria. Lesi spent a few minutes at each table. "You two look like twins."

Carla who had been admiring Freja's straight blond hair nervously smoothed her flyaway red curls. "Oh no. She's Danish and I'm Scottish."

When their manager seemed uncomfortable or confused with that response, Freja jumped in to rescue the conversation. "Yes, she does remind me of my sister. We're both so tall."

That put Lesi at ease. "Well, welcome. This dining room is open every day for breakfast and lunch. Everything is gratis to augment the small stipend you receive as interns."

Freja raised her glass, "*Skoal.*"

The Two Pearls

Lesi raised her glass also. "Of course, since we're in wine country, the wine is also included. Just don't overindulge. You are expected to return to work for the afternoon."

Carla, who didn't drink, even after her time in Chicago, lifted her glass of ice water to be sociable. Still, serving wine at lunch, especially free wine, shocked her.

These surprises were minor compared to the afternoon part of the tour.

Carla never expected to find an animal more engaging than Sasha. Trouble and Mischief were close, but they were cats. Aloof, independent, and with a penchant for knocking things over. At Mdudu Nyama she met *Proandricus skeadi*—a giant earthworm. She expected these blind hermaphrodites to be dull, solitary creatures, but to her surprise, she learned they were social and constantly searching their dark environment for a mate.

As a chemical engineer, she appreciated their novel evolutionary choice. Before meeting these clever worms, she assumed fauna all used continuous processing—moving their food along and performing a different digestive function at each point. On the other hand, flora used batch processing—each cell performed the entire digestive process. Her new best friends were batch processing creatures, each segment being a complete little nutrition factory, processing food, delivering nutrition, and discarding waste. She just loved them. Unbelievable beasts. In the wild, they could grow to several meters in length!

Karina admired the clear sky above the warm Tamil Nadu savannah. With the Western Ghats behind them, the troupe had settled into a comfortable routine. The animals scattered to take advantage of the ample pasturelands. After dinner, the people sat around the dying cooking fire singing traditional songs accompanied on a small *chenda* drum and a *kuzhal* pipe. The elephants contributed their deep rumbles and the mammoths added a playful arrangement of high-pitched trumpets. As the sun dropped behind the mountains, Priya stood up. "Time to round them up for the night."

The animals headed for the temporary paddock attracted by the sound of oats and corn being scattered from plastic buckets. All except for the little ones that always wanted to stay out after bedtime.

Karina turned to Sarita, "Let's get the children." She volunteered for this task every night, not wanting to miss a chance to observe the adorable mammoths.

Sarita picked up her rifle and they headed to find the youngsters while being serenaded by rumbling elephants.

Karina listened to the rumbling. Something was wrong. The rumbles were accompanied by some higher-pitched sounds. "Sarita, did you hear that?"

Sarita held her rifle ready. "That's not a rumble. That's a roar!"

They both ran in the direction of the commotion until they spied the mammoths. Karina saw it first. "Tiger! Sarita, can you shoot it?"

Sarita picked up her binoculars. "Sorry. No. The cat's too close to the mammoths and it's also an endangered species. But I can try to scare it away." She fired into the air.

Karina didn't need binoculars to see that neither the tiger nor the mammoths reacted to the noise. "Again. Again!" Karina urged.

The gun discharged three more loud blasts. Three more pointless shots.

Karina couldn't just stand there and watch the mammoths become a tiger's dinner. She grabbed Sarita's rifle as the orange cat lunged. She shoved it against Sarita's chest. "I don't care. Kill the cat!"

Sarita raised her weapon to her shoulder. But before she could shoot, Indrakshi charged the tiger, hitting him midair, and knocking him over.

Karina nervously smacked Sarita on the back. "Did you see that? My Indrakshi may be a small mammoth, but she still outweighs that tiger."

The other mammoths backed away, but Indrak advanced. Now the two opponents were too close and moving too fast for Sarita to fire.

Karina watched horrified and scared for Indrak. She hoped the tiger would retreat, but Indrakshi taunted him, waving her trunk and trumpeting.

162

Karina held her breath. The tiger attacked Indrakshi's throat. The mammoth's tiny tusks didn't help, but to Karina's surprise, Indrak put her head down and spun around.

The tiger couldn't get a grip on the round, hairy neck, and slipped to the ground with a thud.

Sarita exclaimed, "Wow! I've never seen anything like that."

The tiger advanced once more, claws spread, paws windmilling at the dancing Indrakshi. This time the tired cat wasn't fast enough, and his tail ended under a mammoth foot. He retreated to a chorus of mammoth trumpets and stopped to lick his tail several times before disappearing into the tall grasses.

"Wow!" Karina thought about mammoths and ancient history. "You know, her ancestors lived with saber-tooth tigers eons ago. I wonder if this is how they defended themselves?"

Sarita just grunted.

With the threat defeated, all the animals gathered around Indrakshi and headed for the nighttime corral.

The next morning Karina brought Priya to examine Indrakshi. She found a few superficial scratches on her delicate trunk, which she treated with antibiotic cream. "Karina, cat scratches are notoriously full of bacteria. We don't want to risk an infection. Check her for any other scratches."

Karina stroked Indrakshi's flanks. "Can you please stand still for me?" She ran her hands through the mammoth's long blonde fur. "You were very courageous last night. I need to check you." Indrakshi stood still. Karina imagined that she understood what was happening, but it may also have been because Sarita was feeding her bananas.

Karina checked the ears, front legs, shoulders, torso. "Good girl. Almost done. You're looking good." When she ran her hands over Indrakshi's rump and hind legs, they came back tinted red. She parted the fur around the scratches and Priya treated them with more antibiotic cream.

Priya looked worried. "Karina, did you see her get bitten? Some of these look like bites! Cat bites are much more dangerous than scratches."

"How serious?"

"She could get septicemia. She could die."

"What can we do?"

"We haven't had any other injuries, so I'm going to use our complete supply of antibiotics, TMS or trimethoprim/sulfa, to treat her. We have enough for a half-dozen people or one mammoth. Sarita, stop feeding her those bananas and get my medical kit."

Priya mixed the bananas with some cooked rice to form a thick paste. She broke open six capsules and kneaded the contents into a sweet ball. "Sarita, have you ever played cricket? We need a bowler."

Sarita smiled. "No, but I played some rounders, and I was a fair bowler."

"You are certainly talented. We need your arm. I am going to convince her to open her mouth and you are going to toss this medicine in."

"Okay." She spun her arm around. "I'm ready."

"Don't let your hand enter her mouth."

Priya caressed Indrakshi's chin and ear. "Can you give me a big yawn or smile?"

The mammoth opened her mouth. Maybe that is a laugh. Sarita tossed the medicine in. The mammoth chewed and swallowed.

"Good work. Now we just wait and hope."

Karina stayed the rest of the night with Sarita's rifle to assure the tiger didn't return.

●

A large bird with a yellow body and blue wings swooped across Roshni's path. She followed its flight through the reeds and over the open water, where it hovered. In an instant, the bird dove out of the air and caught a fish, which it swallowed whole. Roshni knelt at the river's edge and drank the cool water. Her begging bowl contained some rice and dried fish; the people in the last village had been generous. She waved to the kingfisher. The bird cackled, *ke-ke-ke-ke-ke-ke*.

After a brief nap to the kingfisher's lullaby, she continued east, wherever the road would take her—her heart set on the journey, not any destination. A car stopped beside her. When the door opened, she felt a refreshing air-conditioned breeze.

"*Namasté*, wanderer. Can I give you a lift? Where are you going?"

She smiled at the driver and sat on the comfortable seat, ignoring the second question, happy to go wherever fate took her. With the landscape speeding by, the ride took on a mystical aura. Kerala was so full of life and beauty.

She turned to the driver. "Why did you stop for me?"

"You looked so peaceful and happy. My daughter recently died, and I needed some of your serenity."

"Karma. I recently lost my son. Perhaps they have been reincarnated together. We behold what we are, and we are what we behold."

When the car stopped at a bridge, the driver said, "This is as far as I'm going. I hope this is okay."

Roshni recognized the bridge. She was in Muvattupula. "*Namasté*, this is wonderful."

●

With so many things on his mind, Kaczka only half-listened to Vadish. "I have charged my three Hindu commanders to organize the celebration of Ganesh's birthday. *Eid-ul-Adha* is also soon, we should include that for the Muslims."

Oh no, thought Kaczka. The research station had always treated the Muslims well; Vadish had seen to that. There was no reason to include them. *Ganesh Chaturthi* was a peace offering to the Hindus. Keep it simple. Still, he needed Vadish's cooperation. Nothing was simple. He asked Vadish, "If we include the Muslins, how about the Christians?" while wondering about the Sikhs, those people that fed Roshni. Were they even a religion?

Vadish frowned, but he got the point. "I see. It will still be a festival. I'm sure all the children will enjoy painting elephants, regardless of their religion."

"Good. I trust you bought lots of neon-color paints."

Vadish nodded.

As a peace offering, Kaz asked Vadish, "Would you like to be the one to invite the crowd that's been at your door for all these years?"

"It is too soon. You do it. They are not ready to forgive me. Maybe later, but not now."

Now it was Kaczka's turn to nod.

Vadish had more to say. "I can understand how they feel about me. We will learn to accept each other. *Inshallah.* God willing."

Kaczka echoed, "*Inshallah.*"

Kaczka walked through the Muslim arch with bare feet, emulating Gandhi. The Hindu crowd seemed surprised to see him. The men moved closer. Light brown faces. Dark brown eyes. Mostly dressed in white, loose shirts and loose pants for the summer heat.

"You are all invited to the celebration of *Ganesh Chaturthi*. It is a few days off, but we're not ready." As he had hoped, the mention of Ganesh's birthday attracted the children, and with them came the women in brightly colored saris.

"First, I'd like to remove all this barbed wire." He pointed to the top of the Muslim Arch and the fencing stretching to the horizon on either side. Everyone followed his gesture. When they realized the armed guards were gone, the crowd exploded, the children cheered, and the drums rolled. Kaczka basked in the excitement. Men, women, and children all volunteered to help remove the hated barbed wire.

He pointed to a stack of cartons. "I also need some children to unpack the paints for coloring the elephants." This was similarly well-received. Kaczka felt confident there would soon be peace with the research station, and even with Vadish.

Inshallah.

●

Priya opened the last six TMS antibiotic capsules and mixed up a ball of medication. Again, Sarita bowled it into the mammoth's mouth. Priya stole looks at Karina, looking for a hint of grief or sadness. Karina maintained a stoic affect. Somehow, this girl whose mother died before she could remember, who'd been kidnapped at twelve, and whose father was gone more than he was around, had raised herself to be a strong, resilient woman.

Priya mumbled to herself. "We're still far from Thondi and we've already used up our medicine supply."

As if in reply, Indrakshi gave a weak rumble and hugged her limp trunk around Priya's waist.

She stroked the sick mammoth, being careful to avoid her tender rump. "There is water and pasture here. We'll rest until you feel better."

The next morning, she reported to the group gathered around the breakfast fire. She could feel Karina's intense stare. "I can't get Indrak to take oats, her favorite, or even water."

She drank some tea before she continued.

"Worse. She has a fever and diarrhea too. This isn't good."

Priya knew what she had to do. "Sarita, take two *lakh* from my box of 5,000-rupee banknotes. Madurai will have a hospital. Buy as many liters of lactated Ringer's electrolyte replacement fluid as they will sell you. Five hundred would not be too many. We also need IV catheters, 16 gauge, at least 40 millimeters."

"That's a half ton of water!"

"Yes, pay them to drive it out here…in an ambulance if necessary. Also, try to get a veterinarian."

She looked at Karina, waiting. "And Karina, she'll need help. Please accompany her."

Karina visibly relaxed, as did Indrakshi who put her trunk in Priya's lap while Priya ate her breakfast of rice and tea. After a short while, Indrak fell asleep, gently snoring. The other mammoths visited, two or three at a time. They chirruped and rumbled and stroked the sick mammoth's flank with their trunks.

The vet arrived in an ambulance.

"Dr. Priya, this is Dr. Nanda." Karina made the introductions. "She has agreed to keep our mammoths secret until we leave India. She drove the ambulance herself.

"Is this your patient?" The vet let Indrakshi smell her hand, and then she took out her stethoscope. While she examined Indrakshi, Priya gave her the history and told her about the two-week course of TMS antibiotics.

After a brief exam, Dr. Nanda reported. "You can see she is panting. Ten breaths per second is pretty high, even for a juvenile. And her pulse is high, over fifty. Let me check her blood pressure."

This idea astounded Priya. She asked, "Do you have an elephant-sized blood-pressure cuff?"

The vet smiled. "No. We put the cuff around her tail."

Priya watched. The reading was 150/100 which would be high for a person, but she had no idea what to expect from an elephant or mammoth.

Nanda frowned. "Her blood pressure is low, too low. You have a sick lady here. Let's start the Ringer's. She is critically dehydrated." Dr. Nanda turned to the sick mammoth. "Stay calm young lady. This might be cold, but then everything will be good." The vet lifted Indrakshi's ear and sprayed anesthesia. The mammoth squeaked but didn't move even when she did the other ear.

Nanda inserted a catheter behind each ear and sutured them in place. "So, Dr. Priya, you understand how this works. Each time a bag is empty, switch in a new one. We want to give her 100 to 150 liters, now. I'll come back tomorrow to see how she is doing."

Priya didn't get any sleep that night. Neither did anyone else. Volunteers switched the Ringer's bags every ten to fifteen minutes. Somehow, the mammoths had also organized a watch rotation. There were always two to three mammoths rumbling and comforting Indrakshi.

The following morning Dr. Nanda returned in an unmarked safari vehicle. When Indrakshi saw her, she trumpeted and walked forward. Priya laughed as two volunteers scrambled to keep up, carrying Indrak's hydration bags so the mammoth didn't tear out her catheters.

Dr. Nanda patted her side and rubbed her ear. "I see you're feeling better this morning." The vet turned to Priya. "Her respiration has improved. Let's continue the Ringer's, only seventy-five liters this time. Your TMS treatment might have saved her, but with septicemia, it is hard to know, because it attacks so many internal organs, lungs, liver, kidney, heart, spleen."

Priya replied, "Sadly, I understand that all too well. I think we've prevented septic shock, but other than that we have to wait."

The vet left, saying, "I'll be back tomorrow."

The night was a repeat of the previous night. Mammoths. Ringer's solution.

The next morning, the mammoths were all trumpeting. And circling Indrakshi, who lay on the ground. Priya feared the worst. She held Karina. "We should wait for Dr. Nanda."

Karina broke free from Priya and ran to Indrakshi. Soon tears were rolling down her cheeks. Priya moved forward to comfort the girl, while everyone else stood back, but Karina brushed her away. After wiping her face with her sleeve, Karina stood tall. "At least she is out of pain. She was brave, defending her brothers and sisters. We must also be brave."

At that point, the trumpeting stopped, and the elephants joined the mammoths, all rumbling and walking slowly in a circle around Indrakshi. First Karina, then the others joined the procession mourning the fallen mammoth.

27. SULUK, MAATALII—QAMANITTUAQ NUNAVUT CANADA

Suluk ordered gro-light bulbs with the refund credit for the shelves she'd previously ordered that hadn't worked for the new closets. Satisfied that she'd used the credit in the best way possible, she went on to look for different shelves, from another site. Ones that would fit.

None of them had realized making nice custom closets for their guest rooms was going to be such a trial. It might have been more cost- and time-effective in the long run to have just ordered the closet fittings ready-made by one of the custom closet companies.

At least response time for searches on the internet was much faster, now that the phone company and Erne-Auco had joined to upgrade everyone's systems. They'd also installed more towers. Results came up almost before she finished typing her search words. It made solving her problem much faster.

Here were some shelves that could be ordered to any size. They were expensive though. Suluk clucked her tongue. Maatalii paused on her way by and looked over her mother's shoulder.

"Wow. Maybe we should get the finished boards and cut them ourselves."

"I looked into that. But the hardware is so complicated, I think it might be worth it to just get these and put our time in somewhere else."

"Okay. Good thought. Oh, I found some wonderful aqua-colored matching comforters and curtains," Maatalii said. "And towels that coordinate with them. Cute polar bears instead of those retro flowers they show everywhere!"

"I saw what you picked out. Those will be very good," Suluk said, thinking it was also very good that they were at the stage of selecting the finishing touches. It had taken them more than two years to prepare the ground, the foundations, and then build the new rooms. Now the Snow House Inn was rebuilt, and they were almost ready to advertise on travel websites. They'd already had inquiries from people who had stayed before. The small local company that ran "Northern Lights Tours" were especially interested in bookings.

Suluk thought about that tour company with a small smile. She had met her friend Ikiaq there. Ikiaq, who was due to be back in town in two or three days. Her smile grew bigger. She had surprised herself that she could be interested in a man so soon after she had lost Opik. Or was three years really "so soon?" It seemed enough time to grieve. She decided not to feel guilty; Opik would understand.

She ordered the shelves to the correct size, hardware included. When those arrived, the closets would be complete. Meanwhile, they could begin offering the rooms, since everything else was done. She picked up the nice digital camera Tarkik had passed down to her after he had received a new one from his father-in-law to be. This girl he had met at college came from a rich mining family. He kept promising to bring her home, but so far, no one in Qamanittuaq had met her.

Suluk went outside, following the new concrete path to the Inn rooms. She took photos from all sides, hoping the winter light was good enough to bring out the modern but comfortable aspect of the rooms. The deep turquoise Maatalii and she had picked really seemed bright against the barren soil of the tundra. They needed to put in a few plants, she decided. Some flowers.

Suluk felt herself grinning as Ikiaq walked into the Inn's lobby area. As usual, he carried a compact toolbox in one hand, and his overnight duffel in the other. She still was unclear on what his job was for Erne-Auco, which required him to pass through her village about twice a month. But she was glad for it. She checked him in, giving him his lucky "room number 14" as he had requested.

Later, she met him in the restaurant so they could chat while he ate the daily special, spicy caribou chili and mushroom-marjoram bannock.

"Did you see my note to Osha about the mammoth ivory?" he asked around a mouthful of bannock.

"Only Inuit artists can carve and sell the tusks," she said, and he nodded. "Is that the *final* decision?"

"It is, although they were very hesitant to give it."

"They are worried about elephant tusks and rhino horns."

"Actually," he said, swallowing, "it's the narwhal they are most concerned about. Just looking at an ivory carving, it's impossible to tell the difference, without a DNA test."

"Why would we hunt endangered narwhal when we have mammoths in our yard that we will be slaughtering anyway?"

"Exactly the argument we used. The Committee knows the Keepers of the Way—including your mother—will supervise tanning the skins, preserving the fur, and harvesting the tusks of each mammoth. In addition, you will use a tiny laser to mark each item produced from the mammoth tusks, just like diamond cutters mark each diamond to identify its provenance, now."

"Very high-tech, for such an old craft."

Ikiaq grinned. "Like Snow House," he said.

"Flattery?"

He laughed, and then she did, caught by the strange juxtaposition that happened so often now: *The People*'s old ways intersecting the new. It fascinated her, like the movable electronic fences they'd finally designed for keeping the mammoths enclosed. Who would have thought they'd have *fences* across the permafrost? With *mammoths* inside?

Some day they would be able to free the herds to run wild across the Arctic tundra. But for now, their plans meant confining the animals to a small area to eat what the tundra offered, and to churn the soil to encourage re-freezing. Of course, it was absurd to imagine mammoths could re-create the Arctic permafrost entire, but slowly they might make a difference.

Ikiaq reached across the table and took her hand in his. They stared into each other's eyes, even after Osha walked past, *tsking* under her breath. Suluk knew her mother had remained a widow for all the years after Father's death with no regrets. But that did not mean Suluk had to. Opik was gone. Ikiaq was here. She could be happy, twice.

As Osha *tsked,* Maatalii smiled at her mother's joy. When Suluk met her daughter's gaze, both she and Maatalii grinned. Osha's opinion was Osha's. Maatalii and others were glad Suluk had found someone. Ikiaq had become her bed friend whenever he was in town, which was just about often enough to suit them both.

She only hoped Maatalii could find a good man for herself, for she deserved joy, as well. Suluk stood up and gave Ikiaq a peck on the cheek as she returned to the kitchen and her duties.

Maatalii's gaze passed over the whole of Snow House Inn, proud of its new incarnation. She was taking more photos for their brochure, trying to capture the mood she and Suluk had discussed, after looking at the unsatisfying pictures both her mother and Tarkik had taken. They wanted the brochure and website to show "cozy," "modern," and "welcoming." Tarkik's had been shiny, colorful, and kind of cheap, somehow. Her mother's were…awkward, oddly framed or focused on the background instead of the buildings. Plus no one had gotten a good interior shot of the rooms. She decided if she took a couple hundred photos, at least some of them should show what they wanted. They only needed three or four good ones.

She heard a car pull into the parking lot behind her, and turned to see who it was. She saw Sivoy walking over from the dog pens, and realized the newish four-wheel-drive vehicle belonged to his friend, the widow Hitty. And sometimes with Hitty, came her son Caiden. Hitty slammed the car door behind her and walked over to Uncle. Maati watched Sivoy give the widow a big hug, and wondered if the two of them were considering something permanent. A more formal joining than her mother had with Ikiaq.

Hitty laughed at something Sivoy said, and they walked together toward the dog pens where wagging tails greeted them. Aput had the bad manners to actually jump up, barking as if he greeted an old friend. Hitty patted his head as Sivoy tried to make him sit down.

Maatalii went back to taking pictures, then heard another car door slam. She glanced over her shoulder to see Caiden walking towards her from his mother's car.

"Heya," he said.

She smiled at him, wondering if she should comment how the sunlight shone on his stand-up white hair like the halo on a Christian angel. Deciding she didn't know him well enough to be direct, she just said, "Hi."

"I wanted to thank you for your idea and your work in promoting our CD," he said.

"Oh, do you think it has made a difference?" She'd linked the band's new CD to some obscure sites for self-produced music, and Inuit arts and crafts, and polar bear preservation sites. The "People of the Ice" disc had earned a number four or five spot on a couple of independent music "top ten" sites.

"It absolutely did," he said. "If nothing else, it's gotten us more airtime on a couple of important playlists, and has resulted in a couple hundred downloads of our single, "The Cub Lives." He grinned. "Linking it to polar bear rescue sites was genius."

She laughed. "Well, probably more annoyingly clever than genius, according to a couple messages I got from them, but I'm glad it worked for you. The Sisterhood is still getting orders for their music, too, which would never have even happened without your studio and your help."

"I'm glad. It's worked well for both of us." He cleared his throat and looked beyond her to the deep turquoise blue of the Inn. "Speaking of which, where's the cub?"

"We moved him out to the area by the caribou herd, to try and get him used to animals instead of people. He's old enough to be released into the wild, we think."

"Oh, I'd like to see him. Maybe he can inspire another winning single," his grin was crooked, self-deprecating.

"Well, *I'd* like to hear more," she said.

"You like our music?"

"Let's say I like, 'The Cub Lives.'" She waved her hands, trying to indicate her uncertainty. "I'm not sure I truly *like* some of the others, but I keep listening, trying to understand what you're doing."

A "that's probably good" kind of expression swept across his face. He said, "Okay, then. We were hoping to talk you into blowing a kind of drone background on a couple of our new songs."

"I just wonder—"she tilted her head, trying to find the right words. "I wonder how people will be able to hear the throat singing behind the..." *really loud* and *thrashy* didn't seem complimentary, but how else to say it? "Um, guitars and drums."

He nodded. "Yeah, it'll be a thrumming effect, maybe not distinguishable as throat singing so much as a rhythm drone. And of course, we'll balance the sounds out electronically, after it's recorded, and we'll maybe not have the bass player on those tracks."

"Okay, well let me know, I'll show up at the studio when you need me."

"Thank you Maati, I'll text you when we're ready."

She watched him walk away, glad that the sloppy-pants sagging revival was over and gone. His butt was cute in the fitted jeans.

◠

"We have a solution for plowing beneath the new restaurant at Snow House," Maatalii announced at the Sisterhood meeting. She glanced around. The group was crowded into the back half of the Gathering Room, as the front half was stuffed with props for the *"Good Book"* play. The Protestant minister who was one of the church's renters had written it for the village children to perform and the congregation had been perhaps overly enthusiastic in creating sets, props, costumes for it. The Sisterhood only had half as many tables for their meeting as usual.

Feeling she'd successfully gathered everyone's attention, Maati went on, "A new family is moving in. Farmers from America," she said.

"They have big enough plows?"

"I think so. They aren't here yet; Sivoy and I just talked to the real estate lady, what's her name over at the post office-real estate place."

"Oh, I know who you mean," someone said. "The red-hair lady."

"Yes," Maatalii said. Like the incoming farming family, the real estate lady was Anglo, and therefore not part of their women's group, though they'd tried to make her feel welcome in the community.

It was a bit shocking that a white farm family would consider coming to this place, but she was happy Snow House might have a way to get some deep plowing done. What Sivoy had accomplished with the borrowed mine equipment for the Inn's new foundation had worked really well. "They asked to talk to some local people before they came, because they wanted to know if there would be any other work opportunities for them on the farming off-season, if they should bring their big equipment."

They had a new Sisterhood member this season: Tarkik's fiancée Jissika, whom they had all finally met. She wasn't shy, that was certain. She interrupted Maatalii to say, "They also plan to try and grow wheat."

"That's crazy. Won't it freeze?" Osha said, pursing her lips.

"Not if the *Hot* keeps going north," Suluk put in. "Which we're all trying to prevent. Maybe they know more than we do."

Osha shook her head. "I read where the tree line has moved another couple meters north. Baby trees all over the place down there. Getting closer."

"Maybe the plows will dig up the trees," someone else said.

"Maybe the sun will go out and the *Hot* will die," snapped Meriwa, "as long as we're wishing."

Everyone kind of corner-of-the-eyes looked at her, then away. As usual, no one had a response for Meri's tart pessimism. Jissika was smiling, as if she'd thought Meri's comment was funny but even she didn't say anything.

Tarkik claimed Jissika was clever and witty, but no one else among the family and friends thought so, rather the opposite. Maatalii didn't feel she knew the young woman well enough to judge.

Maatalii skin-stitched a row of dots into Hitty's wrist, very careful of her work, with all the women watching. So far, she seemed to be doing a good job of copying the design into reality; or at least no one had yelled at her. Yet. She kept her attention on her work.

"Did Sivoy get the barn done?" One of the older women asked. "The barn for these new mammoth creatures?"

"Yes," Hitty and Maatalii said at the same time. Maati gestured for the older woman to go on.

"The barn is done, the supplies are in and the movable enclosures are set up around the caribou, for now. To try them out."

"How can a bitty fence keep a hairy elephant in?" Osha grumbled. Mammoths weren't part of the Ways; Osha was Keeper of the Ways, and mammoths and fences didn't fit into her mindset any better than Inuit rock and roll did. Maatalii hid her smile as Osha shook her head.

Suluk said, "They are used to fences. They've been kept fenced in since they were born, except the journey to get them onto the ship. It is in their minds that a fence is a wall, not a flimsy cage."

Maatalii added, "As long as there is plenty to eat, we expect them to stay within."

"Big mess if they don't," Osha said, and a couple other voices agreed.

"We will just hunt for them, if they get out," Suluk said, a cross tone to her voice.

Maatalii looked up, imagining dagger glares between her mother and grandmother, but the two women weren't even looking at each other. That was almost worse. What was the big conflict brewing between them? Was it just Osha's disapproval of Ikiaq? Because Ikiaq was a miner? Because they made no plans to marry, or did they have plans? Or was there more to it?

"What supplies," Jissika asked. "I thought they were supposed to eat tundra?"

Maatalii explained: "Well, the tundra is changing, and we cannot guarantee there will always be a place with enough grass and moss or lichen. They'll also eat meadow weeds, things like cushion plants and arctic poppies, arctic willow, bearberry," she went on. "But they need a *lot*. The people I contacted, suggested having plenty of hay and grains available for when the tundra doesn't supply enough for them."

"Costly," Osha said.

Meriwa snickered.

"The caribou paid for it," Suluk said. "And the mammoths themselves will, also."

"The caribou meat is also nicer if they get some grains, too, so it should pay off, as we can offer more and better meat," Maatalii added.

"I want to go see the barn and birthing stalls," Suluk said, looking at Maatalii.

"Yes. How about an outing tomorrow, for anyone that would like to come?" Maatalii glanced around the room. "We're letting the *nanook* cub free tomorrow, also; I know some people wanted to watch that."

Osha grumbled something Maati couldn't hear, but she saw her mother glare at the old woman and shake her head. As Keeper, Osha was not fond of new ideas, but it was going to take new ideas mixed with the old to keep Snow House alive. Maati loved learning about the old Ways, but some of them just no longer worked. She had wondered several times if she really was the best apprentice Keeper. She kept trying to adapt the Ways to present circumstances, but the Keeper was supposed to *keep*. Not change.

"Were you ever able to find seals and fish enough for the bear, Maati?" Hitty asked. "I know you wanted to give it experience with something besides caribou meat."

"Just what we need: polar bears attacking the caribou herds," Jissika said.

Maatalii had had just about enough negative commentary, but Osha beat her in replying.

"*Nanook* have always preyed upon caribou. What nation are you from?" Osha said, letting contempt enter her tone.

Several of the women chuckled, and Jissika turned red.

But, after all, Jissika's family were miners. What could they know about the wild? Jissika was used to something quite different from Qamanittuaq and its people. Neither Maati nor certainly Osha had ever been to Fifthslope, the mining camp that had become a rough town, where Jissika had grown up.

Maatalii set the threaded needle to soak in the ink and massaged her hands, which ached from the intricate work. "Sivoy and Ujurak managed to fish some salmon and grayling and char for *nanook*," she said. "They found a beluga carcass up north a ways, and also caught a couple of seals, so we're hoping the cub knows what to hunt for, at least by smell. I wish—well, we all wish we could have found a foster mother for it, but *nanook* have gone far north and east, to find the coldest cold. We did our best."

"Mmm," Osha the Keeper agreed. "Pray it survives."

⬤

The next day a group of about ten people, including a reporter for the local blog, joined Maatalii and Suluk for a tour of the mammoth barn, and the polar bear cub release. Maatalii thought the barn looked like pictures she had seen of big old barns in Canada and the United States, except it was not red. To be large enough for several mammoths, if needed, plus the storerooms for all the supplies she had learned they should have on hand, the barn was huge. Two stories tall and bigger than Snow House restaurant stacked on top of itself, she thought, looking at it. They'd gotten the metal siding in a medium gray, not wanting something too dark and absorbent nor too light and reflective.

Building enough piers to keep the big building up off the permafrost had been an enormous expense. Like all buildings in Qamanittuaq, it had to be on stilts to prevent further melting of the permafrost, even in such an empty building as a barn. It was unheated, but the animals themselves generated heat enough for the times they'd need to be shut in.

The corrugated metal roof was galvanized steel, put down with bolts and battened with rubber between steel beams to withstand blizzard winds. There was a narrow opening beneath the roof and under the eaves for ventilation. Inside, she demonstrated the winches, cables, and pulleys for getting hay up into the loft, and the barrels that held grains for the caribou and the mammoths. They had several simple tools for working with the great beasts, including a portable ultrasound and X-ray system that would help them diagnose injuries and pregnancies—all of which could be used for the caribou, also.

Maatalii had gone for two days to a special workshop near Quebec City, to learn how to use the ultrasound, and had taught Suluk, Sivoy, and Ujurak what she had learned. They all hoped they were ready to take care of these huge animals; they had taken many risks to try this plan for feeding themselves and others, and hopefully also rebuilding the arctic permafrost.

Osha clapped her hands and suggested it was time to release *nanook*. She led the way out of the barn.

About ten meters beyond the barn was the polar bear pen. They'd had a tricky time herding the cub from its old enclosure into the new. Sivoy had worked hard to create an igloo-like cold hut for it to sleep in, since there wasn't enough snow and ice to make a proper den, like its mother would have made. They fed it almost every day, leaving it to fast about once a week, as it might in the wild. They made sure it had access to freshwater, and also some seawater in a shallow pool for romping. Now Sivoy glanced around, making sure cameras were ready to record. People nodded, and he opened the gate, tying it open against the railing so if *nanook* cub panicked and wanted back in, it could easily do so.

Sniffing the air rather like a large creamy dog, the cub wandered along the fence line. Ujurak clasped a big prod they'd gotten for moving mammoths around, and held it ready in case the young bear came toward the group of people.

But it didn't. It wandered as far as the gate, then looked out, as if coming to realize nothing stood between it and the wide-open tundra. Cub took a couple of steps past the open gate, and looked over its shoulder at the group of human people, as if asking, "Are you sure?" Then it ambled further away from the fence, looked in both directions, and abruptly began galloping. It never looked back, as it gradually disappeared among the few humps of un-melted snow and tundra dotted with white flowers and patches of yellow-green lichen. Then it was gone.

Maatalii wiped her eyes with her sleeve, and noticed a couple others did the same. The whole community had cared about the polar bear cub, as if it was a symbol of their entire way of life. That it had survived seemed a miracle, and gave them hope that they could do the same. At least, that was her interpretation.

People went to their cars; no one had come on a slushski: there wasn't enough slush this late autumn. Maatalii decided to walk back, enjoying the cool, bright day. She waved Suluk and Sivoy on, and soon she was alone, heading west into the early-falling sun of the day.

She thought about vehicles for their ever-changing conditions. She and Sivoy had worked on converting the dog sleds to run on wheels for weather like this, when not enough snow covered the ground for a real dog sled. She had read of people in Alaska using their dog teams on such converted sleds, so tourists could get an idea of what sledding was like. The wheels mostly worked, except in places where the tundra had gotten boggy.

She walked off the road to see if she could mark off more of a trail for them to follow for the next batch of tourists who wanted a dog-sled experience. She passed back by the barn, admiring how professional the big building looked. Of course, after the first winter, it probably would not look so nice, but for now, they had gotten good photos for their ads for caribou and mammoth meat. The mammoths would arrive soon.

She passed the restaurant, heading to her little room in the back. They were going to be building a whole new building for the restaurant soon, but meanwhile she and Suluk still lived in the "temporary" ones Sivoy had thrown up for them while the Inn was being redone.

As she neared her door, she glanced past the row of new Inn rooms, past the parking lot, where she sensed movement at the far end of the airport runway. One of the tiny commuter planes was taxiing back toward the corrugated steel hut that, along with two run-down Quonset-style hangars, comprised their airport terminal. Walking toward her from where the plane would have turned around was a young, plump woman.

No. Not plump. Pregnant, she could see as the woman came down the slope into the parking lot, carrying a suitcase in each hand, awkward and unbalanced.

And not just any woman.

Amaruq.

She gasped in shock, and then began running. Ama stopped walking, set down her suitcases and waited for her *uaguk* to reach her. Maatalii laughed as she got closer and closer and could confirm, that yes, it was Amaruq. Their hug was fierce and happy.

Her *uaguk* had come home!

Carla sipped her second cup of black coffee and blinked her eyes, doing her best to stay awake. She stood beside Freja, the only person she recognized. She whispered, "Good morning" only receiving a tired nod in reply. A reveille of chirps and whistles by local birds serenaded the silent, jet-lagged crowd. She reviewed all the horror stories she'd heard about interns being required to wash lab equipment, repeat dull measurements, and do almost any menial labor except cleaning toilets.

She finished her coffee and took in the beautiful gardens, especially the vibrant bougainvillea. She recalled the worms. She loved those enormous friendly worms! She'd be willing to clean toilets to work with those worms.

Freja tapped her shoulder and pointed to Lesedi Marais approaching the group. She smiled an acknowledgment, thinking: This is it. Here we go.

"Welcome to your first full day at Mdudu Nyama. I'm Lesi. I hope you are all recovered from your travels and ready to get to work."

Scattered nervous laughter greeted this. Carla reflected that nerves and time zones prevented much recovery.

Lesi began, "For your intern project—"

When she paused, Carla squeezed Freja's hand.

Lesi continued, "—you will design a process to convert worms into hamburger."

Cheers and applause! Carla hadn't been the only one thinking about a summer of cleaning toilets.

"Best intern project ever!"

Freja said, "*Vidunderlig.*"

Everyone respectfully listened when Lesi continued. "Look at your badges. Evens are on the continuous process team, and odds are on batch processing."

Carla looked at Freja. They were together on the batch team. They celebrated with a high five.

At lunch, the batch team sat together. They all spoke some English. Everyone but Carla was drinking wine, but she talked as much and as loudly as the rest of them. "I'm going to be the envy of everyone in my class when I return to Chicago. Who lets undergraduates design an entire production process?"

Freja added, "Wow! *Ja!* An engineering dream project. During the live worm phase, temperature, oxygenation, pH, and moisture will all be critical. Then during the conversion phase—separation, enzymes, extrusion, and packaging. This project has *en lille smule* of everything."

After that, Carla knew she'd be best friends with Freja. The lady wasn't afraid of details.

A boy, who turned out to be from Johannesburg, bubbled with excitement. "I studied cheesemaking at Joburg Institute of Technology, a batch process that has developed over five to ten thousand years."

Another boy, who Carla thought looked Asian, interrupted with, "Hai! Hai!" before continuing in English, "Everyone read the specifications and we can divide the work at dinner."

The women read the specs while sitting in the rose garden and enjoying the afternoon sun. Freja noted, "A thousand kilos of mince per day."

Carla hadn't wasted her time growing up on a farm and attending school in Chicago, the U.S. meatpacking capital. She added, "That sounds like a lot, but U.S. production of hamburger is four orders of magnitude more!"

When they arrived at dinner, the Asian boy informed them, "You two girls are on moisture control."

Carla normally didn't mind being called a "girl," but the way he said it sounded derogatory and demeaning. She looked at Freja and could tell she'd had the same reaction. The rest of the team, all males, were silent. Before they could reply, the know-it-all from Joburg presented his preliminary system design.

Carla frowned. She whispered to Freja. "Who do they think they are? I'd rather clean toilets than take orders from those arrogant jerks."

Freja gave her a little smile. "We'll show them."

That night Lesi invited them all out to a night of drinking. Everyone had changed out of their professional clothes. The men wore loose, colorful shirts, heavy necklaces, and tight pants. The women wore their hair loose, with bare midriffs, and makeup. Carla happily spotted Freja, who like her, had not changed from her daytime attire.

Freja smiled at her. "I guess we didn't get the memo."

Carla gave her an impulsive hug. "I hope they're not too disappointed when they discover I don't drink."

"Me neither," was the surprising reply.

"What about at lunch?"

Freja laughed, "Æble most. Apple juice."

Lesi led the increasingly rambunctious mob through the streets of Stellenbosch. First, they sampled a few pubs, where Lesi praised the food and warned everyone to eat. Next came a winery, followed by a brewery.

Lesi bragged, "This tour is just a sampling. We have plenty more of everything."

Around midnight, "We'll end the evening at a special place. The Stellenbosch Distillery. Gin. The best gin, just to remind you that the Dutch invented it."

Everyone laughed and enjoyed their drinks, but Carla and Freja never felt the need to join in. Stellenbosch also offered a wide variety of excellent sparkling ciders and ginger beers, some with quite a bite.

The evening ended with the teams trash-talking each other as they stumbled back to their rooms.

"Your batch design is just a glorified model railroad."

"Continuous is just a new name for an assembly line, a failed idea from the 20th century."

"Batches are for bakeries, not serious production. Did you ever hear of a batch petroleum refinery?"

Laughs all around. "Refineries? Yet another failed 20th-century idea." Carla retorted. "We just toured a gin distillery. Perhaps you noticed: it's a batch process. As is beef production." More laughter.

The design meeting was delayed to the afternoon. Freja started, "You all understand moisture control is critical. Too much water and the worms drown. Too little and they suffocate."

Carla continued their slide presentation. "We evaluated the proposed system design." She emphasized the word *proposed* to give notice to the cocky guy from Joburg. "We rejected the climate-controlled enclosure. That approach uses the most energy. Wasteful designs like this brought on the *Hot* in the first place. It would be irresponsible to continue such practices.

The Joburg student said, "That's the way cheese is manufactured."

Carla snapped back. "You said that cheese technology was five-thousand years old. Surely we can do better."

Before he could reply, Freja put up their next slide. "Efficient Controls."

Carla explained how an array of sensors and controls for drainage, water sprayers, turners, and composition of the growth medium would work. Another slide. Freja showed them her mechanical design.

The two arrogant boys who must have felt themselves losing control protested. "The control software will be too complicated. You'll never finish on time."

Freja and Carla smiled at each other. Carla started up a simulation package and ran an animation of the prototype control software. Now the silent men spoke up. "Well done!" and "You are two talented ladies!"

The two arrogant guys meekly asked, "Can you help us with our control software?"

National Women's Day in August released everyone for a three-day weekend. Ashur organized an excursion to climb Table Mountain. Since this was her first opportunity to leave Stellenbosch, she signed up. She and Freja skipped the cable car and hiked to the top.

Lesi scheduled a demonstration day for the end of August. Much like they'd been accused, the batch design looked like a miniature railroad from a kiddie amusement park.

Everything worked smoothly, especially the moisture control. However, the guy from Joburg's design for final packaging failed, spraying hamburger over everyone to joyful cries of, "It's not cheese, is it?" and "Cheesy design!"

Carla, Freja, and two men from Scotland stayed up all night adapting a sausage casing machine for packaging. Though they were all exhausted, the demo went well, or at least as well as the competing continuous processing demo.

The next national holiday was Heritage Day in September which was informally called Barbeque Day. The Mdudu Nyama marketing team took the opportunity for a huge event featuring their hamburger meat. This event included eating competitions, races, dances, and a carnival. The engineers scorned the marketing commotion, and most arranged to be out of town in a preemptive move to avoid being drafted to grill hamburgers or talk to the public on the benefits of worm-based meat.

Carla signed up for another of Ashur's excursions. This one was four days and included a fifteen-hour drive to Namibia. She ended up in Ashur's car with Freja. They were headed to Sossusvlei.

Carla knew nothing of Sossusvlei and little of Namibia. "Are we really driving fifteen hours to see sand dunes? When I lived in Oklahoma, we had lots of them."

One of the other engineers laughed. "Well, I never heard of Oklahoma."

Ashur, who seemed to be the international traveler, said, "I've heard of Oklahoma, but I've never been. I have been to Dallas, Texas. I think that's close."

Carla was surprised that anyone had been to the United States. "*Yebo.* Only a couple of hundred miles." Then she corrected herself. "About three hundred kilometers."

She napped. The drive offered a nice break from her long hours. She also took her turn driving as there were no eRoads. When they crossed the Orange River at the Noordoewer border post, Carla took out her new passport. When everyone else just showed their comp, she apologized. "I've heard the United States will be introducing ePassports soon."

Ashur assumed the role of the trip guide. "We're entering Namibia and about to transition from grapes to the desert."

Freja added, "We're also at the western edge of the Kalahari basin."

When everyone gave her a questioning look, she added, "I looked it up. I like to do my homework." Carla winked at her friend, who had saved their project more than once by doing her homework.

In an apparently internationally recognized joke, one of the engineers asked, "Are we there yet?"

Before Ashur said anything, Freja jumped in with, "Halfway." No one was surprised this time.

After a couple of hours driving through Namibia, Ashur tapped the driver's shoulder. "Break time." Carla knew the drill. The boys would walk off to the left side of the caravan and all line up facing away from the cars. The girls would go to the right and form a privacy wall facing toward the cars. One at a time the women would go behind them and take advantage of the protective barrier.

With the bathroom ritual complete, they all gathered around a plant with wide leaves that looked like it was dying in the desert. Freja exclaimed, "Look at that, *Welwitschia mirabilis*!"

Ashur continued. "Only found in Namibia. Don't let the impression that this is a waste pile fool you. This one is over five hundred years old and others have survived twice as long."

By the next break, Carla had seen enough desert scrubland. She was glad when the driver turned west off the main road. Soon they passed a couple of motels and suddenly they were surrounded by the grandest, pristine, pink-orange dunes. Carla could only say, "Wow!" She realized that she'd seen these flying to Cape Town. "They look so much larger from the ground!"

The sudden transition to something so startling paralyzed her. Eventually, she started taking pictures.

Freja narrated. "This sand has been carried off the Kalahari Desert by the wind. The Namib desert is the world's oldest, over fifty million years."

Later, Ashur announced, "That is Dune Seven, the highest. It is a good place to stop for pictures and facilities."

Eventually, they got to climb dunes and slide down on the warm, soft sand. Carla promised herself she'd return. But for now, this was an excellent climax to her time in Africa.

◡

It was still dark when the truck stopped and announced, Big Bend Dam. Mike's heart pounded when he heard the Missouri crashing through the turbines and the whine of the generators. He jumped out and grabbed his backpack. Sasha gave the lady a goodbye kiss.

Then Mike remembered his manners. "Thank you, ma'am." He offered his hand.

She shook it. "Have a good camping trip, if that's what you are doing."

He watched her get back into the cab shaking her head with a smile.

She commanded the truck's nav system. "Resume the previous destination." The door slid closed and she was gone.

The water rushing through the power station hummed as he ran across the dam with Sasha. He wanted to start the next part of his escape under darkness. The sun glanced across the prairie.

High water had peaked a month ago, but the Big Muddy still flaunted its power. The turbid water rushed south. He moved among the upturned boats and rafts, some with motors. For his purpose, he wanted something small, difficult to spot from the sky, a raft. He rejected brightly colored rafts. Red, yellow, white all would show up against the brown river.

Finally, he saw a faded green one, maybe army surplus. He flipped it over and slid it toward the river. With his pack and Sasha in place, he eased it in. Fortunately, he had a firm grip on the grab rope because the current whipped the raft downstream dragging him behind.

Sasha stood in the raft barking as if to say: climb aboard, you're going to drown.

He held on as the water poured over his limp body. He coughed and gasped as the current tried to strip off his clothes. He had visions of the Troopers finding his corpse floating into the Mississippi at Saint Louis. The waves crashed over him making it hard to think. His hands cramped, and the rope caused blisters and broke them. All he could do was hold on.

Then he was shot out of the narrow spillway and the water calmed. He scrambled aboard. By the time the sun rose, he had passed Dignity, the 50-foot-tall Native woman, and was on his way to Fort Randall.

At Fort Randall, Mike left South Dakota and the Missouri River. He still had a long way to go before reaching Cherokee, but he decided heading due south, cross country, avoiding the well-traveled routes, would be best.

It took weeks of sleeping in fields, hunting rabbits, stealing chickens, and raiding kitchen gardens before he arrived in Cherokee. He slept among the grazing cattle and watched Elzia's house. During the day, the compound buzzed with activity. The first time Sasha saw Elzia, she started to run towards her, but Mike held her tight. After that, she stayed hidden.

At night, the workers disappeared, but Elzia's parents were always home, or when they went out, she went with them. After three days, he was exhausted, hungry, and desperate. *So close, yet so far.* The next morning, market day or church, nicely dressed workers deserted the ranch. His heart beat excitedly as he watched Elzia head for the barn. Still, there were too many people milling around. He didn't dare approach her.

He moved through a feedlot, from feeder to feeder, from pile of manure to pile of manure, paralleling Elzia, approaching the barn. Just when he thought he was close enough to call to her, three men exited the barn. Sasha whined and again moved toward Elzia. Mike rubbed her side. "Go get her, but don't attract any attention."

Sasha stood up, raised her head, and casually strolled across the yard. There were other dogs, but she just ignored them like she'd been here all her life. She stopped at a water trough and took a relaxing drink. She walked through a small group of chickens. They ignored each other.

Mike held his breath as Sasha approached Elzia. She immediately recognized the Newfie. He could see her restrained reaction as she looked around. "Where is he?"

Sasha led her to the feedlot.

Elzia stood next to Sasha and spoke to a pile of manure. "I was worried about you. I haven't been able to connect to you and your picture has been online. They say you are a bioterrorist, causing algae blooms, poisoning fish and livestock."

He raised his head so she could read his lips. "I haven't been online for a month. Electronic tracking. I arrived a few days ago, but you're never alone."

"Come back tonight. There is a big celebration. I'll get out of it." His heart beat a million times a second. He didn't know if he could wait. Finally, he just found a fallow field and fell asleep behind an empty water trough.

She greeted him at the back door, but as he moved closer, she retreated. "You need a bath and some clean clothes. We keep some for the ranch hands."

This was his first chance to clean up since he left Big Muddy at Fort Randall. He got in the shower and ran the water as hot as he could stand it. Sasha joined him, and the water ran as muddy as the Missouri for a long time. He put on the second-hand, but clean, clothes and went to Elzia's room.

She hugged him. "We have so much to talk about. Where should we start?"

He took a deep breath. "How much time do we have?"

She smiled, "Hours, two or three."

"Food. Can you make me a hamburger?"

She gave him an odd look.

"It's been a month of rabbit, stringy, tough, wild rabbits and old, egg-laying hens. And vegetables...farm garden vegetables, mostly raw. I bet Sasha would love some dog food. Kibbles. At first, she seemed to like rabbit meat, but I think she's had enough."

After dinner, he asked, "Are they still looking for me?"

"Oh yes. I see reports on the manhunt, stories about algae blooms, and your picture regularly."

"What should I do? I'm not turning myself in. I don't trust them."

"First, I like your new beard. You should keep it. Second, you should keep cleaned up. It's less suspicious."

"I still have my comp, but I don't dare turn it on."

She went over to her closet where she opened and closed boxes. "Here it is!" She handed him a beat-up comp. "This is mine from elementary school. The camera and speakers don't work. It hasn't had a data plan for years, but if you can find a free WiFi, it will connect."

He handed her his comp. "I can't use this."

She refused his comp and handed him a piece of paper. "Keep yours. It might be useful later. Here's my email from middle school. Use that to contact me."

The conversation stopped. They held hands and looked at each other. Then a bright light shone through her window.

"My parents! They're home."

"Where should I go?" He grabbed the old comp and his backpack and ran. Sasha gave Elzia a sloppy kiss and followed.

She yelled to him. "Canada. Go to Canada."

Canada, he thought. "Good idea. After all, my mother's moving the farm up there. But how am I going to get to Canada?"

She laughed. "You made it here from South Dakota. You'll figure out something."

He gave her a quick hug and disappeared out the back door as her parents unlocked the front.

29. KACZKA, ROSHNI—INDIA, KARINA—SRI LANKA

The former terrorists had taken over the communal kitchen to prepare for *Ganesh Chaturthi.* Never able to resist a new cuisine, Kaczka toured the prep counters. His curiosity took him to a woman in an orange and yellow sari dusted with flour. It looked like she was making dim sum, *xiao long bao* steamed dumplings. He recognized most of her ingredients: flour, ghee, coconut, and cardamom. However, she was grating a large brown block of something. "What is that? Is it some kind of cheese?"

The woman raised it into the air. "Did you hear that? Our famous *chef* asked it this might be cheese!"

That filled the air with merriment. One lady exclaimed, "Do Hindus even eat hard cheese?"

The room responded gleefully with, "No," "Never," "Of course, not."

The woman in the floor-covered sari handed the block to Kaczka. It was heavy and hard, like a brown Parmesan, but it didn't smell like cheese. She pushed it to his face. "Lick it. Taste it."

He couldn't bring himself to lick it, but he broke off a piece to taste. "Sweet!"

"Yes. That is jaggery. Heat the sugarcane juice, add lime to clarify, and pour into molds."

Someone added, "Natural, healthy, and good for the planet. Low carbon footprint."

He took another taste. It was more like molasses than refined sugar. "What are you making?" he asked.

"These are coconut *modaks*, a special sweet for *Ganesh Chaturthi.*" She pointed with her nose around the kitchen. The others are making peanut, chocolate, sesame seed, and mixed fruit varieties."

He took pictures of everything and made notes. This would be another recipe to add to the Future Foods archive.

On the day of the festival, Kaczka wore loose pants and a white linen shirt, the same as most of the men. The men put the five-meter Ganesh Shrine on rollers and the parade followed Ganesh to his resting place in front of the pagoda where they were greeted with a table stacked high with *modaks*. The children rushed to grab one in each hand and ran to the paddock to paint elephants.

Kaczka scanned the crowd to locate Vadish, curious as to how he was getting on with his former adversaries. To his surprise, he found him with the elephants. He had a small girl sitting on his shoulders, painting butterflies on an elephant's ear with one hand, and feeding Vadish a *modak* with the other.

"I'm glad to see you making peace with the former demonstrators. I need to talk. Can you return that lovely girl to her parents?"

When Vadish set her down, she stuffed the remainder of the *modak* in her mouth and took off to join some other children.

"I'm off to Maine, in the U.S. I need to organize the new Mammoth Ranch."

Vadish looked puzzled. "Do you need me to go there?"

"No. I've convinced Karina to delay college a semester to foster those mammoths until I can find them a forever home."

"Then, what's happening to the research station here in Kerala?"

"It needs to be something else. I was thinking it could be a tourist attraction. Imagine this!" He raised his hands pantomiming a marquee. "Elephant sanctuary! Tourist Cabins! Wouldn't that be grand?"

Vadish crossed his arms and took a deep breath. "I think it's time to do something for the people of Kerala."

"I agree. Tourism provides jobs."

"No. We can do better."

Kaczka looked at his comp. He'd have to leave soon if he didn't want to miss his plane. He turned to his driver. "I have to talk to Vadish a bit longer. Fetch my suitcases and bring the car around."

He checked his comp again before addressing Vadish. "What are you suggesting?"

"We have farms, a laboratory, a power station, and even a town hall. Let's make a new town and do something with the lab?"

Kaczka imagined the new town. Families in the bungalows. Children and sacred cows rambling through the streets. Workers, in groups of threes and fives, going to the fields each morning. A farmers' market each weekend. That could work. But—"What could you possibly do with the lab?"

Vadish lit up. "Lots of things. People have been trained at the research station. Maybe IVF, or forensics, or medical tests. Lots of things."

This seemed like a stretch for rural India. Before Kaczka voiced his doubts, Vadish interrupted with his most outlandish idea. "A pharmaceutical company! We could manufacture generic drugs."

"A pharmaceutical company? Are you going to run that?"

"Obviously, not me. But *Inshallah*. God willing."

God willing for sure. With a plane to catch and no time to argue, he left it to fate. His car pulled up and Kaczka jumped in. "*Inshallah*. If you can organize something, I won't stand in your way, but if you can't, tourist cabins!"

As the car rushed to the Muslim Gate, Muvattupula, and the Cochin Airport beyond, stragglers, still walking down the road for *Ganesh Chaturthi*, leaped out of the way. Kaczka noticed a woman with a bundle on her shoulders. He thought he recognized her, but his car zipped by too fast to be certain.

━

It had been a week since she'd mourned Indrakshi. The march across Tamil Nadu had given her time to think. Klara. Indrakshi. Niraj. Fifteen years of deaths. Every night she went to bed with the same thought: Death doesn't make any sense.

Finally, they reached the beach. Karina threw off her shoes and ran across the sand. "Ocean. The Indian Ocean. We're Here!" Some of the animals followed her example and together they splashed in the surf. The ocean stretched to the horizon inviting her to imagine a limitless future. It was time to think ahead, not of the past. As before, she refused to spend the rest of her life in mourning. Many resurrected mammoths needed her. Important adventures ahead.

A fast boat roared out of the surf and a man vaulted onto the beach pulling the mooring line. Karina rushed over to help him pull his boat out of the waves.

Once his boat was secured on the beach, he turned to Karina. He reached out his hand. "I'm Basu. Are you Priya? I saw the mammoths."

She shook his hand. "Those are the mammoths, but I'm not Priya. She's older."

By then Priya had arrived. "Are you Basu?"

He offered her his hand. "Yes, that's me."

With his attention shifted, Karina looked at him. He only wore a dhoti. His bare chest displayed the quiet strength of a laborer. Whatever remained of their journey, she had confidence he would help them the final leg of the trip. He flashed a big smile of brilliant white teeth and bounced up and down with excitement. "Are those the mammoths? Is that really what they looked like? Were they that red, and brown, and *blonde*?"

Karina felt a pang of regret, sorry he hadn't met Indrakshi. She couldn't wait to introduce him to the other mammoths. "Come over here. I'll take you closer, but remember they are wild animals, not pets."

When he followed her, she felt grown up, not fifteen.

Basu walked around them, still bouncing like a child. "I expected more fur on their trunks and bigger ears."

He picked up some hair from the ground. "Wow. I never expected this to be so fine and soft."

He opened his comp. "Can I take some pictures?"

Priya interrupted. "Sure, but don't show them to anyone until we're gone."

Karina took that as a hint, to back away.

After many pictures, he asked, "How can I speed you on your way?"

Priya replied, "We've been traveling for over a month. Hopefully, we're close to Sri Lanka, Talaimannar Pier, and our ship to America."

He laughed. "Close is a relative term."

Karina laughed. He's got a good sense of humor.

Priya was serious. "Close enough for your ships to carry us across the Palk Strait. You did promise to get us to Sri Lanka, didn't you?"

Karina wondered if something she'd done had made Priya grumpy.

He laughed again. "No and yes."

Karina wanted to shake Priya. He's a good guy. Give him a break.

Priya just scowled, "What do we have to do?"

Karina worried, she didn't want to chase him away, but then he stopped laughing and became serious. "You need to get to the Adam's Bridge. The *Hot* has made this easier."

He seemed to be waiting for her response.

Karina mouthed okay willing Priya to respond.

Finally, Priya said, "*Easier* sounds good. Then what?"

"The Thondi-Rameswaram levee, built to hold back the rising seas, has cut the distance to the Adam's Bridge. Follow the levee to Dhanushkodi, a tourist town at the foot of the bridge. I'll meet you there in a week."

"Are we going to walk across the Adam's Bridge?"

"Of course not. The bridge is a maze of checkpoints and border agents. Traffic between India and Sri Lanka, even after years of peace, is tightly controlled."

"Then how do we get across?"

Instead of answering, he ran down the beach and boarded his boat. When he disappeared into the waves, Priya turned to Karina. "Why couldn't he just tell us the plan, instead of making us blindly follow his instructions?"

Karina now understood why Priya had been grumpy and thought less of bare-chested Basu.

They started across the Thondi-Rameswaram wetlands—a wildlife preserve reclaimed by the levee. The marsh seemed to distract the animals from their sadness. The elephants sprayed each other. The mammoths splashed and rolled in the shallow water. Karina was glad to see them playing. She thought, there's so much more to life than mourning.

At first, the mammoths ran everywhere and flushed flocks of herons, egrets, and kingfishers. Eventually, the birds got used to the rambunctious visitors and settled out of reach.

As Basu had predicted, one week later they reached Dhanushkodi. Karina didn't want Priya and Basu to butt heads again, so she suggested, "This place will be swarming with border patrol agents. A girl like me will attract less attention. I can pass as a tourist. Let me go find Basu." Priya agreed. Karina walked into town among the souvenir shops and tour boat captains.

He found her. "Blonde girl! There you are. Right on time."

She knew Priya wanted to know the plan, so she tried to pry it from him. "Will your boats meet us here?"

"Yes, I have three fishing boats coming tonight."

"Three? Fishing boats? We have over a hundred tons of animals!"

"Well, that's what I expected. Let me teach you a little archeology."

"Archeology?" She wondered where this was going but was always eager to learn something new.

"The first elephants got to Sri Lanka, many millennia ago, by swimming."

"Elephants can swim? Really?"

He got serious. "All mammals except some primates can swim. Elephants can swim over fifty kilometers and they're fast—twenty-five kilometers per hour. I assume mammoths are similar."

"Wow. I didn't know that. The mammoths are so big. I thought they'd sink."

He flashed those teeth. "You'll see soon enough. They float and use their trunks as snorkels, so the border patrol won't see anything but a few fishing boats in the dark."

"Perfect. I feel like I'm already on the ship headed for the Cape of Good Hope, and North America beyond that."

◡

When Roshni saw the Muslim Arch, she thought: Is this the end of my quest? The familiar sights filled her with desires: warm meals, clean clothes, comfortable beds, scientists, elephants.

She untied the bundle holding her few possessions, searching for a small sack she'd been saving. She found it—a rice offering for Ganesh. When she passed through the arch, Ganesh, once reaching five meters into the sky, was gone. She'd gone hungry to save something for Ganesh, but he was gone. Like the wrath of Shiva, a panic attack hit her. Her legs shook, tumbling her to the ground. Her heart thundered. Her sweating hand clenched the bag of rice. *Ganesh do not forsake me.*

When consciousness returned, she realized this was the first panic attack since she'd left the docks. Did her desire for the Ganesh Shrine trigger her panic? One thought filled her mind: Desire nothing, give up all desires and be happy.

She emptied her mind and continued east, concentrating on each step: lift, swing forward, heel, toe, shift weight, repeat. A black car almost hit her, but she didn't let it upset her meditation or deter her from her path.

First, she saw the administration building with its tiers of steeply pitched tile and painted a bright red. As she got closer, she saw the Ganesh Shrine. *How did you get there?* She could hear the excitement of a celebration. *Ganesh*

Chaturthi, she realized. Her hand still held the rice offering. Vadish would be nearby and she didn't dare let him see her.

She left her bundle beside the lab and took the *pallu* end of her sari to cover her head and face. When she passed the food tables, she could not resist the delicious *modaks*. When she finally reached the Ganesh Shrine, she dropped the rice into his offering bowl. Ganesh help me, she prayed.

She went around the back of the pagoda and found a place to spend the night. The setting sun lit up the Western Ghats. Tomorrow, I will continue east. She thought about retrieving her bundle, but there were too many people. Maybe tomorrow morning, she thought. Years ago, I arrived here empty-handed. I can leave empty-handed.

"Wake up, Dr. Roshni Teertha."

She opened her eyes, but the rising sun blinded her. Who could have found her? No one had called her by her title in years. "Vadish?"

"Who else? I brought you some breakfast."

She held out her wrists. "Are you going to arrest me?"

He sat down next to her in the wet grass. "Obviously not. Allah has sent you. Kaczka wants to turn this place into a tourist attraction."

She wondered why he wasn't arresting her, and why he was going on about tourists. "I am following my right path. Today I'll continue east to find my Karma. Even if you're not arresting me, Kaczka or the Intelligence Bureau will."

Vadish reached his arms out to hug her, but she backed away and he stopped. *What has gotten into him? Has he forgotten I kidnapped his daughter?*

"The IB has known you were living on the docks for a while, they closed your case. Allah forgives all sins."

She found this hard to believe, but that still left Kaczka. She had also abducted *his* daughter.

As if Vadish had read her mind, he continued. "And Kaczka? As soon as he heard you had to beg for food, you stopped being a terrorist and became hungry. You know Kaczka loves all the hungry people."

Her thoughts went to Ganesh. *What do you want me to do?*

She wanted Vadish to leave and let her eat her breakfast in peace, but he kept chattering on. "I don't want another tourist center. I want something productive that the people of Muvattupula and Kerala can be proud of—a new town and a pharmaceutical company. Kaczka won't let us do it without a chief scientist."

"Are you asking me to be the chief scientist? Again? After all I've done? Will Kaczka agree?"

"Obviously, yes, yes, and yes."

Her heart pounded. She could feel another panic attack coming. Not two in a single day! She reached out her hands and whispered, "Tell me again," before she passed out.

191

When she awoke, Vadish still held her hands and was repeating, "We forgive you."

She still feared this was desire tempting her.

Vadish repeated. "We need you."

She thought, happiness is making other people happy. She looked around the corner of the pagoda and saw the Ganesh Shrine glowing in the rising sun. For an instant, it looked like the statue was smiling. "I'll do it."

Vadish agreed, "*Inshallah*."

30. XIANG BO, ZI MIN—HUIXIAN CHINA

Zi Min and Xiang Bo flew from Hechi to Guilin like old pros. Zi Min's headphones never left her ears, and she rarely looked up from her reader, wholly absorbed in her newest favorite book. Xiang Bo had taken the window seat this trip, and looked out at drought-ridden forests and fields until, quite depressed enough, she turned on her laptop and wasted time with a Solitaire game until they landed in Guilin.

Li's call had sounded frantic. This time the diatom-algae had really escaped. Li's most recent journey to the Huixian fields had sent him into panic mode. He had actually called Mo Chou, who had then driven halfway to Nalai where she'd been able to reach Xiang Bo by cell phone at last.

"He said to tell you he found the white diatoms, live ones, in the ponds. He also found dead ones on the banks of the stream that runs into the Li River."

"That is bad," Xiang Bo had managed, feeling overwhelmed with this news. She had to book flights immediately.

Mo Chou asked, "Do you need me to come feed the chickens?"

"I don't know how long I will need to be gone to clean up this mess," she said. And she needed someone to look after the vat project. "Ugh. Did you say that student that was boarding at the Dawn House still needed a job?"

"Yes!" Mo Chou said, sounding very relieved. "Quan Song. Can *he* do it?"

"Please ask. Then maybe drive him down here. He is, of course, welcome to stay and live in the house here and eat from our garden. I have a project here I need someone to keep an eye on and update me about from time to time. If he doesn't mind driving back to Donglan every day."

"I think his classes are only two or three days a week, so that could work out well for him."

"I can even pay him a small bit, if he does a good job."

That arranged, it had been a small matter to book their flights, drive to Hechi and be on their way to Guilin.

Li was there to meet them and drive them "home," as he'd said. She'd tried to hide her flinch at that. The Cheng family compound still did not feel like her home. Maybe that was her fault, for not allowing Di'e a mother's place in her heart.

She did enjoy Di'e's company, and Ming-Hua's. Li seemed to be trying to reach out, to be friendly and welcoming.

"How are your classes going?" she asked, opening a dialogue between them on a neutral topic.

"Very well," Li said. "I have a full schedule now, three classes each term. Of course, two of them are beginning biology, they always need someone to teach those and the simple labs that go with them. But at least one class each term is in the advanced subjects, sometimes with a specific lab topic attached."

"Those are more fun, aren't they?" she said, remembering how much he had enjoyed working with the higher division students.

"They've been asking me to have you come and teach at least a one-day lecture, or maybe do a seminar on your research projects."

She groaned. "First, I have to fix this one."

"It's definitely not a false alarm, this time. It's taking over the other ponds, even the ones without fish. And then the fish show up in them too, somehow…"

"Dropped by birds, maybe?"

He shrugged, his hands loose on the steering wheel. "Maybe they jump, or there're small breaks in the levees, or eggs somehow get transferred. Besides the birds, we've discovered *xeong* in there too. I've read some papers—what do they call them in English?"

"Raccoons."

"Yes. Fat little wash-bears. They could certainly be transferring both the algae and the fish. But not the rice. Without the rice, the ponds are completely covered in a flat layer of white."

Xiang Bo shook her head. "My governor is definitely broken. I should have come and checked it more closely last time."

Zi Min's voice floated over the seat, "Mama, can I see the *xeong*?"

"They are the same as we have in Nalai."

"There are just more of them," Li said. "Many more. They have taken over from the birds, now that the fish are harder for the birds to see beneath the white skin."

Xiang Bo scowled and said, "Maybe growing food in vats is the right idea. With fields, the people are going hungry, while raccoons get fat."

⬬

Dismay was easy for Zi Min to read on her mama's face as they stared at the white fields at the Huixian site. Zi Min searched for raccoons, but these probably only came out at night, like the ones at Nalai did.

"I think they may have mutated," Cheng Li said.

Zi Min still had trouble thinking of him as "Papa." It did not sound right.

"They're glowing at night," he said.

Xiang Bo's eyebrows went way up. "The *diatom-algae* glow?"

Li nodded.

"Oh," Mama said. "That's very bad. You are right, they must have mutated. I certainly did not design them with bio-luminescence. "I wonder if…" she drifted off.

"The lab is still all set up in the compound," Li said.

Xiang Bo grimaced. "All right."

"I know you think I sabotaged your work, earlier, Xiang Bo. But I would not ever do that."

She turned at looked him in the eye. "No?"

"Not ever." He shook his head firmly. "But I am starting to think Wei might have." His frown and his thoughts seemed distant. "I keep finding odd little discrepancies in his lab notes and reports in my own work. And your trial dishes were in the shared lab at that time, when he was still working here."

Zi Min wondered who Wei was. He did not sound very nice.

"Are you in touch with him?" Xiang Bo asked Li.

Li shook his head. *Papa*. "No, I tried to reach him at his old address, and he's gone."

Xiang Bo opened her mouth like she was going to say something, but Zi Min saw her close it again, and rub her mouth like she did when she was thinking and didn't want to be disturbed.

Zi Min did not understand all the science her parents—that sounded strange: parents—were talking about. But she could certainly sense that something had gone wrong. She waited in silence to be sure they had both stopped talking. Then she said, "Can I come back tonight to see the glow? And the *xeong*?"

Mama gave her a quizzical look and laughed. "Yes. I suppose I should see them, too."

"Maman has planned a special welcome dinner," Li said.

"We will of course spend the evening with her and her meal," Mama said. "We can come back here afterward."

Li nodded.

Grandma—Zi Min would have to get used to calling Di'e *Ya-ya*, now. That did not seem quite right, either. Maybe she could call her *Maman*, like Mama and Li—*Papa*—did. She would have to ask her mother if that would be okay. Maman had obviously worked hard to make a nice dinner to welcome Zi Min and her mother.

But tensions were high, and Mama was obviously worried. Then things got worse. Zi Min heard a loud rapping at the compound gate. Papa left the table to answer it.

"Courier delivery," he said, returning with a big envelope he handed to Mama.

They all stared at her mother as she opened it.

"Oh," Xiang Bo said, reading. "It's a summons from the Party Secretary of Guangxi Autonomous Region." She cleared her throat and scanned the document as the family watched her. "I'm to appear and present a report on the fish-farm project to the Guangxi Party Secretary. Oh, no. It's about 'white, glowing ponds' in the district." Lips tightly pressed together, Mama put the letter back into the envelope and kept her eyes on her plate as she picked up her sticks and took a rather unenthusiastic bite of rice.

Ya-ya seemed so disappointed. Her banquet, made to welcome Zi Min and her mother back to the Cheng compound, had been disrupted by the delivery of the summons.

Zi Min, sensing the unease around the table, tried to put the focus back on the meal, complimenting her Cheng grandmother on the food. Each course was small but tasty, and smelled so good.

Di'e blinked away tears and smiled at her, and Zi Min felt proud she had helped, at least a little.

After dinner, after she helped clear the table and wash the dishes, she ran to her bedroom and grasped the tiny pot of *Ya-Ya* Bai Jaio's ashes. She gulped as she slipped past the bedroom where Li and Mama were talking. She smiled brightly at *Ya-Ya* Di'e and Ming-Hua, even though he couldn't see her, and made her way quietly out to the ancestor shrine.

The real ancestors' shrine!

She bowed to the statues, pots, boxes, and offering dishes that were already there, then carefully placed *Ya-Ya* Jiao beneath the leaves of a big rhododendron plant. She placed the bites of food from dinner she had snuck into her pocket onto a rock beside the pot, promising to get an offering dish soon. When she left, she again bowed to the ancestors, begging them to accept the Zhuang woman they had never met.

Later, Zi Min followed her mother as she walked along the levees between ponds, scooping up tubes of water and white stuff and labeling them.

Li, *Papa,* held a flashlight so Mama could see what she was writing, and then flashed the beam back on the pond for the next scoop.

"Do you think you would like to come to Yangshuo University with me tomorrow, Zi Min?" Dr. Cheng Li asked. Papa.

"Oh. Am I allowed, Papa?"

He smiled at her. "Of course. You would only be able to sit in on my own classes, at least for now, but you might find them interesting. Your...mother says you love looking at slides and data in her little lab at your home in Nalai. You might enjoy seeing a great big lab where the students learn about studies like Dr. Bai Xiang Bo's."

Zi Min bounced on her toes. "I would like that." She almost asked why Mama's name wasn't Dr. Cheng Xiang Bo, but like a flash from the flashlight, she realized that would not be a good question right now.

Li smiled at her gently. "You might want to bring your reader, in case some of the day gets a little boring. I won't mind if *you* read in my class."

She saw Mama look back at them over her shoulder, eyebrows raised. Zi Min hopped over the soggy part of the embankment.

"I'll bring my reader, but I think it might be fun all day."

"Ming-Hua, this is for you to do," Di'e said, holding her older son by the shoulders.

He shook his head. "I am no politician, Maman," he said.

"No one is a politician until they are," she said, voice firm. "You will learn. You will become."

He groaned, spreading his arms out helplessly. "I can barely play in public, much less speak, and to prowl for votes may be beyond me."

"It will be good for you," Di'e said. She would not let him squirm out of this. It could be the answer to their prayers, both for him and for their home. "There is an opening on the Huixian Wetlands Council, which also meets with the Guilin City Council. They have a lot of influence over what happens in this entire area."

Ming-Hua mumbled something she couldn't understand.

"Do you *want* to live in a tiny apartment in a high rise?" she asked, goading him. Of course he didn't; she knew he loved the sounds and smells of the family compound as much as she did, even though he could no longer see them.

"No more than you," he said. "But—"

"Then this is a way to prevent that. You know they have had their eyes on our home, our land, for many years now. We need a voice in Council to stand up for history, for culture."

"I've been sitting in on their meetings long enough to know it's a financial matter, not a cultural one. Apartments mean renters, means money, means income for the Council. Much more than our tiny compound can bring in."

"So, you must present other ways for them to earn. They can be convinced that food production is more important than cheap, crowded housing. I will help you prepare a presentation for them to look at, at how much food we grow here. Certainly Xiang Bo's integrated fish farm ponds are more productive than an apartment building. We have a good argument, Ming-Hua!"

He sighed. "Do you think that maybe Li can help make it sound good? They still don't like that you are half-French, Maman. If Li and even Xiang Bo, with her Zhuang background, are involved, wouldn't that help appeal to the Council? Zhuang can almost always get what they want, even without bribes."

Di'e used her cane to stump her way over to the bench and sit down. The courtyard was drenched in sunlight—the same sunlight that was wrecking the entire province's food production rates. Except for Xiang Bo's white ponds. She cleared her throat. "Maybe. But you still need to be the one to present the information to Council, as part of your application to be a member. Not Li, not Xiang Bo. You."

"Yes, Maman," Ming-Hua said, giving in, as she had known he would. "I will."

Later, Di'e took care of the second family issue she needed to manage that day. Without a word to anyone else in the family, she made her way to the garden shed and found one of the polished granite stone platforms stored there. She took it through the courtyard, and arms quivering, set it gently down in an open space among the stones of the ancestors' shrine.

She brushed the dust off the platform with her bare hand, then moved the tiny pot of ashes she'd discovered that morning onto it. From her pocket, she withdrew a beautiful small blue porcelain bowl—blue for the mountain sky—and placed it to the right of the pot. She placed grains of cooked rice into the bowl, replacing the food Zi Min must have left the night before. She'd caught the cat eating it early that morning when she'd gone out to exercise.

With a smile of satisfaction on her face, she went back into the kitchen and made tea.

"Do you understand what I mean by symbiosis, Zi Min? Mama asked.

Zi Min nodded, feeling proud that her mother wanted to explain her research. "Yes. I read about it in school, and also Dr. Li talked about them in his classes yesterday," she said. She still didn't feel comfortable calling him Li, nor certainly Papa. But Dr. Cheng didn't sound right either. "Dr. Li" didn't seem to bother Mama, at least.

"Okay. Well, in this particular symbiotic relationship, the algae supply photosynthates, which are food to the host organism, which is the diatom in this case. The diatom protects the algae.

"Apparently they work together very well, since this diatom-algae is very...*happy*. I was afraid it might get too happy, back when I designed it. So I put a governor in the DNA that would signal it to stop reproducing once it had filled its pond."

"So that is what broke?"

Mama turned and smiled down at her, where she sat on the floor, petting Ming-Hua's fluffy cat. "You are a very smart little girl. You know exactly what we're talking about."

Zi Min nodded.

The cat's fur was so soft, she could stroke it forever. "Do you think we could have a cat, like this? Or maybe a rabbit? *Ya-ya* Di'e has rabbits."

"I'm afraid those rabbits are for dinner, not pets," Xiang Bo said. "But I suppose we could have a cat at our Nalai house. If we ever go back."

"You mean we might stay here? Forever?"

Mama bit her lip. "I don't know, little one. This is a very big problem to solve. I don't know how long it will take, or what the government will ask of me." She turned back to her fancy microscope. "Maybe I can figure out how to turn this stuff into fertilizer or something."

"I thought it was for food."

"It's not nearly as tasty as the mountain algae. The *Nofu* is great, compared with this."

"The fish like it."

"Yes, they do. I don't know if that's enough, though. It was supposed to do several things at once. Maybe it just doesn't do a good enough job at any of the goals to be worth the problems it's causing by spreading so easily."

"The glowing ponds were pretty."

"That is so, Zi Min. But you can't eat 'pretty.'"

●

"I'm signing her up for classes at Yangshuo. They have a very strong Young Scholars program that she is just right for." Li rubbed his forehead, then looked up abruptly at Xiang Bo. "If that's all right with you," he said.

Xiang Bo's mouth seemed glued shut; she could feel herself blink repeatedly while she thought. Then she realized what she needed to say to him. "Is that what *she* wants? Did you ask her?"

"Yes, and yes," Li said. "She was so excited, she bounced up and down." They smiled at each other.

"Well, that is fine. I am making progress on this—" she waved a hand meaning her research, the diatom-algae and its reproduction rates. "But even if I can find the cause of the failed governor, I don't have any kind of plan yet for putting the genie back in the bottle. It has escaped."

He nodded. "Even if we fix it, releasing the revised version may not stop the original one. By its very nature it will be self-limiting."

They both nodded, acknowledging that part of the problem.

"It's like trying to out-populate a feral cat colony with a neutered one. They can never catch up, much less overtake the wild ones."

"Do you think we can make some kind of phage that could destroy *only the escapee?*"

"I'm not sure I would be willing to release it, even if we could. I can all too easily imagine it changing, mutating so it eats every algae we know of. A bigger disaster than this one. Which at least seems to be very unhappy in saltwater. It may fill up *our* ponds and rivers, maybe all over Guanxi Province, but then it will stop." Xiang Bo said. *I hope.* There was always the possibility that it could change again.

"I cannot figure out what it is gaining from the bio-luminescence. Why did that change become helpful to it?"

"I wish we could just put a microphone down and ask it," Xiang Bo said, then regretted it. Li wasn't particularly fond of her occasional whimsy.

"That would be helpful," he said, a smile crooking his mouth.

Strangely, it gave her hope.

Maybe they could solve this thing. Maybe they could do it *together.*

<hr/>

Xiang Bo dressed in her most conservative business suit for the meeting with the Guangxi Party Secretary and the elected Zhuang Secretary. While the government of her nation generally approved any project that would provide food for its people, she had no idea whether this particular Secretary had any scientific training, and any understanding or sympathy for what she was doing with her experiment.

Li made some calls, trying to find out what to expect from this man, and whether the Zhuang Secretary had an influence at all.

They did not find out much, but still hoped that Xiang Bo's Zhuang heritage would be helpful. Li waited out in the lobby of the government building while Xiang Bo was searched and then escorted into the building to the room where the meeting, or hearing, was to be held.

She'd worked steadily in the days before, examining the diatom-algae symbiote to see what she could learn about the changes in the genetic structure, and specifically in her governor, that had broken down. Other than spreading everywhere, her DAS was doing exactly what she had designed it for. She had to hope that would work in her favor.

About a dozen people filed in and Xiang Bo got her first look at the Party Secretary, an older, severe-looking man in a well-tailored navy blue suit. His counterpart, the Zhuang Autonomous Region Secretary, was an ancient Zhuang woman wearing a traditional collarless, embroidered black jacket that buttoned along the left side. The Secretary had paired her jacket with wide-legged trousers and an embroidered belt. She had omitted the boxy headdress, and instead pulled her gray and white hair back into a smooth bun. She sat down and met Xiang Bo's eyes with a brief nod that was barely a tip of her head.

The Party Secretary did most of the talking.

He surprised her with his knowledge of the details of her integrated fish farm project. He praised the increased levels of food production in the ponds where DAS was growing, which was now over most of the Guangxi wetlands. More fish, more rice, and more vegetables, overcoming the effects of the *Hot* to such a degree that food production in Guangxi had actually increased in the last months. That was news that Xiang Bo had not heard before. *Good* news.

She could feel the "but" coming, though.

"Our national government takes pride in the success of your research, Dr. Bai." His smile was more of a grimace, and Xiang Bo felt the urge to duck under the table she sat at. "However, there is a major problem."

The Secretary flicked his fingers at one of his underlings who tapped keys on a computer. The room lights turned off and a projection formed against the screen at the back of the room. Clearly taken from a drone camera, the landscape of the Huixian area of Guangxi showed green and beautiful as the camera panned. But instead of complementary blue ponds and streams, most of the waterways were a glaring white. DAS white.

Then daylight faded, evening fell, and ponds and rice paddies began to glow. At first dozens, then hundreds of them lit up with the slightly greenish brilliant luminescence of DAS.

"This radiance can be seen from space," the Secretary said. "Other governments of the world have begun to ask what we are doing, here."

The room lights came back up and the projection was turned off.

"They treat every new thing from China as a threat. So far we have explained that this project is a successful integrated fish farm experiment. But we cannot explain the glow-in-the-dark effect. It suggests a lack of control."

"Why did you make it so?" the Zhuang elder asked.

Xiang Bo swallowed, but still found her throat too dry to speak. She sipped from her water glass, formulating her response. "The bio-luminescence was an unintended byproduct of the symbiosis," she said. "It has no purpose, but it also causes no harm."

"Except to draw the eye of other nations," the Party Secretary said.

Xiang Bo could do nothing but nod.

"Here is our judgment," the Party Secretary said. "The grant monies for this project will be sequestered, until we are provided with sufficient evidence that you have this symbiote under control. We require some scientific proof that the bio-luminescence is harmless. We need to see how you are preventing DAS from spreading. You will continue to work at your Huixian headquarters until we receive this evidence."

So. She was stuck at the Cheng compound until she provided proof. Proof that she was fairly certain she could *not* provide. Then she realized...perhaps *one* good thing could come from this.

"Sir, there is a problem."

The Party Secretary raised an eyebrow.

"The Guilin Local Council continuously threaten to buy out the Cheng compound lands, in order to build apartment buildings."

The Zhuang Secretary actually growled. "Fools! Turning good farmland into buildings!" She turned to the Party Secretary. "I thought we had learned our lesson, that we must build where we *cannot* farm. We already have insufficient croplands."

He nodded. "This will be *adjusted*," he said, making a note on the papers in front of him. "The Cheng compound will exist in its present form, untouchable. We will now adjourn and expect a report from you within six weeks."

Xiang Bo nodded her acceptance.

"Is that enough time?" the Zhuang woman asked.

"I cannot say for certain. I have a great many things to check."

"Meanwhile, DAS has begun to spread beyond the borders of this province," the Party Secretary said. "We need to tell the world something positive, Dr. Bai. China does not need to be blamed for another disaster."

PART III — 2058

31. 2054: Kaczka—India, Karina—South Africa, Maine

Karina turned to the good-looking guy in a black, red, and green dashiki seated beside her. After leaving Heathrow, they shared a pleasant chit-chat and dinner before they both slept like experienced travelers until woken by announcements for breakfast.

"Fasten your seatbelts. We have started our descent into the Winnie Madikizela Mandela International Airport. Out of the left windows, you'll soon see Robben Island."

She had made a point to remember his name. "Ashur, I'm spending a couple of days in Cape Town. Robben Island and Table Mountain are on my itinerary."

She noticed his deep brown eyes when he asked, "What brings you to South Africa?"

She enjoyed his accent and tried to guess his age. Late twenties she figured. "Long story."

He took a bite of his airplane croissant scattering crumbs everywhere. "We're not landing for another half-hour. I'm all ears."

"I just graduated from college. This is my graduation present."

"I can't place your accent—"

She thought, no one can. I've lived in too many places.

He continued, "but you're not from here. Why visit South Africa? It is not generally high on anybody's list."

"I've been to a lot of places." She replied modestly. "I've even been to the Cape of Good Hope on a cruise from India to North America."

"Wow!" He seemed genuinely impressed. "But that doesn't explain this visit."

She took a sip of her breakfast tea, a habit she'd acquired in India. "Years ago, my father visited Stellenbosch. His description inspired this visit." She didn't explain how he'd lied to her and shuttled her off to India where she'd gotten abducted.

"Did he go to visit the vineyards?"

She knew Stellenbosch had many wineries, distilleries, and breweries. She thought, if he's just interested in drinking, I'm going to scare him off. "No. He was there to learn about eating earthworms." She expected that to end the discussion.

"Really?"

"Yes. He was a speaker at a conference on invertebrates. He didn't know anything about worms, but he knew mollusks and crustaceans."

Ashur dropped his croissant. "I can't believe this. You're Dr. Kaczka Kowalski's daughter?"

Not sure whether to be proud or embarrassed, she said, "Yes."

He handed her an old-fashioned business card. "I worked for Mdudu Nyama and I still call Stellenbosch home."

Now it was her turn to be surprised. "Really? The earthworm hamburger company?"

"That's the one." He rubbed his hands together. "I discovered I could make more money showing people how to convert their local insects and worms into hamburger. I design factories."

Kaczka would approve. Plentiful food for the poor. She could imagine the two men jumping from one project to another. "You should team up with my father. He would love your technology."

He made an exaggerated gesture offering his hand. "Maybe for another time. For now, I would be honored to be your guide."

After their whirlwind tour, Karina sat with Ashur on the patio of their favorite café in Stellenbosch with a stein of local beer. "Thank you. This week reminded me how much I enjoy exploring new places."

Ashur traced his finger through the condensation on the side of his glass. "I understand how you feel. I had a good engineering job right here, but I wanted to see more of the world. The change to running my own design firm, competing for contracts, and dealing with different cultures was frightening at first, but I'm glad I took the leap."

His wanderlust awakened an excitement she'd not felt during her college years, that had been filled with just academics and mammoths. Her only travel had been between school in Chicago and the ranch in Maine. "I envy your life."

"No need for that. You could join my company. We're always looking to expand."

"How big is this company?"

"Right now, just two of us. Me and a Danish engineer I met at Mdudu Nyama. I'm sure you know how difficult it is to find world citizens, at home with long-haul airplanes and unusual customs."

Returning to her peripatetic lifestyle sounded terrific, but— "I'm not an engineer. What could I possibly do?"

"You have so much international knowledge. I'm sure we'd find something."

She didn't want to just be a travel companion. "Are you serious. Tell me one thing I could do."

He tapped on his comp. "It's here someplace." He rotated from portrait to landscape mode. "There it is, hiding in a sidebar." A few more taps and he handed her his comp."

"What's this? It's not even in English."

He smiled. "You see my problem. This is an email from the C.E.O. to the manager I am negotiating with for an important contract. You said you knew Malayalam. Can you read it?"

She wondered how come he had this email. "Did you steal this? Are you asking me to break the law?"

"No. Of course not. This was sent to me."

That didn't sound right. "Why would they send you something you can't read."

"They sent it to me by accident, so it's mine now."

That seemed suspicious, but she didn't know much about the business world. Maybe this was the way they did things. "This isn't Malayalam; it's Tamil. They are close, but my translation will be a bit of a guess." Tamil had more straight lines. It was a harsher script compared to the graceful Malayalam spirals. This harsh script carried a harsh message. "After some polite pleasantries, it says, *'You better close that deal if you want to keep your job.'* This wasn't intended for you, was it?"

"That's great. Thank you! That manager has been pushing me to lower my bid, but now I know he's bluffing. I'll show him for pushing me around. Now he's going to pay top dollar."

She felt bad for the manager, but the job Ashur offered was real and sounded like an adventure. "Might be fun, but I have to think about the mammoths."

"Mammoths. Really?"

She didn't reply, but if he thought belittling her mammoths would convince her to join him, he was going to be disappointed.

"The project you just helped me with is in Chennai, but before I return to India, I have to check on a factory in Sydney and another in Windhoek Namibia. We need someone like you."

His proposition sounded ideal and made her question how she ended up in Maine. She struggled to recall if she had wanted to manage the ranch or whether Kaczka had talked her into it. She wasn't sure which way it went, but it was her responsibility now. The spying made her uneasy, so she didn't commit one way or another. "You might be right, but I need to catch a plane."

When he let her off at the airport, he leaned closed to her and kissed her cheek. The kiss lasted longer than she expected, while she imagined traveling the world with him. "You have my information. Now that school is over, I'll be at the ranch. You have a standing invitation to visit."

After she was seated on the plane, she called him. "That was a serious invitation. I expect to see you soon."

He laughed and added, "My offer for you to join my company was also serious."

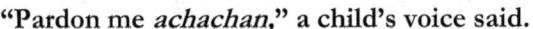

"Pardon me *achachan*," a child's voice said.

Grandpa? Kaczka still hadn't gotten accustomed to being considered old even though he was approaching seventy. He smiled at the little girl that bumped into him in her rush to grab a couple of *modaks* and get back to painting elephants. He felt out of place as he moved around Putiya Pattanam, the new name for the research station. Few people recognized him, and no one stopped to talk. Even Priya had quit attending the festival, occupied with her grandparents and her school in Muvattupula. He had considered skipping *Ganesh Chaturthi*, but with nothing else on his calendar, he'd booked a week in his old bungalow. Now he regretted that decision.

"Kaz, old friend!" Vadish vigorously shook his hand. "I'm so glad you were able to join us."

The energetic welcome made Kaczka feel even older and more out of place. Vadish, twenty years his junior, no longer seemed like a contemporary.

"Make yourself at home. You know your way around. I've got to run to judge the elephant painting."

Kaz explored Putiya Pattanam, New Town. All the signs were now in Malayalam, except for the laboratory building which declared itself to be, "New Town Pharma," in English. The solid sans-serif font advertised an international corporation in a way the Malayalam spirals never could. As another confirmation of his age, the mixture of familiar and foreign disturbed him.

Someone tapped him on his shoulder. "*Achachan*, can I help you?"

He turned around. Roshni wore a saffron and green sari, like the national flag. He couldn't think of anything to say.

She broke the awkward silence, "Kaczka! Would you like a tour?"

"No thank you," he blurted out. Then he remembered the Sikhs. "Can you tell me how the Sikhs feed people for free? They fed you in Cochin, didn't they?"

Roshni paused and he feared he'd offended her by bringing up the time she'd been homeless.

"I'm not the right person to explain the langars. You should visit the Golden Temple in Amritsar."

Grateful for a reason to shorten his visit to New Town, he replied, "Good idea. I'll do that." He found Amritsar on his comp. It was located in northern India, Punjab. He booked a flight for the next morning.

He had to change planes in New Delhi and didn't arrive until dark. After having put off the Sikh mystery for years, his anticipation filled him with energy. He thought maybe I'm not getting old, just bored. He stayed up late researching Sikhs, langars, and the Golden Temple. He discovered that the temple originated with the *sarovar* pool built in 1577 by Guru Ram Das. After only a few hours' sleep, he woke at sunrise.

He left his shoes and comp in the cloakroom and tied a simple orange cloth to cover his bald head. He joined a crowd of Sikhs dressed in turbans, tunics, and loose pants. Together they crowded through the west entrance, the one farthest from the hotels and parking lots.

No pictures or descriptions prepared him for the sight. Straight ahead he saw the Golden Temple. Onion domes glowing in the sun. Gilded stone carvings. Just like a child's fantasy. In the middle of a huge pond, the ancient *sarovar*.

Once he passed through the gate, he stopped. Without thinking, he put his hands together and bowed his head. The enormous open courtyard swallowed all voices and echoes, only leaving the amplified sound of prayer.

He walked slowly to the water's edge, feeling like a small child lifting his head to sneak peeks at the courtyard surrounded by sparkling white stone buildings, columns, and domes. His head turned: gold, white, gold, white in a dizzying progression.

He remembered reading about cleanliness in the temple. Following the others, he stepped into the pond to wash his hands and feet. Even with thousands of visitors, the water was crystal clear.

In a meditative trance, he circled the pond. After an hour he came to a narrow corridor. Compared to the four entrances, each offering that view of the golden temple he'd still not forgotten, the alleyway was simple. It was marked with a sign in six languages, Kitchen or Langar. This was his destination.

Before he entered, he thought, I should wash my feet again. When he checked them, he discovered they were still spotless. Wow! They kept the temple clean, even the floor.

This langar fed 100,000 people a day, for free, for everyone, without discrimination. All that was required was a covered head and bare feet. It was like the scarcity of the *Hot* never reached here. There was enough food for all. In the kitchen, he saw woks bigger than a hot tub. So many people, cutting vegetables, mixing cauldrons of lentil dahl, baking roti, and washing aluminum plates. His first impression was overwhelming and chaotic.

But in a while, someone took his hand, and in pantomime offered him a seat at a low table. With a small rolling pin, he sat rolling balls of dough into flat circles. For an hour, dough balls magically appeared, and circles left for the large griddle called a *tawa*. From his seat, holding his tiny rolling pin, it all made sense.

As he filed into the dining room, he counted 150 people in his group, a good day for any soup kitchen. They seated him on the floor and handed him an aluminum tray. Someone came by with a bucket and ladled dahl on to his tray, followed by someone else with a basket of roti who placed two in his hand. *Did I roll these myself?* He dipped a roti in the dahl and took a bite. It was delicious. He imagined feeding 100,000 mouths per day in cities around the world. Feeling at peace, Kaczka bussed his tray, all the while thinking this is the future of food, Future Food.

The langar was the place he'd always dreamed of. He would build langars around the world.

◖

Karina watched fondly as Ashur shed his jacket and picked up his comp to join her in the kitchen. Their long-distance friendship had grown with many calls, video visits, and email translations. But this was only the third time they'd met in person, IRL, in real life, as her online friends said. She'd met him once in New Delhi and this was his first time to Maine. Sarita thought he was too old, "More of a father than a boyfriend," but to Karina, he was nothing like her father. Sometimes she wondered if she'd grasped him too fiercely, but his smile seemed to say he felt the same as she did: that at long last they'd each found their soulmate.

He looked tired but she knew he shouldn't crash until the sun went down, which wouldn't be for several hours.

He sighed, "I didn't expect the trip to be so long."

She explained, "Any journey to northern Maine is long, no matter where you start from."

He put his suitcase in the spare room and flopped down on the bed.

"Don't you dare. You know better than that. First shower, then something light to eat."

He gave a weak laugh. "Yes, I know your father is an exotic chef. But no earthworms please."

"No worries. I'll whip up an American favorite, Mexican omelet with homemade tortillas."

As he headed for his shower, she added. "After eating comes the tour. No rest until sunset."

"I'm surprised to see you living in a log cabin. I thought they disappeared in the 19th century."

"Don't be fooled by the rustic look. I had it built with the latest technology, satellite internet, solar and wind power with battery backup, and a large freezer with enough food for the worst blizzard northern Maine can imagine." She took a breath and wondered why she needed to justify this to him. Then she continued anyway, "Besides logs are plentiful and excellent insulation."

He tapped his knuckles against the wall. "Solid construction." He walked into the dining area. "How about the furniture? Is it as old as it looks?"

She hugged him with a gentle kiss on the cheek. "Aren't you a smart one? You've figured it out." She carried the breakfast-for-dinner to the table. "A local workshop custom-built the pedestal table, matching sideboard, and eight ladder-back chairs."

He ran his hand along the tops of several chairs. "Nice work. You must entertain a lot."

She pulled out a chair. "Sit here." She sat next to him. "I rarely have guests." She squeezed his hand and served him some eggs and a warm tortilla. "I wanted a smaller dining set," she looked into his dark eyes. "But the carpenter told me that eight was the traditional number. He was a *very traditional* artisan." She tapped her knife handle on the tabletop. "It's all painted with some magic from colonial times, indestructible milk paint, a *traditional* blue."

Seeing her home through his eyes, it felt like an amusement park reconstruction compared to places they'd both visited like Machu Picchu and Angkor Wat.

He ate two servings of eggs and so many tortillas. Afterward, she pulled him to his feet. "You must have been hungry. If you're going to stay awake, we better take a hike."

He gave her a hug and a long kiss. "You sure it isn't time to go to bed?"

She was tempted, but her years of good travel training took precedence. "Later. Let's go." She guided him out the front door and off the porch with its inviting Adirondack chairs to the trail around Cloud Lake. Hiking hand-in-hand through the balsam fir and black spruce, she pointed out the birds and small animals active at dusk. "I'm sorry I don't know all the names. I have guidebooks on the sideboard, but I've never found an occasion to open them." A red fox with three kits was the high point of the hike.

The sun had set when she returned the weary Ashur to the cabin. "Tomorrow we'll take a longer hike through the ten thousand-acre wood to see my mammoth herd."

He gave a weak smile and murmured, "Okay, Christopher Robin," before he fell asleep still dressed and on top of a log cabin patterned quilt from another traditional artisan.

"So, can you tell me again why you're raising mammoths?"

The question sounded friendly, but it made her wonder. "They have lots of uses. Trampling the grounds helps renew the permafrost." She caught herself repeating her father's words by rote. "Though obviously, there's no permafrost in Maine." She continued to parrot Kaczka's presentation. "Valuable fibers. Lean meat. Ivory tusks. Cultural icons. Tourism."

He cheerfully agreed, "I see. Do you get many tourists?"

The short answer was *no*, but she felt obligated to explain, "As you surely noticed, we're far off the main roads. I am talking to some zoos that might exhibit them."

"That's a terrific idea! Those mammoths on exhibit would be great advertising for the ranch."

Strangely, the more positive he was about the ranch, the more she questioned it.

After he left, she again tried to recall how she ended up in northern Maine.

In a dream: *the refugee ship floated into Portland dock after a brief crossing from the Cape of Good Hope.*

Priya stood on the deck, "Sarita and I are continuing to Hudson Bay."

Sarita added, "After that, we're going back to Kerala. No more mammoths."

"Well, I'm staying here. My father wants me to escort the herd to the ranch."

Sarita pulled Karina's hand, dragging her up the gangway. "Don't do it! He'll trap you! Your life will be over! Stay with us!"

"I promised my father. The mammoths need me."

Indrakshi grabbed her other arm and trumpeted, "Come with us to Canada."

As the ship faded into the fog, she heard the faint words from Priya, "Take care of yourself."

Everything she knew and held dear disappeared into the dream fog and an incredible sense of loneliness swept in.

More and more it felt like Kaczka had entrapped her. Less and less it felt like something she had chosen for herself.

The sun was warm on her shoulders, and the baby-to-come also acted like a little heater, so Maatalii shed her jacket. She laid it over the mammoth-fence railing and leaned against it, a little bit sideways to allow for her baby-belly.

"Look! See? They're doing it again!" Nanuq's nine-year-old voice rose to an excited squeal.

"No need to shout, Nanuq," Amaruq said, putting a quelling hand on her son's shoulder.

Maatalii and Amaruq both watched the baby mammoths eat some of their moms' fresh poop, as Nanuq and Basia had said.

"Ew," Amaruq said. "I get why, but it's still disgusting."

Basia, Tarkik's youngest child, also made a disgusted face. She held up her cat's cradle for Maati to do the next move.

At six, and as a girl, Basia was not always welcomed as a playmate by nine-year-old Nanuq, but today she was holding her own. No doubt Nanuq was hoping she'd be so disgusted by the poop-eating, she would run away. But Basia was tougher than that. She peered between the rails of the fence and watched the huge hairy mammoths. Big as old-style ice houses, the mammoths seemed to block out the sun. Certainly from Basia's viewpoint, the creatures must look like mountains, Maatalii thought.

She took the opportunity to teach a lesson to both children. "This is how the babies get the right stuff into their own guts to digest all the weird food they have to eat from the tundra."

"*Like*-en," Nanuq said, pronouncing it carefully.

"Yes, lichen and wildflowers, but mostly grass. Grass is very hard to digest. Cows have *four* stomachs to digest their grass." As she had expected, Nanuq laughed at this idea.

"How many do *mammoths* have?" Basia wondered, looking at her hands and her cat's cradle.

"I have not been able to find out. They don't chew cud, so not as many as cows."

"Can you look? To find out?" Basia asked.

Nanuq roared with laughter. "Look? I am looking! Can I see a stomach? No! You are so stupid!"

Basia's expression was more annoyed than hurt by her cousin's critique.

"Basia is correct, Nanuq," Maatalii said. "There are two ways to look."

"What? You would have to take the skin off." Nanuq said.

"Yes. That is one way. To dissect a dead mammoth and look at the stomach or stomachs directly. There is also another way."

"You can use the baby TV machine!" Basia crowed, shaking loose the strings of the finished cat's cradle pattern from her fingers and putting it in the pocket of her unzipped parka.

"Yes. The ultrasound might tell us how many stomachs the mammoths have," Maatalii said. "Though I do not know what to look for. So, when we slaughter the first animal to make meat, I have asked Suluk if we can look over the carcass to see what is inside them. Though we have decided they probably have just one stomach, like elephants, we need to be sure, so we know better how to care for them."

"Why do we have to ask Grandma before we look?" Nanuq asked, a whiny tone edging his voice.

"They are her mammoths," Maatalii said.

"Why does Grandma have everything, and we have nothing?" definitely whining, now.

Amaruq scowled at her son. "What are you wearing? Where do you sleep?" she asked. "What do you eat each day? And who got you your X-Box?"

"Papa! Papa did!"

Maatalii met Amaruq's gaze above the heads of the children. Amaruq rolled her eyes and shook her head. Niki Pitka had given Nanuq nothing, except the genetic contribution that had started him as a fetus. Amaruq's hard work had earned barely enough to feed and clothe herself during the pregnancy in Churchill. Until she had come home to Qamanittuaq and Snow House, it had been a real struggle. Now Nanuq glorified his imagined father. Maatalii could see tears well in her *uaguk's* eyes.

"No, he didn't, Nanuq," Amaruq said.

Maatalii said, "Your mama provided everything for your papa and you when you lived in Churchill, before you were born. Here, grandma gives you all those things. You will show her respect and your thanks!"

Confused, Nanuq looked from his aunt to his mother and back. "Why doesn't Papa give us things?"

Amaruq bit her lip, looked across the pasture at the huge, hairy beasts the tiny-seeming fence enclosed. "Your papa doesn't want to," she said. "He wants to keep everything for himself. That is why we do not see him. And that is why I do not like it when you are selfish or stingy, like him."

Nanuq glanced up at his mother's face again, then away, a scowl darkening his features.

"Come on," Maatalii said, to break the icy silence. "Let's go pick berries in the greenhouse!" Even Nanuq liked berries.

◠

Jissika was a sarcastic, jealous outsider, Maati decided, and she needn't feel bad about rejecting the young woman's snide opinions.

Only the fact that she was Tarkik's wife gave the Snow House family any reason to try and like her at all.

Maati had spent the morning listening to Jissika's acidic opinions of Maatalii and Caiden's baby's nursery—the decorations and plans and supplies. Jissika had done everything *so* much better and different for her own babies. Finally exasperated, Maati had without a word walked outside into the faint winter sun. Even that was brighter than a room with Jissika in it.

Maatalii and Caiden still shared her room in the old restaurant building which stood beside the "new" Snow House Restaurant, but that was mostly because they both worked there and wanted to stay close. And didn't have enough resources yet for their own home. Of course, a separate nursery would have been nice, but for now, a corner of their bedroom would have to do. She had hung a canvas that Caiden had painted with polar bears and Inuktitut icons to separate the baby's corner. Together, they had painted an old hand-me-down crib and put on the new mattress cover. It was cute; a little shabby, but she had been happy enough with it until Jissika sprang her mean opinion upon every detail.

It had been difficult for her to come to terms with Jissika's different world view. To herself, and everyone at Snow House, achievements were always celebrated by everyone. They supported one another, they cooperated. There was no, "My stuff is better than your stuff." Without a word being said, the consensus feeling of *The People* was: "*Our* stuff is great."

Taking deep breaths, she walked toward the current mammoth enclosure, noticing the bulging bellies of several of the females who were going to be giving birth soon. The mammoths were reproducing faster than anyone had expected. The estimates based on elephant reproduction times had been way off; mammoths were more like bison or yaks in their reproductive time cycles.

She mused on how everyone was reproducing. Like the mammoths, she was pregnant. Her younger brother Yuka was now married, and his wife was expecting. Even Sivoy and Hitty were going to have a little one, which had surprised everyone, especially the new baby's grown siblings.

Maati looked around the Snow House grounds, trying to decide where she and Caiden should put their own house. Yuka had built in town. She wanted to be closer to her mother and her jobs at Snow House.

Now that the new restaurant was finished, the old one was due to be torn down soon. She and Caiden would *have* to move. They had both been stuffing money away, but they had not nearly enough. Of course, Suluk would help them as she had Yuka, because family was family. Caiden sometimes felt resentment that she always expected her mother to help and accepted that help.

Things had been different in Caiden's mining family. She would have to talk to Sivoy and see if he and Caiden's mother Hitty also had problems around their different traditions about money. She knew Caiden had been a little embarrassed that he was going to have a new baby brother or sister—Hitty had gone to the clinic and found out the baby's gender, but had not shared that information with her grown-up children.

As if he could tell she had been thinking about him, Caiden was a sudden presence at her side, like a warm shadow. She gave him one of her sidewise smiles, and he laughed.

"Sneaking up on me?" she asked.

"No, I just finished with the potato soup and wanted to be sure you were okay. I heard some of what Jissika was still spewing."

"Spew, a good word for it. Is she ever happy with anything?"

"Tarkik seems to think so. He's been bragging about how happy they are."

"Well, good for him," she said, trying not to be sarcastic. "Basia seems like a happy child, so maybe her mother doesn't do so much complaining at home."

"Jissika saves it all for us."

"Hmm." She waved a hand at the Inn, the new restaurant and the landscaped grounds and parking area around Snow House. "Do you think we should try to build our house here? We've talked about pre-fab or scratch build, but not where it would go."

"Don't you think we could get our own land?"

"Mother would be hurt. Besides, some Snow House land is something she *can* give us. She doesn't have enough cash to pay us wages for our work, but she still has plenty of land."

Caiden nodded. "I guess so."

"Unless you wanted to be closer to your family? We could build in town, but I don't want to be too far away from Snow House."

"No. I have no reason to be close to Mother. Besides, we can barely afford materials for a house; we certainly can't get a car, or even our own slushski, to get to work from town," he said with a grimace. "I wish our albums sold better."

"I am a little glad you aren't so famous. You would have to go on tour, and leave me here." She gave him a full smile, letting him know she was only half-serious.

"I doubt that will ever become a problem," he laughed. He and his bandmates were quite realistic about their chances for big success. Some recognition, some extra money—those made them happy. Mostly, they made music together because they loved to.

"What about back there?" Caiden pointed to a low slope behind the last section of the Inn, where the separate, two-story suites were located. "We could have a view of the inland tundra in one direction, and overlook Snow House and the town and Lake on the other."

Maati looked at the area, imagining their cozy house there. "That could work," she said. "I'll ask Mama about it."

"We can maybe get the farmers to plow and compact the area for a good foundation."

"Yes, they're looking for work."

◡

The farming man looked tiny in the cab of the huge earth-moving machine. Suluk looked up in awe as he pushed levers and gears and started the enormous thing moving. Yuka was in the cab with him, watching everything he did. Giqa, Sivoy, and Meriwa stood out in the weak spring sunlight, watching with Suluk.

The pale green and tan tundra scrub was swallowed at the front of the machine. Out the back came dark peaty soil and some rocks and shredded plant bits. Suluk felt a pang as the unfrozen tundra was eaten up and spit out. The field-to-be would be planted in a couple rows each of tough grains: barley and spelt and rye, and a new kind of resilient millet, plus triticale and winter wheat. Abbie called it a "test field." The grains would be made available to Snow House in exchange for the use of the land behind and south of the Inn. Depending on what grew best, Abbie's next crop would be just one or two of the sturdiest and best-producing grains.

Not usually superstitious, Suluk said a short prayer to the spirits of the land, asking forgiveness for this intrusion. Truly, they all hoped this plowing would be a temporary thing. One crop, then the plowed tundra would refreeze into permafrost in the winter. It might not hold off the *Hot*, but it was just one of the many things they were trying.

Meanwhile millions of people went hungry and homeless. How could she deny a field of grain?

Suluk sighed, and walked back to Snow House, Giqa and Meriwa moving beside her. Sivoy and Yuka were going to stay and watch, or help as needed, she supposed, not sorry to leave the noise behind.

She scowled as they entered the Restaurant, seeing Ezra Mikigak leaning against the counter. Jissika's brother was just as sarcastic and judgmental as she was; Suluk didn't understand how Tarkik could stand to be in his own house with such family.

"Is Tarkik here?" Ezra asked loudly.

"Do you *see* Tarkik?" Giqa snarled.

Ezra held up his hands in a peacemaking gesture, palms out. "He might be in the back, old man, so I ask. What's your problem?"

Giqa reared his head back and opened his mouth, and Suluk decided to step in. "Tarkik is taking a couple days off to do things at his house," she said.

Ezra's scowl deepened. "Well he wasn't there when I went by," he said in a growling voice.

"So you check on what your brother-in-law is doing, and you aren't even at work yourself?" Giqa sneered.

Apparently this pushed Ezra over the limits of his social graces; he burst into a scoffing laugh. "Listen to you all fierce and snarly! I didn't know you had it in you. Pretty obnoxious for a broken, useless old drunk."

Suluk was shocked at the acrimony between the two. "None of this is welcome in here," she said. "Please take it outside if you are going to fight like musky bears."

Giqa turned away from Ezra and sat down at the counter. "I didn't want to talk to that person in the first place," he said.

Limiting his response to a glare at Giqa's back, Ezra looked down at Suluk, who always felt like a little pebble in front of Ezra's six and a half feet of boulder. "Do you know where Tarkik might be?" he asked in a gentle tone, as if trying to make up for his earlier hostility.

She shook her head. "Did you try calling him? He usually answers his cell right away."

"Yeah, it's been 'not available' all morning."

She shrugged, "He hasn't been around here."

"Can you tell him to call me if you see him? I have a job he might like, up at Fifthslope."

Taken aback, she merely nodded. She still needed Tarkik's help around Snow House, but she could hardly complain if he took a paying job. She'd heard Jissika's complaints about how little money that family had, never mind they never had to buy food, or that they lived in a house that Snow House had built for them.

"He better not take that job, if he wants to keep living," Giqa muttered, without turning around.

"What?" Suluk said. "It's not your say, Giqa!"

"If he goes to the mine, he will be exposed to their physical systems. They are careless. Things happen. Soon your half-son will be a dead son." Giqa turned his head just far enough to meet her eyes, ignoring Ezra. His expression was grim. "I *know*."

"Aggh, your accident was your own fault, old man. Your own drunk fault," Ezra said.

"You forget, I did not drink in those days," Giqa said with quiet dignity. "Only afterwards. There are far too many 'accidents' at the mine."

"What?" Suluk asked again, lost.

Ezra just shook his head.

"*I* wasn't driving the truck that hit me," Giqa said.

Ezra shook his head again and walked out. He tried to slam the left half of the big glass double doors at the restaurant entrance, but the piston-closer slowed it to a gentle click.

Suluk touched Giqa's shoulder. "I know you don't like Ezra, but you don't much like Tarkik either, so what was that all about?"

"Ezra knows," Giqa said, and without another word, turned back to his coffee and plate of bannock.

Behind the counter, Maatalii met her eyes and shrugged. Suluk shook her head and walked back to the kitchen. There was always more cooking to do, and she wasn't going to figure out *that* confrontation. Maybe her friend Ikiak knew; he was pretty open about some of the problems that caused tension between the miners and the Qamanittuaq villagers.

"We're going to be living in forest, if this keeps up," Suluk said.

Osha looked up from her sewing. "What?"

Suluk pointed to the prep-room TV screen where a reporter was showing how far north the tree line had moved. "Forest. Moving north." She finished peeling onions and started on the carrots.

"You need those mammoths to work harder," Osha said. "And more caribou."

Suluk laughed. "They are both doing a good job here."

"Maybe we should move some of them down to where the trees are," Osha said pointing at the map that was on the TV screen.

"They are reproducing quicker than I expected, but I do not have nearly that many animals. Those people down there will have to take care of it themselves."

"Maybe send the farmers down to plow; those plows are pretty good at churning it back to permafrost. Then the trees won't grow."

Suluk nodded, tossing carrot peels into the compost bin. "Maybe."

Their caribou herds were increasing. She had to scramble to buy more fencing for them and the mammoths. Their herds of mammoths had doubled twice in the ten years since the big animals had arrived. Ujurak had had to hire help in the slaughterhouse, because the mammoth meat was selling well all over the world.

But. There was always a *but*. The herds simply couldn't make enough of an impact on the vast Canadian Arctic. Tiny sections of the permafrost were protected, and re-froze every year under their fenced pastures. But the tundra extended for thousands of kilometers in every direction beyond their— comparatively tiny—herds and pastures. In summer nearly all the permafrost was melting, which affected everything else in their living area, from sea life to forests. They had seen it coming and been unable to stop it.

So now they adopted more abandoned polar bear cubs, most recently another set of twins. They'd expanded their sanctuary to allow both sets of twins plenty of room. They were fed caribou and mammoth scraps, but no one had the inclination to hunt the increasingly rare seal pups for the bears. A few of the town's fishermen brought occasional extra fish, but for the most part, Snow House fed the bears and housed them until they were big enough to head out on their own. The older set of twins would be released in another couple of months. Suluk had given Giqa the job of feeding and caring for them, so the old man had something to do besides drink and grumble.

The town children also came with food offerings. Suluk worried sometimes that the bears were becoming too used to humans, that they would forget how to be polar bears. They had been relieved to donate a couple of their rescue bears to zoos, who presumably knew how to look after them and could afford to.

She finished chopping the carrots and scraped them into the pot with the potatoes and onions. Mammoth meat simmered in an adjacent pot, and soon she would combine them for their famous Snow House stew. It was "famous" since Maatalii and Amaruq's school friend had come and reviewed it. He'd been very complimentary.

Wiping her hands, Suluk went and stared out the back window at the slope where Caiden and her Maatalii stood with the builder, laying out their house. It was hard to believe she was about to be a grandmother twice over, with both Maati and Yuka expecting babies soon. Lusa was still unmarried, and didn't seem to be looking, which had surprised her, since her oldest had always loved playing with his little siblings. She shrugged. Maybe he had had enough of that. He was busy making interesting things at the fabrication shop. The manager and owner of the place was probably going to pass the shop along to Lusa when he retired, since he had no children of his own who wanted it. Lusa would have to do the same, if he never married and had children. Well, he was only forty; there was time.

She would be an auntie again soon, too, whenever Hitty and Sivoy's little one arrived.

She glanced away from Maati's house-to-be over to the airport runway, where her eye had caught movement. Someone, a young man, it looked like, was walking toward Snow House. She frowned. She didn't have anyone booked to arrive today, and this was no one she knew. Her eyes followed him across the parking lot, lost him between the Inn buildings.

Then she saw him glance in the Inn office, which was unmanned at the moment with Maatalii being up on the hill and Meriwa at the plowing, and no one expected to come. He read the sign on the Inn door, then continued on to the Restaurant. She walked out front to see him come in. He took off the big backpack he'd been carrying and set it on the floor, nodding to her, a faint smile on his handsome face.

"Is Amaruq Oonark here?"

"I think she is in the back prep room. Who shall I tell her is here?"

He shrugged. "She'll know," he said.

Suluk walked into the back, and became aware the young man was following her. She hadn't invited him to come into their workrooms and kitchen. She felt a sort of fear ignite in her belly. Who did he think he was?

Amaruq looked up from her cutting board. The light in her eyes died as she looked past Suluk to the stranger.

"Oh," Amaruq said. She walked around the shelves. "Niki." She didn't sound happy to see him. "What—? How are you here?"

"Surprised I found you?" he said. "I came to see my son," he said. "You know, the one *you* named Nanuq."

Suluk scowled. This was Nanuq's ne'er do well father, then. A man she had hoped never to meet.

"He's off at school now," Amaruq said. "You should have let me know you were coming."

"Oh, should I?" He moved stiffly, waving an arm almost like he was going to strike Ama. But he stepped back, gesturing to emphasize his words, "I was busy taking classes, and taking care of myself, and *working,* since you just abandoned me. So, yeah. I finished school. I have my Licence. I can get a real job, and I came to get my family back."

"After nine years? Nanuq doesn't even know who you are."

"When will he be home? When does school finish here?" Niki asked.

"At two o'clock," Amaruq said.

"Today? You don't have *away* schools here?" Niki said, disbelief clear in his tone.

"Just for High School," Suluk said, letting the young man know someone of authority was here. Amaruq seemed entirely too...acquiescent, in Suluk's opinion. "The little ones don't need to go away."

Niki nodded. "All right. Where's the school? I can go see him there. I only have two weeks."

"No," Suluk said.

"They don't allow visitors," Amaruq said.

"Well, that's bull," Niki said. "I want to visit my son."

"Public schools don't allow visitors, you know that," Amaruq said, sounding a little more sure of herself.

"Rules can be worked around. I'm sure they have exceptions for emergencies."

"How is this an emergency?" Suluk wondered.

"I'm ill. I need to see him."

Amaruq bit her lip. "Ill?"

"I have two weeks before surgery," he said. "I want to see my son, now. Where is he?"

So demanding, Suluk thought. So hard.

This was not how *The People* behaved.

Abbie put the last batch of cookies into the oven. She dropped into her chair and sipped her now tepid tea. The new house reflected the colder climate. Smaller rooms. Smaller windows. She referred to the compact wood-frame architecture as *my igloo*, even though her neighbors had abandoned the snow-block domes long ago.

In the early years Abbie had made gestures to join the community. She purchased a commercial grain mill and donated flour to school bake sales. In the winter Redd plowed fields as part of the permafrost restoration project. Regardless, no matter how friendly the villagers were, she felt like an intruder.

Her breakthrough came when the grandchildren were born.

"Grandma!"

William and Wendy, two heads of curly red hair, pleasantly filled the already snug kitchen. She hugged the two rambunctious children. "Billy. Dee. What are you shouting about?"

William reached for a cookie.

"Not those. They just came out. Too hot. I'll get you a cooler one."

She stood up, leaning on the table, and walked to the boxes of cookies she'd prepared for sale at Snow House, confident one cookie more or less wouldn't make a difference. "Tell me little ones. What's the commotion?"

As usual, Billy took a bite and chewed silently, letting his younger sister respond.

Dee shoved her cookie in the pocket of her snow pants. "Yuka! Yuka is here! He's going to plow the snow. Can we go with him? Please?"

Abbie looked at Billy, still eating his cookie. "Do you want to go also?" It was impossible to keep him from being overshadowed by his sister. He would have been happy to curl up by the fire with Tasha reading a book. Tasha was their second Newfie, and she loved Nunavut.

He just smiled and nodded.

Abbie went to get a couple more cookies. "Sure, go ahead. Give these to Yuka." Dee grabbed them, and they ran toward the door with the big Newfie following. Before she let them out, Grandma Abbie stopped them to snap their jackets and put on their hats and mittens. Dee wore a faded green snowsuit from a second-hand shop in Churchill. Billy's came from the same place, faded blue. Abbie had purchased new hats and mittens decorated with polar bears from the Snow House gift shop. If the wheat crop was good, she'd get them matching snowsuits next winter.

She put her tea in the microwave to reheat. *Oops.* She had been using the microwave to time the cookies, so she had no idea how long the cookies had left to bake. She checked the oven. Pale white. She sat down and sipped her hot tea.

Grampa Redd came in from outside followed by a gust of fresh snow. After working so hard to outrun the *Hot*, she didn't mind snow blowing into her home. "What are those grandkids running out to do?"

He walked slowly into the kitchen. Once he'd made peace with his need of a cane, he'd turned out a dozen or more on his new lathe. There wasn't a woodworking guild in Qamanittuaq. Some of the canes were plain, but others were carved with ornate Celtic designs. He'd started working on one with seals and birds imitating an Inuit design. She had tried to convince him not to leave them all over the house but had given up. "They're going with Yuka to plow the test field."

He sighed. "I hate to bother you, but could you make me some coffee."

She smiled. "Sure." She could tell his arthritis was acting up or he'd never have asked for help. Thirty-three years they'd been married, and he seemed more distant each year. She felt like he left part of his soul in Oklahoma and with each move, there was less of him with her. Here in the far north, he seemed to be just his lathe, the news, and, of course, his quiet pain.

"Do you want your NSAID cream?"

As expected, he grumbled, "No."

The cream required him to take his pants down, something he preferred to do in private. Their six-room igloo didn't allow for much privacy.

He accepted his coffee. "They've been plowing that field all winter. How long is that experiment going to continue?"

"I heard from Suluk that the permafrost is thicker in the plowed fields than the controls. She says that the field with the mammoth herd is even better."

"Well, that's promising," Redd said in his monotone. "I doubt they'll ever have enough mammoths to save the Arctic. Why do we keep supporting that plowing experiment? It's gone on for years."

Redbird had a good heart. His negativity had more to do with his pain than anything else. "No reason to halt. They recharge the tractor and it's not doing anything in the winter anyway. I think of this as being a good neighbor."

"That must be working. Snow House offered to show my carvings in their gift shop."

She hadn't realized that he talked to the people there, even though they were just a short walk away. She was encouraged to see him getting out and socializing. "That's nice of them. You'd be the only non-Inuit there."

"Yes." He looked down at his cane. "So much has changed. I wonder what kind of world we're leaving to our grandkids." He looked up. "Do you have any extra cookies?"

"Oh, I forgot! Cookies!" She ran to the oven and rescued some very brown cookies. "Wait, I'll get you some good ones." She borrowed three more cookies rearranging them into one less box.

She sighed thinking: two billion people were eating one less something tonight. She was grateful her family always had enough to eat and thankful for her grandchildren.

◡

Dee climbed the ladder into the cab of the large green tractor. Her brother quickly followed. She reached across Yuka and beeped the horn. The sudden loud noise sent Tasha to hide in her doghouse. Dee sat in the copilot seat. She looked over the empty field, dark with dirty snow from all the plowing. "Nothing is growing here. Why are we plowing?"

"We plow the snow, so the ground will freeze."

Billy asked, "Why do we want the ground to freeze?"

Yuka replied, "There's a lot of bad stuff frozen there. When it thaws, that bad stuff is released."

Dee hated when people treated them like babies. She tried to remember the best word. *Sequence. Quest. Question. Non-sequitur. Sequester!* "Sequestered carbon will be released?"

He laughed. "Exactly!"

She didn't like when he laughed at her, but he showed her the tractor engine, the hydraulics, and explained all the controls. He was a good friend.

Billy had another question, "How does plowing the snow help?"

"The snow is like an igloo for the field."

She smiled and found another word. "Insulation."

The cab had heated up, so she took off her mittens and unsnapped her jacket. When she put her hands into her pants pockets, she found the cookies. "Here Yuka. My mom sent these for you."

"Thank you. There are three, so one for me, one for you, and one for your brother."

William didn't look up from his book but reached out his hand to accept a cookie.

She liked machines. She also liked animals. "Yuka? What do you think? Will your mom be auctioning mammoth calves again this year? I want to raise one for Christmas dinner. The mammoth roast at Snow House was yummy."

"The herd is growing. I think the sale will be next week. I'm sure she's already told your mother."

"I'll be sure to clean out a stall."

◡

"One, two, three, four, five," Dee counted the bowls.

"*Atausiq, marruuk, pingasut, sitamat, tallimat,*" William counted the spoons in Inuktitut.

Dee poked her older brother. "English, use English or *Inupasugjuk* will take you away."

William grabbed the spoons. "*Un, deux, trois, quatre, cinq. Inupasugjuk* doesn't speak French."

Abbie liked that her grandchildren were learning the Inuit culture. Maybe that meant they'd stay with her. They were the only outsiders at the Qamanittuaq primary school.

"Besides, I'm a *Tuniit* and I will frighten *Inupasugjuk*."

"No, *Inupasugjuk* will carry your *Tuniit* away to be a doll in her igloo."

Dee shouted over him, "*Inupasugjuk* is a giant. She captures little children to be her dolls. She'll put you in a nappy and rock you in a doll cradle."

"Would not! Would not. *Tuniit* is bigger and he's my friend. He'll smash her igloo and throw her onto an ice floe."

At dinner, the abbreviated family gathered around one end of the table. Abbie took two steps to carry dinner from the stove. Their compact igloo had no dining room. The table tucked into the kitchen. Abbie tried to appreciate how convenient it was to have everything close but couldn't. Redd sat at the head and ladled out fish soup made with carrots and scallions. Abbie missed the dairy cows they'd had back in Oklahoma. Milk was expensive, but she still made a creamy soup for the children. Calcium. The children needed calcium.

Redd interrupted the sounds of slurping soup. "Has anyone heard from Aunt Carla?"

Elzia prompted her kids. "Where is Aunt Carla?"

Dee answered. "Mom got an email from her. She's in San-tea-AH-go. It is summer there. Nice and warm. I wish I were with her."

Billy took advantage of Dee's pause. "Summer. That means she is south of the equator. When it is winter in the north, it is summer in the south." He took a big breath and grinned proudly. "And vice versa."

After the meal, Elzia put the children to bed in the middle upstairs bedroom. She and Mike shared the largest one, leaving the smallest one for Carla whenever she wasn't away on business. Of course, Abbie and Redd used the ground floor bedroom since he could barely climb the stairs.

With Elzia upstairs putting the grandkids to bed, Redd mused, "Our children turned out pretty well."

"Yes, and Carla has a great job." Their daughter worked for Green Dots, a big company in Australia. They sent Carla all over the world, but Abbie wasn't sure what she did. It had something to do with algae or pumps. Mike also did something with algae.

Redd hobbled over to his chair in the small living room, covered his legs with a mammoth blanket, and was carving an Inuit design into a walking stick. He was only fifty-seven, but the years and the cold had caught up with him.

Abbie washed the dishes, drying and putting them away without moving. "Compact and convenient," she whispered to herself. When she finished, she sat with Redd in the living room. "Carla is never home, and now I think Mike and Elzia are going to move away."

For a pleasant change, Redd took the optimistic position. "They seem happy. Both have good jobs. Growing algae is the farming of the future."

"Do you think Carla is happy? Over thirty, still single, no children?"

"Sure. She likes to travel, and everyone doesn't need to have children. We can barely feed everyone. This is a crazy time to add more."

34. Suluk, Maatalii—Qamanittuaq Nunavut Canada

Amaruq's face told a story of terror when she towed Basia into the restaurant. The door closed behind her. Suluk saw no Nanuq.

"Where's—"

Amaruq burst into tears. "He's *gone!*" she shrieked. "Niki took him! He's gone!"

Both Suluk and Maatalii went to her and tried to make sense of Ama's words, muddled by tears and despair.

"Nanuq wasn't on the bus. The other children said he went home with his father," Amaruq said after many starts and stops. "How could he do that? We are not married. That is not his son. How could the school let him take him?"

"Of course it's his son," Maati tried to say.

"No. He never even came to the hospital!" Ama said. "He never even held him, you know that! Nanuq is not his, he is mine!"

Maati engulfed Ama in a hug. Of course she was wrong; Niki was the father, Nanuq was his son, whether they had ever married or not. Suluk was not sure how the Canadian laws applied, when it was a Canadian Inuit child and the father was from Alaska, of the United States. Of course Niki could not just steal his son without telling the child's mother; that part she was certain was wrong.

"He may have some rights. We're going to have to see what the laws say," Maatalii said.

"How can he even want Nanuq?" Amaruq wailed. "He never cared. He doesn't know the first thing about taking care of a child. For nine years, he never came to visit, and now—now he thinks he can just come and steal him?" Ama reached for her *uaguk's* apron and patted her eyes dry. "I will get him back," she said.

"Yes," Maati said. "*We* will get him back."

At this, Amaruq threw her arms around her almost-sister and foster-mother, giving them hug. Maatalii wasn't due for another two months, but she already walked like a mammoth. She turned away, rubbing her back, and Suluk patted her arm.

"Can you watch Basia, Mama?" Maati said. "Tarkik's supposed to come pick her up."

She nodded. Watching them head towards the computers and the internet, Suluk sighed. Having daughters was definitely harder than having sons. She'd had none of these problems with Lusa or Yuka.

What were they going to do about Nanuq?

The sky was gray, threatening rain, and the cold north wind wasn't helping either. Suluk shivered, but held tightly to the middle of the south side of the mammoth fence, while Sivoy moved the back section. The wind blew over her skin just as it blew over her heart: Basia crying, missing her cousin and friend. Maati and Ama frantically searching the internet, talking with social services. Fearing the worst and finding it, that there was no trace of Nanuq.

Still, this mammoth enclosure must be moved.

It was difficult, because the mammoths, like elephants, had a matriarch that led the herd. Each time they split the herd they left a matriarch behind with half the group; then the animals in the new herd had to work out who their new leader was, and with so few that could be considered *elders,* the mammoths didn't have many choices. *None* of them had much experience.

Likewise, the males in the new group vied for breeding rights, and fights seemed constant, often wrecking sections of fence, or requiring a male to be pulled from the herd for veterinary work, which was getting expensive.

Plus they had to move the fences for each herd every few weeks. The mammoths ate up everything inside the fences very quickly. She thought again that a crew of two or three people hired to simply move fences was becoming a necessity.

She tried not to think of expenses. She was going to have to raise the price of their meat or increase the number they slaughtered each year, or she wouldn't be able to feed the rest. And she knew she really needed to hire a permanent fence-moving crew, had known for months. Both she and Sivoy had other things they should be doing, as did the other people helping them today.

Gratitude filled her heart as she thought of all Sivoy did. She could always count on this brother. Unlike some of the others in the family, like Tarkik who only came to work when he wanted something from Snow House or anyone else.

Sivoy signaled it was time for her to roll her side of the fence down to match up the south end, at the same time Caiden rolled the north end, and a couple neighbors took out the temporary sections that closed the gaps during the move. It took only an hour or so for each move, but everyone also had travel time that got longer as the herds moved farther out away from Snow House.

Suluk's arms were shaking by the time she and Caiden clamped the last corner together. It started raining before they got home, of course. Everyone was wet and tired and irritable, and they still had a full day's work to put in.

When she got back inside, she saw Maatalii and Amaruq packing suitcases. Her heart sank as she realized they would be leaving her short-handed, but of course they had to go get Nanuq.

"You found him, then?"

Amaruq burst into tears, so Maati answered. "He was seen yesterday in Churchill by one of *uaguk's* old work friends." She looked at her mother and shook her head. "I know we are leaving you at a bad time, Mama, but we did get the farmer lady to come and help 'til we get back."

Wondering how much help an American farm woman was going to be at an Inuit hotel and restaurant, she just nodded and went to get some cash for the girls to use while they traveled.

Niki's face was red, and he was so angry he was spitting as he roared out his words. "You've had him for nine years! Now it is my turn! You cannot have him back!"

Amaruq pushed Nanuq behind her and back down the hallway. Maatalii tried to squeeze past Niki next to the railing to get back beside Ama, but Niki wasn't having it. He shoved her, and their combined weight made the banister creak alarmingly. Maati stepped back from Niki and to the middle of the hall, one hand grasping for the security of a doorknob on one of the bedroom doors. Inside, Niki's new girlfriend gasped and tried to slam the door behind her, her hand trapping Maatalii's on the knob.

"This's my room," she said. "Stay out."

Since that was the room where they'd found Nanuq, Maati hadn't had any hesitation about forcing their way in the first time. Now they had Nanuq, she cared nothing about the room. The woman seemed more interested in keeping her out of the room than helping Niki regain his son, though.

"Let's calm down, Niki," she said. "Amaruq deserved to know you were taking Nanuq, and where to. It was wrong of you to just grab him and run."

"I didn't run! I took my son and brought him home with me for a proper visit. You have no right to steal him back!"

His girlfriend—Maatalii didn't even know her name—nodded her agreement.

"That is for legal authorities to decide," Maati said. Amaruq wasn't saying anything, just grasping Nanuq's hand in a grip tight enough to whiten the boy's skin. *Uaguk* had warned her that she seemed to lose all volition whenever she was in Niki's presence; Maatalii would need to speak and be firm. Ama had been right. It was weird, because normally Ama wasn't the kind of girl to be weak and compliant. It was like Niki had some magic power over her.

"There's nothing legal that needs to be done," the girlfriend said. "You were never married, there was never a divorce, and there is no visitation rights schedule set up. Niki has his Licence, and I study law too, and I know this is true."

"Social services says there must be a formal agreement about visitation. Whether he is Niki's son or not—"

"Of course he is my son!" Niki roared.

"You have *kidnapped* him from his mother and you can be arrested for that!" Maatalii outshouted him. "Nothing for nine years, and then you just come and grab him—that is neither right nor legal!"

"You are wrong," the girlfriend said, tucking a lock of long blonde hair behind her ear. "I can prove it to you."

"And I can have social services here in ten minutes to back *us* up," Maatalii said firmly. "So for now, Nanuq comes with his mother. We can arrange a meeting tomorrow or the next day where we can work out a visitation schedule—"

"No!" Niki yelled.

To Maati's ears he sounded just like a snotty five-year-old defying his mother. She was opening her mouth to make another suggestion, trying to soothe tempers, when Niki spun around and pushed her with both fists.

His hands impacted the front of her shoulders so hard, she knew there would be bruises. "*You* are the problem," Niki said, pushing her, stabbing his fists at her shoulders again and again. The girlfriend ducked back into her room, shutting the door.

Behind Niki, Maati could see Nanuq clinging to Amaruq's waist, his head buried in her bosom. Poor Nanuq must be so confused and scared. Maatalii planted her feet and pushed Niki's next strike aside, so one fist hit the wall and the other flailed in the air instead of hitting her. Her shoulders hurt, but at least he wasn't hitting her baby.

"You're hurting me," she said clearly, trying to bring him back to his senses.

He kicked her, connecting his boot so sharply against her shin that her whole leg went numb. Tears sprang to her eyes with the sharpness of the pain that followed.

"*You* are making this worse!" he yelled again, and again tried to use his fists against her shoulders. Again she deflected his arms, and took a step back when he raised his foot to kick her again.

"Stop it, Niki!" Amaruq yelled. "I'm calling the police!"

He spun around and stomped the few steps to where Ama was dialing her cell. He shoved Nanuq against the wall so hard he cried out, and then grabbed Amaruq's phone and threw it over the banister. It smacked onto the floor below, pieces flying off.

Even so, someone had called the police. Maatalii could hear sirens of cars stopping outside the apartment building. Maybe the girlfriend had done the right thing, Maati thought. She stepped toward Niki, who was now battering at Amaruq, trapping her against the door at the end of the hall.

"Hey, now," Maati said, catching one of Niki's arms. "This doesn't solve anything, Niki."

He used his trapped hand to grab her arm and yanked, his face so filled with fury he looked a madman. His other hand, meanwhile, released Ama and he hit Maati in the head with his fist. It must have hurt him as much as her, because he shook his hand in the air. She pulled free of him, moving down the hall toward the stairs, hoping to see police on the landing below. She heard boots on the stairs, but did not see anyone yet.

Then suddenly Niki was there in front of her again, pushing her shoulders, kicking her legs. She covered her head with her arms, and crouched down, doing what she could to protect herself.

"I want to go home!" Nanuq screamed.

If Niki was angry before, he became enraged at that cry from his son, and he, pushed and shoved and kicked at Maatalii in a flurry of blows until she felt the floor disappear from beneath her, and she crashed onto the stairs. Momentum carried her down, and she blacked out. Her last sight, Amaruq screaming in horror at the top of the stairs, was the picture her mind closed down on.

◠

Maatalii heard her mother's voice calling her name, and opened her eyes, thinking, *Is it time to get up? Have I overslept?* Familiar faces surrounded her. Caiden grasped her hand.

Caiden? No, she and Amaruq had gone to Churchill, to find Nanuq. And then— She didn't know what had happened then. She knew her whole body ached.

Her womb ached. Her baby!

No, her belly was too flat. Had she given birth?

She met Caiden's gaze. His mouth was tight with worry. That was not a good sign. She tried to speak, but discovered her jaw was wired shut.

"Baby?" she managed to moan out.

Caiden's face collapsed. She glanced at the others: Mama, Amaruq, Aunt Meriwa was there too. They all looked sad.

So. She had lost the baby.

Because…because she had fallen down the stairs when Niki attacked. She remembered now. His rage, the fight, him striking Nanuq and Ama and herself. But that hadn't happened today, or even yesterday. It happened some time ago, because Mama and Caiden had had time to get here.

She could feel tears fill her eyes as she struggled to speak. "How long?"

"A week, *uaguk*," Amaruq murmured. "You have been gone for a week."

"The doctors said you might not ever come back to us," Caiden said, tears sliding unnoticed down his face.

"Nanuq?"

"He is safe," Mama said. "The only good thing to come out of this mess."

"They put Niki in jail, of course. They were going to put his girlfriend in, too, for conspiracy. But I asked them not to," Ama said. "Because she called the police and an ambulance, and we think that is all that saved you. And maybe me and Nanuq, too."

"I hope she learned her lesson about him," Meriwa said, scowling. "Bastard." That wasn't the Inuktitut word she used, but that's what she meant, Maati thought. "You have a concussion, both shoulder blades broken, jaw broken, and your foot is so messed up they're afraid it will never mend properly."

Maatalii could feel the wires in her jaw ache, and her womb cramped and throbbed, and her head hurt. Other things just seemed numb.

"Your baby could not be saved," Meriwa went on, giving voice to what no one had actually yet said. "But they think you can still have other children."

"Can you give us some time together?" Caiden asked, glancing at the others.

They left then, shooed out by what looked like a nurse. When the woman came closer, she saw the name tag. Dr. Benton-Smith, it said. Not a nurse, a doctor.

"Only a few more minutes, hon," the doctor told Caiden, who nodded.

He was crying. "I cannot even hug you," he said. He picked up a corner of her sheet and wiped his face. "We lost a little girl," he said. "But we'll be okay, Maati. We'll be okay."

She was crying, too. She couldn't even feel her arms to lift them and wipe her face. Caiden found a box of tissues and did it for her, then blew his nose and bent and gave a gentle kiss to her forehead.

"Just get well, and come home," he said.

Zi Min graduated from Yangshuo University at age fifteen. Her parents had helped her prepare a stellar application to excellent graduate centers across the planet. No one was much surprised when she was accepted at many, and had the dubious honor of choosing from among them.

She asked her mother's advice when she had come nearly to tears, acceptance letters spread across her bed, and her brain exhausted from arguing with herself.

"I went to the United States, as you know," Xiang Bo had said. "I think research in the States has become a bit of an under-funded backwater these days. Most of the best-qualified graduates are seeking placement outside the U.S. I think you would do well at any number of other locations. The Indian Institute of Science at Bangalore appears in many, many technical articles. Ghent is still good, though a little less modern in its thinking. If you have decided to focus on technology, you will probably want the Swiss Federal Institute in Zurich."

"I'm dropping the tech focus," Zi Min said. "Biology, Food Sciences, Chemistry."

"Our own Jiangnan or Tsinghua University would not be bad choices in that case," Mother said.

"I wish Scripps still existed," Zi Min said. That wonderful research center had died when the States had drastically cut back on government funding of pure research units. Unless food production was the major focus, the funding went elsewhere. Many institutions had closed their doors.

Xiang Bo smiled sadly. "I do, as well. I would be proud to have you go where I went."

Zi Min looked over the stacks of letters and brochures. When she had applied, she still hadn't decided on her exact focus, so some of these were no longer appropriate. She picked up a half-dozen acceptances and dropped them into the recycling bin. That simplified things a bit.

"Do you want more input? Or just quiet to think?" Xiang Bo asked her.

"Quiet, I think."

Her mother nodded and went out, closing the door.

Food Sciences or straight Biology? She loved working with her mother. She loved the idea of feeding the world. And most of the research funding was there. So: Food Sciences. She picked up and disposed of three more acceptances, leaving five. Two were in China. She wanted to go outside the country for her graduate work. That left three. She stared at the University of California at Davis letter, with its enticing financial aid package and beautiful campus. But: the United States, no longer a leader in academics, no longer pushing scientific boundaries, and socially, unwelcoming of foreign students—her acceptance letter had glossed past that fact. She pushed it aside.

That left the University of Wageningen in the Netherlands, or Ghent in Belgium.

She called up photographs of those two choices and imagined herself in each environment. Wageningen reminded her strongly of Guilin. No karst formations against the horizon, of course, but green and flat and filled with ponds. The buildings were blocky and solid, also like those at home.

Ghent, on the other hand, was utterly different. Spiky pointed buildings stacked next to one another, drenched with the feel—and no doubt scents—of European age. There were rivers, or canals, but no ponds. It felt like something new to her. And their research assistantship would provide her excellent opportunities for independent work.

A degree from the ancient University would appeal to conservative grant foundations, wouldn't it?

"Ghent it is," she said.

So, she was on her way. She visited the campus for welcome week. She enrolled in classes and became engrossed.

And then she returned for a visit home, which felt like a giant step backward.

At home, Mama was still struggling with the escaped diatom-algae. Papa was still teaching classes at Yangshuo. *Ya-ya* was still trying to keep the local Council from taking the ancient compound away. It was like being stuck in a time loop.

She lifted the food in her bowl with her chopsticks and looked at her mother. "*Nofu?*" she asked.

"It is, yes."

"It's delicious." *At least that had made progress,* Zi Min thought.

"It's helping to feed the world, at the moment," Mama said, "and making Mo Chou and her supporters rich."

"Did you give up complete control?" Zi Min asked. She noticed her Papa making a face. A disgusted face.

"No, I still have voting rights, and we earn some money from the production."

"But mostly not," Li said in his grumpy voice.

Zi Min sighed. Definitely a time loop.

◡

Di'e walked quietly in the night. The stones of the courtyard seemed to glow in the full moonlight. She joined her granddaughter Zi Min in silence.

Zi Min's shadow now stood taller than Di'e's own. The bright little girl was now a lovely young woman. Di'e tried to celebrate that thought, but somehow, instead, her mind caught on the fact that she would not be making any more sticky-bun hairdos for her granddaughter. It made her feel old, ancient even, and left behind. *But that's what living long means everywhere*, Di'e thought. *It happens to everyone who doesn't die young.*

They stood side by side a few moments, admiring the moon, its white light shining on the courtyard paving stones, the sweet scent of jasmine that grew up the posts of the ancestor shrine floating in the air. Di'e's little cat Tai stropped herself against her ankles, then around Zi Min's, and then made an infinity between the two women, looping endlessly.

Zi Min bent and picked up the cat, breaking the pattern. "It's so beautiful here, *Ya-ya*. I hope we can keep this place safe from the future."

"'*From* the future'?" Di'e asked.

"They're putting up more apartment buildings just north of here. Soon it will be continuous city from Guilin to Yangshuo. Like an amoeba, ready to engulf us, like Chongqing did everything around it."

"Not to beat an old drum again, but it could help if you were married, Zi Min. A political man could go to local Council meetings and stop that sort of thing."

"I thought Ming-Hua was taking care of the Council."

Di'e closed her eyes. She took a deep breath. "He is not...politically strong. In ten years he has built up some favors due, yes, but he does not ask for them to pay up, to help us."

"What happened to Mama's influence with the Guangxi Secretaries?"

"She cannot provide them sufficient proof to calm their fears. We need a forceful man on the local council."

Zi Min half-laughed, half-snorted. "I am not certain I *could* marry such a man, if I even found him."

"I repeat my offer to locate a good matchmaker. I know it is old-fashioned, but perhaps that is what we need: an old-fashioned matchmaker to find an old-fashioned man to save an old-fashioned house," Di'e said firmly. "There are reasons to live within the society the rest of the province enjoys. A strong, conservative Council would work to preserve our history."

"And to *prevent* our studies, here, Ya-ya."

"They know how much income your mother's projects have brought into this region," Di'e said. "They are not stupid."

"*They* see very little of that money."

Di'e fought to control the tremors that now and then took over her head and neck. This was not a good time to appear weak. "I'm certain you can see that if we have weak input into the Council, we will have no influence with them and what they choose to do," she said. But they had wandered off the path she had intended this conversation to take. "So you do not want me to find a matchmaker, Zi Min, daughter's daughter?"

The young woman sighed. "Oh, see what you can find. I will talk to them. But please, *Ya-ya,* make no promises. By myself, I may have found someone who appreciates my work and my mind, instead of just my body and my duties. So I am not entirely sure I am available to marry some Councilman."

"Who have you found?" Di'e wondered. "Another scientist?" *Another elitist intellectual who cares nothing for his surroundings?* she wanted to ask.

"Someone I met at Ghent," Zi Min said.

Definitely an intellectual, then, Di'e thought. "Would he come here to live?"

"She might," Zi Min said. "She's thinking about it."

Shocked into silence, Di'e stood there like an ancestor statue, still as stone. *She?*

Of course most of the rest of the world accepted these things now. China stood alone in its conservatism. *Oh,* she thought, *to be fair, there are all those Muslim nations that also hold out against sexual liberalism.* Or outright *deviance,* most Han Chinese would call it. But China's unstated national attitude had been to ignore the whole thing, to pretend homosexuality did not exist now, just as it "hadn't existed" for the past dozen millennia.

It was, however, quite difficult to ignore when it was brought into one's own house.

She played forward in her mind what would happen if Zi Min brought home a same-sex partner: The Huixian Wetlands Council would excoriate her and her entire family along with her. Ming-Hua would lose his fragile place on the Council. And then the deeply conservative Council would be eager and able to build their coveted apartments and push them off this beloved land. She sighed. *Her* beloved land. The rest of the family did not seem to care as much.

The Council might make so much noise that Xiang Bo could lose her grant monies for research. What would happen to feeding the world, then?

The whole scenario would have the opposite result from Di'e's plan. "Ahhhh," she groaned. How could her family have come to this?

Zi Min reached out a tentative hand. Concern in her voice, she asked, "Are you well, *Ya-ya?*"

"No," she said. "No, I am not." After a moment of silence, she said, "Perhaps I should just sell out, take the money and move to the mountains. Maybe your mother would let us live in Jiao's house."

"I don't think it will come to that, *Ya-ya.* But isn't that Papa's decision?"

"No. It never was, since he does not care. He would live in the field shack if it had a place for his microscopes."

Xiang Bo inserted the last bit of data into her charting program. She printed out the charts so she could check them for errors and presentation strength.

Perhaps she should increase the ratio of temperature change on the vertical axis, and color-code it, so the cooling effects of DAS-covered waters in Guangxi showed in a more pronounced way.

The Secretaries were not scientists, not even the young Zhuang who had replaced the old Secretary. He had a degree in project administration, but it was more business-oriented. She had tailored her presentation to appeal to that aspect of her research: numbers, production rates.

She focused on the positives: DAS may have spread everywhere in Guangxi, but it was definitely providing benefits. Fresh waters were cooling down; that was demonstrable. At the same time, DAS-infused integrated fish farms were feeding a large portion of China. Well, it was, along with salt-water rice developed by the research team that had out-competed Li for funds.

The Council had believed her earlier presentations enough to restore her funding. They had not returned all they had sequestered, which was annoying. Some of those funds had been from private investors, or crowd-sourced ones, like Empty Bowls. The government had no right to take those monies, but they'd claimed "administrative fees," and kept almost ten percent of what they'd been holding back from her. She was pretty certain interest from those funds more than made up for any administrative costs, but it didn't pay to accuse the Party Secretary of stealing research money.

She wanted them on her side. She still hoped to have the Guangxi Council out-power the local Council insofar as land use was concerned; that was more important than a couple thousand yuan.

Besides, everyone knew at this point, that the entire nation of China must not lose even a *mu* more of its cultivatable lands. That the local Council was still trying to absorb the Cheng compound into its stupid apartment-building development was evidence of their profoundly short-sighted greed. The Party Secretary of Guangxi had the power to put an end to that, if he only would.

Xiang Bo spread her presentation across two monitors and looked at the overall effect. She rubbed her mouth, checking each chart. While she knew simple colors and lines were not going to sway the Council's opinions, she also knew there were good and bad ways to present her data. DAS was going to change the world, and she was pretty sure the Secretary could see that from what she had composed, here.

"That is good, Xiang Bo," Li said. She realized he'd been standing behind her looking over her shoulder for some time. "I hadn't understood that you have enough observations to show the cooling trend so clearly."

"I think it's strong enough to make a positive case for DAS, even though I have still not found a way to control it. Instead, I'm trying to show them that maybe it doesn't matter. That we may actually *want* it to continue spreading, as it cools our water and feeds our people."

"But, of course, it must be stopped eventually," Li said.

"Yes. I am working on that. If you have any further ideas, I would welcome them," she said.

Xiang Bo knew something was wrong between Di'e and Zi Min. It was a frustration that she could get neither of them to talk about it. Things finally came to a head when Li got involved.

"Ming-Hua succeeded in getting a vote to go his way, thanks to your suggestion to get some of those Council members to invest in the *Nofu* project," Li said as they got ready for bed. "At least two of the Councilmen have made good money and are inclined to support him. But Maman is still unhappy. Do you know what is going on?"

"I know she and Zi Min are not speaking."

"Maman told me Zi Min may be bringing *her wife* home."

"Yes."

"You knew?" Li stopped buttoning his pajamas and gripped her arm. "You knew and you said nothing?"

Genuinely puzzled, Xiang Bo set down her hairbrush and turned to face her husband. Their marriage had gone better and better as they had worked together to solve the problems of the diatom-algae. But this sounded like trouble. "I did not think there was anything to say."

"This is not Europe! This isn't even the United States, which can't decide if it's prudish or liberal! This is backward China: breeding grounds for all that is conservative. A moment's thought would have suggested you say something about a same-sex marriage coming into this house."

"Since they are to be wed in Ghent, there seemed nothing to say. It would be done."

"It isn't done *here*," Li said. His face was red and he was breathing fast, like he used to do when he got angry. It was like he had reverted to thirteen years ago. "Do you really think the Council is going to give us permits to run experiments when Zi Min and her wife are living here?"

"There's no reason the Council have to know," Xiang Bo said with perfect practicality. "I don't think Zi Min planned to make an announcement. It will look like two college friends working together, if anyone looks at all. And if they even decide to come here. They may stay in Ghent or go to Sweden for that project Zi Min applied for."

Li raised his hands, as though he was stopping traffic. "Maman is already fretting: She is certain we will be thrown off our land if word gets out. How can it be kept a secret?"

"It isn't anyone's business."

"You know better than that."

Xiang Bo shook her head.

It seemed like every time she had part of her life under control and going well, something blew up and she was caught utterly off guard by it. What did Li care who Zi Min married?

And what did it say about their own marriage that he could be still such a mystery to her after all these years?

36. KARINA—SAN FRANCISCO, CHICAGO USA

Karina went directly from the airport to the recycled wedding cake, the name she and Ashur had christened the plastic monstrosities of columns, arches, and domes her father had scattered around the world—his cookie-cutter imitations of the Golden Temple in Punjab.

She could have backed out when he didn't reply to her email, but Ashur had encouraged her to confront her father. This newest langar had just opened overlooking the Golden Gate Bridge. She had no problem finding him in the huge cooking space—copper pots the size of bathtubs stirred with wooden paddles and woks with long handles being shaken over open flames.

As she expected, he stood on a podium flamboyantly attired in a long jacquard silk Kurta. The deep purple stood out from the kitchen staff's white uniforms. Always the performer, he waved a small rolling pin like a baton, surrounded by a group of tourists, sitting cross-legged at low tables, who had paid good money to be allowed to work in the kitchen. With a fake Malayalam accent, he encouraged the crowd. "Remember to dust your rolling pin with flour before you flatten each dough ball."

She laughed to herself as these guests learned a skill most children in the Indian countryside knew before they entered school. A choreographed crew of assistants delivered dough balls and collected thin circles. She noted his smug satisfaction with the activity swirling around him. He cajoled his captive audience with constant chatter. "Well done." "Nice circle." "Perfect thickness." As usual, no one had a chance to speak except her father.

She stood among the sweating cooks flipping the roti on the turning *tawa*. The dough circles puffed up like balloons but deflated by the time they were dumped in big baskets and served to the diners.

She waved to him. She was sure he saw her, but he returned to his stage to recount the *langar origin story* and his epiphany at the Golden Temple. "The most beautiful building in the world...They feed one hundred thousand people each day...Free!"

She had had enough. She wasn't going to listen to this story one more time. "Don't you have any time for your daughter?" she shouted over the cacophony in the kitchen. "I wouldn't have had to fly here if you answered your emails!"

He looked around like he was going to call for security but thought better of it. He approached her with open arms. "Karina, I'm glad to see you. Can I get you something to eat?"

She rolled her eyes. When he got close enough, she hissed through her clenched teeth. "Cut out this nonsense. The show is over. We need to talk."

He gave her a big smile and an awkward hug. "Whoa. I'm busy right now. How about tonight? I'll take you to dinner." When she frowned, he added, "Not here. Someplace else."

She backed away. "I spent twelve hours getting here. I'm not waiting until dinner time, whenever that might be." She picked up a stack of aluminum trays and flung them into an empty wok. The sounds echoed with a satisfying metallic explosion. She saw his eyes open wide, as again he looked around, more concerned about the audience than his daughter. "I'm not leaving until we talk."

He took a deep breath and slowly exhaled. "Okay. Let's go to my office."

She followed him to a plain door. When they entered, she found herself in an opulent room with plastic columns and arches that echoed the wedding cake exterior. Indirect lighting made the room glow. This over-sized room made him look small in her eyes, and a bit foolish. She felt sorry for her father but remained true to her objective.

He spoke to his comp and ordered tea. "Have a seat. We won't be disturbed."

She sat on the sofa furthest from his desk, so he couldn't take the power seat behind that massive piece of carved teak. He set his 'baton' on one of the low tables and leaned forward. She looked at his face, lined with age. First, she thought, He's only seventy. Not that old. When she looked closer, she realized, oh my, he's wearing makeup!

From mammoths to *Nofu* to langars, he had chased one crazy idea after another. Now looking at him with his ostentatious clothes and clumsy makeup, she understood why her mother had taken the precaution to leave her money to Karina and not her husband.

She hid her anger. "While I was still a minor, you took money from my trust and purchased the mammoths. Now I am stuck with a worthless ranch in Maine."

He straightened his back and squared his shoulders. "That's just not true. I've heard the people raising mammoths in Nunavut have been quite successful."

"Nunavut!" Sheer frustration made all her suffering tumble out at once. She swallowed the garble of words, clenching her teeth. "Ah!" she gasped, "You know more about the distant Arctic than about your daughter!"

When he didn't respond, she wanted to hurt him. "After your effort to rescue me from those kidnappers—which I did not need—you abandoned me. You've always had more time for everything else!"

He just looked down and fiddled with his little rolling pin. She had come to deliver a message. As usual, it wasn't getting through. "Listen to me, Father. Listen as if this were the last time you would ever hear any words from me!"

He looked up, met her eyes.

"Mammoths do well in Nunavut, but Maine isn't cold enough. In the year-round warm weather, maturity and estrus are delayed. My mammoths amble aimlessly, despondent, and trapped in an extended prepubescence."

"Well, that's not my fault. No one knew."

They were interrupted by the delivery of a silver tea service with a tray of sandwiches and cakes.

"No one knew?" she asked him. "What gave you the right to spend my trust on *no one knew?*"

She stood up. "Thanks to you I've wasted my life caring for those depressed animals." She walked to where he was sitting. "Remember Sarita? She's married, with two children, and living in a big house in Mumbai."

He leaned back against a large cushion. "Are you done feeling sorry for yourself?"

Ashur had prepared her for this moment. She wouldn't let Kaczka brush her off that easy. "I want you to buy the mammoth ranch. You owe that to me for your failure to fulfill your fiduciary duty as a trustee."

He seemed offended by her indictment. He picked up his rolling pin and tapped it on the low table. "First, while your friend raised a family, you were in college. You have a degree in Animal Science and an M.B.A." He paused before adding, "Your trust had plenty of money for your years in school. Most people your age are drowning in debt."

She'd prepared a rebuttal, but she felt like a bully attacking the sad, old man that sat before her.

He seemed worn out when he tapped the table again. "Second, you own ten thousand acres in Maine and a herd of mammoths! Granted, not as big as the herd in Nunavut, but fifty-two is the second largest herd on the planet." He smiled at his little joke delivered in that fake accent.

This surprised her. The herd had just reached fifty-two with a recent birth of twins. She realized that even if they didn't talk, he was keeping in contact.

He tapped the table again and said, "Third," but he didn't continue. He looked run down and confused, unable to remember what he'd planned to say next.

He'd worked so hard and had so little to show for it. She grabbed a small cake and some tea to give him a chance to gather his thoughts.

He looked at her. "As you accurately stated, you didn't need me to rescue you when you were kidnapped, and you don't need me to do anything now. You've always been intelligent and independent." He closed his eyes. "I remember you holding your own when you were eleven and the next youngest person was twice your age. You could talk to scientists and engineers; you were fearless."

She drank some more tea. He hadn't contradicted her. Some of the old feelings for a father returned. She recalled their travels. The research vessel exploring deep-sea hydrothermal vents. Visiting seven continents before she was seven.

He continued. "You are right. Something changed after the kidnapping. I realized that you didn't need me. You were growing up and could take care of yourself."

She took another sandwich. Inside, she wanted to be angry that his nice words simply were excuses for his neglect, but she couldn't find the necessary pain and hurt. She was just ready to give up on him.

"I'm not going to tell you what to do with *your* mammoth ranch."

She realized he truly didn't care about the animals. It was up to her to decide to sell or not. And she realized she had a lot to think about before she decided. After wiping her hands, she dropped the fine Egyptian cotton napkin onto the little table. She took the few steps to where her father was now standing and shook his hand. "All right, Father. I'll take care of the mammoth ranch my way." He opened his mouth to speak but she preempted him. "Good-bye," she said. She picked up her comp and walked out, leaving him standing there. She was finished with him.

Across the bay, the Golden Gate Bridge opened, the cables hung loose, and two ships sailed through the gap, their superstructures reaching high above the roadway. The drawbridge retrofit had been all over the Internet but seeing it IRL took Karina's breath away. As the Marin Headlands separated from the San Francisco Peninsula, she thought about her father. He had made one point she couldn't deny. Twenty-five was too old to be running to him for answers.

Thunderstorms canceled Karina's flight to Boston, marooning her in Chicago. She stalked through the corridors, hiding in souvenir shops, bookstores, and restaurants, avoiding eye contact, and blending into the crowds. She relived playing stowaway, invisible and independent, twelve years old again.

An all-beef hamburger served on the fluffiest bun, a combination of climate-changing food and cancer-inducing industrial manufacturing appeared on a cardboard tray. For today, she'd be more like Ashur and not listen to Sarita, her father, her college professors, or anyone. As one of ten billion, she wouldn't even care about the *Hot*.

She took her snack and found a small table hidden behind a large trash bin. From there, as she had hidden on the RV Riftia, she observed, answerable to no one. Singles, couples, families. They looked like ants following scent trails.

Newly-free Karina made her first independent decision in over a dozen years.

She searched "Cloud Lake property for sale," until a picture caught her eye. It showed a nice-looking lady in a purple calico dress, with blond braids, a cowboy hat, and high-heel boots. Her four-wheel-drive displayed two signs: *Clayton Lake Realty* and *Residential Snow Removal.* Karina thought, local, independent, perfect.

Her comp connected and the lady with the braids answered.

Karina ran her fingers through her hair. "I'm in Chicago right now, but I have a property on Cloud Lake. I just sent you a link."

The lady said, "Karina Kowalski Mammoth Ranch? Are you Karina?"

"Yes, that's me."

Karina watched her scan through the slides.

"Do you want to sell?"

"Yes."

"Did you say that your ranch was on Cloud Lake?"

The lady emphasized both *ranch* and *lake* as if she didn't think either word could be accurate.

"Is it a working ranch?" The lady stopped at a picture of the office with dioramas and a stuffed mammoth. "This looks like a museum. Is it a tourist business?"

"Ranch. Museum. A little bit of each. We have a herd of woolly mammoths."

The real estate lady flipped through the pictures. "Mammoths? Are these holograms? Aren't they extinct, like the dinosaurs?"

Karina didn't want to dive into the mammoth story, so she took a deep breath and started over. "We have three more cabins like this one. They can be set up as rental units."

Now the lady smiled and opened a private window on her comp.

Karina continued. "Also, about ten thousand acres of meadows, forests, and ponds."

The real estate agent tapped furiously. "I can work with that," she said. "and zoned commercial, I see."

Karina circled back to the mammoths. "The herd is about fifty mammoths. The babies are small, two to three hundred pounds, like a black bear."

The lady's eyes got big, "And the adults?"

"Big. Really big." Karina couldn't figure out what to say next.

"Bigger than a moose?"

Now Karina knew she was in trouble. "Way bigger. Five to ten times bigger."

"Oh." The real estate agent thought for a minute. "I see. I don't think we can generate any interest until you remove those things." The lady mumbled to herself, "bigger than a moose," and shook her head incredulously. Then she said, "For sure. They have to go."

Before she finished her meal, her comp buzzed. "Hello, Ashur. I was just speaking to someone about selling the ranch."

"Have you translated the last Malayalam document I forwarded to you?'"

Between the meeting with Kaczka and talking to the real estate lady, she had forgotten. "That's the next item on my list. I'll do it before I board my plane to Boston."

"Where are you."

"O'Hare. Chicago."

"Can you leave the ranch on its own for a while longer and meet me in Paris? I have a negotiation where I can use your skills."

She had two quandaries. The ranch. The mammoths. No one would want them both. Karina now knew she could sell the ranch, and she'd figure out something to do with the mammoths. After all, she'd survived being kidnapped, and the biggest flood in the history of southern India. How difficult could it be to place a few huge, hairy mammals?

She didn't like it when he preempted her plans, but she looked forward to Paris, a welcome diversion from Maine. "Sure, I'll change my reservation. See you soon."

Carla hardly recognized her shy nephew as he ran across the Qamanittuaq airport tarmac and up the stairs for his first airplane ride. Before she could stop the excited seven-year-old, he had explored the galley and made friends with the pilots.

"I'm going to Africa. It's winter there."

She cajoled him out of the cockpit of the thirty-two-passenger turboprop. "We need to be in our seats or we're not going anywhere."

He bounced down the aisle and she buckled him in next to a window.

"Look! Here come our bags. I see mine!"

Carla repeated this frenzied boarding routine in Churchill, Winnipeg, and Toronto. Each larger aircraft injected William with another jolt of adrenalin. She rejoiced when he collapsed over the Atlantic Ocean, so they could both get some rest before the London layover.

When they eventually arrived at their hotel in Swakopmund, Namibia he staggered like a small drunk. She removed his clothes, dressed him in his pajamas, and covered him with a blanket. "Rest, Billy. You've had a long couple of days."

Carla marveled at his rapid recovery. On the first day of her assignment, he had brushed his teeth and dressed before their breakfast arrived. She wondered whether it was the travel or being away from his sister, but he had exploded into an adventurous child. With no objection, he ate a breakfast of mielie pap, a corn porridge. She took pictures to send to Elzia of her cautious son eating hard, spicy veldt bread, dipped in olive oil with thick slices of goat cheese. *OMG. #WorldTraveler.*

When they arrived at the algae processing operation, William looked up at his aunt and stamped his bright orange boots. He shook with excitement. "Ready, ready, ready! Let's go!"

They stood at the edge of one of the huge settling reservoirs, the size of a dozen swimming pools.

Billy pulled at her hand. "Where is all the green gunk coming from?"

"That is algae. It grows in the ocean."

Green Dots' technology farmed algae in the ocean rather than the vats used by others. Huge volumes benefitted Green Dots' approach, but the ocean-grown algae harvest came with many by-products that needed to be removed.

He bounced up and down. "I remember. You can see them from space. I counted the green circles when the plane landed. Twenty-seven!"

"Right," she lied. There were actually fifty-four of the two-kilometer diameter colonies. Aerial photos of these algae farms were ubiquitous in her company's publicity and gave them their name: Green Dots.

She continued. "Big hoses connect the algae farms in the ocean to these settling tanks."

He looked up at her with a mixture of admiration and confusion. "Settling tanks?"

Then he remembered, "Ocean waves mix everything up. The green gunk rests here, so the algae can float to the top and the seawater, fish, sand, everything else can settle to the bottom."

Smart kid, she thought, almost reconsidering her choice to remain childless. "Then what?"

"The top layer, the good stuff, goes to filters and centrifuges to extract the algae. Everything else goes to a water purification system."

He smiled. "People eat the top layer and drink the rest."

Close enough she thought.

William's eyes darted back and forth over the green slime that remained after the reservoir had been drained in preparation for Carla's visit. He held onto her tool belt. "Aunt Carla. Look down there. I see little fishies. Silver and shiny. And an octopus!" He ran to the access ladder.

She grabbed his arm before he could scamper down. "Wait for me. It's slippery. Do you remember why we're here?"

He pulled her to the ladder. "Separator mucked up. Pumps clogged. No one knows why. No one knows what to do."

She attached their safety lines and they climbed down the ladder. Even though children weren't allowed, she took him anyway. After they'd flown her first class, paid for the best hotel, and knew her daily rate, no one told her how to do her job. Besides, child labor was still prevalent in Namibia. Regardless, he was learning a lot and enjoyed the novelty. When Dee got older, she'd take them both.

She watched his slow progress and the tight grip he maintained on the ladder feeling proud that he'd learned the safety procedures better than some of those hot-shot young men and women that worked in the plant.

From her diagnostics, she knew the algae outflow was the problem. Pumps were failing too often, and replacement parts were expensive enough to justify her visit. While a seven-year-old could understand the concept, the engineering complexity overwhelmed everyone. Friction and abrasion. Mohs scales. Titanium alloys. Bernoulli equations. Eddy currents.

While she walked to the sludge pump housings, Billy chased herring. Even in just a dozen centimeters of green gunk, the silver fish easily slithered away from him. He continued to pursue them, getting covered in algae and laughing the entire time. "Fishies! Fishies!"

She looked up. Technicians in blue, green, and red jumpsuits to match the Namibian flag and managers in suits circled the reservoir. This was her favorite part—she called it *diagnostic theater*. She signaled for the overhead crane and started loosening the bolts. The nuts were twenty centimeters and weighed a kilogram each. Using a wrench with a two-meter handle, she removed them. After an hour, the pump was dismantled in the center of the reservoir.

The standard procedure called for the pump to be repaired in place, but in this case, a new pump was lowered, and four technicians installed it.

"I got one! I *got* one!!"

Everyone laughed as the green child proudly held a herring over his head. Then the fish gave one final spasm and escaped. Undeterred, he hunted for another one.

They raised the damaged pump for delivery to the maintenance building. She also collected several samples of sludge in polyamide collection tubes. She'd send them back to a lab in Sydney for analysis. Hopefully, either the pump or the samples would solve the mystery.

"This pump is fried." Carla could smell the distinctive odor. As she examined the disassembled parts, she played a little game: *Which part failed?* The air had an acrid taste. She was confident that this meant the motor had burned out. She wouldn't know positively until she completed her postmortem.

Green Dots pumps rarely failed. Billy's excitement had clearly shown that input included lots more than algae suspended in seawater. Fish, mollusks, crustaceans, and plastics were all expected. They used cutter pumps to macerate everything into a smooth slurry. Green Dots' patented centrifuge technology separated the algae biomass from the waste materials.

She arranged the pump parts in an orderly array on the workbench. She could see that the impeller and cutter bars shone, heat-treated tungsten carbide ready for work. She moved down the long table using her hand to waft samples of smells, a technique drilled into her by her high school chemistry teacher. Everything smelled like the beach until she came to the motor.

Yuck! She rushed to the sink to rinse her mouth and wash her eyes. *Definitely the motor. But why?*

Three managers in suits stood back from the workbench talking among themselves in a local language. She gave them a brief report. "The motor burned out, most likely some obstruction downstream. Since it's already Friday afternoon, and I need the results from the lab, we'll continue on Monday morning."

Since they had the weekend free, she took an excursion to the sand dunes she'd visited during her internship at *Mdudu Nyama*. William cheered when they finally reached Sossusvlei. "Sand drifts! People are climbing the sand drifts. I want to climb too."

He turned to the driver. "At home, we have snowdrifts. No one is allowed to climb them."

She almost said, Sand *dunes*, but instead stayed with his word choice, "Well, these sand drifts are safe."

He became excited. "Climbers! More climbers."

When they stopped at a lake with picnic tables, William jumped out and pointed. "Look! A lake in the middle of the desert."

The driver responded. "Well, it rained over there." He pointed to the east. "And the river overflowed. Soon the water will evaporate, and the lake will be gone."

Billy grabbed a sausage sandwich and started chasing the small brown and white birds that collected around the temporary lake.

The driver remarked, "Dune larks." Carla talked to him about dune animals until William returned for some cookies and a juice, both in glass containers. The driver explained that there was a large fine for bringing plastic or paper into the area. "Those 'Leave nothing but footprints' slogans failed, but strict rules and strong enforcement worked."

Billy returned. "That ranger took those people's bag of cookies and made them leave."

The driver raised his eyebrows in Carla's direction as if to say: Served them right. They packed up their lunch and started up a dune ridge. Everyone carried a steel water bottle. Billy started off running, but then slowed down and waited. "Aunt Carla? Do you have a boyfriend?"

She didn't want to discuss her social life with a seven-year-old. She wondered if he had heard Abbie and Elzia talking about her, not that being single over thirty was that unusual. She ignored the question, but he stopped walking and just stared at her with his enormous blue eyes. She smiled and straightened his hat. "Not really. Do you think I should have one?"

The guide kept walking.

Billy whispered. "You need a boyfriend to get married."

Still trying to keep the discussion light, she hugged him. "Do you want to be my boyfriend?"

He threw his armed around her legs. "Yes. Yes! Could I?"

That was not the response she expected. She peeled his arms back and took his hand. "Oh dear. Don't you think you're a little young for me?"

Together they ascended the dune. From the top, they had a panoramic view of the valley. Billy excitedly pointed to a distant group of oryx. "Unicorns! Look at them." A few minutes later he stopped to watch beetles burrowing in the sand.

Carla thought that the boyfriend discussion had passed, when he moved close and again whispered, "I wish you were married."

She was baffled. Why would a seven-year-old child be interested in boyfriends and getting married? She looked to the driver, who gave her a palms-up, I-don't-know look. She took a deep breath.

The driver jumped to his feet. "Okay, let's all hold hands and we can run down the side of the dune. Billy screamed and stood up. Each adult took a hand and they careened down, sand flying everywhere, sometimes falling and tumbling, everyone laughing.

"Oops. I lost my water bottle."

Carla could see his bright orange canteen halfway up. The driver immediately moved to retrieve it.

Billy asked, "Do you think you're getting married soon?"

She decided that he wasn't going to forget this. "Tell me, William. Why do you want me to get married?"

He hugged her and she could see a few tears. "I don't want to go to China. I want to stay with you."

She smiled and carried him over her shoulders to the car. "What's wrong with China?"

He looked at the ground. "I don't know. It's just scary."

"When we get back to the hotel, we can download some books about China. I'm sure that after you read them, you won't be frightened anymore."

The driver looked puzzled. "But you won't find many children's books about China."

"No problem. He's a really good reader." She turned to her nephew. "Aren't you?"

He broke out a big smile giving Carla the impression that he'd answered this question before. "I am an extraordinary reader with a gargantuan vocabulary and prodigious comprehension."

The driver just said, "Okay then."

Monday morning the technicians inserted the remote inspection robot into the long pipeline that connected the settling reservoir to the algae processors. Carla figured that a burned-out pump meant something blocked the pipes. The question was what and why? Green Dot systems were often installed in remote, low-tech locations. The systems were designed to be maintenance-free. When something went wrong, they sent for Carla.

Two technicians watched over her shoulder. One asked, "What are you looking for?" The other pointed to a shiny spot and suggested, "Is that it?"

After her discussion with Billy, she wondered if they were flirting with her. She glanced at them. *Boys.* They were too young. Soft skin. Pudgy cheeks. Not shaving yet. Then she considered. These guys might never shave. Still, they were too young. More likely they wanted a job with Green Dots.

Marketing had drummed into her that in addition to the geeky tech stuff, she should always be selling Green Dots. She had stock options, so when the company did well, she benefitted.

"Okay, guys, let's see if we can solve this. Did you inspect the intake screen?"

"Oh yes, Momma Carla. We check the screen every week. Sometimes we have to scrape some tiny mussels off."

That answered her question. "Momma" was a sign of respect, but also signaled that they saw her as older. They weren't flirting.

The shorter young man said, "We've been trained. We know that the pipes are polished. Rocks or shells—"

The tall one interrupted, "Or crabs or fish."

"—can scratch the surface."

The pipes were tougher than rocks and shells, but it never hurt for the techs to be hypervigilant.

"Yes," the tall one added as if this was a contest, "Nicks and scratches give bacteria and algae—"

This time the short guy interrupted, "and even mollusk larvae—"

"—a place to attach and disrupt the flow."

Final round to the shorter technician: "Laminar flow. Efficient systems have laminar flow, no turbulence."

Bonus round to the tall one. "The intake screen protects the pipes. We take good care of those screens."

"Excellent. Full marks for both of you. Let's go back to the monitor."

Carla switched over to autopilot. She could inspect pipes in her sleep. She'd been after the developers to create software to automatically inspect the pipe walls, but they always had other priorities. So here she was slowly guiding the inspection robot with two eager technicians looking over her shoulders. The light frequencies varied from infrared through ultraviolet. Each time the light changed, she quizzed her students.

"Did you see something?"

"Is that a scratch?"

"What about that shiny spot?"

Slowly the inspection proceeded. She thought about Billy and those two technicians who called her, "Momma Carla." She distracted herself from the tedious monitoring by wondering: *Am I getting old? Is it time to stop traveling? Should I settle down?*

Both technicians yelled, "Over there! Look! Mussels!"

"Good eye! Well done." She saw no reason not to praise them, even though Billy could have found the ten to twenty-centimeter shells and the mystery was unsolved.

"Can you disconnect that section of pipe and bring it to the lab. We'll examine it after lunch."

"Yes, Momma Carla," and they both went off on her quest.

"Did you have a nice morning reading about China?"

"Oh yes. It is pretty interesting. I like rice and I bet I'd be great with chopsticks. They are just like the people from Snow House. They eat a lot of fish. I like fish."

Carla congratulated herself. He just needed a couple of books.

Billy pointed to some Chinese calligraphy. "Look at this. Their writing is even stranger than the Qamanittuaq school. But! They write with paintbrushes. I'd rather use a brush than a computer."

On the way to the lab, she passed two managers.

"Good day. I hear you found something."

"Yes, we found mussels growing in the pipes, but we don't know why."

A manager wearing a Green Dot necktie said, "I knew you'd solve this. We planned a celebration dinner tonight at the best restaurant in Swakopmund."

She looked at him. *Cute. Is he flirting?* She turned to William without accepting the invitation. "Let's go. We need to get to work."

Billy smiled at the manager. "I like your tie."

When she walked into the lab, the techs stopped their work and looked to her expectantly. She wondered if they had skipped lunch to please her. She could brush aside the people back in Australia and the local managers with their cheery, but anxious, status queries, but these trusting and hard-working techs—she didn't want to let them down.

"We pried the mussels from the pipe. They came free easily. All that remained was a thin coating of fine algae."

She looked at the spot, hoping to see the problem. Unfortunately, it looked good. She turned to the techs' puppy eyes, reminding her of Tasha. "Did you see any scratches?"

"No, nothing. Why did the algae grow on the polished surface?"

She put her head into the seventy-five-centimeter pipe. Even with a bright light and a magnifying glass, the pipe looked flawless.

This was a bigger mystery than she expected. The fancy dinner would have to be delayed. Sometimes small algae colonies got a hold when the flow was interrupted. "Let's look at the logs."

Both technicians smiled and opened the logs on their comps. The short one eagerly asked, "What are you looking for? I can run a search."

"Were the pumps turned off? In the last month? Ever? When was the last time the pumps were stopped?"

"This is one of our best reservoirs. It hasn't been interrupted for over six months."

The other tech, looking a bit guilty, asked, "Is that why the motor burned out? Should we have given it a rest?"

The manager with the Green Dot tie joined them. "Almost done? Ready for a nice dinner?"

The technicians were silent. William answered. "Sorry, sir. Not yet."

"The little boy is right. We might stop soon and wait for the lab results, but the mystery is unsolved."

The manager walked away, and the technicians looked to Carla.

She was still puzzled, but she gave them something to do. "Our problem is under that film of algae. Make a fifteen-percent solution of algaecide in acetone and clean that spot. No brushes, cloths, or anything that might scratch the finish."

For the next hour, they delicately cleaned. No complaints, just periodic looks to Carla for encouragement.

"All clean. Looks perfect."

Carla confirmed their assessment. "Let's call it a day and wait for the lab report. I'm sure it will tell us what we need."

They both looked disappointed. She didn't know what to say, so she just bowed and backed away—Japanese style. She knew that wasn't the local custom, but it was the best she had for these gung ho young technicians.

By the time she got back to the hotel, she was hyper-anxious. Something was wrong. Algae fouling an algae processing system would be a conundrum. They belonged in the system, just not attached to the pipelines. She sent emails back to Sydney. With the time difference, she expected a reply by her morning.

She was worn out, so she went to the hotel restaurant where she and Billy could get American comfort food. Mac and cheese, cheeseburgers, fries, and hot fudge sundaes.

After dinner, William hugged her. "Don't worry Aunt Carla. My dad says you're the smartest. You'll figure this out."

She patted him on the shoulder. "Your dad's pretty smart too. Those people in China want him to help them with their *Nofu* bioreactors."

Billy nodded and Carla proudly hugged the little boy who knew more about algae than most people.

She thought about how she and her brother seemed to end up in out of the way places. Rich countries did not find algae flour palatable. Rich cities did not want to see huge industrial plants or green dots from their beaches.

She wondered if it was time to cash in her stock options and retire? Especially if she couldn't solve this problem. News of the Green Dot systems not being able to process algae could kill the stock price. Had she stopped being a loyal employee, or was she just weary of life on the road?

When they finished their dinner, she noticed the empty bowl that had contained Billy's smooth, gooey mac and cheese. It reminded her of her father and all the people that might go hungry if the Green Dot systems stopped working. For Redbird and all his handmade empty bowls, she had to solve this.

The next morning the technicians cut a small section of the pipe and prepared it for the scanning electron microscope. The scans showed many small scratches, too small to be seen visually. "Sub-micrometer damage," she pronounced.

A preceptive technician asked, "Are those flaws enough for the algae to attach to the pipes?"

She reluctantly admitted, "Yes," while silently adding, but it shouldn't be possible. Diatoms normally had a Mohs Scale hardness of six, or maybe seven, like sand. Green Dots systems were prepared for this.

She feared *super diatoms*, the *Bigfoot* of the algae business. Rumors of *mutant diatoms* metabolizing the increased levels of carbon dioxide to synthesize silicon carbide popped up regularly, often blamed on rogue scientists in China. The distance to Asia made this unlikely in western Africa.

Just then, her comp beeped, and an overnight lab report demolished her confidence. The sample contained something with a hardness in the seven-plus to eight range. *Super diatoms* from China or not, something was hard enough to scratch the pipes.

Everyone stared at her as she studied the attachments. The evidence was undeniable. She tried to hide her panic. "Something out there," she pointed west to the unseen Atlantic Ocean, "is damaging your pipes."

They all stepped back and looked to her. "What should we do?"

She put on a brave face. "No problem. These colonies are easily removed. With regular monthly inspection and cleaning, you should never have this problem again."

The techs did not reply, just stared over her shoulder. She turned around to see the manager with the green tie behind her. With her best confident, corporate stance, she reached out her hand. He shook it and she discouraged further discussion with, "I'm looking forward to the dinner tonight."

The next couple of days were exhausting. New maintenance procedures released globally. She found an article on scratch-resistant comps. All new pipes would be coated with synthetic sapphire with a Mohs Hardness of nine, just like comp screens.

Solving hard problems. Saving the company. She remembered why she loved her job. On the flight back to Qamanittuaq, William kept saying, "I knew you'd do it. You are the smartest. I want to be like you when I grow up."

38. XIANG BO—HUIXIAN CHINA

"The frustules are opalescent," Zi Min said, looking up from the electron-microscope.

"Yes, at close examination. In the fields, they still appear white in the sunlight," Xiang Bo agreed. "The opalescence is part of the nano-structure, and is linked to the bio-luminescence."

It was amazing, Xiang Bo thought, that her daughter stood here having this discussion with her. She looked at her no-longer-little daughter with a sort of awe. Zi Min had turned her childish enthusiasms with *new* and *different* to the work of feeding the world. Here she was now helping her mother solve the problem of the escaped diatom-algae symbiote, after all these years. Xiang Bo wanted to bounce on her toes, herself.

Zi Min spent another few moments making adjustments, then announced: "I agree with you. The reproductive governor you inserted is intact. I believe the change lies in these other structures. Horizontal gene transfer that led to the luminescence in DAS."

"Good," Xiang Bo said, smiling. "Tomorrow we'll look at the luminescence structures, then. HGT may indeed be the mechanism, which I believe had something to do with making the organism more tolerant of variances in pH." She pulled a loose lock of hair back behind her ear and tilted her head, waiting for her daughter's reply.

"That makes sense. It could propagate to more ponds, which it obviously has done," Zi Min said, biting her lip. "We can probably fix it, but...*should* we?"

Startled, Xiang Bo slid off her lab stool and faced Zi Min. "What? Of course we should! This blasted symbiote is so successful, it's taken over the entire province! What happens when it shows up in Mumbai?"

"Well, yes; it will probably spread. But isn't that what we wanted? A fast-growing *Hot*-tolerant food source for all of China that we can share with the world?"

"It's doing that already. Think about this, Zi Min: Given adequate nutrients and sunlight, DAS doubles itself every day by asexual binary fission."

"Yes, of course."

"Well how long do you think it will take to spread all over the world?"

"Not long, if there was nothing to stop it, but it dies in saltwater!"

Xiang Bo took a deep breath. "It does now, yes. But look how it has adapted to new environments already. One more simple gene transfer could remove that limitation. I believe we are back to the original problem: the governor is not governing as I designed it. The self-limiting original I planned has escaped, and it is now free to infest every freshwater system on the continent! It will destroy even the eco-systems which *do* work to provide their local peoples with food."

Zi Min's lips twisted, and she shook her head. "I just do not think that is such a problem. *People will have enough food.* They will simply have to learn to enjoy the things we can grow in the integrated ponds. Who doesn't like barley, corn, and soybeans? Sweet potato, squash, cabbage—"

"But—"

"Melons," Zi Min went on, overriding her mother's voice, "tilapia, mullet, catfish, even trout."

"The point is, they will have very little choice. My blasted symbiote will consume every freshwater system, possibly in the entire world! Do you think they will thank me when there are no blue-water lakes left *anywhere?*"

"They will thank you for the food they are eating," Zi Min said, certainty strong in her young-adult voice.

⌣

"I think we have perhaps created a monster," Xiang Bo said over Li's shoulder.

"Hmm?" he said, still staring at the news reports on his screen. "Your symbiote is not a monster."

"I mean Zi Min."

"*What?*" he turned around and looked up to meet her eyes, shock apparent on his face. "Again?"

It had taken years for him to get over Zi Min's marriage to Lotte. But that wasn't the problem.

"She doesn't care if DAS takes over the world's freshwater."

"It hasn't done anything of the sort. It has spread across Huixian Valley. It isn't even in Nalai, you said yourself!"

"Yet."

Li flicked his fingers, as if brushing off that problem. "No. I agree with our daughter, in this, *baebae*. What good are blue waters if no one is here to see them, because all the peoples of Earth have starved to death?"

Xiang Bo stood silent a moment. "There will come a day when people forget they were ever hungry."

"That would be a good thing, don't you think?"

Li reached up a hand to clasp hers. She clenched her fingers spasmodically around his. Her other hand came up to cover theirs.

She said, very softly, "Perhaps, then, *I* am the monster, for creating it. It will be as bad as Ice-9. Vonnegut's end of the world."

Li made a noise deep in his throat. "What? Some silly science fiction writer imagined a nonsense weapon that has no analog on the planet! Your integrated fish farms are a reliable food source in this disastrous climate, and bear no resemblance to a weapon. Ancestor's sake, Xiang Bo: You should be proud!"

She could feel her body slump as she stood there, shoulders drooping, head down, hands clenched. She did not feel proud. She could feel disaster looming. She could feel it coming like an enormous black cloud that would obliterate the sunlight, forever.

"You are being foolish, woman. Don't do this to yourself."

But she could feel it, feel the room darken as they stood there.

Xiang Bo realized she had fallen asleep in the lab again, when she woke to the morning light, birds singing out in the courtyard. She sat up, ungluing from her cheek the zip drive that she had rested on…for how many hours?

She had been working tirelessly, but was still no closer to creating a governor that could stop the spread of DAS.

Maybe she should go back to their original thought, a dozen years ago. Li had suggested a phage that would hunt down the algae and eat it, or destroy it. For good reason, Xiang Bo had not wanted to risk releasing such a thing into the environment. It might create even worse problems, eating up *all* the *good* algae on Earth—including those used for food.

Even if they let DAS do its worst, it would still be better than utter destruction of the earth's biomes, which all rely on algae in some form. DAS could crowd them out, but it would not extinguish them like a runaway phage could. But after all these years DAS still had not done so. It had spread, yes. But it didn't destroy.

She had begun to believe her daughter and her husband were both right. That even if it did "take over the world's freshwater," people would be glad of the food they could obtain from DAS.

Then she had seen a small article in her news feeds. A curiosity. A report of a strange white algae infesting the lakes where normally pink flamingos fed. The brine shrimp that were happy to live in the enormously saline waters of the Rift Valley Lakes and other salten seas and lakes were dying off. The flamingos were turning white.

Some of them glowed in the dark.

The article writer had been amused by glow-in-the-dark flamingos. But Xiang Bo wasn't amused. She knew, she *knew* what had caused the phenomenon. DAS had hitched a ride to Africa.

And it was now *saltwater tolerant*.

She shuddered, and returned to her work with a vengeance.

Suluk's heart clutched as Maatalii appeared in the doorway of the small airplane. Maati looked weak and thin. Beside Suluk, Caiden grunted and ran up the stairs to help his wife come down them, her every step shaky and uncertain. Caiden glanced at Suluk, anguish in his eyes. It was as if the wrong Maatalii had been sent home; surely this was not their sturdy, funny Maati.

Later, inside at the restaurant table nearest the kitchen, Suluk watched as Caiden tried to get Maatalii to eat some of Osha's bannock, still warm from the pan. Maybe that humble nourishment would help restore her real daughter, she thought. Caiden and Maati were talking in soft voices, but she still heard Caiden say, "I was angry that you risked yourself and our child. Then I saw you looking half-dead in that hospital bed, and I knew you had done the right thing, helping family. I would have been unhappy if you were so selfish that you would not go."

"Of course I had to go. For *uaguk*," Maatalii said, her face looking sad. "But the price was so high, I am thinking I was wrong to interfere."

Caiden shook his head and squeezed her hand, Suluk could see Maati squeeze him back, their fingers whitening in the grip. Holding on. "I should have gone with you. I could have stopped some of it. I almost lost you, too, which couldn't have been what Amaruq wanted, either. At least Niki is in jail, where he cannot do more harm."

Their voices dropped to a murmur, and Suluk felt she was spying, so she went back to the kitchen and chopped fresh mammoth meat for the stew of the day.

That done, she gave Maatalii a hug as the young couple passed by on their way to their almost-finished small house out back. Maati laughed about something Caiden said and then turned her head to smile back at her mother as they went out the back door.

"*Ajurnamat,*" Suluk said, as she went into her little office. "It can't be helped."

A hamlet up near Resolute had begun raising musk oxen, importing a starter herd from Greenland. The more she read about it, the more Suluk despaired. This was direct competition for Snow House.

Like those in Greenland, the musk ox fur could be spun into a soft warm yarn. Garments woven from the cloth were selling well, much better than those from the coarser mammoth wool. The best they could do with the mammoth yarns were sturdy rugs.

Worse, the musk oxen meat, like mammoth meat, was leaner than beef, and was a less expensive alternative. Increased production by the northern Inuit was going to cut into her meat sales, of both mammoth and caribou.

Muskoxen meat had gotten good reviews. Of course, her products had, as well, but production was limited, since their primary goal had been to repair the tundra, not produce alternatives to beef.

Like the mammoths, the musk oxen were good at churning up the soil, helping the permafrost re-freeze. They ate the same grasses, lichen, and mosses that the mammoths ate. Their horns could be carved and looked similar to mammoth ivory. In Suluk's opinion the horn was not as nice, being grainier, and it tended to yellow more as it aged. But in all, they were definitely competition.

She slowly turned the pages of her accounting book, looking at how the income numbers had fallen at the same time expenses for Snow House and all its derivative businesses had risen.

As beef became the caviar—or the white truffles—of the *Hot* economy, she could expect her mammoth and caribou meats to increase in value. She just needed to sell more. Meanwhile, she might need a loan. Would their local bank loan money on such a business as Snow House Inn and Restaurant? She bit her lip, as she looked up interest rates and considered value. It would be a gamble, betting on Snow House to increase its profits, that was certain.

She could not begrudge the Resolute people their musk oxen herd, not when those people hadn't even *chosen* the site of their home. They'd been moved there by the Canadian government in the High Arctic Relocation program. They'd nearly starved while trying to learn to live as Inuit had lived for centuries. The *Hot* did not affect them quite so much up there—they did not seem to have to rescue many abandoned polar bear cubs, for example—but with fish numbers dropping, alternative protein sources became more and more important all over the world. The Resolute group were just trying to survive. They were doing it with the *Umimmak* from Greenland.

Of course, she was only trying to survive, also. As were her family and her town.

She sighed and closed her accounts book. Something was going to have to improve soon, or Snow House was going under. What would all her family do then?

By her second day home, Maatalii was feeling much stronger. She felt she could work. She was smiling as she opened the door to find Amaruq standing there, hand raised to knock.

Uaguk's greeting was not what Maati expected.

"I need to talk to you," Amaruq said, her face cold and unfriendly.

What was the problem? Maatalii wondered, closing the door after Ama entered. She walked over to where Ama now stood in front of the small solar-powered stove and heater, rubbing her hands. Maati sat down in the rocking chair—the one that was supposed to have held her and her baby—and waited for her sister-friend to speak, fighting tears.

"I kept wondering how Niki found us. I had never told him where I was from. He only knew it was one of the small villages here in Nunavut."

Maati nodded. "I never even spoke to him while we were at school together; it was apparent he did not like me." Which was one of the reasons she had never understood why Ama had loved him, had gone with him. As time passed, seeing what the man had been like had made that puzzle even more inexplicable. Until she had personally seen the hypnotizing magic-like hold Niki had had on *uaguk*.

"Well, I found out who told him." Amaruq's face was still closed, still cold.

"Told him? I assumed he had found you on the internet or something. He did know your name, from your school registration, yes?"

"He knew my name, of course. But, no. It turns out he and my very own brother, Tarkik, know each other. Tarkik told him."

"What? How?"

"When Tarkik was buying supplies for Snow House, he met Niki, who had access to some linens and cleaning products that were probably stolen. Tarkik was able to buy what Snow House needed and pocket the money he saved, so he was fond of Niki. I guess he still is, for that and other reasons."

"Okay...but why would Tarkik tell him *now*? He knew all these years..."

"They hadn't had much contact, once Tarkik stopped buying supplies. But he said—Tarkik told me—that Niki had been looking for his child on the internet. Tarkik finally saw one of his posts, and told him where we were."

Maatalii frowned, taking in what Ama had said. "I still don't really see why he would help Niki like that, if it meant betraying his own sister."

"Well. It turns out he has a similar problem. A lost child." Amaruq spun and bent over, grasping her own upper arms. As if she were falling and needed a strong grip to save herself.

"What?" Maatalii said, confused.

"Tarkik met a girl when he was away at college, before Jissika. She got pregnant, and even though Tarkik offered money, she would not abort the child: she wanted it. Then she disappeared. Tarkik didn't know where, and he never saw her again. He has a child he's never seen, so he had some sympathy for Niki."

Prickles covered her arms. Even so, how could one of the family betray his own sister? Tarkik must have known it would mean trouble for Ama, yet he had told Niki anyhow.

Amaruq squeezed her eyes shut tight. "I still cannot believe you did your *kakiniit* without me!" she said in an abrupt change of subject, waving a hand at Maati's arms. Maatalii stared at her in disbelief.

"Ama, you walked off and left me without a word. I did not know where you were. I did not know *how* you were. I did not know if you would ever come home! And you are hurt because I tattooed my arms while you were gone, for *months?*" Maatalii shivered at the strangeness of it all. "I think Niki has some kind of magic spell over you, that is the only explanation I can find."

She looked closely at her *uaguk*, searching Ama's face for an answer. Amaruq licked her lips.

"Thank you for helping me get Nanuq back," she said. Then she turned and walked out, slamming the door behind her.

Maatalii got up and walked to the front window. She pulled back the still-unhemmed curtain and watched as Amaruq walked away. *Uaguk* got smaller as she walked, as though she were shrinking, as though her self and her love were fading into the tundra.

Maati shivered again, rubbing her arms. Then she walked back to her rocker, turned up the heater, and sat down, fingering her forearms where her skin-stitched pattern spoke of her strength and family and love.

She did not feel strong, now. She was tired and sad, and very, very, confused. Why was Ama angry at *her*?

◡

Tarkik glanced at Suluk and smiled.

"All ready to go?" he asked.

She finished tucking her long parka around her legs and set the pile of papers in her lap. "Yes," she said, reaching behind herself to grab the seatbelt and fasten it.

She smiled a little as she watched her nephew and foster son. Tarkik was so proud of his new car, and happy he had a chance to use it on behalf of his family. He'd been making good money working for Erne-Auco mines, and seemed to like his job well enough.

"What is this machine you drive at work?"

"It's called a loader," he said. "I mostly move dirt around."

"You know how to drive it?"

"They trained me." He glanced at her. "I know Giqa and some of the others don't much like the mining company, but they're pretty good people. At least, they've been good to me. Jissika is so pleased with the extras we've been able to buy, and I like the work. It's been a good thing for us."

"I think Giqa still expects Sedna to rise up and flood out the mine."

Tarkik shook his head. "Maybe she already has; we've had a lot of trouble with water seeping into the lower levels." He cleared his throat, then his frown turned into a smile again. "But that's what gives me a job, so that part's good."

"I am glad." She thought about the upcoming meeting between Erne-Auco and the KIA—the Kivalliq Inuit Association, which she herself represented along with several other locals. She hoped Tarkik didn't get into trouble for driving her to the meeting. She did not plan to support the company's request for an expansion license, feeling the KIA needed to set stricter controls on environmental damage.

━●━

"We provide jobs for many locals," The Erne-Auco officer said, clearly confused. "Our mandate is to offer at least 50% of our positions locally before we even look anywhere else, and we train the ones who need it, too."

After glancing at her fellow KIA members, Suluk decided she should answer this. "We are aware of this and of the care you take with both our social and environmental needs." She held up the pages of the licensing request. "Nevertheless, this impacts another 10,000 hectares of Inuit Owned Lands. How much of the tundra do you need to destroy, before it is enough?"

Other Inuit present in the group nodded at this. That was the main question, wasn't it? Where and when would it stop?

One of the other mining company executives leaned forward, tapping on the table. "You ask this, when you authorize plowing up the tundra all around Qamanittuaq?"

All the Inuit laughed.

"How is that okay, but what we do is bad?" the man went on, trying to ignore their amusement.

"That is to *help* the permafrost," the oldest Inuit representative said. "During the summer, the snow and ice cover reflect sunlight and limit the depth of the permafrost thaw. That is good. But now we have very little snow and ice in summer. That is bad. There is nothing limiting the depth of the thaw."

The mining people all nodded. They got that part.

The Inuit Elder went on: "In winter, the snow insulates the permafrost like a blanket. It keeps it warm, so it does not freeze like it should. That is bad."

"But— I give up!" the man said. Sweat dotted the pink scalp beneath his comb-over. "How can ripping it up help it refreeze? That's just… counterintuitive."

"When the tundra is churned up, like by caribou hooves, that clears away the insulating snow, and exposes the chunks of dirt to the cold winter air. This helps the permafrost refreeze. That is good." The Elder glanced around the table, to see if the anglo mine bosses were understanding him. He nodded and continued, "And now it is churned by mammoth feet and farming plows as well as caribou hooves."

"But us digging up the tundra doesn't do that? Why?" The Erne-Auco man honestly seemed to be trying to understand, Suluk thought.

"Maybe in a few places in your gold mines you have noticed it freezes up fast. But you keep digging, down and down; that does not accomplish the same thing."

"Well, we will put the tundra back when we finish," one of the other mine people said. "We always do; it's part of the terms of our contracts with you, and it is emphasized in that proposal," he lifted his chin towards the papers the Inuit all had in front of them.

"*When* the Fifthslope mine is finished and the lands restored, *then* we will consider this new uranium mine," the Inuit eldest said, in firm tones. "But not until then."

All the Inuit nodded at that. They were agreed on this. The Erne-Auco men bit their lips, but they had no further arguments. The meeting broke up.

Glad she hadn't had to be the one to state the KIA decision, Suluk gathered up her papers. She put her KIA Business Development Fund application on top, that the Elder had brought for her as she'd asked.

Maybe they would give her money. Maybe that was how she could pay for mammoth feed and fencing. The Association had helped other local businesses, they had a fund for it. And Snow House was certainly a local business that needed help. The application was one of the main reasons she had gone out of her way to attend this meeting.

The Inuit all shook hands with the Erne-Auco people and filed out. Everyone was polite, nobody looked happy, but at least the meeting was finished. Suluk made her way outdoors, to see the aurora shimmering overhead. Green curtains, with a few streaks of pink sheeted across the sky, like a wide river of light. While sometimes silent, tonight the parking lot was quiet enough to hear flickering crackle sounds the aurora was making, in which she could almost hear voices. *Voices of ancestors and gods.* Are they angry, or approving? she wondered.

She brought her gaze down and found Tarkik standing by his new car in the parking lot, ready to drive her home. She waved and went and got in the car. He had even warmed it up. Tired, she leaned her head back and snoozed most of the way home.

The lights of Snow House Inn's reception area woke her, and she gathered her things and waved good night to Tarkik as he started the car again and drove away.

40. ABBIE, ELZIA—QAMANITTUAQ, ELZIA— OKLAHOMA

Abbie stood in front of the aging printer, "You can do it. Just a few more pages." It couldn't hear her, but as it spat out each warm sheet of paper with a hiss and a slight grinding sound, she imagined its struggle to support the needs of Qamanittuaq primary school. The kindergarten classes made the most demands, with many pages of letters and pictures to teach the two alphabets the children had to learn. The worksheet she coaxed from the valiant printer had a picture of an igloo, even though the people in Qamanittuaq all lived in wooden houses. It had the English word Igloo along with its French equivalent *Iglou*. It also had a word in Inuktitut syllabics that started with a triangle—Δ. When she started volunteering at the school, she had hoped to learn to read their alphabet. Only a few words of the strange writing had managed to penetrate her aging brain.

Before the printer finished, the two o'clock bell signaled the time for winter dismissal, less than an hour until sunset. Abbie paused the multilingual igloos and headed for the kindergarten. Reversing the morning routine, she helped the children exchange felt moccasins for their kamiks. A few children wore traditional boots handed down from grandparents, but most wore brightly colored ones insulated with some puffy filler. Their parkas were the same mix. Most of them could dress themselves, so Abbie's primary job was to match each piece of clothing with the proper child. Most of the name labels were written in Inuktitut syllabics, but even though she couldn't read them, she quickly learned to match the labels with the children.

She thought back to her arrival when all the round faces with dark eyes and straight hair looked the same. Now she had no trouble recognizing thirty different five- and six-year-olds. Beyond the physical differences, so obvious, though indescribable, each child had a unique personality. Of course, she smiled to herself, no one had any difficulty recognizing William with his pale skin and curly red hair.

Between volunteering at the school and taking care of Billy and Dee, her days and her heart were full. Elzia worked as a waitress at Snow House and had made friends with other young mothers, often joining them sledding down the hills surrounding Qamanittuaq in the winter and exploring the lakeshore in the summer. Redd had made a few friends with the older men who congregated around Snow House, but, true to form, he tended to be solitary. She proudly thought that the five of them had successfully made their transition to Nunavut. William and Wendy were even learning to speak Inuktitut.

Mike and his sister Carla traveled so much that they had not become part of the community. They were tolerated much like the crews from the monthly ships from Chesterfield Inlet with necessities like canned foods, solar panels, and lumber, and the weekly airplanes from Churchill with luxuries like fresh vegetables and tourists. Abbie's grandchildren celebrated the arrival of their father or aunt, always accompanied by small gifts and exciting stories of the world beyond, often tropical, and always populated with strange animals and customs.

Abbie had applied for Canadian citizenship and easily imagined her small family living in this cold village on the shore of Qamanittuaq Lake. She dreamed about a time in the distant future when her descendants would be bonded to this place, as Redbird's had been to their adopted home in Oklahoma, now so far away in space and time.

Elzia cherished her evening time with William and Wendy. Tonight, they shared the family room with Redd snoring in his recliner in a discordant duet with the news. The whole house smelled delicious as Grandma McGilvery baked pumpkin and apple pies in the kitchen.

Elzia's children tucked in close to her around her comp displaying the faces of their distant Oklahoma grandparents. Billy and Dee were excited to speak to them. They hadn't flown south in over a year and Elzia's parents had never found time from their ranching chores to fly north.

Dee kicked her feet up. "Look at my new kamiks." She rotated her feet. "See. From Snow House. The best. Warm and waterproof." She reached across her mom and poked Billy. The grandparents laughed as she encouraged her brother. "Show them your new boots."

William took off his boots and held them in front of the camera. "Can you see these? They are mammoth skin. A hundred years ago there were no mammoths. Now we have a whole herd."

At the mention of mammoths, Dee interrupted. "I got a mammoth calf to raise this year. We're having a mammoth roast for Christmas. We might even make some money selling the extra meat."

Elzia's mom turned her camera to the mudroom in Oklahoma lined with shiny black boots with metal clasps. "Those are our winter boots. These days we have more mud than snow."

With the camera back on the grandparents, Elzia's dad added, "Send us some mammoth steaks. They were tasty, a little like deer, but with more marbling."

The call ended with lots of I-love-you's and See-you-soon's. "Will you stop in Oklahoma on the way to China?"

Elzia said, "Of course," but the real answer was more complicated. She closed with, "I love you, and will let you know when we've made our travel arrangements."

She intended an extended stay in Oklahoma, but she needed to speak to the McGilverys first, a task she'd been putting off.

Elzia watched Abbie set the table. This was usually her children's chore, but tonight was special. Eight place settings. The grandparents, Elzia's family of four, Carla back from somewhere, and Yuka as a guest. With Redd's arthritis getting worse, the family needed help, and that usually meant Yuka.

After everyone took their seats, Abbie held hands with her grandchildren. Elzia noticed this and followed her lead. Soon everyone held hands around the table. Elzia didn't know what to expect. The McGilverys didn't go to church and Abbie only said grace on Thanksgiving. Elzia bowed her head and waited.

"Thank you, Lord, for the food we are about to eat, and for those who are here to share these blessings. We are grateful for our wonderful family together around this table. Amen."

Everyone, including Dee and Billy, echoed, "Amen."

Elzia served them fish and chips. The Inuit often ate raw fish. She knew the Japanese did also, but her family didn't. After that prayer, she thought she should say something. She looked to Mike to see if he wanted to start, but before they figured it out, Carla began.

Carla took a drink from her glass, "I am also glad to have the family together because this might be the last time I'm here for a while."

Elzia was surprised but kept a calm face. She wondered if Carla had a boyfriend and was getting married. Or was she pregnant? She never mentioned any boyfriends, nor spent more than a week or two in the same place.

Carla continued, "You know I have been traveling around the world for years. I appreciate that you've made a place for me here as my home base, my foundation."

Elzia gasped. She looked at her sister-in-law with concern. *She's leaving. Abbie is going to be upset.*

"Green Dots has offered me a job in product marketing in Sydney. They figure I know more about our customers than anyone. This is a great opportunity and a promotion."

Elzia wanted to clap and say, maybe you'll meet someone if you settle down, but she looked at Abbie's disappointed face and kept quiet.

The table was silent, but this wasn't an occasion for cowards. Elzia kicked Mike.

"I feel this isn't the best timing, but you all know I've been considering a position in China. Well, after my interview in San Francisco, we went to Chinatown for Dim Sum, and I agreed to join them for a year, with an option for an additional year. They have one of the only algae products to break into the American market. To quote my sister, this is a great opportunity and a promotion."

Elzia had never seen her mother-in-law looking so sad and she still had her own announcement. She couldn't be blamed for Abbie's children deserting her. Still, she felt bad. "The children and I will stay in Oklahoma. Mike and I agreed that he should get settled before deciding if we should follow. We don't even know if they have a school where he is going."

Abbie cried. Billy and Dee hugged her. "We love you, grandma."

Then William turned to his mother. "Are you and daddy getting divorced?" Elzia hadn't expected this question. Divorce was rare in Nunavut.

She hugged her children. "No divorce, but we're going to stay with the Oklahoma grandparents while daddy explores China."

Billy bravely announced, "I want to go exploring."

Dee added, "Me too. I could be like Sacagawea."

After Elzia and Mike put the children to bed, they put on their parkas and kamiks and walked to the barn.

Mike attempted to be cheerful. "Well, that went as well as we could have expected."

"I'm sorry Carla is also leaving. Abbie is stuck with only your father. Maybe with all of us gone, he'll perk up."

"I don't know about him, but I think it will be good for Carla to settle somewhere. Leaving Oklahoma upset her, and I feel she's never recovered."

Elzia took her hand from her mitten and slipped it into Mike's. "I don't want to break up our family. Can't we go with you?"

"I explained this before. They encouraged me to come alone. I'll be staying in a one-room shack near the factory. I know nothing about housing, shopping, schools, or hospitals. It doesn't sound like a good place for families."

Elzia got more upset the more she thought about it. Now she wondered if she should have pushed back harder, not let him take the job in China. "You said you'd call us every day."

He got quiet like he always did when they argued. At times like these, he reminded her of his father. "I will absolutely call every day. The one thing I know is that they have fast Internet."

At that point, Tasha showed up. Elzia hugged her. "I'm going to miss you too."

They walked back to the house in silence.

◡

Abbie stood with Tasha as Yuka drove Carla and Mike and Elzia and her grandkids to the bus terminal. Tasha leaned against her leg and raised her paw to touch her hand. "Yes, Tasha. This is a sad day."

She could hear the whine of Redd's lathe. He seemed lost somewhere else, turning out empty bowls, and mourning for hungry people on the other side of the globe. Abbie turned to Tasha, "Let's go inside."

The big Newfie took up most of the sofa. Abbie took her spot and the affectionate dog rested her head on Abbie's lap. Abbie looked into the large eyes and asked, "Do you think I made a mistake moving so far?" Tasha licked Abbie's hand. Abbie scratched the Newfie's ear. She found the weight of the large head strangely comforting. In a cheerful voice, she offered another question. "Do you like playing with your *qimmiq* friends?" At the mention of the Canadian huskies, Tasha looked to the door and wagged her tail. Abbie smiled for the first time that day. "Well, at least this is a good place for you."

She got up and took out the flour and sugar and set up the large mixer. She'd promised the ladies at Snow House some more cookies. *I think I'll try to spend more time over there. Drinking tea. Learning Inuktitut. Helping at the Qamanittuaq school.*

Dee and Billy ran to greet the Oklahoma grandparents. Dee drove the luggage trolleys in wild circles. William wanted to ride the luggage carousel. Elzia, with the help of g'ma, did her best to keep them out of trouble, while g'pa rounded up their luggage. Four suitcases. Three boxes. One old-fashioned trunk. Plus, their carry-ons.

Elzia watched in awe as her father stacked everything on a freight carriage and herded it toward the parking structure. After living with Redd so long, she had forgotten how active and fit someone in their fifties could be. Maybe it was healthier to live in Oklahoma. More fresh vegetables. Less fat.

G'pa wrangled everything into the bed of the truck. Elzia sat in the front seat with g'ma. The kids sat in the backseat with g'pa. Elzia noticed the different color palette. In Nunavut everything was white. Even with only five hours of daylight, Qamanittuaq felt sparkling. The drive to Cherokee seemed brown, dusty brown. Bare fields. Unpainted houses. Dirty cars. She was glad that none of this discouraged her children.

Dee broke the uncomfortable silence. "G'ma. Can I raise a steer? I know they're not as big as mammoths, but they are tasty."

"We don't raise cattle anymore. They required too much water. For a while, we tried fishponds, but they also needed too much water." She laughed. "Isn't that silly, trying to raise fish in a desert?"

Ever curious William asked, "Is this a desert? I don't see any cactuses."

"Cacti!" Dee corrected.

G'ma explained, "This is a different type of desert. We get some rain in the winter. Sometimes we even get snow."

That set the two children off.

"We get plenty of snow back home."

"Our favorite place is called Snow House."

"We also have lots of fish."

Elzia wondered if her children would stop chattering. She smiled when g'ma joined the discussion. "Well, we raise chickens. Lots of chickens. Dee, would you like to raise your own chickens, and maybe a turkey for Thanksgiving?"

Elzia could see Dee trying to imagine chickens, until she finally figured it out, "Fluffy feathers! Chickens would be nice!"

Elzia didn't feel as resilient as her children. Even though she knew the climate had changed, after all, she'd grown up with climate change, it was still disappointing to see it. No winter wheat. No cattle. Somehow the empty fields made her miss Snow House and Mike, especially Mike. She wasn't one to regret her decisions, but something like regret made her shiver. *I should have not given in. I shouldn't have let him go to China alone.*

Carla took in the familiar sights as her plane approached the Sydney airport. The Harbour Bridge. The Opera House. The Royal Botanic Gardens. Everything looked as expected, except the harbor was unnaturally white. Not whitecaps. Uniformly white. It was summer in Australia, so it wasn't frozen. Carla puzzled over the strange appearance as the airplane landed.

This mystery was resolved at the Green Dots marketing meeting the next day.

"I assume you noticed the white surface on Sydney Harbor?"

Carla nodded.

"Those are *your* super diatoms. They might have originated in China, but that's not important. As you discovered, they are now found around the world."

"Everywhere?" Carla wondered aloud.

"Yes. All of our systems are operating at reduced capacity."

Carla noticed an empty bowl on the table and thought of her father. "What are the impacts on the global food and water supplies?"

"There are no issues in Australia, but many places are reporting shortages and the U.N. has been organizing relief efforts."

Carla thought of all the people she'd met. Those technicians with hungry parents and children, working two jobs and depending on inexpensive algae flour. They depended on Green Dots to keep them fed and healthy. Green Dots supplied the cheapest food. Those customers didn't have an alternative.

She also worried about Billy and Dee. *What kind of world are we leaving for the future?* Now she was glad she didn't have children.

41. KARINA—MAINE, BOSTON MA USA

Karina sat at the Mammoth Ranch computer. She ordered supplemental oats and veterinary supplies. Her comp flashed for an incoming connection. "Karina Kowalski Mammoth Ranch," she answered.

"Hello. This is the kindergarten at the Clayton Lake School. I'm sorry for calling with such short notice."

Karina smiled. Maybe a bus full of five- and six-year-olds would visit. Laughing, curious children could be pleasant, and she certainly needed the business.

"We had planned to go to the Caribou Children's Museum, but the bus had a mechanical problem."

Karina didn't mind being the backup. "I understand. We're closer." She didn't even pretend that the ranch might be busy when booking the tour.

With the eyes of a six-year-old, Karina prepared for the school visit. She hung up the white *Mammoth Research Station* lab coats. Her prize acquisition scavenged from the lab in Kerala was the pipetting robot. She filled the source containers with colored solutions. A quick test verified the robot would create cute images of plants and animals in the sixteen by twenty-four grids. The tiny pipettes sucking up colors and shuttling them over to deposit them into the microarrays mesmerized the children wearing the lab coats.

The other popular hands-on display was a jumble of mammoth bones, mostly ribs and legs. Children marveled that the bones were bigger than they were and even built sculptures. A perennial favorite was the dioramas made from shoe boxes and shipping cartons by previous students. Karina's proudest acquisition was a large oil painting of the mammoth herd by a local artist. Finally, she printed a stack of coloring pages for the children to take away as souvenirs.

She sat at the information desk drinking a cup of tea and admiring her little museum. A mailing tube reminded her of a poster she'd ordered for the climate exhibit. Next to *The Blue Marble*, she hung *The Blue Snowball Rising* showing a pale blue earth from behind a pearly white moon demonstrating the strange algae that now flourished around the world.

A car pulled into the small parking lot. She greeted any visitor with anticipation. The real estate agent with blond braids and cowboy boots took two long strides and stood directly facing Karina. "This is Karina Kowalski Mammoth Ranch, right? And you must be Karina."

"Yes, and you're with Clayton Lake Realty. I didn't get your name when we spoke last time."

The lady didn't respond but headed for the office.

Karina had to run to get to the door first. She held it open and said, "Welcome," even though she now felt wary of this aggressive woman. As the lady walked around, Karina imagined what she was seeing. Her charming displays faded under the lady's critical appraisal.

"Quaint," the woman said with disdain in her voice. "I didn't expect much, and this confirms my original evaluation." She pointed to the painting. "I can't list this place until you get rid of them." She tapped the largest mammoth for emphasis.

Karina still didn't know her name and decided she didn't care. She reached out her hand, "Thank you for visiting. I'm not interested in selling right away." With her other hand, she opened the door for the woman to leave.

◡

When the conservation community finally recognized the mammoths as more than a curious science experiment, Karina received an invitation to the International Conference on Endangered Mammals. A few months later, she waited for mammoth seventy-seven to arrive in an empty animal enclosure at the acclaimed Franklin Park Zoo in Boston.

Karina wiped the sweat from her brow and shaded her eyes. Finally, she saw it. A blue truck stirring up a cloud of dust. Her heart raced as the refrigerator on wheels came clearly into view. *Aroostook Fisheries* in red lettering and grinning lobsters with eerie smiles confirmed that seventy-seven had arrived.

Given the heat and humidity, she regretted bringing a mammoth to Boston. Regardless, she directed the truck driver. "Backup. Cut to the left. Good. Good. Okay. Open the door. Pull out the ramp."

Karina watched the mammoth take a few tentative steps in her direction until he raised his trunk and smelled the air. She could almost hear him thinking what she felt. Too hot. The mammoth backed away into what little cool remained in the truck.

Karina found a hose and held up a bubbling stream. "Come on. You want a drink." She turned to the driver and handed him the hose. "Don't worry, he's as gentle as can be." The driver didn't look convinced, but he held his position as directed.

Karina cautiously walked up the ramp and spoke to the mammoth. "You're right. Boston in the summer is no place for an arctic beast like you. It's even too hot for me." She nudged his big head toward the driver and the hose. "See. He's your friend and has some nice water for you."

The mammoth reached his trunk toward the water but didn't move. "We need to find you a new home. All the biggest zoos attend the ICEM."

The mammoth flipped his trunk in the air and trumpeted. The frightened driver jumped, squirting a stream of water, and soaking the mammoth and Karina.

Karina retreated, but seventy-seven resigned himself to his fate and left the truck. Seventy-seven, she thought. Why didn't we give him a cute name? Animal shelters always assigned cute names. She recalled that Priya had given names at the beginning, but something happened during the exodus from India, and they all had numbers now.

Karina stayed with seventy-seven. She secretly hoped that this zoo might keep him. Many zoo-goers and zoo directors visited. They had a lot of questions.

"This is a baby. Adults get as big as elephants."

"They don't live in jungles like elephants. They are arctic animals."

For the zoo directors, she added. "They'd need a cooled exhibit space like your penguins and polar bears."

"They mature younger and reproduce more quickly than elephants."

She displayed pictures of mammoths in the snow surrounded by fir trees and lying down to nurse babies that were born smaller than elephants.

At the end of the conference, she met with directors from Boston, New York, Cleveland, and San Diego. The San Diego director summed up the consensus. "We needed a major fund-raising effort to exhibit polar bears in our warming conditions. These mammoths are ten times bigger. We just can't afford it."

In the end, she loaded seventy-seven and headed back north following the blue truck with the grinning lobsters. Her anger at her father for this ill-considered experiment returned. She refused to let it upset the scenic drive. Bad enough she had to clean up his mammoth mess, she wasn't going to waste any energy being mad at him.

A lush green lined both sides of the eRoad. Different plants caught her eye. A maple with sharp, pointy leaves. An oak with soft, rounded leaves. In the undergrowth shiny poison ivy vines and sassafras mittens. As she got closer to home, the bright green faded into the grey-greens of conifers.

Her comp flashed with a message from Ashur. She let it wait, unopened, preferring not to interrupt the scenery.

Back in Maine, Karina spoke to zoos in Europe and South Africa. Somebody in Siberia had expressed interest, but he wanted a *good-faith* deposit of twelve million dollars before he would visit. That sounded like a scam, so she cut off negotiations. She applied for grants from two endangered species groups. A lawyer had offered to set up a charity for the mammoths. He had only asked for a two-million-dollar retainer as if she had that kind of money.

She even looked up the contact information for a couple of pet food companies, but she hadn't spoken to them. After some confusion, she set up a meeting with Snow House, her last and best hope. She took it as a good sign that Snow House hadn't asked for any money.

Karina waited anxiously for the visit. She reread their emails. The two people visiting were Amaruq and Maatalii. She wondered whether they were men or women. All she knew for sure was that they lived close to the Arctic Circle. That would be good for the mammoths.

A car pulled into the parking lot. They're here, she thought. When she opened the door, she saw two women. "Welcome. Are you Amaruq and Maatalii?"

They nodded and introduced themselves. Karina thought they looked like twins, but she noticed that Maatalii had tattoos on her wrists.

Karina couldn't imagine how these two young women would be able to rescue a herd of mammoths when nobody else could, but she tried to be polite. She shook hands. "Welcome to the mammoth ranch. How was your trip?"

Maatalii replied, "Long. We've been traveling for two days."

Amaruq added, "You live in a remote location. Qamanittuaq is bigger."

"I understand. Sometimes I wish I lived closer to a big city." Karina then asked, "Do you know anything about mammoths?"

The sisters suppressed laughter from some private joke. They looked at each other deciding who would answer this hilarious question.

Maatalii had the biggest smile. "We maintain the largest mammoth herd anywhere. Our herd is more than twice the size of yours."

Of course, Karina castigated herself, *I knew that.* She recovered with, "Would you like to see the mammoths. They are just down the road."

Amaruq smiled again. "We passed them when we drove in."

Karina restrained herself but inwardly cheered. *These ladies are perfect. I will make this work, whatever the cost. I've got to move on. Move on without these mammoths.*

Before Karina could say anything, Amaruq's smile turned into a frown. "They are a despondent group."

Karina worried that they might not want the mammoths if they thought they were sickly. "It's our weather."

Maatalii agreed but still seemed less than enthusiastic. "Getting between here and our home was difficult for us. I can't imagine how we'd move that herd of mammoths. This is worse than when Priya herded them across India."

Karina almost said, "I know. I was there." She thought of all the dead ends she'd investigated. "Don't worry about moving them. I'll take care of that." She figured she could transport the mammoths by sea. After all, that's the way they arrived.

"That helps. We'd like to go visit the herd close up and will give you an answer tomorrow."

⬬

271

A few weeks later, Karina awoke from her uneasy sleep. The mammoths were restless all penned into the corral. She worried about them. She went out to check that they were okay for the sixth or sixteenth time that night. She counted them. They were all there.

Dawn arrives in an hour, was her first thought. And, *I've been up all night* quickly followed. The shippers with their eleven eighteen-wheelers would arrive soon. She put her head down for a short nap.

She dreamt of floodwaters rushing to the Arabian Sea. *I'm not in Kerala. This isn't a dream. That noise isn't water.* She shook her head and sat up. She listened again. The truckers!

She sprang up and ran outside. "Good morning." She tried to appear awake. "Are you here for the mammoths?"

A kid, possibly still a teenager, handed her a comp, "Sign here." The kid added, "When no one answered the door, we packed up the animals."

The trucker woman brushed her curly black hair from her face. "Gosh, ma'am. What kind of elephants are those?"

Karina, now alert, smiled. She enjoyed nothing like curious visitors. "Those are mammoths. They're going to their new home in the Arctic."

The woman—Karina had looked more closely, and she seemed more like in her thirties—replied, "I don't know anything about that. We just take them to the docks in Portland."

Karina walked out for her final farewells. She signed the comp and watched as the woman and her partner climbed into the cab of the first truck. The other driverless trucks automatically followed, just like a train of elephants! Karina watched until they were out of sight.

With the mammoths gone, Karina had moved to a B&B in town, not wanting to spend any more time at the deserted property than required. She would have immediately left Maine, except she needed to sell the ranch.

She arrived early for her appointment with a real estate agent. The office had a musty smell, so she opened the windows to air it out before the man showed up. She also dusted the display cases and scooped up the mail piled on the floor and placed it on her desk. While she waited, she drank a large latte along with a breakfast sandwich and a shortbread cookie that she'd had the good sense to bring with her.

After breakfast, she sorted through the mail. Junk mail. More junk mail. A few bills, electric, Internet, and gas. In the middle of the mound, she found a large envelope from a lawyer. She tore it open and started reading.

She scanned the cover letter. *Bankruptcy. Langars, Inc.* What a surprise, she thought sarcastically. Then she wondered why the letter had been sent to her. She checked the envelope. *Karina Kowalski Mammoth Ranch, Inc.* She continued. *Real estate lien.* Then it hit her. Her father had used her ranch as collateral. Along with losing the plastic wedding cakes, he'd also lost her ranch.

She picked up one of the ladder-back chairs. She thought, specially made by a local craftsperson, painted with indestructible blue milk paint. She smashed it against the table. It just bounced with an unsatisfying twang. She cursed the chair and her father and the lawyers before heaving the sturdy chair through a front window. A satisfactory crash resulted as the chair continued onto the front porch before bouncing into the gravel parking lot. As long as she had chairs and windows, she yelled at her father, "You stupid, selfish, irresponsible…" and threw them through the triple-glazed windows.

Finally, she kicked over the entertainment monitor and collapsed on the sofa. She called the real estate agent and canceled her appointment. The lawyers could deal with the broken windows and everything else. She sprayed gravel as she spun her wheels. She didn't look back for fear that she'd return to set the place on fire. The past had been taken from her. She had no way to go but forward.

Careening from side to side on the backwoods roads, Karina vented her frustration on the rented car. She pushed hard on the accelerator and the car drifted around a sandy curve, throwing a cloud of dust into the air. With a tight twist of the steering wheel and a tap on the brakes, the rear wheels skidded, and the speeding vehicle headed towards the entrance of the eRoad. In a few minutes, the car seized control of the steering and pedals. The eRoad had taken over, but tension still controlled Karina's fists and shoulders.

When her comp buzzed, she almost threw it out the window. She ignored the ID display. "Hello! Who's this?"

"Ashur here. Did you get my email?"

Like a flash, she saw the pattern. No matter what she was doing, he needed her to be doing something else. "Get someone else to do your spying. I'm busy." She broke the connection and blocked him. She'd go forward but without some man telling her which way to go.

Maatalii folded some hand-me-down baby clothes and set the stack into the shelves in the baby's room. As much as she missed and mourned her lost baby, she knew it was time to move on. She was glad she had this new little one to focus on; it helped her let go. And this time she had a bright new room for their child, in their snug new house.

She heard soft footsteps, then Caiden came up behind her and rested his forearms on her shoulders.

"How are we doing? Enough tiny baby clothes?" he asked, looking over her shoulder.

"I think so. I'm so grateful we have our own washing machine. I can wash the dirty things right away, so we always have some clean; we may not have many choices, but we have enough. All the women tell me babies outgrow these tiny outfits so fast, it makes no sense to buy more. Look, these have been used by three babies already and they still look new."

Caiden looked and grunted. "It's nice to be able to surround him with already-beloved clothes and wraps."

"*Her,*" Maati said with a sideways grin.

Caiden shrugged. "We'll know soon enough." He walked over to the crib, its mattress covered in a printed yellow and green sheet, also recycled. "Your brother Lusa says he is almost finished with a *People's* style mobile to hang over the crib. Polar bears and such, for our baby to look at. That will be new, just for us."

"Oh, that will be nice. I had no idea he was doing that."

"Oops," Caiden said, not looking embarrassed at all. "Maybe I wasn't supposed to say anything."

"I'll act as surprised as I am pleased, then," she said, laughing. She turned to face him, and they stepped closer to one another and hugged around the baby bump.

Over Caiden's shoulder, Maati saw out the window a pair of white RCMP cars arrive at the front of Snow House Inn.

"What's that about?" she asked, waving a hand.

Caiden turned and looked. He frowned. "Nothing good, I'm thinking."

"May we have all Ticasuk and Oonark family members gather in a private room, please," the police officer said.

Maatalii saw her mother step forward. "Room 101 is empty," Suluk said.

Suluk kept the room empty so they could use it as a flex space: office, meeting room, guest bedroom, crafts workshop, or storeroom. Even with a dozen people, without any furniture it did not feel crowded.

The Two Pearls

With a lot of whispers and mutterings, Maati, Suluk, Meriwa, Osha, Amaruq with Nanuq, Yuka and Sivoy all shuffled into room 101. Only Lusa was not here. Maatalii thought Caiden should come as well, but the police had waved him back. "I'll watch the front desk, Maati." he said. "I'll be close, if you need me."

She needed him *here,* not close, but she nodded and he walked away.

The patrolmen closed the door and another RCMP officer, the leader, stepped to the center of the room. That one looked around at the people in the room, glancing at each family member. "I am Lieutenant Kilabuk," he said. "I may not know you individually, but I do know Snow House is a vital member of our Qamanittuaq community." He took a deep breath and glanced around the room again. "I am sorry to have to tell you, but Tarkik Oonark has died in an automobile accident early this morning."

Of course the whole family reacted, talking in shocked tones among themselves.

But Maatalii couldn't seem to process the words; it was as if the man was speaking another language.

Tarkik? Dead? She had seen him the day before, when he came to pick up Jissika. The couple had seemed so happy, and so alive together, it just did not make sense that he was dead.

"Does Jissika know?" she asked.

"We have informed the Mikigak family already."

This provoked more exclamations and discussion.

"What happened, do you know?" Amaruq asked.

The Lieutenant held up a hand, and waited until they quieted.

"Black ice," he said. "The car slid off the road into a deep pond. Tarkik did not escape. Jissika Oonark has identified his body. She will contact you with funeral arrangements. Again, I am so sorry to bring you this news."

Still numb with shock, Maatalii looked from face to face around the room. They grieved; they believed Tarkik was dead. She still felt as if she was frozen.

It seemed so ironic that after all their fighting against the *Hot,* it should be *ice* that killed her cousin.

Mama had an arm over Meriwa's shoulder, and Ama hugged her waist. Maati's aunt's eyes were so flooded with tears she could not see where she was going. Suluk guided her out the door and down the hall, where a small seating area and table covered with greenery and flowers from their greenhouses were arranged.

Caiden, who was suddenly there, reached for Maati's hand and led her to a quiet hallway. They stood together, clutched in a warm embrace.

"Poor Tarkik," Maati managed to say. "He was so happy with his family and his job and his new car."

"He was," Caiden said, enclosing her in a hug. He patted her shoulder, still hugging. "I am glad he was able to enjoy it all, after so many years of feeling not good enough."

Maati pulled away from him far enough to examine his face.

"Do you really think he felt insufficient?"

Caiden nodded. "He shared with me a couple times that compared with his sister and cousins, he had never contributed enough. And Jissika's expectations were high. His job at the mine solved most of those things for him, and he was learning to be content."

"That is good, then," she said.

Aunt Meriwa appeared in the hallway with Lieutenant Kilabuk, trailed by Ama and Suluk. "Are we cursed?" Meriwa asked, her voice gravelly with grief. She abruptly stopped walking and the Lieutenant came close to crashing into her. He stepped back, giving her room as Meri flung her arms out. "Maatalii, go find that old shaman, the Feather Reader."

Maati opened her mouth, but nothing came out. She understood her aunt's shock: Tarkik was Meriwa's foster son, after all. But what was a shaman going to do? He couldn't answer Meriwa's prayer, to make Tarkik un-dead. He couldn't answer *why*.

"Where does he live?" Caiden asked.

"He used to be in that shack up by Giqa's house, but I think he has taken to camping in the old way, on Arluq Island," Meriwa said.

Maatalii bit her lip. Were they going to have to waste time finding the old man? A shaman could not bring Tarkik back to life. Nothing could.

Surprising her, the Lieutenant spoke up. "He usually leaves the island when winter starts, but I believe he is still over there. At the east end, by the fishing wharf."

"I'll see about a boat," Caiden said.

Maatalii, not really thinking that this whole shaman visit was a priority, put a hand on her husband's arm to stop him. But then, maybe her aunt was right. Maybe Snow House was carrying a curse, and it wouldn't hurt to cleanse the air.

"Actually," Caiden said, "we can probably use my family's boat. Nobody will need it, and nothing's frozen yet, so it should be safe enough. I can row over."

"Take Sivoy or Lusa with you," Mama suggested.

Meriwa nodded and grasped the police officer's arm as they walked to the front door. "*Soon*, Caiden," Meriwa said over her shoulder. "Before something else awful happens."

Suluk stood still as the others went outside.

She still did not believe Tarkik was dead.

How could he be dead? She had just seen him, a few hours before.

Had she been the cause of it? She shouldn't have asked him to drive her to the meeting and back. It was too much; he had been tired, he hadn't seen the ice.

She shook her head. She had been the last one to see him alive.

But he had been alert and cheerful when he'd waved goodbye, watching as she made her way inside Snow House before he drove off. He had *wanted* to drive her. He had wanted to visit his family, and he loved driving his car.

She took two steps and sat down, dropping into a chair with a *flump*; the chair hadn't been locked open, but it did so as she landed, clacking with a hard-plastic sound. She'd meant to put away all these folding chairs, but somehow she'd overlooked this one, a stray among the over-stuffed lobby seating.

She could smell the flowers she'd placed on the center table herself that morning. Ever after she would link the scent of tiger lilies with Tarkik's death.

She knew she had to let go of blame.

Suluk nodded to herself. "Tarkik drove slowly," she said to herself, remembering. "He told me sometimes that road is icy; he did not want to slide off."

She could not really blame herself without claiming herself to be some kind of powerful magic-wielder, to be a cause of such things. Truly, she had no power over her family; they made their own choices.

Lately, a number of those choices had turned out badly.

Amaruq's choice of Niki and Churchill.

Ama's choice to hide Nanuq from Niki.

Maati's choice to go with Ama to get Nanuq back.

Even, long ago, Opik's choice to chase after caribou.

And now, Tarkik's choice to drive the road to Fifthslope four times. She had not forced him—she hadn't even asked him, he'd volunteered. But if she wasn't responsible, what was?

Maybe Meriwa was right, maybe they needed a shaman.

Maatalii was a little embarrassed to be standing outside in her bare feet, holding hands with her siblings and cousins and their spouses. Feather Reader, the old shaman, seemed like something from an ancient story—a fiction and a fraud as he shook a bundle of kelp and seal bones above each person's head.

She noticed some of their neighbors were staring at the ceremony from behind the curtains in their windows.

Nobody did this kind of thing anymore. It was not only terribly old-fashioned, it was based on traditions—or *superstitions*—that most Inuit no longer believed in.

Nevertheless, Mama and Aunt Meriwa wanted to be certain there wasn't some malevolent curse upon Snow House and their family. Maati tried to think of it as an insurance policy. It couldn't hurt, and it might help, however foolish they might look for these moments.

But as if to prove to them that it was indeed profound foolishness, the following morning they were greeted with another disaster. Amaruq ran into the restaurant with tears in her eyes.

"Someone has attacked us, Maati." She gasped and barely got the words out. "They destroyed the greenhouses." She held up a handful of limp carrots and a head of ripped and crushed lettuce. "They tore up *food,* Maati, as if they didn't care that people would go hungry without it!"

The utility room door thumped shut and Maatalii turned to see Caiden kicking his boots off, a dark scowl on his face.

"I think we can salvage some of this," he said, walking in in his socks, thrusting a crate of tumbled and bruised vegetables at her. "Sivoy didn't hear or see anything, because he's been out chasing the caribou and mammoths someone also let out of their fences last night. I'm going to call the police."

Mama walked from the kitchen out to the counter with a plate of food for a customer sitting there. Suluk arranged the man's silverware and asked if he needed anything else. As Maati looked carefully at her mother, she could see Mama had heard what Ama and Caiden had said.

They all walked back into the kitchen together.

"Who would do this?" Mama moaned. "Why?"

"Why?" Caiden repeated, voice harsh. "Because they are jealous of our success." He shook his head. "Snow House has not starved like some have. We have even given food away to help others. Some people resent such obvious signs of accomplishment."

"But we have worked hard for this," Amaruq said, voice wobbling into a wail by the end. "They could always do the same."

Caiden shrugged. "They could. But it is easier to blame than do." He met Maati's gaze. "Don't go out there until I can clean it, okay?"

"It says 'shame.' " Amaruq mumbled. "The runes they wrote on the door, they say 'shame.' But what?" she looked at each of them, fists clenched. "Shame for what?"

Some of her bewilderment was addressed at the Sisterhood meeting that week. Maatalii and Suluk were still trying to make sense of it.

"I've heard rumbling that you take advantage of other Qamanittuaq families," one woman said. "In spite of the fact that you've given crates of food to several different families when they've been stretched too thin."

"And Snow House sends other kinds of help, when needed," someone else said.

"But you ask for help, too, like with the fences, all the time," a third woman put in.

Meriwa shook out a new bundle of embroidery floss and unwrapped a meter of it. "So that's reason to destroy a source of food?" She threaded her needle, not looking at anyone. "We ask for help sometimes?"

"Maybe the greenhouses were easier to attack than Snow House itself," Jissika suggested. "Sometimes it kind of looks like the Tikasuk-Oonark fortress."

Suluk shook her head. "I cannot see where we have ever put ourselves forward as some kind of leaders. As if we were 'better than.' It has always been my intention to cooperate with others and I believe my children—our children," she said, glancing at Meriwa— "have always done so, too."

Jissika sighed. "Well, releasing the polar bear cub you hand raised was turned into a big local news story."

"*We* didn't do that!" Ama cried out.

"No, you didn't," one of the other Keepers said. "But it looked bad for you, as if you sought praise for your environmental work."

"Work which we should *all* do, and yet, *don't!*" Meriwa said, her usual tartness coming out sharply.

"I think the point is," the Keeper said patiently, "that you have the resources to do so, while others don't. So there is resentment."

"So you are saying we try too hard?" Maatalii said, starting to feel very angry at the turn the whole conversation had taken. "So we should sit around and drink beer instead of building greenhouses?"

"Everywhere the townspeople turn, there is Snow House," the Keeper said. "Sometimes that hurts." She turned the cookie dough she had been stirring out onto a floured board on the table, began lightly kneading it.

There was a silence among them, while they digested that statement. It was so quiet in the room, they could hear the thread being pulled through the taut canvas as Meri stitched a bird onto her wall-hanging. A snow bunting, in white, gray, and tan.

"Yet they resent being asked to be part of it, too," Amaruq pointed out. "I've invited several of you to try your hand on a plot inside our biggest greenhouse. Instead of joining in, someone destroyed it. How is that being one of *The People?*"

"I'm not excusing them," the Keeper said. "I'm trying for clarity here."

"It almost sounds like you know who was involved. Who did all that?" Meriwa grated.

The old woman bit her lip, shaking her head. She poked her finger in the middle of each cookie she'd cut out, then placed an imported almond into each of those center dents. They were for the church service, Maati knew. That Keeper made cookies each week so there would be a little treat for anyone who showed up to the Sunday service.

"Breaking up the greenhouses, destroying innocent vegetables and fruits and flowers. Letting caribou and mammoths go loose, possibly to their deaths when they cannot find enough wild graze or browse. How can clarity help them?" Amaruq asked.

"I wish I knew," the Keeper said. "I do not understand it myself."

⌣

Sivoy's legs seemed to give out beneath him as he closed the gate on the most recent batch of mammoths he'd rounded up. Suluk knew he was exhausted, he'd done most of the work of re-catching the mammoths and caribou alone.

It made her furious that this kind and gentle man, who had helped everyone in town at some time or other, was asking for help and not getting it. She yelled at people about it, then realized she was making matters worse. If Qamanittuaq resented them so much, yelling at them was never going to help.

Caiden had offered to help Sivoy, and had even gone out on a couple occasions to look for lost stock, but Suluk wanted him to put the greenhouses as his priority. Ama and Maati must restore their greenhouses as much for the family's morale as for the food they'd eventually be able to grow and harvest again.

Maati's pregnancy was advanced and she couldn't do much. Surprising them, Jissika had volunteered to come help out in the Snow House restaurant.

Jissika, who seemed the most tired and saddest of the entire family. Suluk was both startled and warmed to realize the young woman may have genuinely loved their Tarkik.

Suluk wiped off tables in the restaurant, watching out the window.

Caiden came out and helped Sivoy spread food around the corral for the hungry animals. Most of them had lost enough weight they could see ribs. Sivoy had found several groups of caribou that had starved on the tundra, their bare bones lying white in the sun. The *Hot* had destroyed everything they might have eaten, out in the wild.

Suluk shook her head. That made her angry, too, that people here, people *she knew,* would do this to their animals because they were angry at Snow House.

What was happening to *The People* and their ways? When did Inuit become *envious?* They had always shared. That was the *Way*.

At least Lieutenant Kilabuk had offered to help.

The money for replacing the solar panels and heaters for the greenhouses was, she hoped, going to come from a grant by the Kivalliq Inuit Association. Given the attitude of most folks in town, she worried that the KIA vote might go against her, against her family. Then what could they do?

The Two Pearls

Sivoy suggested putting strings of lights out there in the new and repaired greenhouses. They could help with the warmth, at least. Even if they weren't full-spectrum light, they might be better than winter dark, for the new plants.

Hearing that, Kilabuk had offered his vote and said he would speak in favor of bestowing the community's funds upon the greenhouse restoration. He still did not know who had been responsible, and no one in the community spoke up with information.

And now Lieutenant Kilabuk looked tired as she felt. She could see rings under his puffy eyes. "We're still working on it," he said.

"I know," she said. "We thank you." What else was to be said? He did not know any answers, either.

How could Qamanittuaq turn on them like this?

Why?

She was horrified to watch hunger and envy shatter their town to bits.

43. Abbie—Qamanittuaq, Mike—China, Carla—Sydney

Abbie struggled to adjust to the empty house. Before Elzia and the grandkids departed for Oklahoma, Billy and Dee had awakened her each morning by jumping out of bed right above where she slept. The hardest times were before and after school when the house had always echoed with purpose and chatter. She missed making lunches, helping with kamiks and parkas, and locating school assignments.

Even though Mike and Carla had settled on the other side of the planet, she still found herself planning for their return. The worst was after dinner when Redd settled in front of the news, and she poured two cups of tea, one for Elzia who also would not be back.

She volunteered at Qamanittuaq school and hung out with the ladies at Snow House, but without her own family, she felt disconnected. Even Redd seemed to be affected. He moved slower and slept more.

She occupied herself learning to make dinners for just the two of them. At first, she made normal dinners and divided them into halves or thirds to be eaten later. Eventually, she learned to use smaller pots and bowls. She served on saucers. Eventually she adjusted and the refrigerator stopped looking like a mismanaged soup kitchen.

She sat with two small plates of fried fish and a few Brussel sprouts each waiting for Redd. They didn't speak much during the day, so she made a point to eat the evening meal together. After ten minutes, she walked to the door looking toward the barn and his workshop. When she unlatched the door, Tasha pushed it wide open. "Where's your daddy?" she asked the excited dog. The Newfie slobbered and panted.

Tasha ran toward the barn but stopped halfway. Abbie followed. There was Redd sprawled on the ground. "No!" she screamed. She fell onto the cold ground while Tasha walked in worried circles. She opened his parka and placed her head against his chest. She could hear his heart and feel his breathing. *He's alive!*

He twitched. "What's going on?"

"You passed out."

He pulled himself up. "Maybe you can walk me into the house."

She didn't let him see her shaking as she steadied him into the kitchen. Tasha never left his side and sat at his feet under the table.

"You're going to the doctor tomorrow."

"I'm fine. It was just low blood sugar."

"Eat your dinner." She felt fear swirling through her body, shaking her legs, making it hard to breathe. Her heart pounded in her chest. She promised herself she wouldn't burst into tears when he needed her strength. She'd lost everyone, but she wouldn't lose him. He wasn't even sixty yet.

After dinner, she put him to bed, further frightened when he went without a fight.

She ignored the mess in the kitchen. She and Tasha snuggled together on the sofa watching the news while tears dripped down her cheeks. Only Tasha watched the news. Abbie searched medical sites for emphysema, syncope, and stroke—lungs, heart, and brain.

She fell asleep dreaming of clouds of wood dust billowing from his lathe. *He should have worn a face mask.*

Throughout the following days, a small voice kept saying: He told you not to leave Oklahoma. She found it hard to believe that a short while ago she had applied for Canadian citizenship.

Mike's plane descended through the clouds to the Hechi airport. He had expected terraces and green rice paddies, but all he could see was a large city, bigger than any in Canada.

When he disembarked from the airplane, the cold hit him. He stopped on the tarmac to dig out a hat and gloves from his carry-on. Pulling a small suitcase behind him, he followed the other passengers to the terminal.

By the time he reached the luggage stacked on the floor, he knew he hadn't brought enough winter clothes. He grabbed a trolley and collected his suitcases. The signs were in Chinese and another script he didn't recognize. Maybe Mongolian or Tibetan.

He pushed his trolley to the curb, rubbed his hands together for warmth, and waited.

Finally, a miniature pickup truck stopped in front of him.

"Mister Mike? *Nofu?*"

Mike gave the driver a big smile and nodded his head vigorously. "Do you speak English?"

"*Shi, shi.* My name is Quan Song, but you can call me Quan."

"Okay, Quan." Mike realized he was shouting. He tried again in a more conversational voice. "How far are we going?"

Quan paused. "I get confused with miles. Maybe 125 miles."

"I understand kilometers. How many kilometers?"

"Eighty."

"That's better. Only fifty miles. So, maybe one hour?"

Quan laughed as he loaded the luggage. He circled the truck bed again and again tying everything in place. "That is an American joke, right? Two or three hours."

When they left the airport speeding along on a four-lane road, Mike was sure Quan was making a Chinese joke. Tell the new guy, two or three hours.

However, soon the truck turned off the highway to a gravel road, and it became clear why Quan tied the luggage.

Mike was still hoping for two hours when the road turned to dirt, and holes, and rocks. Mike now hoped to make it in three hours.

The rough track was too noisy for conversation, so Mike, exhausted from the long flight, stared out the window. The countryside reminded him of the tundra: empty. But this was mountainous, not flat. He had left the city behind, but still no terraced rice paddies. Maybe he should have done some more research before accepting this job. He did congratulate himself for not giving in to Elzia's entreaties for the family to join him. This place did not look family friendly.

He noticed a few ponds that looked like they were frozen, but the wind stirred up waves, so not ice. He wondered if the diatoms he'd been reading about created the illusion.

He shouted, "Are those that crazy diatom algae?"

Quan replied, "*Shi, shi.*"

Mike didn't give it another thought because *Nofu* was different, not diatoms, and grew in vats.

After three hours and twenty minutes, they parked in front of a cinderblock building with a corrugated steel roof. Quan untied the luggage and carried everything inside. He flipped a switch and LED lights lit up across the roof peak. "Nothing but the best for you."

Mike took in the single room. Bed. Table. Two chairs. Sink. A single-burner stove attached to a propane tank. A microwave oven.

Mike hid his disappointment. The cement walls were a faded green, the same color as the furniture. He admired a colorful rug on the floor. Three drawings of Chinese calligraphy decorated the wall. "What do those say?"

Quan pointed to each in order. "Healthy food." "Clean environment." "*Nofu.*" "Those are from the company. You can get more if you want to send them to your family."

There was a single electrical plug. It had a strange Chinese socket, but he had come prepared with an adaptor. Basic, he thought.

Quan ran across the room and opened a door. "Composting toilet. Latest technology." Quan handed him a laminated card with cartoons that Mike assumed to be instructions. "Also, an indoor shower." Quan pulled a lever and water streamed from a grate in the ceiling to a drain in the floor. "The tank is on the roof, so sometimes hot and sometimes not."

"Most likely cold," Mike whispered to himself as he opened the small refrigerator. He saw beer and juices, some eggs, cheese, and sausage. A loaf of bread and a jar of American peanut butter were on the counter. That's what the label said, in English, American Peanut Butter.

He was ready for a nap but remembered one last thing. "Internet?"

Quan ran around the room like he was looking for something and finally said, "American joke." He opened the door and pointed to a tall tower about a quarter of a mile down the road. "Wireless. Everywhere. No password!"

He recalled telling Elzia that the conditions would be primitive, but the Internet would be great. He was right.

Quan left and Mike collapsed on the bed.

Mike had the next day off. He got up early and took advantage of the wi-fi tower. "*Ni Hao* everyone in Oklahoma."

Elzia held the camera pointing at Dee and Billy.

"Daddy, are you in China?"

"Yes. Do you want to see where I live?"

Both children shouted.

He turned the camera around to show them his room.

"Is that all of it?" William asked.

"Yes. Some people have families, even bigger than ours. They live in the same size building, just with more beds."

Outside he held his comp high to show a small village, a factory building in the distance, and filling all the open spaces: white ponds and desolate fields.

He walked down to the river. Dee told him about her chicks, and Billy talked about his second-grade teacher.

Elzia sent the children away. "We should be there with you."

Mike felt bad, but he wanted to take care of his family, and that tiny cinderblock shack wasn't it. "You saw how primitive the housing is. Let me get settled."

It didn't sound like she was even listening. "Oklahoma has changed. Drought. No cattle. No wheat."

"The children cry every night. William doesn't like his school and has stopped reading. Dee doesn't have any friends."

He considered offering to leave China, but what if she said yes?

She turned off the camera. "Think about it. I love you."

It sounded like she was going to cry.

He said, "I love you, too," and that was the end of the connection.

After sausage and fried eggs for dinner and a cold shower, he walked back to the riverbank. This job in China that had seemed so exciting now just felt foolish and lonely. The cold wind sounded like Elzia's sad voice, *we should be with you, should be with you, sh-h-h.*

Carla looked around her flat at the foot of the Sydney Harbour Bridge—a kitchenette, bathroom, and sleeping area. Each morning, she was awakened by cargo cranes and tugboats. Too late, she discovered that the city cost more than her salary. She missed solving million-dollar problems. No one offered weekend junkets or welcome or farewell dinners of appreciation.

Beyond losing her travel perqs, the expense of living in Sydney surprised her. At the beginning of the twenty-first century, ebullient investors had hoped to turn the Sydney docks into an upscale destination, but the needs of international shipping—container ships and warehouses—won out. The few abandoned hotels had been converted into cheap flats, now the best she could afford.

The banging of shipping containers woke her up. She warmed a pasty for brekkie and filled her walking mug with real coffee. Even including the luxury of imported coffee beans, breakfast from her kitchenette still stretched her paycheck. She stretched it even more by walking the five kilometers to Sydney Uni and the Green Dot offices.

When she arrived, the office was deserted. Oh no, she thought, today is the big meeting and I'm late. She dropped her backpack and cup at her desk and ran to catch up to the group already on the way to the meeting, hoping no one would notice.

She bumped into her friend Ingrid, who pretended to be knocked off balance. "G'day mate. Slow down. Did you forget to wake up on time?"

"No, of course not. You know I live on the docks. No chance to sleep late."

Ingrid and Carla walked together to a University auditorium. Green Dots security people checked everyone's IDs. They took seats in the back like troublemakers. On the stage were the big managers.

"Today Green Dots are announcing a major milestone. We are combining with three major algae companies from Vancouver, Riga, and Cape Town."

Ingrid turned her comp for Carla to see. "Look at the stock going down. This is not good news."

Carla nodded, "That super algae problem turned out to be worse than I expected."

A new manager had taken the stage. She was explaining about *redundancies*. Carla turned to her friend, "Redundancy?"

Ingrid frowned. "Mate, we're being thrown out on the street. Sydney, Riga, and Vancouver are all being shut down."

Carla replied. "I could live in Cape Town."

"You're not listening. Some of the engineers will be given that chance, but Cape Town already have plenty of marketing people."

"Ingrid, what are you going to do?"

"We have a caravan. My husband and I have been thinking about exploring the Great Sandy Desert. Our children are at a great age to travel."

Carla didn't have a husband, children, or even a caravan. That night she looked out of her converted hotel room at the moon reflected off Sydney Harbour. She reheated a take-away shepherd's pie and spread Vegemite on toast. This wasn't how she'd imagined spending her thirty-second birthday, but she found some sweet Anzac biscuits which she dunked in warm milky tea before turning in early

She didn't know how to contact Mike in China, and her mother had enough to handle with Redd's emphysema. Suddenly, the world seemed so large and she seemed so alone.

The next day, Mike's comp beeped in the middle of a meeting. *Elzia.* "Excuse me." He stepped into the hall.

He looked at the time and spoke softly. "Are you alright? It's the middle of the night there."

"I've been on the Internet since the children went to sleep. I can borrow some money from my parents and fly to Hechi. We can be there in three days."

He knew she could do it. When he wanted her to join him in Canada after she graduated from college, she did it against the advice of her friends and family. He also knew that with her science degree she could get a job. *Why don't I want her to come here?* He didn't have a good response. "Please. Can you wait one week?"

A timer popped up on the screen and started counting down. At 167:58:32 she said, "Okay. One week. 168 hours."

At 167:55:21 she said, "I better get some sleep. The kids will be getting up soon." The screen went blank.

He thought about the children crying at night, Elzia searching for flights to China. He hoped tomorrow would bring some inspiration.

The factory had a status meeting every morning. A table at the side of the room offered hot tea, cut fruit, and a big bowl of *Nofu* accompanied by an assortment of sauces in every color of the rainbow. He hadn't eaten much on his day off, so he grabbed a tea, slices of pineapple and melon, and a bowl of *Nofu* with some purple sauce which he hoped was berry.

He was sipping his tea when the room went dark and the presentations started. The slides, projected on the wall, were in English, but all the discussion was in Chinese. Everything seemed routine until the slide that announced. *Batches infested by DAS: three. Production lost: two thousand gallons (six million litres).* The numbers didn't match, so he assumed that the larger liters-lost was the correct amount. This was the problem they brought him to solve.

He asked a lot of questions.

Quan explained in English. The others around the table listened and several interrupted to correct him in Chinese. It seemed everyone understood English, but no one felt comfortable speaking it.

"DAS sometimes forms colonies in the vats of mountain algae—"

Mike had read enough to know the rest of the story and didn't have the patience for Quan to translate it into English. Mike summarized rapidly, "— where it outcompetes the other algae and you have a vat of silvery, crunchy, diatoms, not fit for human consumption."

"Exactly." Quan didn't seem offended by the interruption.

"Perhaps the next step would be a tour of your incubators."

Mike expected the production operation to look like the ones he'd seen in the United States: large vats, miles of stainless-steel pipes, and colorful control monitors. He anticipated the soft hum of pharmaceutical pumps and biological incubators with dim lights and a few operators dressed in spacesuits—looking like a futuristic temple or a classic science fiction movie.

Entering the *Nofu* building, he was blasted with hot humid air and the cacophony of acres of plastic drums rolling to the sound of splashing and ball bearings. Hundreds of people ran around. More than anything else, this reminded him of his soda bottle incubators back in high school.

Inspectors tagged mature drums with red flags on bamboo poles. Next, a team would open each drum and apportion it into four daughter drums to be placed on available rollers. Other drums were marked with green flags. These were picked up by forklifts and taken to another building to process the mountain algae into *Nofu*.

He waved his arm toward the door, and shouted, "I've seen enough."

Back in the conference room, he asked, "What have you tried?"

Quan tapped his comp and a slide appeared on the wall.

"Handwashing, positive pressure, filters, lockers, lunchrooms, showers."

Mike assumed *lunchrooms* meant that they stopped workers from eating lunch in the facility, and *lockers* implied that workers weren't allowed to bring personal items inside.

Compared to the hyperclean and sealed processes used in the pharmaceutical industry, this operation was like growing algae in a waste recycling plant. If this had been a hospital, all the patients would have died of infections.

He didn't say this. Instead, he temporized, "Let me do some research and see what I can find." He really had no idea, short of blowing up the factory and starting all over.

That night he had nightmares of the Vienna hospital where doctors went directly from autopsies to baby deliveries. Of course, the death rate was enormous. Even after Ignaz Semmelweis showed the doctors the data in favor of handwashing, the gentlemen doctors were offended to be accused of transmitting diseases. Learning from history, Mike realized he'd not only need to find a solution but one that would be accepted.

He woke up early to connect to Oklahoma. As soon as his comp connected, he saw the timer on the screen. 130:21:52. Time was running out.

On the Oklahoma side, William grabbed the comp and ran out of the house. The screen bounced and Mike could hear Dee shouting. "Wait until you see what we found!"

When the picture stopped moving around, Mike gasped.

Elzia laughed at his surprise. "I didn't believe it either. My parents saved your high school experiments. Do you recognize those test tubes and all those soda bottles and tubing?"

"Yes. Yes, but what is that doing in your parents' barn?"

"Your mother couldn't take it to South Dakota, and the buyers wouldn't keep it. But the recyclers wouldn't touch it. Everyone called it a biohazard."

Mike sighed. "People can be so stupid."

"So, my parents took it. It got put into the back of the barn and everyone forgot about it. Cool?"

Mike gasped, then shouted, "Do you see any test tubes labeled 147?"

"Calm down, kids. Give me the comp and see if you can find any test tubes that say one hundred forty-seven. One. Four. Seven."

Dee sounded offended. "I know my numbers!"

"I found it!" William grabbed a handful of vials and showed them to the camera.

"Careful. Careful." Mike pleaded from an impotent ten thousand miles away.

Calmly, Mike explained what he needed, and Elzia made suggestions.

When they said goodbye, the timer read 129:55:32 and Mike finally relaxed. He slept a solid eleven hours that night.

The next day, he collected samples of mountain algae and put together a small lab with incubators and micromanipulators. The *Nofu* factory had some of the equipment he required, but the rest had to be borrowed from an in vitro fertilization laboratory in Hechi.

When the express package arrived the next day from Oklahoma, it was labeled: baked goods. Hidden among dozens of cookies were three test tubes with labels in a high school boy's careful printing: 00147.

He placed the contents in separate vials and added different nutrient solutions. He hoped he could revive the algae, but worst case, he could extract the DNA. After placing the vials in an incubator, he called Oklahoma.

The timer showed: 79:32:11.

"I got the package. Thank you."

"No problem." She seemed as excited as he felt. "We did have to drive all night to get it to the Dallas airport, but Dee loved the adventure and William got to miss school."

When she mentioned William's skipping school, he remembered how unhappy everyone was in Oklahoma. He didn't say anything. The timer turned over to 79:30:00.

"I love you. I've got to get back to work."

He was counting on a miracle. He read about horizontal gene transfer in algae. Evidently, that was what caused the problems with DAS. In vitro fertilization and horizontal gene transfer both moved genetic material from one cell to another. With the IVF equipment, he inserted Mighty 00147 genes into mountain algae. Nothing died. He had created viable hybrids.

The next morning, he returned to the *Nofu* building.

"Okay, Quan. Bring me an infected drum and a half-dozen empty ones."

He seeded all six drums from the contaminated one. To three he added the hybrids of mountain algae and Mighty 00147.

The next morning, they checked the drums. The untreated drums were the characteristic silver of DAS. The treated drums were a healthy green.

Quan slapped his back. "Congratulations! How did you do that?"

"I did it a long time ago. I have no idea how."

"What did you do?"

"I made the mountain algae stronger than DAS."

"I didn't think anything could beat DAS."

"Seems that's not true." He thought for a moment, then, "Quan," he said, and waited until he was certain he had the man's attention. "Make sure you don't let the mountain algae 147 out."

Quan bowed, nodding. "It's secure," he said.

That afternoon he called Oklahoma again. 26:12:56.

"I was hoping you'd call. Did you ever wonder how that 147 grew so well?"

"Yes, but I'm mostly a hands-on empirical type of guy. More of an engineer than a scientist. My thing is to make it work, but *why* is outside my job description."

"Well, you do recall that I'm the one who went to college? I am a scientist."

Dee chimed in. "I want to be a scientist like mommy."

Mike responded. "And Billy. What do you want to be? Do you want to build things like daddy?"

William responded. "I want to raise mammoths in the snow!"

"Anyway," Elzia continued, "I did a literature search, and scientists have discovered a more efficient photosynthesis process, one that works better with today's increased carbon dioxide. I bet that's what you discovered long before them."

"I remember saying that. I wanted to call it *chlorophyll m*."

She read the timer. "25:58:21. Should I purchase our tickets?"

"NO. I think this was the only reason they needed me. I'm coming home."

A week later, the treated drums were not green or silver. The various hybrids had all died. Mike flashed back to high school and all the experiments he had run before finding 147. His initial success with mountain algae had been encouraging, but he realized that more crossbreeding and possibly years of experimentation might be necessary before a real solution was found. In the meantime, people depending on *Nofu* were going to be hungry.

Mike went back to his concrete-block room. The challenges kept piling up, but at least Elzia and the children would be joining him. Misery likes company, he thought.

The next morning, he called Elzia to tell her to buy the tickets to Hechi.

He expected her to be happy, but instead, she sent the children to be with her parents and started crying. "Visas. Last week I applied for visas. They turned us down."

Mike disconnected the call feeling like he had been time-shifted back to high school. Alone without a plan and his only hope in some plastic container of microscopic beings. Microscopic beings that could care less about Mike.

44. Xiang Bo, Zi Min—Huixian China

Xiang Bo's frustration grew as she examined the mosaic of genomes related to DAS. Each genotype, or *xenolog*, of the diatom-algae-symbiote had its own horizontal gene transfer history that traced back to a cenancestor. However, those HGT contributions were difficult, almost impossible, for her to trace.

She still believed identifying the cenancestor could be the answer: she could modify the reproductive regulator to stop the spread of DAS, possibly even destroy it. But the network of ancestor genes was so excruciatingly complex and changeable she despaired of finding the thing that needed to change. She simply did not have sufficient background in bioinformatics.

Zi Min did. But Zi Min did not believe DAS was a problem.

Xiang Bo leaned back in her chair, resting her head on the chair back while she stared at the ceiling in thought.

Perhaps she could find a way to degrade DAS using safe microbes. It was going to have to be by using something unique to her diatoms, which meant she needed to work with the silica transport proteins. Those were not found in any other diatom or algae species, and were very different from food sources, such as rice. They ought to be safe.

The cells of DAS were united into linked colonies by siliceous tubes. She knew some species of bacteria could accelerate the breakdown of silica. If the DAS colony mats were broken up, the symbiote might have trouble surviving, and it would certainly slow its spread. The small clumps were also more vulnerable to predators and probably to variations in climate.

What she did not know was if she could control such a bacteria without destroying anything desirable. The whole point of integrated farms was to raise food, including vegetables and fish and edible algaes together in a symbiotic relationship. There was a very real possibility that to break one part of that relationship meant breaking the whole thing, resulting in less food, not more.

The National Government Secretary had been so delighted with the success of DAS and her integrated fish farm system that he had encouraged the Chinese Ministry of Commerce to formally sell and export the system to places all around the world, at least those with enough water to support such systems. Some areas of both central Africa and India now employed integrated fish-farming as a major part of their agricultural output.

Meanwhile, DAS spread, even in the colder waters of the Arctic. She had seen a photo essay about the "whitening of Nunavut."

While that cooling had not made an effect on the *Hot* globally yet, or at least she had no proof of that, she did have historical evidence that it *would*.

DAS would kill the *Hot*. Eventually. A fair bit of her research monies was now targeted at projecting how long it would take to bring the *Hot* back to a neutral point, world-wide. She was confident that would happen. She must present her data in such a way that the National and Guangxi Councils believed that it would happen, too.

She picked up an article she had run across earlier, about preventing horizontal gene transfer. It seemed some multicellular eukaryotes had an inbuilt mechanism to prevent HGT. If she could find a way to link that to DAS's reproductive system, she could halt the mutations, preventing DAS from learning how to grow in every micro-ecology on Earth.

⬭

Zi Min flung a memory cube at Xiang Bo's desk, startling the older woman. Zi Min said, "I saw you working on DAS again; I have found many, many articles that show how beneficial it is.

"It's in the vat algae we made: *it destroys edible algaes*. How is this good?"

"I am aware," Zi Min said, rolling her eyes. "I'm on the phone with Mo Chou every day. But I'm speaking of DAS in the wild. You are still stuck on trying to stop it, and I'm telling you it's too late, *and* it doesn't matter!"

"Of course it matters, Zi Min. DAS has increased the ocean albedo. Have you looked at climate data about the effects of such massive cooling globally? We are going to go right from the *Hot* to an ice age!"

"Yes, I understand. But that is many years away." She pointed to the memory cube. "Plug that into your comp," she said.

Xiang Bo let out an audible sigh and picked up the cube. She fitted it to the reader slot of her comp and watched the screen come up with diagrams of CRISPR off-target base editors.

Zi Min allowed herself a small smile as her mother leaned closer to the screen, following the research report's diagrams. "Try the adenine base editor," she said, trying not to sound too smug.

"That's what I originally used," Xiang Bo said.

"Yes, but Dr. Li said you've used the cytosine line for your governors."

"That's the only way I could make them work—" Xiang Bo squinted at the screen some more. She tapped a stylus against her teeth with a quiet click. "Maybe," she said. "Maybe that would work."

⬭

"It's in the oceans. It's in the Arctic!" Li's voice carried all the way from his office out into the courtyard, where Zi Min had been talking quietly with Lotte.

"Oh," Lotte said. "I guess we knew that was coming."

Zi Min nodded. "He was distracted for a while, talking to Mo Chou and trying to solve the vat algae problem. But that wasn't going to ever keep him from seeing the news," she said.

Xiang Bo walked out into the courtyard looking dazed. "Too late," she said. "All that work, and it's too late to stop it."

"Maybe it will kill itself," Lotte offered, "the sea will get too cold, and DAS will die."

Xiang Bo shook her head. "Nothing kills it," she said.

"Not even the American's Mighty 147," Li said.

"I thought that had cleared DAS from the vats?" Zi Min said, putting her arm around Lotte who had shivered at what Xiang Bo and Li said.

Her papa met her gaze and shook his head. "Quan Song called last night. DAS came back," he said. "The vat algae are dying."

Di'e came into the courtyard, shutting the gate behind her. Her hands were full of green tea leaf twigs. Sensing the tension, she stopped and looked at them all clustered together. "What's wrong?"

Zi Min told her the news.

"I thought that it was good that it cooled things down," she said, her frown showing her puzzlement.

"It is, *ya-ya*, it is," Zi Min said.

"It's good for a while, *Maman*," Xiang Bo said. Zi Min watched her grandmother's face, to see if she understood, "but then it will cool the Earth too much, and we have no way to stop it."

"Ah," Di'e said.

They all jumped as the big iron outer gate clanged shut. Zi Min was first to see it was Ming-Hua walking in, his guide dog leading him down the side yard toward the family in the courtyard. Zi Min was astonished to see tears on her uncle's cheeks.

"What now?" Li asked.

Ming-Hua's despair was like a virulent virus spreading gloom over the compound. "They voted—" he shook his head, "the Council voted to re-zone our compound for apartments after all," he said.

"Fools! They can't grow food in apartments," Li said.

"The Council are pressuring me to get you to sell," Ming-Hua told Di'e. "I'm afraid if we don't, they will just seize it and do what they want, and we will have nothing at all."

"Don't give up yet, Uncle," Zi Min said. "Lotte and I have a plan."

"Can you stop DAS?" Xiang Bo asked.

"No. But we can maybe keep the compound," Zi Min said. She would never forget the expression on her mother's face: as if she mourned for the world. Xiang Bo looked shattered. She hugged her mama and Lotte together. "We'll figure something out. We will."

PART IV — 2068

45. Suluk, Maatalii—Qamanittuaq Nunavut Canada

"To be honest, I never believed we'd get this thing built," the construction contractor said. Kitiqmeot Builders, his hat said. Suluk had mostly interacted with him over the phone; she was not used to his face yet.

"Oh?" Suluk said. "Why is that?"

They both turned and looked at the new Snow House Auditorium and Arena. Ama's Nanuq had designed the magnificent building while he was still in High School.

"Sometimes these award-winning designs are just too impractical. Insufficient thought is put into basic factors like plumbing, air circulation, proper support for free-standing sections." He glanced at her and smiled. "I don't see anything wrong here, but you know, there have been some structures that fell down, or always had problems, like windows blowing out in a big storm and such like. Or the sponsoring agency goes bankrupt, or changes their mind."

Suluk nodded. "We discussed all that before we began. We would not stop in the middle. Though, I still think it should be named Nanook Hall. It's not really part of Snow House."

"And it looks like *nanook*," the builder said.

"Does it?" Suluk wondered. She'd been told that, but she couldn't really see it, even allowing for the stark representative strokes of typical Inuit art that Nanuq had supposedly used in his design.

"You need to be farther away, for it to take shape."

"Hmm. I will look next time I take the dogs out," she said. "Meanwhile..."

"I'll send my crew over tomorrow to finish the cleanup. There's a couple of details inside to be dealt with also, but you can have your people begin setting up for the conference now."

"Good. Thank you."

"Thank *you!*" He turned and shaded his eyes, looking over the building, the parking area and the rest of Snow House, now looking small off to the side. "Contracts like this keep us alive. And it was fun, too!" His smile made his eyes crinkle almost shut, and Suluk was once again glad she had picked his bid from the pile she had received offering to build Nanuq's multi-purpose auditorium and arena.

She spent the time walking back to Snow House composing an itemized list of what still needed to be done before the start of the ICC—the Inuit Circumpolar Council meeting. Sometimes the all-Inuit organization was just called the Arctic Council. Snow House was hosting the meeting this year, the first time the Council had gathered in three years.

The Two Pearls

The primary meeting agenda item was still Climate Change. But they had some new presentations, also. Suluk herself had accepted the request by some Chinese scientists to come and host a presentation about DAS, the diatom-algae that was working so well to re-freeze Arctic waters.

They needed to agree on a pre-*Hot* level of ice and glaciation to allow before stopping DAS. Suluk wrinkled her nose, trying to remember what the Chinese scientist had said.

If she understood things correctly, a predator algae would be released that would stop DAS from working. If all went as planned, the permafrost, ice sheets, and glaciation would return to a stable level, and global cooling would stop. The global climate change would stabilize.

When to release that algae was what the ICC needed to discuss. The Arctic communities' agreement would be formalized and presented to the U.N., and a consortium of world scientists would effect stabilization.

Also at the ICC meeting, there was a subcommittee on resurrection science and ecology that was mostly concerned with the mammoths. She had already asked Maatalii to attend that one.

Mammoths versus native species, she thought. There were still a lot of Inuit who believed the mammoths were destroying the habitat of "native" species, further contributing to their decline, despite several reports that had demonstrated the exact opposite.

Suluk had seen for herself how the mammoths helped the other species. Their big feet helped the permafrost freeze in winter, and uncovered browse for smaller animals in summer. Once the mammoths had passed on in an area, it was repopulated by hares, foxes, various rodents, birds and passing caribou. Maati would do a presentation showing what they had observed over the years.

Oh, she needed to add the notice about WiFi availability throughout the Snow House buildings, and itemize what display and computer functions were available throughout the meeting center.

She was proud that Nanuq's Snow House Auditorium and Arena was the perfect place to host the conference, and indeed, one of the few within the entire Arctic that was large enough. Previous meetings had been held in southern parts of Scandinavia, because the more northerly districts seldom had large enough facilities. Suluk remembered one she had gone to with Osha when she was quite young. The local restaurants had actually run out of familiar foodstuffs, and the Inuit had eaten beef and chicken for the first time in many of their lives, because that was all that was available.

She smiled, knowing Snow House would not have that problem. There were many dishes all the Inuit would be familiar with, whether from Alaska, Canada, Greenland, or Russia. And she had brought in a chef from Mongolia who was familiar with many Asian cuisines, to help back up her Snow House cooks and prepare foods the Chinese scientists might enjoy. She had been pleased at how excited the woman had been to learn of the menu ideas, and the availability and variety of vegetables at Snow House.

Maatalii met her at the door. "The children are all off to school, Mama," she said with a smile. "I'm ready to help."

Suluk smiled back. She loved her three grandchildren, but they were a big distraction to her thought processes, and she needed to focus on the conference and what she had left to do.

They got busy on the list of details, figuring out logistics and timetables that needed to be met for a smooth conference. Suluk thought Maati was just as excited as she was for all these different peoples to come to Qamanittuaq.

To *them*.

What a difference from ten years before.

◡

Maatalii spent the following morning running errands. It was wonderful to see how enthusiastic the entire town was about the Conference. First she made certain the other two small hotels in town were prepared to accommodate any overflow.

One of the owners, originally from a mining family up at Fifthslope and now settled into Qamanittuaq even including into the Sisterhood, took her on a brief tour of her six available rooms. She showed off her new linens, including the special towels Maati had ordered so that each attendee had a practical keepsake to take home with them. Meriwa's embroidered *nanook* mother and cubs decorated the hem. Maati made sure the woman had one of the towels for herself, too, as a thank you for her part in the preparations.

The third small hotel, which would be hosting the resurrection scientists, had installed some large paintings of the mammoths, that Maati had commissioned a local artist to create. The rooms here looked great, too. Maatalii loved that the community was working together, as *The People* should.

As she drove her slushski back to Snow House, she mused that Qamanittuaq had come back together *better* than it had been before. Before Tarkik's death and the icy jealousy that had shattered the town.

Now the Sisterhood had two new Keepers, besides Osha and her student Maati, and Jissika's grandmother. Like Maati, Jissika was learning the Ways as a Keeper's apprentice, but now the entire Sisterhood sat in on their learning sessions as well. They'd all come to realize having the Ways in the hands of a single person was not the best way to pass the traditions along to new generations. There were too many chances for too many stories to be lost, if a Keeper passed on before they'd taught all their stories. The lessons now were shared by all four Keepers and their apprentices, taught to all the women who wanted to hear, to learn, and to pass on their histories, their hunting and drinking songs, their myths and Ways.

Maatalii was startled out of her reminiscence by the sight of Caiden standing with the children in front of the school. Had her errands taken so long that school was over already? He must have walked over to the school to get them. They all piled onto the slushski for the ride back home. Maati was swamped with drawings, graded papers, homework assignments, and excitement as she guided the slushski into the Snow House parking area.

"I want to go see the new mammoth babies!" Tonraq, her youngest said, and his siblings chimed in.

Maati laughed. "Maybe Papa can take you over; I still have a thousand things to do."

"A *thousand?*" Tonraq said, a doubtful tone in his voice.

Maati waved a hand, as if her exaggeration was not that serious.

"Oops," Caiden laughed, and rumpled their smallest son's hair. "At least hundreds!" he said, grinning at Maati.

"Basia is going to come over and help you guys with your homework tonight," she announced. She glanced again at Caiden. "I really am swamped."

He nodded. "It's nice, but I'll be glad when this is all over and things get back to normal," he said.

Maatalii agreed, eyeing the new runway that had been paved just the week before. Even the airport was preparing for ICC, but she knew Mama hadn't paid for that upgrade. She wondered who had.

◡

"We may need to release another group of animals to the wild," Suluk said as the family stared at yet another broken fence.

"Yes. The bulls are crowded too close together, that's why we're getting all these fights," Maatalii said.

"I want to get this done and out of the way before the conference," Suluk said. Escaped mammoths were the last thing they needed to have interrupt the ICC meetings.

"Easy enough," Sivoy said, swinging a new top bar into place, while Caiden fastened down the other end. The two worked so well together.

"I want to pick them, Mama. May I pick them?" Tonraq, of course, who was just six, thought the world revolved around him.

"They kind of have to pick themselves, Ton," Caiden told him. "But if you pick one of the bulls, we can let him out and then see who wants to follow him."

Tonraq bit his lip, and then pointed to one of the biggest of the mammoth bulls. "That one," he said.

Sivoy climbed the fence, and stepped off onto a smaller female's back. Using a length of pipe with a board on it as a sort of portable blinder, Sivoy guided his mount over to the bull. While he worked to separate the big animal from the rest of the milling herd, Caiden and Maatalii got ready to open the gate, while Tonraq got in their way of course.

Using the same system they'd been successful with before, they eased the bull outside the fence, where it stood still, not aware of its freedom yet. Or, where it waited for some females to join it.

Years ago, after Amaruq and Maatalii had gone to Maine and arranged for the *other* herd of mammoths to be shipped to them, Snow House became the sole owners of every mammoth alive. Which included almost 600 animals now, even with culling the herds for meat sales and previously freeing two groups of about twenty animals each into the wild.

They watched and waited while the ninety or so animals in this pasture sorted themselves out. About a dozen mammoths, including several large females and a few young males, separated into a cluster by the gate and the waiting male outside it. The rest stood in the far corner or moved in a swirling line between the two groups.

Sivoy, still on his female mount inside the fence nodded at Caiden to open the gate.

This process still astonished Maati; the big animals just *knew* what they were doing. The small group of mammoths by the gate exited and gathered around the bull outside, while the remaining mammoths whuffed and stayed inside, swishing their tails, or shaking their heads so that spittle flew through the air in bursts lit by the afternoon sun. Sivoy guided the female he rode back to the fence as Caiden and Maati fastened the gate closed. Sivoy handed out the blinder-board guide and hopped over the fence. The female he had 'ridden' snorted and rejoined the large group that remained.

Maatalii tilted her head at the released bull and his little herd. Then she pointed toward the wide-open spaces of the tundra. Slowly, as if making it clear it was *her* idea, the biggest female in the bull's group led them away. By the time everyone had made their way back to the barn to clean up, the small group of mammoths had disappeared from view. Maati hurried to update her records book, listing how many animals had been let go, and her best estimate on their ages and origin. This particular group had been part of the Maine herd, which was still behind their original herd in reproduction levels, but which were healthier and apparently happier here than they'd been twenty degrees further south.

Snow House had already released most of the caribou they'd once had. Fencing the herds in to protect and feed them when the permafrost declined and the tundra died off as a result, had been the only way they could think of to save them. Now things were better.

The *Hot* wasn't entirely gone, but it was fading. Climate change had slowed, then stopped. Now they saw signs it had begun to reverse back to cooler, healthier levels. Some alarmists claimed it was leading to an Ice Age, but that would take many years. The mammoths should thrive out there, as the first two released groups had, and all the caribou, according to their random counts, ranger reports, and drone and satellite imagery.

As they returned to their various duties, Maatalii saw Sivoy stop at his little dog graveyard. He always paid a visit to Aput's grave. It was as if the other dogs knew he honored their old leader. They did not bark and jump in their usual rowdy way until he had gone into the kitchen and returned with their food. That was their signal to return to their usual bumptious joy: Honor time was finished, now it was Feeding time.

Caiden joined her at the door into the restaurant prep room. He put an arm around her waist as they watched Sivoy and his dog ritual.

"I'm sorry he lost Hitty so soon after he found her," she said. "And for you, that your mother is gone so young."

"Cancer has no respect for age, or anything else," Caiden said. "It got Giqa, too."

"I always felt he'd had a good long life. Your mother did not have her full share."

"Nor did Tarkik," Caiden pointed out. "We don't grieve for him as much."

Maatalii made a face. "Well, Ama does, but that's to be expected. If I lost Lusa, I'd be much more upset."

Caiden shrugged. "Things work out, Maati. Tarkik is gone, but Jissika is happy anyway."

"Seems so. She has certainly been helpful here," Maatalii said. "Well," she turned and went into the prep room, "we've got a lot of pot pies to make and get frozen for next week."

"Mmm," Caiden said, licking his lips, "mammoth pot pie."

"Oh, don't worry," Maati laughed. "There's always some that don't look so nice, that we'll get to eat."

Caiden's big grin showed his appreciation of that.

46. KARINA—INDIA, GERMANY, CALIFORNIA

A flash of sunlight illuminated the saloon's dark basement for the brief time the door opened. With the return of the artificial night, the frantic socialization resumed. The outside world had admitted a man in a white shirt and tie, khaki slacks, and short gray hair. While he looked around trying to adjust to the darkness, Karina ran across the crowded room. She started to hug him, but he stood stiff. She stepped back and shook his hand. "Vadish! Thank you for coming all the way to Cochin."

He looked around uncomfortably. She'd expected the younger military man from her childhood, but he had aged. Of course, she had also aged, but in her mid-thirties, she still fit in.

"Would you like to walk along the harbor instead?" she suggested.

Looking relieved, he returned to the door and once again filled the room with bright light. She followed, surprised at how fast he moved.

Along the Mattancherry waterfront, cranes shuttled containers to and from the cargo ships casting shadows across the shore like frantic clouds dancing in a storm. Karina settled Vadish on a bench far enough from the industrial turmoil where they could talk.

"How is everything in Putiya Pattanam?

"Fine."

"Is Roshni still running New Town Parma?"

"Yes."

She wanted to ask about her father, but with his monosyllabic conversation, she didn't feel comfortable. She looked for something else to talk about. "Do you see your grandchildren often?"

Now he came to life. "*Até. Até.* Sarita invites me to Mumbai every fortnight for Saturday tea." He turned on his comp and showed her pictures. "Here is Teja. She is the top bowler for the cricket team at her high school."

Karina admired the athletic teenager.

He continued with pictures of Teja in a sari and another sari. Nair playing rugby. Another picture of his grandson in a nice suit receiving some academic honor. He also had pictures of Sarita and her husband at fancy dinners, and their house, cars, and servants. She needed to do little more than nod her head and murmur "*Até. Até,*" every once in a while.

Finally, she interrupted. "I haven't seen my father in ten years. Have you heard from him? Do you know where he might be?"

Vadish became quiet again. "Your father—" He paused as if trying to find the right word. "Your father had many interests." Another pause. "His interests changed." A longer silence. "Always going forward. He had little use for the past."

Karina understood. Her father had not returned to Kerala or even kept in contact with Vadish. She'd have to go elsewhere to find him.

"Good evening. Welcome to Spaetzle and Wurst. Are you alone?"

Karina nodded her head. She held her copy of Priya's bestselling memoir, *Mammoths, Resurrection, and Exodus.* Just carrying a paper book set her apart as a serious person, but the heavy, non-fiction tome additionally warded away lonely men.

While she read the large paper menu signaling a fancy hotel restaurant, a tall woman with a red ponytail approached her table. In mid-western American, the redhead asked, "I see you are reading Priya's book. Could I join you?"

Karina nodded, uncertain why this American woman would know Priya, and even more curious why she would use that familiar address to a stranger in Berlin. "Sure. Do you know Priya?"

The woman sat down. "I'm Carla McGilvery. Years ago, my family lived near Qamanittuaq."

Karina hadn't met anyone who could pronounce Qamanittuaq in ages. "Do you know me?"

"Oh yes. You're Karina Kowalski. Your picture's in Priya's book."

The two women had a congenial dinner, exchanging stories. Carla owned a business retrofitting water purification plants to respond to DAS. "Most people thank DAS for defeating the *Hot*, but my customers are less sanguine about the abrasive silicon organisms that damage their equipment."

Karina recounted her life as an international trade negotiator, an occupation that took advantage of her peripatetic childhood. "Now that the ACE hegemony has been ended, people with experience in other cultures are in high demand."

Carla smiled in agreement, but wondered, "ACE?"

"Oops. Sorry about that. That's our acronym for American-Chinese-European."

As it got late and the restaurant began setting up for tomorrow's breakfast, Karina ventured, "Have you run across my father?"

"You don't see him regularly?"

"No. We haven't spoken in years."

"Oh." Carla continued. "I don't know, but I hear rumors of a food truck with the strangest menu, mostly algae, insects, and worms, but surprisingly good."

Karina allowed herself to hope. "Do you think it might be my father?"

"Good question. During the height of the *Hot*, everyone experimented with alternate protein sources. I even spent some time with a company that made hamburger from worms in South Africa."

Karina almost mentioned Ashur but didn't. He was ancient history. "So why do you think this might be my father? Is there something special about this truck?"

"Yes. This food truck—I saw it last month in San Diego—is special in two ways. First, it keeps changing. The city. The menu. The name. The artwork. The costumes. The people who know of it, have given it the sobriquet, The ADHD Chef."

"That sounds like him."

"Also, the service is slow as you have to listen to his patter, and on random days, the food is free."

Karina hadn't been so happy since Maatalii agreed to take the mammoths. She canceled her appointments and booked a flight to Los Angeles.

Cabo San Lucas. Newport Beach. Palos Verdes. Sausalito. Mendocino. Portland. Seattle. Vancouver. Karina hired detectives up and down the west coast. Rumors of The ADHD Chef popped up everywhere. All fascinating, but not her father.

Finally, one day she received a connection from Santa Rosa. "Karina. He's here. One hundred and one percent positive. Medieval Faire in Guerneville. Ye Olde Famine Feasts. Hurry. This is the last weekend."

The gypsy wagon occupied a prime spot on the main path. It offered a mixture of traditional Faire fare like turkey legs and large beef ribs, along with a variety of exotic vegetarian choices that were only invented in the 21st century. The eclectic food truck was decorated in non-authentic neon colors. Karina identified the motifs to be from children's *Ganesh Chaturthi* elephant art. Her search had ended. She'd found her father.

Kaczka wore an over-sized purple turban, a robe embroidered with dragons, and outlandish slippers with curled toes. With his Malayalam accent, he told a story of chimeric beasts, feeding hungry crowds, and fighting evil spirits. That's him, she thought with pride. Always flamboyant, and always feeding people.

When he spied Karina, he turned back to the people in the mobile kitchen. "Feed the peasants and the gentry for no charge until no victuals remain." He ran to Karina and gave her a big hug, but then he released her and seemed sad. "Are you still mad at me?"

She didn't want to get all emotional, but still, she choked as tears ran down her face. She felt embarrassed that he thought she'd still be angry about his bankruptcy and losing her mammoth ranch. She hugged him. "No. The past is past. I've been searching for you. You big buffoon! Do you know people have been looking for you?"

"I'm glad you've been able to forgive me. What about Ashur?"

Her father never ceased to amaze her. The ADHD chef for sure. "How do you know Ashur?"

He adjusted his turban and spoke with his fake accent. "Ashur? Did I say Ashur? Who is Ashur? And do you still hate him?"

She recalled their good times in Stellenbosch, Paris, and Maine, but she also remembered how he was always trying to use her to cheat people. "I don't know."

"Well after you broke up with him, he contacted me. He said that you suggested this. We teamed together on a few deals, but I quickly saw he was more interested in making money than feeding the hungry. I sent him away."

"That's him alright. Always watching out for number one." She didn't want to waste any more of her life on him, so she changed topics. "Let's talk about something better. The California Zoological Society has erected a monument in your honor, but they have been waiting to dedicate it until you could attend. Do you realize how many people have been helped by the mammoths? Everyone knows that you started the program."

Now he smiled. "Oh good. I'm getting tired of this food truck thing. Do you think they might need a chef?"

Karina laughed at her father's short attention span and eagerness for something new, anything new. "They're a zoo, not a restaurant."

"I know. I'm ready to prepare food for additional species. I'm sure other species would benefit from some variety."

"I'll tell the CZS we're on our way."

"But Ashur?"

"Him again? I thought we were through with the self-centered narcissist."

"A few years back, he contacted me again. He has started a non-profit to help poor communities deploy small-scale protein conversion systems."

"Well, I suppose that's better."

"He is partnered with Freja, a Danish engineer who was also from Mdudu Nyama."

She wondered if she was feeling jealousy.

"Of course, she is just a business partner, as he tells me every chance he gets. He's only interested in you."

Now Karina didn't know what to think. "Why don't you invite him to the unveiling of your statue."

Her father gave her a gentle hug. "I guess that is fair."

People crowded around the mammoth enclosure. One newborn mammoth attracted the most attention by spinning in circles until she became dizzy and staggered across the artificial tundra. Karina recalled Indrakshi's fight with the tiger.

For the unveiling ceremony, Kaczka had worn one of his outlandish costumes, embroidered silk, and a matching turban. He addressed the crowd in a phony accent. "Many years ago, in the wilderness of India, we started with DNA from Wrangel Island, and today mammoths are in many zoos and saving the permafrost everywhere around the Arctic Circle."

Karina stopped listening as he recounted the flood and the exodus.

"Karina?"

She turned around and was face-to-face with Ashur, dressed in worn overalls and smelling of manure. "What are you doing here?"

"Looking for you."

She said, "My father warned me," with disdain in her voice while crossing her arms and backing away. "You need a shower."

"I know. The zoo needed help, so I volunteered. I should still be mucking the mammoth stables, but I didn't want you to leave before I spoke to you." He pointed to the crowd, obviously getting thinner as her father continued his story. "I knew once Kaz got started you might leave."

Obviously, he was right. As her father droned on, she examined Ashur from the straw in his hair down to his muck boots. Seeing him as a stable hand reminded her that he had forsaken his greedy lifestyle. When he smiled, her affection for him returned.

"If I take a shower, can I take you to dinner?"

She uncrossed her arms but didn't move closer. He still smelled. "It's a date."

At dinner, they agreed that she should return his hospitality and guide him through California.

Their excursion began in San Diego with a private tour of the RV Riftia.

"Can I share the driving?"

"Not a good idea. We'll be taking the Pacific Coast Highway. It's scenic, but with narrow lanes and lots of curves. It's never been retrofitted to be an eRoad, so not the best place to learn to drive on the other side of the road."

They took a week to reach San Francisco, where they turned east and headed for Yosemite.

"This is the Central Valley. It provides half of the fruits, vegetables, and nuts grown in the United States."

"I can drive here."

"Perhaps on the return from Yosemite." It wasn't the roads. Something else made her not trust him driving. Trust. She enjoyed spending time with him, but she didn't trust him! His sudden conversion from cutthroat businessman to compassionate engineer didn't ring true. When the eRoad seized control, she collected her courage. "Tell me why you decided to abandon the lucrative factory business."

She'd feared he'd be defensive or angry, but he tilted his seat back and stretched his legs out. "It started forty-four years ago. I wasn't born in South Africa, I was born in Kibera, the largest slum in Nairobi."

Karina had seen Kibera, a half-million souls living in shacks without electricity and only the most basic communal water and sewage service. She tried to recall what else she'd been told by the guide on one of the many busses that toured through the slum. Kaczka had built a langar just outside Kibera before he went bankrupt.

"Can you imagine being hungry, and dirty, and your family members dying of diseases while watching busses of tourists passing through all day describing your misery in different languages?"

Karina felt embarrassed about her tour even though it was over twenty years ago. "That must have been terrible."

"Yes. So terrible that after we moved to South Africa, I suppressed all memories." He got quiet.

For lack of anything else to say, she announced the different nuts as they sped across the Central Valley.

"Almonds."

"Pistachios."

"Walnuts."

"Not too long ago, I won a big contract to build a hamburger factory in Kenya. On the first visit, I discovered it was to be built in Kibera. Bulldozers were going to clear out the shacks. The families that had some clean water, and some electricity, small improvements accumulated over many decades, were going to be displaced to start over."

She noticed tears running down his cheeks.

"My childhood came back to me. I remembered that I still had family living there. That is when I changed my direction."

She held his hand and kissed the tears from his face. "The next city is Los Baños, the bathrooms. We can switch drivers there."

Even after the *Hot* went away, Karina, Ashur, and their children joined a generation of leaders who considered themselves to be stewards of Earth, vowing to never return to the old normal. Their children visited all seven continents before they were five, travelling only via carbon-negative vehicles.

Dee dressed for the first day of high school. Abbie and Elzia had taken her to Oklahoma City to outfit her for the new school year. A special treat since the latest fashions were unavailable in Cherokee. For her splurge, she had gotten purple and orange button-up boots. Both grandma and mom had thought them to be ugly, so she refused to leave until she had them. To go with the boots, she chose a dress in the popular Victorian style with lots of ruffles and underskirts and a large straw hat with silk flowers that matched the boots.

"You nervous about your first day of high school?" Billy asked.

Dee wasn't the least concerned but recognized Billy's attempt to be the good big brother. She decided to be a good little sister. "Do you have some advice?"

He sat on her bed. "Be prepared to be recognized. Mom and Dad made strong impressions, what with leaving and returning."

"Yes, the middle-school teachers also remembered them." She reflected that Cherokee epitomized a stereotypical small town. Everyone knew her parents and grandparents. Even more, total strangers stopped her to tell her how much she looked like her mother.

"Who do you have for homeroom?"

Dee made a disgusted face. "Miss Perry."

He mirrored her look. "Everyone keeps asking when she's going to retire, but she could last to see your children."

Dee punched his arm. "Don't say that. After high school, I'm leaving town—only returning for Christmas and the July 4th barbeque."

He reached out to shake her hand. "Me too,- sister. Me too."

Dee strode into the social media office on club day. The editrix sat behind a pedestal desk with her name and title displayed in a florid script, orange on purple. Editrix, a nice Victorian erudition, Dee thought. She admired the beautiful dress the Editrix wore, with a bodice consisting of multiple layers of blue and green crochet lace. Dee offered her calling card and introduced herself.

The editrix took the card without looking at it. "Yes, I know who you are. What brings you to our club?"

"I'm a writer. I was editrix-in-chief for the middle-school social media club."

Now the other girl examined the calling card as if there might be more information there beyond Elzia McGilvery. "This is high school. The ninth-graders usually monitor the comments section for inappropriate content and respond in cases where cutting-and-pasting is sufficient."

Dee had hoped for a more welcoming response but came prepared. "In middle school, I started a thread about famous graduates. You need something like that. Let me do it."

She stood silent as the editrix said, "Ninth-grader. McGilvery," before tearing the calling card into four quarters.

The two girls stared at each other. Dee wasn't going to move until she received an unambiguous response. They both waited until the seated girl broke out into a big smile. "Good show. Give it a go."

Dee collected her passwords and set up her profile. As she left the club room, she said, "Cheerio," and made a list in her head of people to interview, starting with her famous relatives.

Her dad had refused to be interviewed for middle school, but for high school, she hoped for better cooperation. She had an ulterior motive. Interview or no interview, he rarely talked about himself. Each year he seemed more like his father, Grandpa Redd. Most days the two men retired to the woodshop. Even with the discovery that hybrids derived from his algae could forestall another ice age, he had become withdrawn.

She figured this could be a way to break through his silence.

"But Dad, Grandpa, this is for school. It's important."

Mike just grunted. When she turned to Grandpa Redd, he also grunted.

Fortunately, Grandma Abbie and her mother supported her efforts. Each morning at breakfast, and each evening at dinner, one of the women said something. They cajoled. They pleaded. He wouldn't budge.

Abbie tried another tack. "Redd, you wanted to return, and we even repurchased your family's land and graveyard. You got your history. Help Dee get hers."

He just grunted.

Elzia added. "You've been generous sharing the family stories. Please convince Mike to do the same."

Both men harrumphed and retreated to the living room.

Dee finally accepted his refusal. For October, she posted something about Redd's family coming to Oklahoma over the Trail of Tears, and for November, something else about Elzia's family moving up from Texas to raise cattle but switching to wheat when the climate cooled down.

Unexpectedly, on Thanksgiving, her dad came in from the workshop and sat down next to Dee. She smiled at him and flounced her skirts.

Mike began, "I started with algae from our farm pond."

Dee linked to a video of the pond behind the refurbished dairy barn. "This exact pond, right?"

He nodded.

Oh, Dad, she thought. You're going to have to do more than nod.

She tried a different approach. "What do you call your algae?"

Again, she received a short answer. "147."

"How did you pick that number?"

"It was the next one."

Dee got frustrated, but she had put so much effort into getting the interview, she wouldn't quit.

"How did it get to China?"

"Your brother."

"My brother?"

That did the trick. He started talking, talking so much. Fortunately, she recorded it all on her comp.

He recounted how grandma McGilvery had left 147 in Oklahoma when they moved north. Then her other grandmother had rescued it and stuck it in the back of her barn.

Dee remembered. "Billy and I searched for it and mom drove all night to Dallas to send it to China!"

"Yes. I should have known right there. Those algae survived over ten years stored in a barn. By right, everything in those vials should have been dead, but not 147. It wasn't the answer, but it had the genes to get there."

She noted the pride in his voice, and he seemed more like the dad she remembered from their time in Nunavut. After that, he told stories about Longhorns and Dusters and meeting Elzia.

When he stopped talking, she prompted him with, "I was born in Canada. How did we end up back here?"

"Do you remember seeing The Two Pearls photograph? The one with the earth covered by DAS shining white in the sunlight, looking like a twin of the moon?"

Her mother came into the living room and made eating motions with her hand. Dee knew dinner time had arrived. She waved her away. While her dad talked, Thanksgiving dinner could wait. Her mother backed away and gave her a thumbs-up, good-job gesture.

She returned to her dad, "Sure, that picture is famous."

"Well, everyone who saw it thought of the impending ice age from so much sunlight reflecting back into space. DAS seemed unstoppable. Everyone was obsessed with the irony that the *Hot* would end in a *Cold*. The reasons were as varied as those suggested for the *Hot*, ranging from the wrath of God to greedy corporations to arrogant scientists."

She didn't want to break his momentum, so now she chose a single word response. "Yes."

"Well, everyone knew DAS originated in China. At that time, you and Mom lived in Oklahoma, while I camped out in a tiny cinderblock shack in a remote Chinese town."

"Were you working on finding a way to control DAS?"

"Oh no. My job had to do with *Nofu*. A strain of algae used to make cheap, nutritious flour. People were still hungry because of the *Hot*."

"So?"

"Well DAS contaminated the *Nofu*. Fixing the *Nofu* production became my primary goal, and 147 seemed like it might help."

"What did all this have to do with DAS?"

"Not much, but public opinion divided into two groups. Doom: The world will end. Science: The scientists will save us. No one expected some farm boy who only graduated from Cherokee High would have the answer." He paused. She thought he wiped a tear from his eye. "Only your mom saw that possibility."

"So, what happened next?"

"Elzia told Grandma McGilvery that the climate would be set right. So, Grandma McGilvery bought her old farm back for almost nothing, since Oklahoma had reverted to desert. Of course, as your mom had predicted, Oklahoma is once again a breadbasket to the world."

"And DAS?"

"Oh yes. DAS. My 147's DNA ate up DAS, and the Earth was saved from an Ice Age. Who would have guessed?" He laughed and they both headed into the dining room for Thanksgiving dinner.

Abbie didn't need to look at the clock. She could hear her husband and son snoring in the living room. A glance out the kitchen window revealed the full moon high in the sky. Mostly, time didn't matter because three generations of women filled her kitchen and her heart. Granddaughter Dee commanded seven mixing bowls arrayed on the kitchen counter: Three apples, two pumpkins, a mince, a peach. Measuring, mixing, tasting, spicing. Dee's energy mixed the magic potions, but everyone tasted and suggested. Abbie luxuriated in the warmth of the oven and the sisterhood.

Carla and Elzia, daughter and daughter-in-law, commandeered the large kitchen table to prepare the crusts. Abbie felt lucky to have the table that Redd's grandfathers had fashioned from an ancient red cedar. She had thought it lost when she left it for the new owners. They had not appreciated the rustic slab and mismatched legs and had dumped it in the back of the barn. They had intended to burn it for firewood, but the daunting task of chopping it up had saved it until Abbie returned to rescue it.

Abbie took the role of honor, mistress of the oven. All night she baked each pie to perfection until the sun rose to shine on seven beautiful circles of golden-brown. All completed just in time to place the stuffed turkey into the warm oven.

Midafternoon, William stopped playing long enough to set the table. Elzia's parents showed up, bringing a case of sparkling cider. Carla and Elzia collected dishes from the kitchen counters, oven, and refrigerator to cover the table with the roast turkey, string beans, sweet potatoes smothered in marshmallows, freshly baked biscuits, two gravy boats, and many salt and pepper shakers.

Abbie had intended to save the Christmas salt and pepper shakers for a surprise in December, but she couldn't wait. It had taken two visits to the Tulsa flea market, and three more to Oklahoma City, but she had found the exact shakers from Carla's childhood. Just one more thing to make the return to the family homestead perfect.

Redd sat at the head of the table. Everyone else sat along the sides, leaving her the position of honor opposite Redd. She poured sparkling cider. Before the festivities could start, there were still two empty seats: Dee and her dad. Abbie went into the living room to collect the two stragglers. When she saw them sitting close and talking intently, she exercised her matriarchic power and figured a way to delay Thanksgiving dinner.

Abbie raised her goblet. "Many years ago, when we left, I never expected to return," she began. "When I heard Oklahoma had become too hot to even raise cattle, I feared for civilization. Were we going to follow the dinosaurs? But here we are together, feasting on the bounty of a healed planet."

William tapped his goblet against his grandmother's. "And not a single dish made from algae or worms in sight."

Everyone laughed, even Redd.

Abbie watched Elzia's mother grasp her glass and look around to see who'd speak next. Abbie nodded to her and she began. "After Elzia, my only child, left for Canada, I prayed. I never prayed so hard, but the prairie dried up and the cattle suffered. Even worse than watching our savings dwindle, the animals became sick and weak from want of water and grazing land. Many a night I cried myself to sleep." Her husband put his arm around her shoulders as she held back tears, dabbing her eyes with her napkin.

He continued. "First Elzia returned with the grandkids. We were embarrassed by our farm's condition. But now that the rains and the McGilverys have returned, this is a joyous Thanksgiving. We are happy to be raising wheat." He paused. "And a few head of cattle, of course."

Abbie looked towards the living room. Still no Dee and Mike. She looked to Redd but could see he had nothing to add. She kicked Carla under the table. Carla picked up the salt and pepper shakers. "I'm happy these have returned. They can come home, but I cannot. While I'm glad to celebrate with my family, I have a life beyond the farm. Along with my friend Karina, we are part of the new generation: citizens of Earth." She winked at William and he winked back.

Abbie saw Dee and her dad approach. She just wanted to hug everyone, but instead, she carved the turkey.

48. MAATALII, SULUK—QAMANITTUAQ NUNAVUT CANADA

Maatalii and Meriwa took seats in the big auditorium as Dr. Bai Xiang Bo set up her presentation computer. Suluk had originally planned to attend, but decided at the last minute she needed to watch over the Inn. She'd sent Meriwa in her place.

Likewise, Amaruq had bowed out, claiming other responsibilities.

"Besides," she'd said, "you must remember how good I was at falling asleep in the big lecture halls."

They'd laughed at that and hugged and then gone off in different directions.

Maatalii fully expected to be confused by the details of the science, and she suspected that had played the biggest part in her mother's change of mind, and possibly Ama's also. Dr. Bai's one-paragraph précis in the program was confusing enough. Beside her, Aunt Meriwa looked around, admiring the seating and the beautiful wood ceiling that Nanuq claimed had perfect acoustics. She had come because she wanted to watch the people. Particularly a certain shy Chinese scientist she had met in the Snow House Inn lobby.

Dr. Bai filled the auditorium's screens with diagrams, photographs, and charts. Most of the explanation of DAS—Diatom-Algae-Symbiote—was well beyond Maati's genetic sciences and chemistry comprehension. But it was fascinating to watch the maps as the symbiote spread across the world, and to see the changes it made to different landscapes.

Its primary benefit seemed to be the way it sequestered carbon and reflected sunlight. Best of all was the efficient way it chilled the Arctic Sea, re-creating ice shelves even in Hudson Bay and the Great Lakes in America. There were small ice floes on their own lake that spring, and she knew that meant there were plenty of places for *nanook* to den, and to hunt the recovering seal populations.

Thriving in both fresh and sea water, DAS did not have much direct effect on the permafrost soils in the tundra. But the cooling of the Arctic waters meant more snow in winter, and colder temperatures that froze the tundra to depths up to a half-meter already—a number that was expected to continue increasing until the predator algae was released and DAS was stopped.

Dr. Bai's English was excellent, but they also had brought in interpreters for the Inuit who only spoke Inuktitut. Maati listened in both languages, to help clarify some of the places she became confused.

"The 'predator algae' is a misnomer," Dr. Bai said. "The term was coined by the popular press. But its function certainly mimics that of a predator," she said. "When it is released, DAS will die, fairly rapidly, all around the world. We will need to do this to stop the cooling before DAS creates an ice age."

There was murmuring in the audience at this.

"The Diatom Algae Symbiote is itself edible, and whales, many fish, and shellfish have consumed it as they would krill or shrimp. However, the shell is gritty and the flavor is too salty and fishy for most people's taste. It can be harvested and processed and used to make a protein-rich cracker. I would like to say it is up to each nation in the world to decide what to do with their DAS. However, once its predator is released, we expect the destruction of DAS to spread as rapidly throughout the world as DAS itself did. Once that happens, DAS as a resource will be gone."

Dr. Bai looked around the room, meeting people's eyes here and there. "For the future, we have ensured that viable samples of the symbiote and its predator have been placed in seed banks around the world should it ever need to be used again. It is also possible it will be useful in terraforming other planets as our species moves out into the universe."

She smiled and looked around at individuals in the audience again. "Questions?"

Most of the questions were very specific and Maati left.

The main thing she learned from the presentation was that the savior of their Arctic climate was a very tiny thing, to have had such a huge effect on their world.

◝

Suluk shook Lieutenant—no, now Captain—Kilabuk's hand. With her other hand, she presented him a check repaying the loan Snow House had received from the KIA, the Kivalluq Inuit Association, to help build the Conference Center—just as they had previously repaid the loan for repairing the greenhouses. As one of the administrators, Kilabuk's influence had helped. The Association monies were made available to assist all local businesses, not just Snow House. Without that help, a lot more people would have starved to death during the worst of the *Hot* in the Arctic.

Erne-Auco mines also supported Qamanittuaq; they'd paid for the airport repaving, in time for the ICC. They'd also supplied the local high school with the latest high-tech equipment: computers, lab supplies, and diagnostic gear, and a green-clean system for the high school swimming pool that Snow House had also donated to. Qamanittuaq teenagers no longer had to leave the town to get a quality upper-division education. That made everyone happy.

Suluk was aware E-A was hoping for a change in the permit vote. And she was happy to consider that, if the mining company continued to recognize its responsibilities to the community. They could all work together for a better Qamanittuaq.

Suluk cleared his empty coffee cup as Captain Kilabuk headed out, thinking she sounded like she was writing advertising copy. But things were good; she was not at all ashamed of that.

Maatalii was able to sit in on the last few sessions the resurrection scientists held. Their primary focus today had been the mammoths and what their place was and should be in the future, versus the rest of Arctic wildlife, so Amaruq had joined her.

"I'm surprised most of you seem to think they are disruptive," she said after the meeting. Several of the scientists clustered around her, both seeking information on mammoth numbers from her, and to suggest alternatives to releasing the animals into the tundra.

"I think most people just want things to get back to what they were before the *Hot*," one of the older men said. His graying hair made Maati want to respect him, but she wanted data, not opinions.

"That seems unlikely," she said. "The *Hot* will diminish, but can things ever be the same again?"

"Certainly not if there are mammoths consuming the food supply of the caribou and other native species," the woman who had led the recent session said.

"Mammoths *are* a native species," Amaruq said, frowning. "The ecology was balanced at one time, *including* them."

"Yes, and then the mammoths went extinct. Caribou, seal, polar bear, lemmings, Arctic hares, all of the others, did not. That suggests the mammoths do not belong."

"If you ignore humans hunting them into extinction!"

"That's only one theory," one of the other scientists said. "More likely is that they were too large, and the ecosystem could not sustain them."

"If that happens, then we will know for certain," Maati said. "For now, we know they are creating areas where the permafrost refreezes faster than anywhere else in our colder winters now, and where the ordinary plants of the tundra regrow fresh and ready for all creatures—from mouse-sized on up—to eat. The caribou survived the first time when there were many mammoths. We see no reason they will not survive this time as well."

Amaruq spoke up, "We are surprised this is becoming such an issue, when there are so many animals and plants that have gone extinct because of the *Hot*. Why aren't you worrying about those?"

"We are," someone said.

"We do," someone else said at the same time.

"Then why this fuss over mammoths?" Maati wondered.

"They're the model for possibly bringing back other things," the lead scientist said. "The first ones to exist. If it turns out the mammoths are harmful to the present environment, then there is less likelihood we will be able to make a case for the return of the dodo, for example, or Amur leopards."

"It seems like it was humanity's fault for those extinctions," Maatalii argued. "It certainly wasn't because of the mammoths."

"The spread of DAS and its effects have clearly demonstrated how little we understand Earth's ecosystems in a global sense," the gray-haired scientist said. "Everything interacts with everything, and we can't predict adequately what the impact the introduction of resurrected species will be when there are so many chaotic variables."

Maati shrugged. "Well, I think if you look closely at the Mammoths, you will see they have not been harmful."

"Perhaps a better focus might be human birth control," Amaruq blurted, surprising even herself, apparently. She put a hand over her mouth, face flushed.

Maatalii picked up that thread, as Ama settled herself, "Most of the extinctions on earth have been human-caused: hunting, destruction of habitat—plain human greed."

While no one disagreed with her, the scientists talked over each other, making various statements about the impact of returning extinct species to the biosphere. They broke into arguing twos and threes.

Clearly the issues were complicated and there were strong opinions on both sides of the question. She realized nothing was going to be settled here and now, and especially that she was late picking up the children from school, again.

Maatalii waved goodbye and left the room; Amaruq followed quickly behind her.

"Are they trying to take the mammoths away?" Ama asked. "After all the help they've been?"

"I don't think they can, Ama," she said. "I just think of those drone pictures Caiden took of the permafrost." She remembered the photos of the fenced pastures and even the grazing areas of the small herds that had been released to the wild. "You could almost see the frost returning to the tundra, radiating out from the mammoth places like icy stars, connecting to other stars. Even the smaller places the caribou have churned are the centers of ice stars, like frost spreading on windowpanes."

Ama nodded, climbing onto the slushski behind Maati. "I remember. It was like a creature growing and spreading. Like the permafrost had been reborn."

"How could restored permafrost be bad?" Maati said. "I don't think they realize how important that is. Even the polar bears are doing better."

Suluk helped Maatalii get the children dressed to go outside. It was getting cold after sunset again, after so many years of frighteningly balmy weather. Once they got to the Auditorium it would be warm, of course, but walking over from Snow House restaurant was going to be chilly. It was wonderful.

"I'm so glad we suggested an early Winter Games meet to end the ICC conference," Maati said, zipping up Tonraq's parka.

"Mom! I don't need gloves, too!" Ton said, hiding his hands in his pockets.

"Well, put them in your pockets so you have them," she said, handing him the gloves again. "It may be pretty cold when we walk back." She realized Tonraq had never seen a true Arctic Fall season. The *Hot* had reigned his entire life. At his age, how could she expect him to understand something he had never seen?

"And you can get cold when you sit at an ice hockey game for a couple of hours," his great-grandma Osha told him.

He made a face, but obediently put his gloves in his pocket.

They were joined in the Inn lobby by Meriwa and the Chinese scientist she had adopted. The white-haired fellow wore eyeglasses, which would probably steam up as soon as they walked outside. Maati hoped he would be warm enough in his light down jacket and knitted wool gloves.

Meriwa had a firm grip on his arm, she saw. It was a puzzle how the two were getting along, since he spoke very little English, and no Inuktitut, and Meriwa, of course, no Chinese at all. But smiles work, she thought as the two grinned at each other and followed Suluk out the door.

Maati herded her children out and they walked along the path. Solar lanterns lit their way. The chrysanthemums they had planted to trim the walkways for the ICC conference were beginning to brown from the frost. Snow House looked quite different from years ago, but it was the same chilled air she remembered breathing deep into her lungs. She smiled at her family's rosy cheeks as they walked toward the Arena where they would join Caiden, and *uaguk* and her family, and Ama's new boyfriend. She saw Sivoy standing by his dogs, and waved. He waved back and joined them. They would all be together to watch the game, and it was good.

49. Di'e, Zi Min, Xiang Bo—Huixian China

Di'e greeted the small tourist group with a bow and a tiny smile of welcome. These were Americans, they never knew what to do in response. Half of them matched her bow, others smiled or reached out a hand as if she would shake hands with them. The tour guide said something to them in English, then Di'e turned and led the way into the compound.

The small tour bus parked outside the gates as she had asked, but not far enough back that she could shut the gates. She would just have to hope the family pets stayed inside today: goat and dog and cat. All three would probably be sleeping in the sunny courtyard—at least until the tour group arrived there. Of the human residents, Di'e knew Zi Min and Lotte had locked themselves in the room everyone called the lab. They didn't need to greet the tourists.

As a China Historical Monument, the Cheng family compound was no longer at risk of being torn down to make way for apartments. They even received a small donation of money from each group that visited, for maintenance of the site.

They received only a few visitors each month—this was one of the more desirable "private, secret" tourist destinations. Only tour guides in the know knew how to set up a visit. With the number of visitors thus limited, the family wasn't overwhelmed with constant tourists—but they had achieved a guarantee of survival for the compound.

Besides leading the group on the tour, Di'e also prepared a small tea ceremony with sticky buns for a snack. Ming-Hua played traditional music for the visitors while they sipped tea.

Sure enough, when they returned to the courtyard after visiting the ancestor shrine, the tortoise-shell cat was curled up on the bench in the sun. Nominally Lotte's pet, the cat suffered occasional pats from visitors, before yawning, stretching, and ambling off. The goat and dog had vanished. Not out the gate, she hoped.

The guide explained the tea ceremony while Di'e poured. Ming-Hua came out of his room, pipa in hand. Di'e sighed to see a spot on his silk jacket where he had spilled something. He obviously hadn't noticed it. Fixing his eyes did not mean he always remembered to use them. He would be embarrassed later to see it, that he had performed with it soiled that way. She glanced at the group, then back at her son as he smiled at the visitors and then sat down on a drum seat.

The guide introduced him and explained a little about the instrument. Di'e's English was now good enough to recognize the word "plucked" as the guide spoke a few more words, then bowed to let Ming-Hua know she was finished speaking. With a dramatic flourish, Ming-Hua placed the pipa in his lap and stroked the strings. The tourists actually stopped whispering and listened as her oldest son then played a traditional love song.

A little brown bird that liked to perch in the pink azalea began to chirp in time with Ming-Hua's music, as if they had trained it to sing. The guide looked at Di'e in startlement, but all she could do was give a tiny shrug. The bird was a volunteer. It looked like maybe some kind of a lark, but she had forgotten most of what she knew about bird types.

From chirps it broke into a short melodic sequence, flicked its tail, then flew off with a *swish* of its wings. Another tiny vote for the specialness of their home, Di'e thought. She would remember to thank the ancestors for that short, sweet gift.

☕

Zi Min smiled as the taxi delivered Xiang Bo and Dr. Li to the compound gate. She had stayed at the Huixian Fields compound with Lotte while her parents attended the Arctic Conference, and then stopped in Brussels, Belgium. There they received their Gaia Award, along with Mike McGilvery, who had flown in from Oklahoma. The award acknowledged the creation of DAS and its...antidote, and their effect on the *Hot* and its reversal.

She had watched her mother struggle with controlling the diatom-algae symbiote for years. Zi Min had had no interest in stopping DAS. Now she was glad she had not helped. The American man that Mo Chou had worked with had discovered—or created—the algae that could stop DAS. He'd found it many years before, never knowing that it was good for anything. If DAS hadn't managed to get into the Donglan vat algae works, they might never have known its effect on the rapidly spreading white symbiote. It stopped the spread of DAS without hurting the other algae.

Her parents also had gone to Geneva for another conference that had been limited to 100 on-site attendees, where they received recognition from NOAA, and Xiang Bo had clarified the structure of DAS. Thousands of scientists had teleconferenced to watch those proceedings, so everyone knew what the plan and timing were for the release of Mr. McGilvery's DAS-destroying algae.

Videos included simulations of the clearing of DAS from the world's waters, which satisfied the concerns of scientists and citizens the world over. She and Lotte watched the conference together for a second time that evening, after the family dinner.

Lotte switched off the holo-TV and turned to Zi Min with a frown. "Why didn't you go with them? Isn't all this your field as well?"

Zi Min shook her head. "Only in a very small way; think of a Ven diagram where the circles overlap only by a sliver. Similar, but not the same."

Lotte grunted. "I like the teleconferencing, though. It means in-person conferences are becoming a thing of the past. And good riddance."

"Unlike *this* zoo," Zi Min said, meaning the tourists.

Lotte picked up the dishes and peeked out the door, to see whether the tour group was gone yet or not.

"They should have cleared out by now," Zi Min said.

"What's going to happen when *ya-ya* dies?" Lotte said, turning to face her wife. "*We'll* have to deal with the tourists."

"Oh, Lotte. You'll be able to wear the beautiful old silk historical costumes you admire so much. It will be lovely," Zi Min said.

Lotte's face brightened a moment, then her scowl returned. "But I'll look silly with my blonde hair. You'll have to do it!" She laughed as she went out with their plates.

Zi Min turned back to the TV-holo screen area and re-lived in her mind the projection of Earth's return to "normal." It would be nice to have blue water again. She recently had seen a photograph of the "The Two Pearls" — white moon, white Earth. No longer The Blue Marble, Earth and her oceans had been coated in a thin layer of reflective white that was clearly visible from space, as The Two Pearls photo had shown.

But soon Mr. McGilvery's DAS-killer, the result of years of experiments using 147's DNA, would be released, and all the diatom-algae symbiotes would die off, falling to the oceans' floors, and taking along their sequestered carbon. Presumably, it would clear from lakes and rivers as well, though those might require individual inoculations. Earth would return to its blue marble state. She hoped it would happen fast enough for her to see it; her whole life she'd lived in the *Hot.*

◡

Xiang Bo got her points across to the mostly un-scientific Arctic conference attendees, and made clear what decisions had to be made. She felt their trip had been worthwhile.

Her one regret was that Mike had not been able to join them at that conference. She tried to make his contribution clear.

He had met them in Geneva, where they presented their information and then had addressed hours of questions from scientists and politicians around the world.

Mr. McGilvery's DAS-killer, an HGT hybrid of mountain algae and DNA from his high school discovery 147, or whatever its new designation was, was in production at Donglan, China, and various other locations around the world. As soon as it was released, DAS would begin to recede. Confined tests indicated it would spread as fast as DAS had originally, if not even faster.

That actually made release dates more difficult to assess, but if that was the worst problem they had reining in her world-chilling symbiote, she would be happy. She was tired, but content. Now she could make plans for the future, because there would *be* a future.

Li planned to use most of his portion of the prize money to support his mother's family compound, to ensure it remained untouched and untouchable by the local Council. It meant bribes to national historical societies, which he could now make more generous, and could save for more in the future. The money also could be spent on maintenance of the old buildings, and fixing things like the front gate, which had broken again. The hinges weren't up to carrying the weight of the heavy gates. That and other issues were a non-problem now, they just needed to get the work done.

Li also paid off the loan he had taken to repair Ming-Hua's eyesight. It left a little money to splurge on a rain capture and purification system for the compound. Groundwater was contaminated with DAS, which would clear eventually, but meanwhile clean drinking water from the bountiful rain would be wonderful.

Xiang Bo still hadn't decided what to do with her own share of the award. She was tempted to gift a large portion of it to the orphanage in Changle.

Or...perhaps she could *buy* the land and building outright, and put a goodly sum into the bank to support it.

Yes, she thought. Then she could add a school with regular teachers.

She went to her comp at the little desk in the hallway where she usually worked. She looked up costs, including construction costs to repair and upgrade the building, and salaries for qualified teachers in the area. She looked into savings plans to fund a scholarship once a year to a student— most likely a girl—for University.

She felt Li's breath on her neck as he read over her shoulder.

"Oh," he said. "Is that where Zi Min came from?"

"Yes. I think I can support a school as well as the orphanage. And possibly a scholarship."

"That sounds like a good plan," Li said.

She turned and met his gaze. Li's gentle smile was in his eyes more than his mouth, but she could see it.

"I can help with the investments, if you would like," he offered.

"I would love your help," she said. "Thank you."

She turned back to her comp, but her eye was caught by the view from the bedroom window to her right.

Outside, in the bright sun of the courtyard, Zi Min bent and kissed the top of Lotte's head. On the bench by the azaleas, Ming-Hua petted the tortoise-shell cat who stropped herself against his knees, and then against Di'e's. In the shade of the ancient willow tree, the dog and goat lay curled together, asleep. She smiled at the peaceful view.

She was home now. They all were.

TO THE READER

Please accept the authors' gratitude for finding and reading our book.

We are independent authors and appreciate how difficult it is to select our book from the flood of offerings. As independent authors, we are significantly dependent on reader-to-reader recommendations.

If you enjoyed our novel and wish to support independent writers, we would appreciate any posts on social media, and especially an all-important Amazon review.

You might also be interested in **Darwin's Paradox: An international science mystery** by J. Oestreicher and D.R. Oestreicher

Available from most online booksellers: ISBN: 978-0-9631755-5-7

http://amzn.to/2k8qJgi

Thank you.
   J. and D.R.

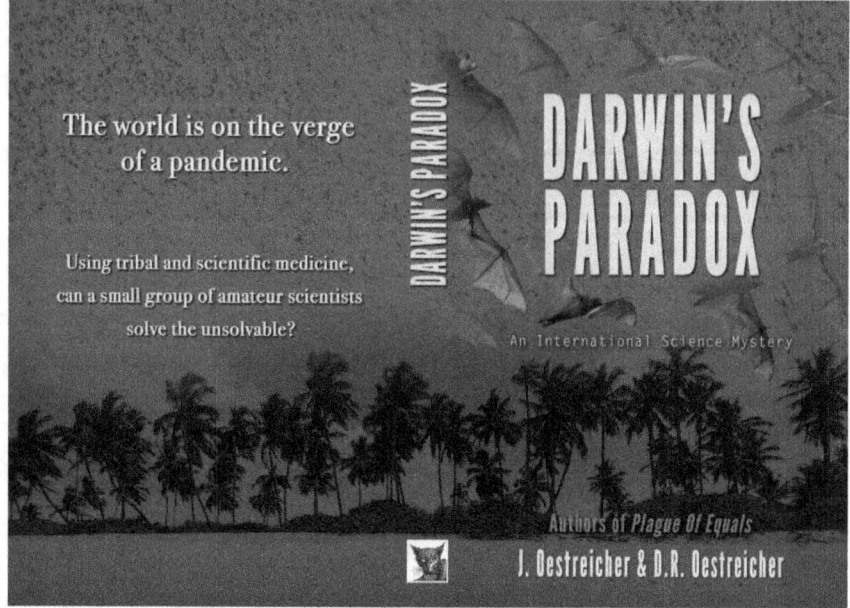

The world is on the verge of a pandemic.

Using tribal and scientific medicine, can a small group of amateur scientists solve the unsolvable?

DARWIN'S PARADOX

An International Science Mystery

Authors of *Plague Of Equals*

J. Oestreicher & D.R. Oestreicher

PROLOGUE

CAMROSE, ALBERTA CANADA

On the first day of kindergarten, Natalie Jenkins packed Ian and his three-year-old sister Lindsey into her pickup and headed to the elementary school. Shortly after her daughter was born, she received a small inheritance which enabled her to get a divorce and move 100 kilometers south of Edmonton just outside the small city of Camrose amidst a vast agricultural parkland.

Best decision ever. Clean air. Locally grown organic food. No crime. Friendly neighbors.

When Ian returned home from his first day of school, he complained of a sore arm. Natalie assumed something happened at school. She didn't believe in overprotecting her children. Ian had had his share of bumps and bruises, but after dinner he held his arm and rocked back and forth. He also had a slight fever, so she gave him some ibuprofen.

That remedied his condition until the next morning when he woke up crying. The pain now extended from his hand to his neck. He was trembling as she drove past the elementary school to the hospital in downtown Camrose. As she negotiated the short drive through city streets, she was grateful she hadn't chosen a more remote place when she was escaping her ex and urban living.

The doctors immediately checked Ian into a room in the intensive care unit. This prompt care did not soothe her. Instead she was frightened. Triage demanded they see the most serious cases first. Not a good sign. She loved Ian as much as she hated her ex whom he unfortunately resembled.

As they rolled him away, she followed and made the magical wish that Ian could exchange whatever he had with one of his parents, preferably her ex. She observed the lengthy exam until she remembered Lindsey was alone in the waiting room. Exercising her personal mommy triage, she rushed back wondering what people were thinking of the mother who had abandoned her three-year-old.

She was hyperventilating, but relaxed when she saw the outgoing Lindsey regaling a gray-haired couple with stories about her bear and her moose, Fatty and Patty. The three of them, Lindsey, Fatty and Patty, had been fast friends and had had so many wonderful imaginary adventures that Natalie could ignore that the adorable stuffed animals were Christmas gifts from Lindsey's father. Ian's father. She no longer acknowledged any personal relation with him.

Fortunately, the vagaries of the oil field industries had sent him miles away, so such gifts arrived via Canada Post, and visiting was out of the question.

She was glad she decided to retrieve Lindsey when she did. The doctor returned shortly after. Again, this prompt action made her nervous. Even more concerning, the doctor didn't talk right away. First, she asked the nurses to watch Lindsey, and then led Natalie into a consultation room. After closing the door and offering a glass of water, the doctor sat behind her big desk. She spoke in a quiet voice, almost sounding like a funeral director, "My first thought was allergies, but Ian didn't respond to diphenhydramine, an antihistamine."

Natalie's frightened mind darted about while she tried to prepare herself for the bad news. She noticed that the doctor wore no makeup except for pale pink nail polish and possibly some clear lip gloss. Wondering whether this indicated a serious demeanor or a lack of care, she missed some of the explanation and what else the doctor had considered. Eventually, the doctor dismissed her, but kept Ian for "further observation." The terrified mother picked up Lindsey and, following the doctor's advice, rented a motel room in town.

After another anxiety-ridden consultation, she decided to stay in the hospital. The motel was just not close enough. She sat in the waiting room with Lindsey sleeping on her lap. Poor Lindsey woke up every few hours when the nervous mother went to check on Ian.

During the night, Ian developed tremors and spasms. He had trouble speaking. The night shift didn't want to do anything until the admitting doctor arrived in the morning.

Natalie seemed to mirror his symptoms. She was so scared and angry that she could barely speak. She tried to control her shivering to not scare poor Lindsey.

For just a moment she wished Lindsey's father had been there to share the responsibilities, but then she recalled, he had never shared the responsibilities when he had been there. That was never going to change.

Nothing happened until morning.

When the doctor arrived, everything went quickly. Several other doctors examined Ian, and they made consultation calls to Alberta Health Services. First to Edmonton, then Calgary, and ultimately to Sick Kids in Toronto.

The doctors considered epilepsy. Natalie had to run to keep up with the gurney taking Ian for an electroencephalogram. Little Lindsey was exhausted, emotionally and physically. After spending the night, Natalie found it easier to leave Lindsey under the nurses' watchful care. By this time everyone knew Fatty and Patty, and some of the nurses even contributed new adventures to the continuing saga.

Fortunately, or unfortunately, she couldn't think straight anymore to differentiate good news from bad news: it was not epilepsy.

By afternoon, she took Lindsey out for a healthy meal. She brought back Ian's favorite, KD, but he would not eat anything or even drink water.

Worse, he now had a rash and was itchy. She heard rumors about parents who had not vaccinated their children. Ian had had all his shots, but she now worried about measles, mumps, and chicken pox.

The doctors reassured her, "Ian's safe from those childhood diseases."

At this she just blew up, "Safe? Safe you say? What the hell is happening to him? Do something!"

They did something. They gave her a tranquilizer and had an EMS ambulance take her and Lindsey to their motel for the night.

———

Ian's symptoms worsened for a week until the doctors told his nearly catatonic mom that Ian was brain dead and they were taking him off life support.

She, Lindsey, Fatty, and Patty cried all the way home, not the least encouraged that the doctors, who could not help Ian, examined them both and assured them that they both were well.

The doctors put together a complete chart to send off to the Health Surveillance and Epidemiology Division at the Public Health Agency regional office in Edmonton.

Unknown to those doctors, medical examiners around the world received similar death charts. In Atlanta Georgia, the Centers for Disease Control (CDC) and, in Stockholm Sweden, the European Centre for

Disease Prevention and Control (ECDC) both numbered their cases in double digits.

LILY

KATHERINE, ARNHEMLAND, AUSTRALIA

Lily ducked her head and wiggled the screen of her computer, trying to angle it away from the glare. Then she tried laying an unpainted canvas across the corner of the screen to block the light. "Casuarina Café" glared backward in bright purple letters on her screen. She finally scooted her chair to the end of the table and turned the computer screen sideways to the sun and the neon sign in the window.

Obrey said his customers liked the light, and he wasn't going to put in shades just to make a bat-cave for her, but Lily was pretty sure he just didn't want to pay for shades. It's not like there was a huge clientele in the shop; Lily was often the only one there, like today. He probably didn't have the cash. He drifted out from behind the counter and looked over her shoulder.

She put the last photograph of her newest artwork up on the Cooperative's sale site and typed the painting's description, size, and title into the boxes on the Coop's form.

"More bats," Obrey said.

"Of course," Lily said. "They are selling much better than my yam paintings."

"Because you do not love yams, as you love bats?"

"Maybe."

"You are so good with the colors; I am always impressed."

"Thank you." She knew he was doing his daily compliment, but it was still nice to hear her work praised.

"How many did you sell last month?"

"Three."

"A good month, Lily."

"Mm."

She saved her work, glanced through her other offerings on the site, then went to her **Bat Chat** page. Obrey drifted away. She found her mind changing gears with an almost physical growl: art to healing. Obrey to Ariq. Bats were the constant.

With the eight-and-a-half-hour time difference, she never knew whether she'd find Ariq online, but there he was.

 ***Dreamtime*: Just updated my Coop page with a new painting.**

 ***Mongol Bataar*: Nice!**

Dreamtime: **Another bat dreaming. I went out with my healer friend; she talked a bit about some leaves I had not heard of. I want to do a painting, but I am afraid to ask her if I can.**

 Mongol Bataar: **?**

 Dreamtime: **The last time I did that things did not turn out well.**

Lily's heart ached when she thought about the old women in Ngukurr she had been studying with. She still did not understand what she had done or said that had been so wrong. There was so much about her people she did not know. And there were so few willing to teach her.

 Dreamtime: **How are things in New Mexico?**

 Mongol Bataar: **Not good. We had a death among our rehab patients with absolutely clean toxicology reports. Several others are ill with what looks like the same thing.**

 Dreamtime: **You are sure it is not simply old age?**

 Mongol Bataar: **She wasn't old. In her sixties, but that's not old. She had orthopedic surgery, nothing life-threatening.**

 Dreamtime: **Is your surgery pure?**

 Mongol Bataar: **I've done more tests, but there's nothing. It almost looks like rabies, but none of my patients or staff have been outside. And, anyhow, how could they all have been bitten by the same rabid animal—and not know it?**

 Dreamtime: **The illness was the same as before?**

 Mongol Bataar: **Almost identical.**

 Dreamtime: **Mm.**

 Mongol Bataar: **Any alternative treatment suggestions from the Outback?**

 Dreamtime: **Send the list of symptoms in as non-medical language as you can manage. I'll need to translate it for my mentor. Maybe she has some ideas.**

 Mongol Bataar: **Sure. Worth a shot.**

Dreamtime: ?

 Mongol Bataar: A try.

 Dreamtime: Mm.

 Mongol Bataar: I looked at your new painting. I like it a lot.

 Dreamtime: Thank you.

———

Lily paid Obrey for her coffee and her computer time and headed out, her portfolio in one hand, her paint box in the other. She walked to her aunt's house, studying the way the red dust puffed up around her bare feet. It was always fascinating, how light and fluffy it was. At her mother's apartment in Darwin, there was often dark mud instead of dusty dirt. Here in Katherine, it alternated between very wet and very dry.

One of the first things she had done when she had gotten computer access was looked at maps of the Northern Territory, and then Australia, and then the world. In New Mexico, where Ariq lived, it was very dry and sandy. But the bats lived everywhere. There were bats for every environment, just like people.

When she turned the corner to her aunt's street, she was abruptly faced with a wall of people and vehicles. An ambulance was parked in the driveway of June and Papa Araminty. People in uniform were talking to her aunt Olivia and some other people who lived on Honey Ant Street. Lily saw her cousin Pana and waved. They met a little away from the crowd, and Pana put her hand on Lily's shoulder.

"It's June Araminty, is sick," she said.

"She was fine yesterday when I saw her."

Pana shook her head. "Not now." Lily's heart seemed to squinch up tight, and it was hard to breathe. June had been the one to tell her about the art Coop, and how to show her paintings online, and what kinds of prices were reasonable. June also was an artist, but she did modern paintings, in bright acrylics with no dots or x-ray styles, not like the more traditional things Lily had been doing.

Pana cleared her throat. "She's such a nice lady."

"Yes, she is."

They watched as the paramedics rolled June out on a narrow bed and into the ambulance.

"She's going to hospital?"

"I think she doesn't want to. She keeps asking for your Auntie Pearl."

"Does Pearl know?"

"She was here. She argued with the medic. I think she went home."

"I'm going to find her."

"You want me to put those in the house?" Pana reached and Lily handed her the portfolio and paint box.

"Thank you, Pana. I will be home soon." Her cousin nodded and walked through the crowd toward her mother's home, using the paint box in front of her to open a space between people. Lily could see Pana's fuzzy dark blonde head like a beacon in the mostly dark-haired crowd.

Pearl. Lily retraced her steps to the corner, took two left turns and walked until the street turned into a lane, and the lane into a path through the paperbark trees. The path ended at Pearl's house.

She could hear Pearl muttering to herself as she walked into the lean-to where Pearl had bunches and trays of herbs drying.

"Auntie Pearl?"

"Hey, Lily. You see all that mess out there? "

"They're taking June Araminty to hospital?"

"She does not even want to go, but there is no telling those people. They know so much."

The old woman looked up as Lily approached. Lily held her arms open and she and Pearl gave each other a big hug. Lily patted Pearl's shoulder.

"Maybe we can go later, and see June," Lily said, watching Pearl's face.

An eyebrow went up in the round, plump face. She looked at Lily. "You think we can take her some bush tucker?"

"Of course. She will be much happier with that than whatever the hospital tries to feed her." Lily grinned, and Pearl grinned back, hiking up her skirt so she wouldn't trip on it. Lily had been meaning to sew some new elastic into the waistband. The skirt was still good; it just didn't stay up around Pearl's waist anymore. As usual, the shirt the old woman was wearing didn't match the pattern in the skirt at all. Lily wondered if that was her artist's eye flinching or her mother's fashion influence. Pearl obviously didn't care.

"Let me see what I have here," Pearl said, and Lily stepped up closer to watch or hand her things. "She has bad fever, shakes, dry skin like a croc mummy." She pushed past Lily and started pulling things out of her drying racks. "You come help, now, see what I make."

"Yes," Lily said, and did so, taking careful mental notes on what Pearl was gathering and what she did with it. June Araminty was going to have a nice bush stew, that was what.

DR. BRIAN

——— 🦇 ———

OMO'A, FATU HIVA, MARQUESAS ISLANDS

———

R℞ His daughter broke his heart for the second time. This time, because she wasn't dead. After years of searching, mourning, and therapy, he had had her declared legally dead and had moved on with his life. Now, there she was, alive, dancing in the South Pacific.

Doctor Brian, as he preferred to be addressed, had awakened when the sun rose over Fatu Hiva streaking through the volcanic peaks. Geologically young enough to trace jagged and sharp lines, but old enough to be covered in eroded lava as shown by the lush green vegetation, the mountains made a dramatic silhouette for sunrise.

His therapist, fearful of antidepressant dependency, had recommended the cruise. Now, after a week of serene oceans, tropical islands, and good food, he hadn't thought of his disappointing career and lost family for days.

After a room service breakfast of papaya, mango, banana, and pineapple accompanied by the blackest espresso flavored with Tahitian vanilla, he boarded the tender to visit Omo'a.

With no goal, he walked around the island and through the small town. He noted the obligatory post office with its ATM, a small food store that sold staples and a selection of candy for the children, and a clinic. A turtle—terrapin? —with a shell the size of a VW bug hood wallowed in damp sand, strands of seaweed draped over its neck. The palm trees, advertised on every website, swayed in the breeze. A few white clouds scudded across the very blue sky. Children were out in the schoolyard. There couldn't have been more than a couple of dozen of all ages.

Beyond the school yard, on the way back to the beach, was a small tourist market. He had no one to buy souvenirs for, but he still ambled in that direction, attracted by the sound of drums.

As he approached his seventieth birthday, he tired easily, so he gratefully took an empty spot on a shaded log, pleasantly surprised to find himself next to Jake, a friendly salesman he'd met on the ship. Jake's movie-star good looks weren't hurt by his scruffy unshaven jaw and bed-head hair—if that was what the young people called it? Every time Doctor Brian saw Jake, he felt compelled to smooth his own balding white hair and finger-comb his beard. He knew he was a long way from a "silver fox" the ladies might go for, but he wasn't ugly, either. At least not until he sat next to Jake. They waved to each other and returned their attention to the next group of dancers. Though the dancers dressed alike in palm skirts, colorful floral tops, and bare shoulders, they ranged in age from pre-teen to grandmothers.

A thirtyish woman with blonde hair and a deep tan attracted both Jake and Doctor Brian. Brian noticed her bright smile captured the attention of several other men in the audience. When she looked in their direction, Jake smiled back at her. As Brian stared at the long curly hair, the smiling face, he could feel his body tense. He was sweating and having trouble breathing.

This dancer reminded him of his ex-wife, the one who had turned his daughter against him. The two of them had disappeared twenty years ago, without even a "goodbye." In his mind, they had both earned the title of "bitches." They were impulsive and cruel—at least, they had been to him.

After years of therapy, he was beginning to let go; he was still not good at it. Since they had left long ago and were declared dead, one of his therapists had recommended a funeral. He purchased coffins and headstones. They were "buried" together, and he visited the graves annually on the anniversary of their disappearance. They couldn't be here, could they? They were dead.

His reverie ended with a loud drum roll. The dancers raised their hands and waited for the music signaling the dance to start. As with many of the dances he'd seen on the cruise, footwork was minimal. The hips kept pace with the increasing tempo of the drums, and the arms told the story. He stared at those arms, especially at the blonde woman's right arm. Against a dark tan were four distinctive v-shaped, white scars.

When he realized that he wasn't breathing, he gasped one long breath and leaned forward, shuddering. He recognized the scars as the unique signature of an external fixator. The exact pattern of scars left from repairing his daughter's arm after the accident. There was no doubt, now, the dancer was his daughter. Penelope was alive.

"Penelope!" he shouted.

She looked at him, their identical green eyes locked. She stopped dancing and blinked. He saw recognition in those eyes.

After the barest pause, she looked away and resumed dancing.

He jumped up and sprinted across the open sand between the tourists and the dancers. He reached his arms toward her. "Penny...*Penny*. It's your father!" He gulped back tears. "Time to come home."

This was a scene he'd dreamt of so many times. Sometimes during a hurricane, sometimes with explosions. Never with dancing. Always with Penny looking younger—as young as she'd been when he'd last seen her. And always with her arms out, rushing into her daddy's arms. He had never thought it would happen, but hope had lingered.

"Penny. Penny! Come home," he kept repeating.

As he approached her, she looked scared and backed away. "No. No!" she repeated louder and louder competing with the drums.

Brian felt a rush of movement behind him. Jake grabbed his arm, his shoulder. "What are you doing, Brian? Let's go sit down. You're upsetting her."

No, Brian thought. No one would interfere with his reunion, not after all these years. With strength that surprised himself and Jake, he swung his arms and knocked the younger man down.

He spun, picking up speed, and ran closer to the stage and Penny. Just as quickly, two large, bare-chested drummers stood between him and the frightened woman, big arms raised to block his charge. When he tried to push past them, one of the men hit him with a large drumstick. That was the last thing he remembered.

———

He awoke in what seemed to be the ship's infirmary. Jake was at his side, legs crossed in a stiff-looking straight-backed chair, a ratty paperback book in his hand.

"Ah! You're awake!"

Brian blinked, rubbing the lump on his head and wincing when he touched a tender spot.

Why was Jake here?

"Now, the reason they didn't treat you on the island is that woman you attacked is the town doctor. And that is just the beginning of your troubles. The cruise ship was ready to send you home. I promised to keep an eye on you; you can't walk around unaccompanied."

"Where's Penny?"

"The island woman? The doctor you attacked?" Jake shook his head. "She has no interest in seeing you."

"But—she's my daughter."

Jake's eyebrows rose at this, and he shook his head. "Maybe you should stay in the infirmary awhile, man."

But the nurse disagreed, needing to clear the bed to take in people who "are really sick." They kicked Brian out.

At dinner that night, Brian went on and on about his drunk wife, the accident, Penny's broken arm and long rehabilitation, the divorce, shouting, recriminations, lawyers, until one day, his wife and nineteen-year-old daughter were simply gone.

When dessert arrived, Tahitian vanilla creme brulee for Brian, and terrine of citrus fruit and Campari sorbet for Jake, it seemed like Jake had had enough.

"Listen, even *if* she is your daughter, she doesn't want to see you. Eat something to take your mind off her."

Brian was going to object, but instead he muted himself with a spoonful of heavenly custard.

Conspiratorially Jake whispered, "I recall you worked in drug research. Ever think of going back? I have a feeling there is going to be a sudden demand." He set down his spoon. "Let's go out on deck."

Research? This just depressed Brian more. From his worthless family, the conversation was shifting to his worthless career. Thoughts of his sore head and his resurrected and obviously hateful daughter both clamored for attention. He didn't want to listen to Jake's sales pitch. But he could use a friend. And what had Jake said about having to accompany him? They squeezed past other travelers out onto the deck. They leaned on the rail. Blue on blue, the sky, the sea.

Brian knew he could slip over the railing and not be missed until the ship was miles and miles away. It would be a fitting end to his lackluster life.

"Listen," Jake said. "I sell sequencers, expensive, high-speed sequencers. Do you know anything about DNA sequencers?"

Brian just sucked on his lip, feeling like a senile old man, and thinking of how the Pacific Ocean could swallow him.

"I am getting rich, very rich. These machines, hundreds of thousands of dollars each—people are buying them by the boatload. Labs that last year had no budgets are buying four or five at a time." Jake paused to glance at Brian. "Something big is going on, really big. I bet you have connections. Find out what."

Well, it wasn't exactly a sales pitch. Maybe Jake was right. Doctor Brian had done drug research for thirty years. If something big was happening, they'd be glad to see him. They'd need him.

The tablelands forest started to hum and chirp with life as soon as the tiniest edge of the sun lit the horizon. Nga Lind stretched and lay in the comfort of her bed for a few more moments, looking out the window. The forest had been cleared next to the mission buildings to reduce the fire hazard, but she could still see trees.

She was used to getting up early, but lately it seemed as though going to bed at the end of the day kept getting pushed later and later while rising time remained early. It was amazing, but she had no surgeries scheduled today.

Of course, the clinic's visitors would come along with sundry problems as the day went on, but at least she wasn't starting off already behind. And Halid was more and more helpful. She smiled thinking about the village headman's son. Halid seemed to be deciding he wanted to be a TC, too, and go to Maputo to get the training. Meanwhile, she was acting as his mentor because she wanted to help him and because he was helping her. A lot.

Two days ago had been a real horror, with two surgeries in the morning—setting and stitching a compound fracture that had come in during the night, and removing the wen from a villager's baby boy's ear. That had been interrupted by an emergency appendectomy.

She'd only had time to look at three people in the clinic after that. She'd set Halid to cleaning instruments while she wiped down the tiny clinic surgery. She'd sent him home, and then stole the time to eat a bit of leftover dinner before she fell into bed and sleep.

She stared at her mother's beloved flowered wallpaper that covered two walls of her room. Linnea had sold vegetables from her garden at the river trade camp for months to pay for the stuff, which had been ordered all the way from Johannesburg. Nga smiled, remembering the day the whole family had worked together to wallpaper this room and her parents' bedroom.

She could hear chickens clucking outside her window. She should get up—but the extra minutes abed felt luxurious.

Her rule was to stop at suppertime, or 6:00 P.M. She had to implement rules, or she'd have been in the clinic all day and all night, too. After 6:00 each evening, she was only available for life-threatening emergencies. The villagers could go to the traditional healer, Imrane. Who also happened to be her brother-in-law. Who also happened to dislike her intensely. He was fiercely traditional.

She needed help, but not Imrane's kind of help. She was the only technically trained healer within several hundred kilometers. People from five nearby villages came to her for help. God forbid if they ever had some kind of plague, like that rumored in northern Zambia. She wasn't even a doctor and she was swamped. What would a serious disease do to Mozambique's shaky medical system? She couldn't even imagine trying to deal with something like Ebola.

When she had gotten her Technical Surgeon's training in Maputo—after her little sister Mezi had almost died in childbirth— there had been promises of funding for more *técnico de cirurgia*—TC—like herself to be trained and sent north. But Niassa Province was a long way from Maputo. All the new TCs seemed to get lost well before they got up here. And she was willing to bet they'd never seen a real M.D. in the entire Niassa province.

"*Nej, du överdriver*—" no, you're exaggerating, she told herself in her native Swedish. "Surely there's one in Lichinga. She's just buried under her patients, so you would never see her." She laughed softly, tossed the covers back and went to brush her teeth.

At breakfast, Linnea asked little Muluzi to say grace. Imrane scowled at her, eyes bulging, a grimace twisting his lips. That was the image frozen in Nga's head when she closed her eyes and bowed her head. Mu, always willing to please his grandmama, complied in his piping five-year-old voice. "Most Holy High Father, bless this food and our people, and lead us into the light of Christianity and protect us all," he said. "Amen."

After they had all murmured their Amens, Mu added, "Let's eat!"

His father scowled at him, then, but Mu just grinned and reached for the steaming bowl of corn porridge. Sometimes it seemed that Imrane was determined to show a severe face. The Yao villagers often laughed, and Muluzi and his big sister and his mother laughed with them, but their papa mostly scowled.

Nga kept glancing at him. Were his eyes bulging more than before? She wondered if he was in pain, but of course the man was never going to ask for her medical help. She had diagnosed Grave's disease and tried to get him to go to Lichinga for tests and medicine, but he was handling it himself, he told her. Whatever he was treating himself *with*, it had not seemed to make much improvement. The man was too thin and was sweating even as he sat here in the cool kitchen.

Mezi asked Teleza to pass the eggs. More solemn than her little brother, the little girl reached carefully for the plate of scrambled eggs and used both hands to pick it up and pass it to her mother.

"It's so nice to have you with us this morning, Nga," Linnea said.

"It's nice to have a hot breakfast," Nga said with a quick grin at her mother, serving herself a spoonful of the porridge. "Nothing scheduled this morning and no one in line at the clinic."

"Because I took care of them last night," Imrane growled.

"Who came in?" Nga wondered.

Imrane glared at her. "Kofi's arm itches. I told him to break the cast off, his arm is healed and the plaster is unnatural."

"Ah. And did he?" she tried to say it in a pleasant voice, curious what Kofi had decided.

"He did not. He says it has to stay until Monday." Imrane shrugged his slender shoulders. "What can a few more days do?"

"It's just to make sure his arm is completely healed," Nga said. So it doesn't go all crooked like Botte's did because you convinced *him* to take his cast off after only a week. But it wouldn't do to say that aloud and start a quarrel at the breakfast table. Nga caught her mother's glance, the pleading in her eyes. Linnea had had a hard time getting Mezi's family to join them for meals. Nga would not ruin that. She smiled at her mother then focused on her plate. Her father cleared his throat.

"We will need some help from the villagers to clean out the classrooms," Anson said. School would be starting up again in a couple weeks.

Linnea nodded. "Some of the children want to help with that," she said.

Their new teacher for the lower grades, Miss Anderson, had just arrived and was settling in. The older teacher, fifth to tenth year, had been here for several days, and was in her quarters behind the school building. The teachers did not have a real kitchen in their cottage, and Nga was surprised neither of them had joined them for breakfast. Linnea Lind traditionally fed the teachers and half the mission personnel at her big kitchen table. Perhaps they had eaten earlier.

Back in the clinic after a pleasant breakfast, Nga washed her hands and put on gloves and a gown. Using tongs, she removed her instruments from the glutaraldehyde bath one at a time, drying them and packing them into clean plastic pouches. Then she put them into their appropriate drawers and bins. Maybe someday they'd get an autoclave, but for now, the chemical bath was the best system they had for sterilization.

Giving thanks for the regular delivery of supplies—like the plastic bullets of hydrogen peroxide and boxes of gloves—she reached for a new pair of gloves, then emptied a bottle of hydrogen peroxide into a small tub of tea-kettle-boiled water. She used a new sponge, wiping down every working surface of her little clinic: exam table, countertop, cabinets, the plastic-covered chair. She emptied out the water, prepared a new batch with another bottle of peroxide, and repeated the procedure, finishing with the floor. She'd been rushed when she'd wiped things down last night, and hadn't had time to do a good job, lately. She was content as she sat outside on the stairs, enjoying the dry-season sun as the floor in her little clinic dried.

Halid showed up wearing only his hand-me-down jeans. His feet were dusty. She pointed at them, and he grinned, walking around to the outside washing station. He rinsed the dust off, and put on booties, careful to only step on the clean mats as he came back to her.

As she stood up, ready to go back inside to do her planned inventory, she saw a stranger approaching, one of the Luambe village boys leading the woman, who was limping along very slowly. She also saw Imrane looking at the woman, but he scowled and turned away. If she hadn't gone to her own village healer, she wasn't going to want a strange one to help. Clearly she had come for the medically trained clinician. Nga tried not to smile. She would have been happy to share treatment with Imrane, if the man wasn't so determinedly unpleasant. The combination of Western medicine with native treatment could be very powerful if they worked together. That did not seem likely to ever happen, though, not with him.

Halid called to the village boy and they chattered together as the old woman finally arrived, cradling her swollen wrist. Arthritis? Or broken? Nga went to work.

It was almost dusk when more strangers arrived in the village. Again, they passed the round village houses and approached the square mission buildings. It was a young couple, with a child. They might have been European tourists with their backpacks, sunglasses, and water carriers, but they shouted greetings in a Malawian dialect of Chiyao, the villagers' language. It was close enough to the Luambe dialect that Nga could understand them. Halid appeared at the edge of the village, looking at her.

The newcomers were saying something about plague. About leaving before it was too late. They seemed to be in good health.

Nga waved Halid off. She closed and locked the clinic door and walked out to speak with the strangers. Several of the Luambe villagers had surrounded the little family, and soon people from the mission joined Nga and the strangers, Halid among them.

"What plague, what sickness," Nga tried to ask in a space between rapid conversations between villagers and strangers. Everyone else stopped talking to listen to her.

The wife looked at Nga. "You are TC, yes?"

"I am," Nga said.

"Did you hear about Zambia, about the sickness there?"

Nga nodded. "I heard, but not very much."

"People are running from Zambia to Malawi now, sneaking past the borders."

"And then they take boats across the lake or walk through the trees to Tanzania, or to here," the man said. "Maybe they are sick, or maybe they are ahead of it."

The wife nodded. "Zambia has more than 700 dead already. My friend is a TC there. Or she was. She died last week."

Seven hundred dead? Nga knew they were isolated here, but she thought at least one of the mission workers would have heard about this on the news. Were these people confused? Or was the government suppressing information, trying to avoid panic or bad press? Zambia had its problems.

"What are the symptoms?" she asked, interrupting a villager who had begun to ask about a friend in Malawi.

"We hear it is a fever, dehydration, weakness. Nothing helps, none of the medicine Suzy tried seemed to help anything. Then she got it, and she died."

"Anyone recover?"

"Not that we heard. The only thing to do is get out of the way. We're going on to Pemba. None of the coastal towns are reporting any problems. You should go too," the young woman said. But Nga shook her head.

"My place is here, helping the villagers."

"If you wait too long, it'll be too late," the man said. "Think of the children," he hugged his son. "We thank you for the water. We'll be on our way."

Nga and Halid waved good-bye as the little family moved on. They planned to go south to the highway, then east to the coast. She couldn't help but wonder if they weren't going to be at greater risk on the coast than Luambe village would be, isolated up here in the high tablelands.

ARIQ

ROSWELL, NEW MEXICO

Ariq Temuujin mentally reviewed the checklist for his presentation: architectural model of E-Ro city, laptop, projector, backup copy of his PowerPoint slides. He touched his waist to check he hadn't forgotten his belt and had zipped his fly. On a straight stretch of road, he looked down to check that his shoes matched. He leaned over to the rear-view mirror to confirm he hadn't nicked himself shaving. There wasn't a lot to shave, but on mornings like this, he couldn't be too careful.

His father had named him after his ancestor Ariq Böke, Genghis Khan's grandson, Kublai Khan's brother. Warrior blood flowed through his arteries, but today Ariq didn't feel it. For the hundredth time, he reminded himself that the Khans ruled the greatest Asian empire, feared by all, east and west, over 5,000 miles from Budapest to Shanghai. How could he allow a planning commission in the tiny town of Roswell, New Mexico, home of UFOs, aliens, and cheap souvenir shops, to rattle him?

Calmed down, he took a deep breath and turned onto Richardson Avenue. City Hall was just ahead. His hands had a death grip on the steering wheel. He hit the brakes to avoid hitting a crowd of protestors. "Earthlings Go Home," "Roswell for Robots," "Spaceports not Hospitals."

Avoiding the crowd, he drove right past the brick City Hall and around the block to enter in the back. Ariq Böke died a coward's death as present day Ariq snuck into the meeting room. To assure a stealth entrance, he left the magnificent model of the planned E-Ro city in his SUV.

Corporate expected Ariq to expand the ROC from twenty-eight beds to a health complex with hundreds of beds, plus luxury hotels, shopping, and recreation for their well-heeled clientele. PopulistHealth had been quietly buying up land east of Roswell, naming the project E-Ro, wanting it to remind their customers of SoHo in New York and SoMa in San Francisco. Eventually, they planned a thirty-six-hole golf course.

Ariq sat through the small-town planning commission deliberations to approve additional plastic aliens on Main Street, opening another theater to screen classic science fiction movies, and expanding a garage by adding another mechanic's bay.

He opened his laptop to review his presentation one more time when his chief financial officer Martina Hirsch arrived. She'd graduated at top of her MBA class from a third-rate college–but a 28-bed clinic in the desert wasn't exactly a resume builder. As usual, she dressed professionally, high collar, pale green suit, and impeccably-groomed short blond hair. She would assist with changing slides and answering detailed financial questions.

After a short break, the Mayor, Susanna Smyth, mispronounced his name. "Erik Tem-u-hin. I see you've brought your projector. That must mean another presentation. Our other business has run long, so I'd appreciate if you can make this brief."

Ariq walked to the lectern between the rows of chairs and the committee members seated at desks. He took a calming breath. "Thank you. I will do my best. As you know, PopulistHealth successfully completed the multi-million-dollar conversion of the abandoned East End Elementary School, and the twenty-eight bed Roswell Orthopedic Clinic is up and running."

One of the members, a dairy farmer named Jorge Casales, wearing a string tie with a turquoise slider and a straw cowboy hat, interjected, "Orthopedic Clinic! We already have a perfectly good hospital. I can't even recall why we approved a clinic for out-of-state rich people."

Ariq paused. "Your regional hospital is excellent. PopulistHealth considered that as a benefit of selecting Roswell, and now we can be an economic growth engine for Roswell and all of Chaves County. We've also helped local people. Remember that infant with pyloric stenosis? We– "

"Yes, yes, that was for one of your own nurses, wasn't it? You pick and choose and only take care of your own."

Ariq did a double take. That was Dee, short for Delores, Fuentes, who interrupted him. She wore her trademark embroidered shirt and braids, the image prominently displayed in front of her popular bakery and on all their pink boxes. The clinic was a good customer and generally she supported them.

At this point, Mayor Smyth hit her gavel. "Let's skip the presentation. You're here to ask approval for a six-story medical facility. We discussed this at lunch yesterday and decided that we're not approving anything taller than the dome on the courthouse."

Ariq frowned, imagining the planning commission eating tacos and burritos at the Star Track Taqueria while discussing the future of a multi-billion-dollar corporation's investment in their small town.

"But we've been talking with the planning staff for over six months and they never said anything. Besides you already have buildings taller than the courthouse."

The courthouse, over 100 years old, had a beautiful beaux arts dome covered in green tile, so he could understand wanting to keep it visible. But the commission's arbitrary decisions frustrated him. He looked to Martina for support, but she ignored him, concentrating on setting up the projector which clearly would not be necessary. He silently thanked the Buddha that he'd left the E-Ro model in the car. Today was not the day.

While he considered his next move, a small group of protesters ran into the hearing room dressed as aliens and shouting, "Shut it down. Shut it down!" The voices behind the plastic masks seemed to be high school students or younger.

The mayor's gavel came down again. Dee spoke up. "That's enough. We gave our word. We are not shutting anything down. But we are also not expanding until we understand the full story. We think you have more plans than you are saying."

Ariq looked toward Marti. She shrugged her shoulders. It seemed like the E-Ro plans had leaked.

"We do have bigger plans for the Roswell community. I came to present those today."

Jorge didn't seem to be interested, "Roswell is a city of culture and traditions with a sound economic foundation based on agriculture and aerospace. We do not need rich people escaping from big cities." Many heads nodded their agreement.

Ariq had walked into a trap. They'd set this up over tacos and burritos. This was a disappointing day for Ariq Böke's many-times-great grandson.

Martina hung up her cell and wrote a hasty note to Ariq. He read the note and stopped. He stood limp in front of the committee, lost, wondering what his ancestor would do. In that lull, one of the aliens, a short one, maybe preteen, ran to the front of the room and grabbed the note, handed it to Mayor Smyth, and stood by hopping up and down.

The note said, "Another death last night. Two more sick. Must find a way to isolate guests."

When PopulistHealth planned the ROC, they chose Roswell as a place for families: low crime, good schools, museums, and clean air. All plusses when recruiting doctors. They also wanted isolation from sick people and strange diseases. They targeted people scared of MDRs and able to afford travel. Big city hospitals had a reputation as incubators of multi-drug resistant diseases. ROC wouldn't have any sick people at all.

Unfortunately, in the last few weeks, guests at ROC were getting sick…and even worse, dying. The clinic was not prepared to deal with this crisis. First, they needed more space.

Susanna passed the note to the other members.

Ariq spoke before they could. "An unknown disease has infected some of our guests. We have been in contact with the CDC in Atlanta. Diagnosis is difficult, as we have guests from all over the United States, and internationally. The sickness is a mystery. One person—no, two now—two people have died."

Their friend Dee seemed shocked, "When were you going to tell us? Is this like that movie? Outbreak? Are the feds going to bomb Roswell?"

Ariq shook his head, regretting that he'd accepted this job when he could have had a nice position in Denver. Maybe he should have stayed in Med School as эмээ wanted. He didn't use that mechanical, English word—grandmother. Only эмээ expressed the warmth and tradition that she embodied.

He sighed. "No one is going to bomb Roswell! But we do need more room to quarantine potentially contagious guests."

Clearly, they weren't going to approve the new hospital; the E-Ro project was dead for the moment.

A good general knew when to call for a strategic retreat. There *was* something that would help, and getting an approval, any approval, would break their development moratorium. He'd use their concern based on Hollywood hype to his advantage.

"Next to the old elementary school, there is an abandoned motel. I think it was called The Area 51 Hideout."

He looked around. He had everyone's attention. Even the aliens were listening and nodding, antennas and springy eyes bobbing. "With your approval, we could convert the motel rooms to be private rooms to isolate our guests from each other and the people in town. We could institute BioSafety Level 1 protocols immediately and increase the level if recommended by the CDC."

The committee smiled at "isolate," and again for "BioSafety Level." Would the planning commission go for this, at least?

The mayor looked at her watch, turned left and right to her committee members, and used her gavel one last time, "Motion seconded, passed, meeting adjourned."

Ariq wondered what had just happened. Were they telepathic aliens? They hadn't even voted. But he wasn't going to argue points of order. Martina gave him a quick smile. Within a few minutes, they had gone from total prohibition to consent to acquire and renovate a second property. Martina knew as well as he did that corporate in Minneapolis had acquired the Area 51 Hideout long ago, and the refit was virtually complete. The approval was after the fact, but important.

He looked toward Marti and folded his hands together, like closing a book. She packed up the projector and stood to leave.

He looked at the committee. "Thank you. As you now know, we have our work cut out for us."

He turned to go.

Jorge stopped them. "Just one minute. We hear that you have been housing bats in one of those old classrooms."

Ariq waited to see what the dairy farmer and amateur veterinarian would say next. The last thing he wanted was to discuss his small Chiropteran Research Center, really a grandiose name for a collection of a few hundred local Mexican Free-Tail bats and a handful of other species.

Jorge continued, "We have not approved anything like that."

Ariq gave a non-committal, "I understand," and continued to walk out with Martina at his side.

They would live to fight another day.

ACKNOWLEDGMENTS AND CREDITS

Many people and organizations (knowingly and not) contributed to this work of fiction. Acknowledgment here does not imply an endorsement, review, or even knowledge, of this book.

We must mention these two who still believe this book is about cats.

Special thanks

Dr. Josh Brower of the Sioux Falls Woodworking Guild answered our questions about the future of woodworking.

Thanks to the advanced readers who are responsible for the improvements from the earlier version and have nothing to do with the remaining issues: Jill McElderry-Maxwell; Peter Rodes Robinson, RodesScholar@gmail.com; Alistair James, Husband, father, engineer, Dragon and Sikak; and J L Blenkinsop, author of *Worlds Of Yifan* and *The Technical War* series.

Cover graphics

NASA, adjusted for DAS.

Chapter graphics

Empty Bowl by Icons Bazaar from the Noun Project 1715778
Mammoth by Dan McCall from the Noun Project 1049036
Polar Bear by RULI from the Noun Project 1494152
Rice Bowl by Mikicon from the Noun Project 317655
Wheat by Creative Stall from the Noun Project 177713

ABOUT THE AUTHORS

The authors grew up in Oakland, CA and Long Island, NY before meeting in Salt Lake City. J. raised three wonderful children while making time to publish poems and short stories. D.R. researched Silicon Valley startups. Today they live in Southern California with their two cats. They enjoy international travel, reading, and writing, and gathering a different perspective from the magical minds of their grandchildren.

www.ingramcontent.com/pod-product-compliance
Lightning Source LLC
Chambersburg PA
CBHW051230260626
47162CB00002B/347